W9-BMZ-691

DEAD OF NIGHT

ALSO BY JONATHAN MABERRY

FICTION

The King of Plagues
The Dragon Factory
Patient Zero
Rot & Ruin (for kids)
Ghost Road Blues
Bad Moon Rising
The Wolfman
Dust & Decay (for kids)

NONFICTION

Vampire Universe
The Cryptopedia
Zombie CSU
They Bite!
Wanted Undead or Alive

DEAD

OF

NIGHT

A ZOMBIE NOVEL

JONATHAN MABERRY

 St. Martin's Griffin ❦ New York

DEAD OF NIGHT. Copyright © 2011 by Jonathan Maberry. All rights reserved. Printed in the United States of America. For information, address St. Martin's Press, 175 Fifth Avenue, New York, N.Y. 10010.

www.stmartins.com

ISBN 978-0-312-55219-0 (trade paperback)
ISBN 978-1-250-00089-7 (hardcover)

10 9 8 7 6 5

THIS ONE IS FOR GEORGE A. ROMERO FOR RAISING THE DEAD.

AND, AS ALWAYS, FOR SARA JO.

ACKNOWLEDGMENTS

A number of good people provided invaluable information, advice, and assistance during the research and writing of this novel. In no particular order they are: Michael Sicilia, public affairs manager with the California Homeland Security Exercise and Evaluation Program; Detective Joe McKinney, San Antonio PD; filmmakers Mike Watt and Amy Lynn Best; Rodney Jones, Tim Hanner, C. J. Lyons, Scott Michaleas, Colin Madrid, Tony Faville, Laura Freed, Tonia Brown, Lisa McLean; parasitologist Carl Zimmer; ethnobotanist Dr. Wade Davis; comparative physiologist Mike Harris; Dr. John Cmar, Instructor of Medicine at The Johns Hopkins University School of Medicine and an infectious diseases specialist at Sinai Hospital of Baltimore, Maryland; Dr. Richard Tardell, specialist in emergency medicine (retired); and computer guru Jeff Strauss.

Thanks, as always, to my agent, Sara Crowe; my editor, Michael Homler; Joseph Goldschein, M. J. Rose, Don Lafferty, Doug Clegg, and Sam West-Mensch.

Thanks as well to my good friends in the Horror Writers Association, International Thriller Writers, Mystery Writers of America, and the Liars Clubs.

And thanks to the winners of the *I Need to Be a Zombie in Dead of Night* contests: Shanc Gericke, Sheldon Higdon, Nick Pulsipher, Wrenn Simms, Kealan Patrick Burke, Michael McGrath, Andy Diviny, Jillian Weiner, Byron Rempel, Elizabeth Donald, Peggy Sullivan, and Paul Scott.

PART ONE

THE HOLLOW MEN

All concerns of men go wrong when they wish to cure with evil.

—Sophocles

CHAPTER ONE

This is how the world ends.

CHAPTER TWO
HARTNUP'S TRANSITION ESTATE
STEBBINS COUNTY, PENNSYLVANIA

He was sure that he was dying. It was how he imagined death would be. Cold.

Darkness flowed slowly into the edges of everything. As if the shadows under tables and behind cabinets were leaking out to fill the room. Soft. Not painful.

That part was odd. In his dreams—and Lee Hartnup often dreamed of death—there was pain. Broken bones. Bullet wounds. Deep knife cuts.

But this . . . this wasn't painful.

Not anymore. Not after that first bite.

There had been that one flash of pain, but even that was beautiful in its way. So intensely painful that it possessed purity. It was beyond anything in his personal experience, though Hartnup had imagined it so many times. With the quiet people with whom he worked. The hollow people, empty of life.

The police and the paramedics brought him demonstrations of every kind of pain. Brutalized and beaten. Crushed in car wrecks. Suicides and murders. Even the old people from the nursing homes, the ones everyone believed died peacefully in their sleep. Hartnup knew that they had experienced pain, too. For some it was the rat-hungry gnawing of cancer; for others it was the mind pain that came with having memories carved out of their brains by the ugly scalpel of Alzheimer's. Pain for all. Pain was the coin that paid the ferryman.

Even now Hartnup smiled at that thought. It was something his father once said, back in the days when Lee Hartnup was the assistant and his father was the funeral director and mortician. Old John Hartnup had been a poetic man. Humorless but given to metaphor and simile. It was he who had started calling the bodies in their cold room the "hollow men." Well, hollow people, to be PC. People from whom the sacred wind of life had fled through whatever crack the pain had chipped into them.

And now Hartnup felt his own sacred wind trying to blow free. The wind—the breath—was the only heat left in him. A small ball of dying air in his lungs that had nowhere to go. There wasn't enough left of his throat for Hartnup to exhale that breath. There would be no death rattle, which amused the professional in him. He knew that some other mortician would hear it when preparing his body.

Of course, it would not be a mortician right away. First it would be a coroner. He had, after all, been murdered.

If you could call it murder.

Hartnup watched the liquid darkness fill up the room.

Was it murder?

The man . . . his killer . . . could never be charged with murder. Could he?

If so . . . how?

It was a puzzle.

Hartnup wanted to cry out for warmth, but of course he could not do that. Not with what was left of his throat.

It was a shame. He was sure that he could manage at least one really good scream. Like the ones in his dreams. Most of his dreams ended in a scream. That's what usually woke him up in the night. It's what finally drove his wife into leaving him. She could take the fact that he worked with the dead all day, and she was sympathetic to the fact that his work gave him nightmares. But after eight years she couldn't take the interruptions to her sleep two or three times a week. First it was earplugs, then separate rooms, and finally separate lives.

He wondered what she would think about this.

Not just his death, but his murder.

He heard a noise and wanted to turn his head. Could not.

The muscles of his neck were torn. Teeth and nails. He couldn't feel the wounds anymore. Even the coldness was fading. His body was a remote island, separated from his mind by a million miles.

The noise again. A clatter of metal, then the singsong of tools dropping to the tiled floor. Retractors and needles and other items. Things that he wouldn't need any longer.

Things that would be used on him in a few days.

He wondered who would prepare his body for the box? Probably that schmuck Lester Sevoy over in Bordentown.

Another crash. Then a sound. Like footsteps, but wrong somehow. Awkward. Disjointed. Like a drunk trying to stagger slowly across a barroom floor.

Lee Hartnup knew that it wasn't a drunk, though.

He didn't have a name for what it was.

Well . . . that was not exactly true.

It was a *hollow man*.

The room was darker now. Shadows were closing around him like a body bag being zipped up with him inside.

A simile. Dad would have liked that one.

Hartnup felt his body shivering. He felt the vibration of it but not the actual sensation. It was hard to understand. He knew that his flesh was trembling because his vision was shaking, but he felt no puckering of goose bumps on his flesh, no actual intensification of cold as his skin tried to retreat from it. And yet the vibration was there. The shaking.

He wondered at it. It was so violent that for a moment he thought that his body was going into convulsions. But that would have affected his eyesight, and he could still see as normally as the darkness allowed.

His head lolled on his ruined throat and he marveled that there was enough structural integrity left in his neck muscles to move his head so violently.

Then all at once Lee Hartnup realized what was happening.

It wasn't a wave of cold shivers. The cold, in fact, was nearly gone. It seemed to flee as the darkness grew. It wasn't convulsions either. The movement was not caused by any muscular action or nervous flutter anywhere in his body. This was purely external.

He was being shaken.

No . . . "worried" was the word. The way a terrier worries a rat. That's what was happening.

And yet not . . . This wasn't a hunting dog trying to break the neck of a rodent. No . . . This was something else. Even down there in the darkness, Hartnup realized how wrong it all was. He could not feel the teeth that clamped onto him. He was beyond the sensation of pressure or pain. All that was left to him was the savage movement of his body, and the uncontrollable lolling of his head as the hollow man bit at him and tore him to pieces.

The cold was gone now. The darkness closed over him, shutting out all light. Even the trembling vision faded into nothingness. Hartnup could feel himself die.

He knew that he was dead.

And that terrified him more than anything. More than the man on the gurney. More than when that man had opened his eyes. More than that first terrible bite. More than the cold and the darkness. More than the knowledge that he was being eaten.

He knew that he was dead.

He *knew.*

God almighty.

How could he be dead . . . and *know?* He should be a corpse. Just that. Empty of life, devoid of all awareness and sensation.

This was something he had never imagined, never dreamed. The wrongness of it howled in his head.

He waited in the darkness for the nothingness to come. It would be a release.

He waited.

He prayed.

He screamed in a voiceless voice.

But he did not become a corpse.

He became a *hollow man* instead.

CHAPTER THREE
MAGIC MARTI IN THE MORNING
WNOW RADIO, MARYLAND

"This is Magic Marti at the mike on a crisp, clear November morning. Coming at you live from both sides of the line, here on WNOW and streaming live from the Net. Your source for news, sports, weather, traffic, and tunes. The news is coming up at half past the hour, so let's take a look out the window and see what Mother Nature's cooking up . . . and darn if she isn't cranky today. Looks like we can wave good-bye to the sunshine, because there's a whopper of a storm front rolling in from Ohio. It parked itself over Pittsburgh last night and the Three Rivers got pounded by two inches of rain. Ah . . . getting pounded by two inches makes me think of my first husband."

Sound of a rim shot and cymbal.

"This is a slow-moving storm, so we can expect to see the first drops later today. This storm is clocking sustained winds of thirty miles per hour with gusts up to fifty. Button up, kids, this is going to be a bad one."

CHAPTER FOUR
SWEET PARADISE TRAILER PARK
STEBBINS COUNTY, PENNSYLVANIA

Some days have that "it's only going to get worse" feel, right from the moment you swing your feet out of bed and step flat-footed into a pile of cold vomit. Even then, feeling the viscous wrongness of that, you know that the day can get worse.

Desdemona Fox knew that it was going to be that kind of day. She was an expert on them, and this one promised to be a classic.

The vomit belonged to the long-haired, lean-bodied, totally gorgeous piece of brainless trailer trash who lay sprawled on the floor with one tanned leg hooked over the edge of the bed. Dez sat up and stared down at him. By dawn's early and unforgiving light he still looked ripped and hunky; but the stubble, the puke, and the used condom stuck to his left thigh let the air out of last night's image of him as Eros, god of love. The only upside was that he'd thrown up on his own discarded jeans instead of the carpet.

"Fuck it," she said and it came out as a hoarse croak. She coughed, cleared her throat, and tried it again. It was louder the second time, a bit less phlegmy, but it carried no enthusiasm or authority.

Dez picked up her foot, fighting the urge to toss her own cookies, and looked around for something that wasn't hers that she could wipe it on. There was nothing within reach, so she wiped it on Love God's hip.

"Fuck it."

Sounded better that time.

She got up and walked on one foot and one heel to keep any residual gunk off the carpet. She rented the double-wide and didn't feel like losing her security deposit to that prick Rempel over a stained carpet. She made it to the bathroom, turned on the shower, set the temperature to something that would boil a pot full of stone crabs, and stripped off the T-shirt that she'd slept in. It was vintage Pearl Jam that had seen better decades. Dez took a breath and held it while she stepped under the spray, but her balance was blown and she barked her shin on the edge of the stall.

She was cursing while she stood under the steaming blast and kept cursing while she lathered her hair with shampoo. She was still cursing when the hot water ran out.

She cursed a lot louder and with real bile as she danced under the icy spray trying to rinse her hair. Rempel had sworn to her—sworn on his own children—that he had fixed that water tank. Dez hated him most days, but today she was pretty sure that she could put a bullet into his brainpan without a flicker of regret.

As she toweled off, Dez tried to remember the name of the beefcake sprawled on her floor.

Billy? Bart? Brad?

Something with a *B*.

Not Brad, though. Brad was the guitar player she'd nailed last week. Played with a cover band. Retro stuff. Green Day and Nirvana. Lousy band. Guitar player had a face like Channing Tatum and a body like—

The phone rang. Not the house phone. Her cell.

"Damn it," she growled and wrapped the towel around her as she ran back to the bedroom. What'shisname—Burt? Brian? She was sure it started with a *B*—had rolled onto his side and his right cheek was in the puke. Charming. Her whole life in a single memorable picture.

Dez dove onto the bed but mistimed her momentum so that her outstretched hand hit the phone instead of grabbing it, and the cell, the clock, her badge case, and her holstered Glock fell off of the night table onto the far side of the bed.

"Shit!"

She hung over the bed and fished for the cell underneath, then punched the button with her thumbnail.

"What?" she snarled.

"And good morning to you, Miss Sunshine."

Sergeant JT Hammond. He was her partner on the eight-to-four, her longtime friend, and a frequent addition to the list of people she was sure that right now she could shoot while laughing about it. Though, admittedly, she would feel bad about it afterward. JT was the closest thing to family she had, and the only one she didn't seem able to scare off.

"Fuck you," she said, but without venom.

"Rough night, Dez?"

"And the horse you rode in on."

JT chuckled softly.

"Why the hell are you calling me so goddamn early?" grumbled Dez.

"Two reasons," he said brightly. "Work and—"

"We're not on until eight o'clock."

"—and it's not as early as you think. My watch says that it's eight-oh-two."

"Oh . . . shitballs."

"We didn't set out clock last night, did we? Little much to dri—"

Dez hung up.

She lay there, hanging over the edge of the bed, her ass in the air, her weight resting on one elbow.

"Oh, man!" said a slurry voice behind her. "Now that's something to wake up to."

Dez didn't move, didn't turn around.

"Here's the morning news, dickhead," she said very loudly and clearly. "You're going to grab your shit and be out of here in ten seconds, or I'm going to kick your nuts up between your shoulder blades."

"Damn . . . you wake up on the wrong side of—"

"Ten. *Three*. Two . . ."

"I'm out."

There was a scuffling sound as Brandon or Blake or whoever the hell he was snatched up his stuff. Then the screen door opened and banged shut. An engine roared and the wheels of a Harley kicked gravel against the aluminum skin of the trailer.

Dez shimmied back onto the bed, turned over, and sat up. The room took a seasick sideways turn and then settled down. She looked around at her bedroom. Stark, cheerless, undecorated, and sparsely furnished. So much of it reminded her of herself. She closed her eyes. Insights like that she didn't need on her best days. Today it was just mean.

She opened her eyes, took a breath, and stood up.

Love God had left a trail of puke droplets all the way to the front door, and she didn't have time to clean them off the carpet. Rempel would be delighted—he hated returning a security deposit.

"Fuck it," Dez said to the empty room. Her eyes stung with unshed tears. She got dressed in her last clean uniform, twisted her blond hair into an ugly approximation of a French braid, and buckled on the gun belt with all the junk and doodads required by the regs. She grabbed her hat and keys, locked the trailer, and stepped into the driveway.

The parking slip was empty.

She screamed "Shit!" loud enough to scare the crows from the trees.

Buck or Biff or whoever had driven her home from the bar. Her car was four miles down a dirt road and she was already late for work.

Some days only got worse.

CHAPTER FIVE
PINKY'S DONUT HEAVEN
STEBBINS COUNTY, PENNSYLVANIA

Sergeant JT Hammond's first name was really JT. His father's idea. JT had a sister named CJ and a younger brother named DJ. Their father thought it was hilarious. JT had not sent him a Father's Day card in eleven years.

JT sat in his cruiser and waited for Dez to come out of Pinky's with coffee. After he'd picked her up at her place and dropped her so she could retrieve her car, they arranged to meet at the gas station convenience store on Doll Factory Road to have some coffee and go over the patrol patterns for the day. Stebbins was a small town, but they shared patrol duties with the three other towns that made up all of Stebbins County. The county was the size of Manhattan but 95 percent of it was farmland, with only seven thousand residents. JT preferred to start each shift with a "game plan" for patrol, backup, and tasks. That way, if all that went on the duty log was parking tickets, a couple of DUIs, and accident reports, then at least all the i's would be dotted and t's crossed.

However, today was likely to be the kind of day when attention to detail was going to matter. If the storm was anything like the weather service was predicting, then all of the officers would be working well into the night, shepherding people to shelters, closing the schools early, coordinating with fire-rescue and other emergency services to pull people out of flooded areas, and who knew what else.

Their cruisers were parked in a V, front bumpers almost touching. JT's unit was a seven-year-old Police Interceptor with 220,000 miles on the original engine. The vehicle was spotless, however, and was the only car in the department's fleet of six that did not smell of stale beer, dried blood, and fresh urine. JT was fastidious about that. He had to be in the thing eight hours a day and sometimes double that, and tidiness mattered to him. His house was just as clean and had been ever since Lakisha had died. JT's kids were grown and gone—LaVonda was saving the world with Doctors Without Borders and Trey was a state trooper over in Ohio. Living neatly was the only way that living alone was bearable.

By contrast, Dez's cruiser was newer and uglier. Mud-spattered, dented, and tired-looking even though it was less than two years old. She drove it hard and ached for high-speed chases. If it was up to her she'd be driving a stripped-down monster truck with a front-mounted minigun and a couple of rocket pods.

At least three times a year JT offered to help Dez detail her car and also clean and decorate her trailer, but that suggestion was invariably met with the kind of enthusiastic vulgarities usually reserved for root canals and tax audits.

JT looked at his watch and tooted the horn lightly. Dez peered out of the dirty store window. He tapped his watch and she gave him the finger.

JT smiled, settled back, and opened the copy of *JET* he had been reading. He was halfway through an article on black superheroes in comics and wanted to finish it before Dez came out. Not that she would jab him for reading such an ethnic-specific magazine—after all, she had every one of the Blue Collar Comedy Tour DVDs, and there was nothing whiter than that stuff—it's just that Dez tended to bust on JT for his love of comics. JT was pretty sure that Dez had never been a kid.

Donny Sampson, who owned a tractor parts store on Mason Street, came out of the store with a blueberry Slurpee in one hand and a Coke Slurpee in the other. He was laughing out loud, and JT guessed that it was one of Dez's jokes. Donny always liked a filthy story, and Dez was a walking encyclopedia of them. Donny saw JT and saluted with a Slurpee cup; JT gave him a nod.

Dez was taking her damn time, so he settled back, but instead of reading the magazine he laid it in his lap and stared through the windshield at the closed door of Pinky's, thinking about Dez. They were often paired for patrol and, since neither of them had family living close, they usually did Thanksgiving, Christmas, and the Super Bowl together. Nothing romantic, of course; JT was old enough to be her father, and she was very much like a niece to him. Maybe a daughter if she would pull the goddamn Democratic voting-booth lever at least once before the world went all to hell. In his way, JT loved her. Felt protective of her. She was tough, though. She laid a pretty comprehensive minefield between her and the rest of the world. The rest of the guys in the department hated and feared her in equal measures.

Dez was a very good cop, better than a small-town police department deserved, but she wasn't a very nice person. Well, maybe that was unfair. She was damaged goods, which isn't the same thing as being bad natured. That, and she was way too deeply entrenched in the nihilistic and often self-defeating mentality of rural small town America. She cursed like a pirate, drank like a Viking, and screwed the kind of people the two of them usually arrested—providing they were well built, well hung, and in no way interested in any species of "committed relationship," especially since the last time she broke up with Billy Trout.

That was a damn shame, too. Billy Trout and Dez had grown up together and had been a hot item more times than JT could count. They were never able to make it work, which frustrated JT because he knew—even if they were both too damaged to see—that the two of them had real magic together. JT never liked to use a phrase like "soul mates," but he couldn't find a better label. Shame they were like gasoline and matches whenever they were together. All of the guys Dez dragged to her lair were clones of Billy; but saying so to Dez would be exactly the same as saying "Shoot me."

So, instead of a lover, Dez Fox had a partner. A middle-aged black man from Pittsburgh with a college degree in criminal justice and a set of well-used manners that had been hardwired into him by his librarian mother. Dez, on the other hand, was pure backcountry Pennsylvania; a blue-eyed blonde who could have been a model for fitness equipment if not for what JT personally viewed as an overactive redneck gene.

The radio buzzed. "Unit Four, what's your status?"

JT lifted the handset and clicked the Send key. "Dispatch, I'm code six at Pinky's. You got something for me, Flower?"

Flower Martini, twenty-eight-year-old daughter of love generation boomers, was the dispatcher, secretary, booking photographer, and court stenographer for the Stebbins County Department of Public Safety. She looked like Taylor Swift might look if her career took a sharp downward turn past a long line of seedy country and western bars. She was still cute as a button, and JT was pretty sure she had her eye on him, age and race differences notwithstanding.

"Yeah," said Flower, "Looks like a possible break-in at Hartnup's Transition Estate."

She overpronounced the name, giving it a nice blend of wry appreciation and tacit disapproval. The Hartnup family had been morticians in town for generations, but in the mideighties, during the New Age inrush, the son, Lee, had given the place a makeover. Changed the name from Hartnup's Funeral Home to the trendier "Transition Estate." Nondenominational services and a lot of Enya music. It actually sparked a rise in business that drew families from as far as Pittsburgh. Now, with the New Age covered in dust, the name was a local punch line. People still died, though, and the Hartnups still prettied them up and put them in the ground.

"Cleaning lady called from the mortuary office," said Flower. "Witness is a non-English speaker. All I could get was the location and that something was wrong with the back door. No other details, sorry. You want backup?"

"Dez is with me."

"Copy that."

There were only two units on the road at any one time despite the size of the county. Unit One was reserved for Chief Goss and Unit Three was in reserve.

"We'll investigate and call in if we need backup."

"Respond Code Two. Proceed with caution . . . JT." There was the slightest pause between "caution" and his name, and JT thought he heard Flower start to say "Hon—." She called him "honey" off the radio all the time and was constantly getting yelled at by the chief. She was the mayor's sister, and it was more than the chief's job was worth to fire her.

"Roger that."

JT clicked off and then tapped the dashboard button to give the siren a single "Whoop!" A moment later the door to Pinky's banged open, and Dez Fox came out at a near run, a white paper bag between her teeth and two extra-large coffees in paper cups in her hands. She handed a cup through the open window then leaned half inside and opened her mouth to drop the bag in his lap.

"What's the call?" she asked, looking irritated that police work was interfering with the ritual of caffeine and carbs. JT knew that it was sacred to her.

"Possible break-in at Doc Hartnup's place."

"Who the fuck would want to break into a mortuary?"

"Probably a drunk. Even so, I could use some backup."

"Yeah . . . let's do 'er, Hoss . . . But lights, no sirens though, okay? My head's held together with duct tape right now."

"Won't make a sound," he promised.

Dez reached in and took the bag back and carried it with her to her cruiser.

"Hey!" JT yelled. She gave him the finger again. When she looked back, JT stuck his tongue out at her and Dez cracked up, then winced and pressed a hand to her head.

"Owwww."

JT leaned out the window. "Ha!" he yelled.

A few seconds later Dez blew out of the parking lot in a spray of gravel. She hit the blacktop, punched the red and blue lights, and the big engine roared as she rocketed north on Doll Factory Road. JT sighed, snugged his coffee into the holder, and followed at a discreet seventy miles per hour.

CHAPTER SIX

GREEN GATES 55-PLUS COMMUNITY
FAYETTE COUNTY, PENNSYLVANIA

The old doctor sat on a hard wooden chair in the kitchen and stared at the phone. The call from the warden at Rockview Prison—where the old man worked as the chief medical officer—had been brief. Simply the warden conveying an interesting bit of information. Six words stood out from that conversation.

"We transferred his body this morning."

Those six words, so casually spoken, were like knives in the doctor's chest.

We transferred his body this morning.

Forcing his voice to sound calm, forcing himself not to scream, the doctor had asked for, and been given, the names and phone numbers of the mortician who had arrived to take the body and the relative of the deceased who had made the arrangements. A relative the doctor had not known existed. No one had known. There were not supposed to be any relatives. The corpse was supposed to go into the ground after the execution. It was supposed to be in the ground now.

"Oh my god," the doctor whispered.

He got up from his chair, walked like a sleepwalker into the living room, up the stairs, into his bedroom. He opened the closet, reached up onto the shelf, removed a zipped case, opened it, and stared dazedly at the gun. A Russian Makarov PM automatic pistol. He'd bought it new in 1974. When he had defected, the CIA took the pistol away, but eventually returned it to him. A sign of trust. He sat down on the edge of the bed. There was a box of shells in the case and three empty magazines. The doctor opened the box and began feeding shells into a magazine. He did it slowly, methodically, almost totally unaware of what he was doing. His mind was elsewhere. Miles away, in a small town where a mortician would be opening a body bag.

"God," he murmured again.

He slid the last bullet into the magazine and slid the mag into the frame. He closed his eyes, took a deep breath and held it for ten seconds, then exhaled it slowly as he pulled the slide back to feed a round into the chamber.

The gun was heavy and cold.

It would be quick, though. He knew where and how to place it so that death would be certain. All it would take was a moment's courage. If courage was the right word. Practical cowardice, perhaps.

Two cold tears boiled out of the corners of his eyes and rolled unevenly over the lines that age, anger, and mania had etched into his cheeks.

He weighed the gun in his palm.

"May God forgive me for what I've done," he whispered.

CHAPTER SEVEN
HARTNUP'S TRANSITION ESTATE

The mortuary was tucked a hundred yards down a winding dead-end road that had been officially renamed Transition Road. The road was bordered by lush evergreens and rampant wildflowers. It always cracked Dez up that there was a big yellow "No Exit" sign right at the turn.

The owner was Lee Hartnup, known as Doc—not because of any medical background, which he did not have, but because he had a PhD. It didn't matter that his doctorate was in literature with a minor in philosophy, the fact that he had a doctorate at all put him in a very small club within the Stebbins community.

Dez liked Doc. He was a bit of a stiff at times but he was "real people."

There were several small functional buildings tucked behind a faux mansion used for viewings. There were no lights on and no cars in the lot. The mortuary was around back, so Dez and JT looped behind a thick stand of pines to the service lot. Two cars were parked near a functional-looking rear door. The aloof gray nose of a Cadillac hearse peered out of the shadows of an open garage. A second hearse was up on blocks near it. Dez and JT pulled their cruisers side-by-side, blocking the parked cars. They opened their doors and studied the scene for a moment, then got out.

JT raised his chin at the larger of the two passenger cars, a four-year old silver Lexus. "That's Doc Hartnup's. Other one must be the cleaning lady's."

The second vehicle was a Ford that was so old and battered that it was virtually impossible to tell the model, year, or color.

The rest of the lot was empty, the morning quiet except for a light breeze that stirred the treetops. The red and blue of their dome lights slashed back and forth across every reflective surface—window glass, the polished skin of the mortician's car, the dead headlights of the vehicle on blocks.

"Looks quiet," said Dez.

JT keyed his shoulder mike to channel one. "Dispatch, units on scene. Can you provide location of the witness?"

"No, hon," said Flower. "I mean, negative. I told her to wait in her car, but she hung up."

"Copy that." JT turned to Dez. "Flower said she told the cleaning lady to stay in her car. Maybe she went inside."

They unsnapped their sidearms as they approached the mortuary, each of them fading to one side to be out of a direct line if someone fired through the door. They came in on good lines of approach, working it like they worked every potential crime scene. The town may have been a no-Starbucks wide spot in a farm road, but they took their jobs seriously.

The cleaning lady had been right. There *was* something wrong with the back door. Dez saw it first and nodded toward it. JT leaned over and saw that the door was a half inch into the jamb but not far enough for the spring lock to engage.

"How do you want to play it?" he asked quietly. They didn't speak in whispers. The sibilant ess sounds of whispers carried farther than ordinary voices speaking low.

Dez studied the door. "No sign of force. Lock's intact. But I don't like it, Hoss. Boy Scout motto," she said.

He nodded and they drew their guns. Glock 22s with a round already in the chamber and a fifteen-round high-capacity magazine in the receiver. They both lived by the "Be Prepared" wisdom.

This felt good to Dez. Just the thing to erase the memories of the Love God laying in his puke on her bedroom floor. This kind of entry—or a call to a bar fight or serving a warrant on a child molester—made her blood pump. It made her feel like crawling out of bed in the morning had some purpose. Dez knew, however, that JT hated this part of police work. He was at the opposite end of the evolutionary scale, and Dez knew it. JT actually believed that the "peace" in "peace officer" meant that the job was all about keeping things dialed down to a no-violence, no ass-kicking state.

JT keyed his shoulder mike. "Dispatch, Unit Four. Hold the air and stand by."

"Copy."

"I'm on point," said Dez. "You, me, left, right."

Dez put the toe of her shoe against the door, mouth-counted from three and pushed. The door swung inward on silent hinges. Dez and JT faded back for a moment, and then went in fast; she cut left with him covering her, and then he was inside, checking behind the door and clearing the corners. Guns were up and out in two-handed grips, eyes tracking together with the light.

They were in a large utility room, a shed that had long ago been built onto the house. There were cabinets and an industrial washing machine on one wall, shelves with cleaning supplies on the other. The far wall had another door and this also stood ajar.

"I've got blood," barked JT.

"I see it."

It was impossible to miss. A handprint, small, a woman's, pressed flat on the wall by the door. Blood trails had run all the way to the floor. That hand would have to have been soaked with blood to leave trails that long. Dez felt a familiar shift inside her head, as if a switch had been thrown. It was something she first experienced midway through her first tour, and it happened all the way through her two tours in Afghanistan. When she tried to describe the feeling to a sergeant over a bottle of Beam in a tent in northeast Afghanistan, the scarred vet said that it was part of the warrior mind. "It's the caveman mind, the survivor mind," he'd told her. "It's when you realize on a deep level that you just stepped out of the ordinary world and are walking point through the valley of the shadow."

Dez had tried to explain this to JT once, and though he understood on an intellectual level, the bottom line was that he'd never been in the military, he hadn't walked the Big Sand. And in thirty years on the job, he had never fired his service weapon and had never taken fire. That made a difference, even if neither of them ever said so aloud. He was smart and did everything by the book, but on some level he was a civilian and Dez could never claim that exemption ever again.

The mind shift changed her body language; weight easing onto the balls of her feet, knees bending for attack or flight, eyes blinking less often, hand readjusting on the grip of the Glock. She was aware of it on a detached level.

JT peered at the blood and then leaned back. He gave his lips a nervous lick. "I do not like this, Dez."

"Liking it's not part of the job, Hoss."

Dez used two fingers to turn the knob, and this time JT kicked the door—*hard*. Then they were moving fast, rushing into the main preparation room, checking corners, watching each other, tracking everything . . . and stopping dead in their tracks. The interior lights were on, fluorescents gleaming from stainless steel tables and dozens of medical instruments.

There was no movement in the room, but everything was wrong.

A gurney lay on its side by the open cold-room door, sheets and straps were tangled and askew. Beakers and bottles had been smashed. The delicate instruments of the mortician's trade were scattered like pickup sticks. Everything—walls, floor, debris—was covered with blood.

It was a charnel house.

"Jesus H. Christ," breathed JT, and for a moment his professional calm drained away, leaving in its place a shocked spectator. The air was thick with disinfectant, old meat, and the sheared-copper stink of fresh blood.

"Clear the fucking room, Hoss," snapped Dez, her voice as hard as a slap.

JT immediately shook off his shock and moved around to the far side of the room, kicking open closet doors, checking the cold room, making sure that the prep room was as empty as it looked.

Except it wasn't.

"I got a body," he called, and Dez cut a look his way. "Ah, geez . . . It's Doc."

Fuck.

"Gunshot?" Dez barked.

"No . . . Christ . . . I don't know. Knives maybe . . . This is bad. He's all messed up."

Dez was not looking at the dead mortician, however. She clicked her tongue, and when JT looked up she ticked her chin toward a door on the far side that led into the mortuary offices.

"Blood trail," she said. JT forced his emotions down and locked the cop focus back into place. He hurried to her side. He had his gun ready and his eyes open, but Dez could see fear sweat popping out all over his face.

There were two sets of footprints. Bare feet and shoes. The bare feet were male and large, easily size twelve; the other set was smaller, though still large for what was obviously a woman's work shoe.

The marks were scuffed and swirled as if the two figures were dancing as they exited. Violent struggles make the same patterns.

"Fuck," growled Dez and kicked open the door.

They rushed into the office, shouting at the tops of their voices.

"Police! Put your hands on your head! Police!"

Their shouts bounced off the walls and died in the still air.

As with the prep room there was only one person in there, and as with the other room the person was already dead.

JT stopped in his tracks and stared at the body. "God . . ."

Dez crossed to the only other exit, a front door. The barefoot blood trail went outside and vanished into the grass lawn, beyond which was a stretch of dense forest called the Grove.

"We got someone on foot." She backed away from the door and called it in. "Dispatch, Unit Two, we have multiple victims. Suspect at large and possibly on foot in vicinity. Roll all available units and crime scene."

Then she closed the door, flicked on the overhead lights, and crossed to where JT stood staring at the victim. The dead woman sat slumped backward in a wheeled leather desk chair that was parked in a lake of blood.

She was dressed in a blue cleaning smock that buttoned up the front. She had gray support hose and sponge-soled shoes. Her dark hair was pulled back into a tight bun; reading glasses hung around her neck on a cheap junk jewelry chain. Her name tag read OLGA ELTSINA.

Dez guessed that Olga was probably fifty. Russian. At least five foot nine, easily two hundred pounds. Arms like a shot-putter, tree-trunk legs, bowling-ball breasts. Not pretty by any standard, with thick lips and a bulbous nose.

What had been done to her was unspeakable. There was no point in checking for a pulse. There wasn't enough left of her throat to bother. The skin below her jaw was a ragged ruin. Strips of flesh hung from her cheeks, her arms, the tops of her breasts. There were pieces of shapeless meat on the floor and stuck to her drab uniform.

Dez slid her flashlight into its belt holster, bent, and peered at the wounds. They were strange. Not one clean cut. No puckered bullet holes. No gouges like you'd see from a claw hammer. The skin looked shredded.

Dez heard a faint gagging sound and half turned to JT.

"If you're going to hurl, do it outside."

He looked gray but shook his head.

"Take a breath, Hoss," Dez advised, and he did. Slow and ragged.

"God," he gasped and mopped sweat off his face with his sleeve. "I've seen every kind of traffic accident. I've seen decapitations and . . . all that. But, Christ, Dez, I think those are *bites*."

"I know," said Dez softly. "Doc, too?"

JT nodded. "The door was ajar . . . You think a bear got in here?"

She studied his face for a moment. "C'mon, JT . . . this wasn't any fucking bear. There'd be slash marks with a bear."

"Coyote?" He sounded more hopeful than speculative.

Over the last decade several packs of coyotes had repopulated rural Pennsylvania. They were vicious, violent creatures, and they'd taken a serious toll on the house pet population. However, attacks on humans were extremely rare, and their bites looked like dog bites. Dez leaned as close as possible without stepping into the pool of blood.

"No," she said as she straightened. "Wasn't a bear, a coyote, or a fucking Bigfoot, and you know it."

JT was panting like a runner. "Dez . . . you don't think these are human bites, do you?"

It was clear to both of them—to anyone who'd ever seen the blunt bite signature of human teeth—what kind of bites these were. Dez kept a poker face. "Forensics will take castings," she said.

Dez stepped back and walked into the other room to take a look at Doc Hartnup. He lay in a rag-doll twist on the bloody tile floor. JT drifted up behind her.

It hurt Dez's heart to see him like that. Doc was one of the good guys.

"JT, look at this," she said, pointing to the bulge in the left rear hip of Hartnup's trousers. "Looks like his wallet's still there."

"Car keys are on a peg by the door," JT said. "Perp left in his own car."

"He was barefoot when he went outside. *If* those are the perp's footprints." Dez shook her head. "We need forensics and detectives on this. This isn't falling together for me. There's a lot of valuable stuff in here, and there's a flat-screen and Blu-ray in the office. Why not take them?"

"Maybe he didn't have time. We might have spooked him and he went out into the Grove."

Dez nodded. That was an ugly possibility. The Grove connected to the state forest half a mile from there.

"Tell you what, Hoss," she said, "It's going to be a circus here soon. We have to start a log on this and I don't want to screw anything up. Go get your camera from the cruiser."

JT gave a distracted nod but didn't move.

Dez straightened and snapped her fingers under JT's face, startling him.

"Yo! You in there? If you need to bug out, then bug out. Go sit in the car, whatever; but don't lose your shit in here."

JT gave her a five-count stare.

"You cool?" Dez asked, her tone quiet but not soft, her blue eyes hard as metal.

He drew in a long breath through his nostrils and gave a curt nod. "Yeah. I'm cool."

Dez grinned. "Okay—then put on your big girl panties and let's be cops."

JT gave a half laugh. "Okay. Sorry. It's just that—"

"When you get the camera," Dez interrupted, "bring the shotgun. Just in case Cannibal Lecter comes back. We don't want to offer him a pork sandwich."

That squeezed a fraction of smile from JT's pinched features. He headed outside. Dez fished in a pocket for gum and popped two pieces of Eclipse from the aluminum blister pack and crunched them thoughtfully between her teeth.

Poor JT, she thought as she stood in the doorway, watching him for a few seconds. Under every other circumstance he was nominally in charge, and Dez knew it. They both knew it. He was better at most aspects of the job. They were both good with it. He'd been on the job longer, too; but her five years in the military made all the difference in how they were reacting to the horror of this moment. While JT was rolling along the back roads of Stebbins County, Dez had been playing hide-and-seek with the Taliban in the Afghan hills. She was never Special Forces, but she humped her share of battle rattle over miles of desert, working everything from Haji patrol to scouting IEDs to dodging red-on-red fire, working in the first wave of American women to go into battle side by side with the men. She'd seen every kind of carnage and mayhem modern weapons could create and carrion animals could make worse. Had it been any other guy but JT losing his shit on the job, Dez would have torn him a new one. JT was like family; different rules applied.

Her thoughts drifted from JT to the crime scene. This was big and it could easily get out of hand. If the perpetrator had gone into the Grove, then that would mean putting together a massive manhunt. Beyond the lawn and the Grove, the state forest was an easy place to get lost and stay lost; not to mention the tens of thousands of square acres of farmland in Stebbins County. Hundreds of farm roads, fire access roads, country lanes, trails crosses and game trails to follow. If the killer was even half smart, it would take a hundred men with dogs and helicopters to run him to ground; and even then it might take days to do it. Days they might not have if the coming storm was as bad as they were saying on the news.

She turned away and looked down at the corpse.

Doc Hartnup . . . Damn.

Dez had known plenty of soldiers who had been killed in battle or by things like land mines and suicide vests; but she had never known anyone who had been murdered. She was surprised that it felt so much worse.

"This is fucked up," she told the dead man. JT returned a moment later with the camera. He also carried a Mossberg shotgun, which Dez would die rather than use because the weapon was loaded with beanbag rounds. She thought they were sissy rounds and once remarked that it was the lethal-force equivalent of giving the perp a blow job. JT knew different—the beanbag round would put anyone from a badass biker to a spaced-out meth head on his ass—but that wasn't enough for Dez.

Dez took the digital Nikon. "I'll document the scene," she said.

"Why don't you walk the perimeter? Figure out where the perp went so we can get some boots on the ground in pursuit. I'd like to bag this dickhead before shift ends so I can spend all night beating the living shit out of him in the holding cell. Sound good?"

He laughed, and it was clear he wasn't sure if she was joking.

"And, JT," she added, "keep your eyes open. This asshole might be outside. He just killed two people . . . Don't get into a debate with him." She punctuated her remark with a sharp nod toward the weapon he held. JT jacked a round into the shotgun and went outside without a word.

Dez went into the adjoining office, stepping gingerly over the bloody footprints, and stood on a clean section of carpet, aiming the camera toward the doorway. She took shots that established a clear trail from the prep room into this one. Then she bent over and took close-ups of the bare footprints. She took incremental overlapping pics so that they could be lined up later to show an unbroken progression from one killing room to the other.

The flash popped everything into moments of brightness that reminded Dez of the starkness of the skies in Afghanistan.

Flash.

Dez shot the handprints on the wall. She shot the blood spatter on the lampshade and across the desk. She shot the pool of blood around the wheeled office chair. She turned and straightened to take photos of the vic.

Flash.

And the cleaning woman was standing right there.

Right.

There.

Flash.

Dez stared in absolute and uncomprehending horror at the big Russian woman standing two feet away. Eyes open to reveal nothing. There was no hint of awareness or pain or anything in those bottomless black eyes.

"I don't—" Dez began.

And the woman snarled and lunged at her.

CHAPTER EIGHT
HARTNUP'S TRANSITION ESTATE

The woman slammed into Dez with full weight, grabbing her hair, driving Dez backward, and then they were falling. The woman snarled—a weird gargling impossibility that came from her ruined throat—and darted her head forward even as they crashed onto the coffee table, exploding it into a thousand fragments of wood and decorative inlay. The impact tore a scream from Dez as the woman's two hundred pounds came down on her and items on her utility belt punched into spine and kidneys and ribs.

She heard the woman's blood-streaked teeth clack together an inch from her ear. Dez jammed her forearm under the woman's chin as the teeth snapped again and again, trying to bite her face, her ear, her windpipe. Black clotted blood dribbled from the corners of the woman's mouth and splashed on Dez's cheeks and shirt.

"Get off of me you crazy bitch!" Dez screamed, twisting her body to try to escape the crushing weight.

The Russian kept trying to twist her fingers into Dez's French braid. The woman straddled Dez, massive thighs blocking her from grabbing her weapons. Yet for all of the woman's bulk she was strangely limp, as if her muscles were half-asleep and sagging. It was a horrible dead-weight quality, and it made escape much harder.

There was no real plan to the cleaning woman's attack except to pull Dez close enough to bite. She snarled and hissed and bit the air, squirming to get her chin around the barrier of Dez's forearm. Fending off those teeth was immediately exhausting because it meant that Dez had to push away most of that slack, squirming mass.

The woman tried to spit at Dez, expectorating a viscous mass of dead blood at her, but Dez twisted away. The black goo splatted on the floor, and out of the corner of Dez's eye she could see something like maggots squirming in the muck.

"Christ!"

Dez finally managed to pull her right arm free. The camera was still attached to her wrist by its lanyard; Dez grabbed it and smashed it with all her strength against the woman's temple. The impact shot pain through Dez's wrist; pieces of metal and plastic flew everywhere, and the force knocked the Russian woman's head away. But that was all it did. There was absolutely no change of expression on the woman's face, even though a flap of skin as large as a silver dollar flopped down onto her cheek. The wound did not bleed . . . and there was no reaction at all to the blow or the pain that it must have caused.

A growl burst from low in Dez's chest as she swung again and again, hitting with the camera every time, mashing the woman's ear, splitting her eyebrow, grinding into temple and eye socket and sinus. The jagged edges of the broken camera tore the woman's face to red ribbons.

But they did not slow the woman's attack at all. She did not even attempt to block the blows. She kept trying to bite, her cold fingers continued to scrabble and grab. The woman spat more black blood at Dez, splattering her uniform shirt.

"JT!" Dez screamed as panic surged up inside of her.

Then Dez pulled her heels close to her own buttocks, bent her knees and placed her soles flat on the ground, then she abruptly snapped her hips upward in a reverse bronco buck-off. The sudden upward thrust bounced the Russian woman's body into the air, and Dez instantly rolled sideways, using the turn of her hips against the inside of the attacker's thighs. Leverage won out and the woman fell sideways.

Dez immediately rolled the other way, spinning onto her side and kicking out at the woman with both feet, catching her in the chest and face and knocking her back against the sofa.

The woman was not even stunned. She flopped back from the point of impact, flopped onto her hands and knees, and began crawling toward Dez.

"Shit!" Dez rolled onto her back and drew her Glock. "Fucking *freeze!*"

The woman snarled and snapped her teeth together—and lunged. Dez fired.

The bullet caught the woman in the upper chest, punching a black hole through the breastbone an inch below the clavicle. The force sent the woman reeling back on her knees, arms flailing like a supplicant in the throes of a religious mania. There was no pain on her face, no sign that she even noticed the .44 round that had punched through her body. Her lips curled back from bloody teeth and she dove once more at Dez.

Dez screamed and fired.

The second round caught the woman on the side of the chin and blew a hole out past her ear, spraying the sofa with blood and flecks of gray matter.

The woman paused, her feral expression dissolving into vacuity, her mouth losing the firmness of its snarl.

And still she did not go down.

Dez felt the world spin around her. Two shots at this range. *Two shots.* Chest and face. There was bone and brain tissue on the goddamn couch. This was impossible.

It could *not* be the truth.

With bizarre slowness, the woman came on, throwing herself at Dez's legs, grabbing at her thighs, teeth apart to bite.

Dez bent forward and slammed the hot barrel against the woman's forehead.

"Fucking *die*!"

She squeezed the trigger. Once. Twice. The woman's head exploded. Skull fragments and strips of dura mater and brain pulp blew back against the sofa and the wall and the floor lamp.

The woman . . . collapsed.

All at once.

Just as JT burst through the door from the prep room with the shotgun.

CHAPTER NINE
HARTNUP'S TRANSITION ESTATE

"Dez—are you all right?" JT demanded as he rushed to her.

"I . . ." Dez's voice faltered on the first word as she saw the gore that was splattered on her legs and gun hand. She saw the squirming larvae and went into a hysterical fit, slapping the stuff off her clothes. "God!"

"Are you hurt?"

"No—help me the fuck up!"

JT hooked a hand under her armpit and pulled her out from under the corpse. Dez's heels scrabbled at the blood-soaked floor as she backpedaled into JT. He lost his grip on her ten feet from the corpse, and Dez fell hard on her ass and sat there, staring, mouth open, shaking her head. Her gun fell from her hand and she made no move to pick it up; so JT did.

"What happened?"

His question seemed to be coming from another room; it was tinny and distant and Dez wasn't sure if he was really there. JT came around and squatted down in front of her. His face twisted into a frown of doubt and he snapped his fingers the same way she had done to him—God, was it only a few minutes ago? On some remote level Dez understood that she was in shock, just as she was aware that she was thinking about being in shock. Her mind was fragmented as it tried to crawl away from the precise reality of what just happened.

"I . . ." Dez began again, but didn't know where to go with it. She shook her head.

JT rose and helped Dez carefully to her feet, took her by the elbow and guided her across the room to a niche filled with filing cabinets. He still held her Glock in his other hand.

"Dez," he said softly, "what happened?"

"She attacked me," gasped Dez.

"No," he said, shaking his head, "Listen to me, Dez . . . the chief and the forensics people are going to be here soon. We need to have a story. We need to tell them something they're going to believe, so I need you to tell me what really happened. Why did you discharge your weapon? Was it accidental? No," he corrected himself, "I heard four shots. We can't sell that as accidental. Dez—did you see the perp? Did he come back? Is that what happened—you saw him and fired?"

Dez kept shaking her head. She pushed a strand of hair from her eyes with trembling fingers.

"Give me something, Dez," pleaded JT, his eyes clouding with the beginnings of panic. "We have to make sense of—"

"She fucking attacked me!" snarled Dez.

JT took a step backward. He looked at her, his eyes searching hers, then he turned and looked at the woman. When he turned back, his eyes kept meeting hers and darting away.

"Dez . . ."

"No, goddamn it. That Russian bitch attacked me."

"Okay, okay, I hear you. She attacked you. But . . . how?"

"What do you mean, 'how'?"

"Come on, Dez . . . She was dead. She—"

"Of course she wasn't dead, dumb-ass!"

"Dez, her whole throat was torn open. We both saw it—"

"Then we saw it *wrong*." Dez took a steadying breath. "Look, JT, I did not imagine that woman tackling me, and I sure as hell didn't put four rounds into her for shits and giggles. She. Came. After. Me." She spaced the words, slow and loud.

JT raised his head into an attitude of listening. Dez heard it, too. Sirens. "Look, Dez, you know I have your back, right? That's unquestioned. I'll tell any story you want me to tell. Screw the chief and screw everyone else . . . but you got to give me something to work with. We can't spin a fairy tale."

"JT . . ."

"They're going to blood test you," he said. He dropped the magazine and ejected the round from the chamber, then thumbed the round back into the magazine and slid it back into the receiver. He didn't return her weapon, however. "What's your blood alcohol—"

"Fuck you."

"No," he said firmly. "Don't close me out. I'm on your side, remember? How many ways do I have to say it? But you have to tell me what happened here."

Dez pointed a finger at the corpse.

"She could not have been dead, JT. No way. I don't care how it looked. We made a bad call on that. You want a story, then that's the story, and it's the truth. She tried to fucking bite me."

"Bite you," JT repeated without inflection. He crossed to the corpse, squatted down and touched the backs of his fingers to her cheek, her forearm, the inside of her wrist. As he rose he flicked back toward the prep room where Doc Hartnup lay. He walked back slowly to Dez, his dark features lined with concern and doubt.

"Yes, she tried to bite me. Guess biting's a frigging theme around here."

"Her skin's pretty cold, Dez."

"I don't care if she's packed in ice, JT. She had me pinned down and I punched the shit out of her and told her to back down and I might as well have been pissing up a rope. She came after me and tried to tear my throat out."

"So you shot her."

"Yes, I fucking shot her."

"An unarmed woman."

"Yes," Dez snapped.

"A seriously injured unarmed woman."

"Ah—Christ, JT."

The sirens were close. Turning off of the highway onto the access road.

"You shot her four times, Dez. How many shots does it take to—"

Dez suddenly shoved him, and JT staggered backward into the row of filing cabinets. A vase of gardenias fell off and smashed on the edge of a secretary's desk. Before he could recover his balance, Dez snatched her Glock out of his hands and shoved it into her holster.

"I never thought you'd turn on me, JT," she said bitterly. She wanted to punch him, to knock him down and stomp on him. She wanted to cry, too, but she would eat her own gun before she'd do that on the job. Even after what just happened.

JT got slowly to his feet, his eyes flicking from her face to her gun hand. "You're scaring the shit out of me, Dez. You're acting irrational here and—"

"I'm perfectly rational. I didn't lose it and I'm not drunk. Or hopped up on anything. You want to Breathalyze me? Fine, and when it comes up clean I'm going to shove it up your ass."

"Calm down, Dez. I didn't say—"

The sirens were right outside now, the wails filling the room with implications. Dez closed her eyes for a moment as she heard car doors open and feet crunch on the gravel. Voices began yelling as the front and back doors banged open and officers from Stebbins and two neighboring towns flooded into the mortuary.

"Dez," JT said slowly, "you know what they're going to say.

They're going to look at the body. They're going to take her tempera-ture and test lividity and do the science that's going to show how long she's been dead. And then they're going to match that against our re-sponse time on the call logs. Then they're going to look at those bul-let wounds."

"So what? Let them look!"

"Come on, Dez. . . . You shot her four times. How come none of the wounds bled?"

Dez took an involuntary step back as if JT had punched her. "What?"

JT pointed. "Corpses don't bleed. Either you killed her on the first shot, in which case they're going to want to know why you kept shooting—and from different angles and distances—or you killed her with the head shots and they're going to ask you to explain why the perpetrator you shot in the chest didn't bleed." He shook his head, and his voice had a pleading note to it. "What do we tell them, Dez?"

There didn't seem to be enough air to breathe, and Dez could not answer his questions. Her chest was tight with tension, her heart hammered with fear. She looked down at the dead woman, following the line of gaze of the arriving officers, seeing the extremity of the violence. Seeing the blood and pieces of human debris as if through their eyes.

Jesus Christ, she thought, *this is it for me. If JT doesn't believe me, then no one will.*

Wild panic flared in her, and she looked around as if hoping to see a door marked "EXIT." But one door led back to the charnel house of the prep room and the other was the route a killer had used to flee this insane crime scene.

Then that door suddenly opened and Chief Martin Goss waddled through the door from the prep room and into the office. He was a short, fat man with boiled red skin that was permanently coated with hypertensive sweat.

Goss's eyes went from JT to Dez to the corpse and back again. He looked at the gore splattered on Dez's uniform.

"Holy Jesus jumped-up Christ," he said. "Dez—are you okay?"

"I'm fine," she mumbled.

"You sure? We have paramedics inbound—"

She nodded. "I'm good, Chief. Just shook up."

"JT?"

"I'm fine. I was outside when this went down."

Goss licked his lips. "Your call-in said that there was a suspect on foot?"

JT showed him the tracks of the bloody bare feet. "Prints disappear near the edge of the lawn. Looks like the suspect was heading west, but that's a guess."

Goss nodded curtly, clicked his shoulder mike and relayed the information to the rest of the team, ordering a search and advising extreme caution. He also called the state police and requested their assistance. The staties had more men and they had choppers. Other officers, including Paul Scott, the county's forensics officer, flooded into the place. Scott flicked a brief glance at JT and Dez and then went into the other room, his evidence collection bag in hand.

Then Goss turned back to JT and Dez. "Okay . . . now tell me everything that happened."

Dez started to speak, but her words came out in a jumble. She could hear the panic in her own voice.

JT stepped in and took a swing at it. Despite his earlier reactions, he appeared to have reclaimed his calm, and he gave the report in quick, clinical police jargon, from the moment they parked the car, to the handprint in the utility room, to finding Doc Hartnup's body. Goss's eyes narrowed for a moment, but he didn't interrupt; Dez watched his face, trying to read him.

JT said, "Believing this to be an active crime scene, we did only a cursory examination of the second victim and determined that she was dead. I went outside to do a walk-around while Dez—I mean Officer Fox—began documenting the crime scene in here with a digital camera. The, um . . ." he paused only a second, Dez had to give him that much, "second victim was apparently still alive and proceeded to attack Officer Fox in a very aggressive and irrational way. Officer Fox was compelled to use deadly force to protect her own life."

The officers had all stopped to listen to this account. Their faces registered varying levels of confusion, doubt, and disgust. Paul Scott came back in and bent close to whisper something to Goss. The chief looked at him, went and peered into the other room, and then came back and studied the faces of both JT and Dez. His face was clouded with confusion and doubt.

He's not buying it, Dez thought. *I am well and truly fucked.*

"That's it?" asked Chief Goss slowly, his eyebrows arched almost to his hairline. "That's your story?"

"That's the way it happened, Chief," said JT.

Dez nodded. Her clothes were splattered with blood, her hair was in disarray, and she knew that she must look like a crazy woman.

Goss pointed at the dead woman. "Did you inflict those injuries on her throat?"

"Of course not," Dez began, but JT touched her arm.

"She appeared to have sustained some injuries when we arrived on the scene, Chief," said JT. "As I said, we did a cursory examination and—"

"Did you also do a *cursory* examination on Doc Hartnup?"

JT winced at the inflection Goss put on "cursory." "Yes, sir."

"Did you determine that he was *probably* dead or *apparently* still alive?"

"Dead, sir," said Dez.

"Really?" Goss said slowly. "The cleaning lady attacked you in here?"

"Yes."

"What about Doc Hartnup?"

"Sir?"

"Did he attack you, too?"

"No," said Dez. "JT told you, the doc was already dead when we got here."

"Really?" Goss went and pointed into the other room. "Then where the fuck is his body?"

Dez shot JT a look and then the two of them hurried over to the entrance to the prep room. There were several officers in there and blood everywhere. Some of it was red, some was black, like the sputum the Russian woman had spat at her. Tiny worms, like maggots, writhed in it. A set of bloody footprints led from the large pool of blood on the floor to the open back door.

But there was no body.

Doc Hartnup was gone.

CHAPTER TEN

He answered the phone with, "Fishing for news with Billy Trout."

His voice was dead, his body slumped into an executive desk chair that he swore once belonged to the misogynistic serial murderer Gerald Stano. He called the chair "Old Sparky" after the much different seat by which Stano exited the world in a Florida prison execution room.

"This you, Billy?" The caller was a man with a Mississippi accent.

"Mmh," grunted Trout. He was six clues away from finishing the *New York Times* crossword. Thirty-eight down was a six-letter word for "parasite." He tried "lawyer," "ex-wife," and "editor," but none of them would fit.

"You still doing those weird news segments?" asked the caller.

"Hence the clever way I answer the phone," murmured Trout with disinterest.

"Still paying for the good stuff?"

"Depends. Who's calling?"

"It's Barney Schlunke."

"Ah," said Trout and filled in the clue: "I.N.S.E.C.T." He tossed the paper onto his desk. "You still in Rockview?"

"*At* Rockview. Inmates are in, staff are—"

"I know. It was a joke. We saw each other yesterday. . . . What do you want?"

"Yeah, I tried to talk to you yesterday at the execution, but you ducked out before I could get free."

What a shame, thought Trout. "Talk to me about what?"

"A news tip."

Trout snorted. "The only news around here is the storm and I'm not a weatherman."

"Not that kind of story. Look, Billy, I wanted to know if you're still paying the same rates for tips as you used to?"

"If it's something good I can give you seventy-five percent."

Schlunke snorted. "You going cheap on me?"

"No," said Trout, "the economy blows, or don't you read the papers?"

"Who reads the fucking papers? News is free on the Internet."

"And you wonder why I've cut my rates?"

"I want the same rates as before."

"Can't do it. As it is seventy-five percent is my kids not eating."

"You don't have kids."

"I got alimony and both of my ex-wives are immature. Works out the same."

"Believe me," said Schlunke, "this is worth the regular rate—"

"This *is* the regular rate."

"—plus another twenty-five percent on top."

"I can't afford to feed a drug habit."

"I don't do drugs."

"Then I can't afford to feed your Internet porn habit, Schlunke."

"God, I can't tell you how much I missed being your straight man, Billy. Maybe I should be doing drugs, 'cause I must be having a psychotic episode. I mean . . . I think I'm talking to an actual reporter who wants an actual goddamn exclusive. But . . . hey, maybe that's just the magic mushrooms talking."

"That's sidesplitting," yawned Trout. It occurred to him that Schlunke was one of those rare people who looked exactly like his name. He was a big, sloppy, shambling lump of a southern boy who came to Pennsylvania because Mississippi wasn't redneck enough. Trout grudgingly conceded to himself that Schlunke had sent three or four good stories his way over the years. "Okay, okay," he said, "you tell me what you have and I'll tell you if it's worth full price."

"Full price is one hundred and twenty-five percent of your old rate."

"Just tell me."

"Word of honor?"

Trout smiled as he glanced around the newsroom. It looked like a Hollywood set dresser had made sure there was every possible stereotype and sight gag appropriate to a regional paper sliding down the greasy slope to the septic tank. Stacks of bundled papers. Two-thirds of the desks empty; the other one-third buried under clutter so comprehensive that it had long ago morphed into a single eyesore rather than a collection of unique and separate pieces of junk; wall clocks that were still set to the wrong hour of daylight saving time; and one other reporter asleep with his heels on his desk and a John Grisham novel open on his chest.

It depressed him. He could remember a time—not that long ago— when coming to work filled him with excitement. Of course, back then he believed that journalists were the good guys and the voice of the people—and that the truth actually *mattered*. Time and the economy had beaten most of that out of him. Now it was a job, and soon it might not even be that.

Regional Satellite News was one of the hybrid services that had begun to crop up during the rise of twenty-first-century Internet news and the death spiral of print. Trout and his fellow reporters fed news stories to over forty print papers in Western Pennsylvania— none of them first rate—and they fed video stories to the Internet and, on good days, to services like the AP. The had very few "good" days here in the hinterlands of Stebbins County.

"Really," said Trout. "You'd take my word?"

"Ha! How's it feel to be someone else's straight man?"

"Fucking hilarious. How's it feel to hear me hang up?"

"You won't. Not with what I have for you."

Billy Trout tapped the eraser of his pencil on his desk blotter for a three count. "Okay. One twenty-five. But this had better be worth—"

"Two words for you," said the prison guard. "Homer Gibbon."

"I got two words for you. Yesterday's news."

He heard Schlunke chuckle.

"You do know he's dead?" Trout said. "Oh, wait . . . as I remember you were fucking there when they gave him the lethal injection and, another news flash—so was I! Gosh, how long ago was that? Yesterday? No, I lie . . . It's twenty-three hours and—"

"—and there's more to the story if you'd shut up and listen."

"Okay," sighed Trout. "This is me shutting up."

"Ever since Gibbon lost his last appeal and the execution date was set there has been a neverending media shit storm. Reporters camped out in the parking lot. I don't know how you snagged a ticket to the show—"

"I have friends in low places."

"—but once that asshole was dead, the party broke up. Now, new chapter. The official story was that Gibbon was going to be buried in some nondescript hole on the prison grounds."

"Fair enough."

"But that's not what happened."

Trout's interest perked up by half a degree. Homer Gibbon was the state's most notorious serial killer. He had been convicted on eleven counts of murder and was suspected of having actually killed more than forty women and children in Pennsylvania, Ohio, New Jersey, Maryland, and Virginia over a seventeen-year period. Although he had never formally admitted to any of the murders, he was convicted on an evidentiary case so compelling that the jury's deliberation had lasted only two hours. Appeal followed appeal, but during the last appeal forensic evidence from a cold-case murder in Scranton irrefutably tied Gibbon to the rape and murder of a diner waitress and her two-year-old daughter. The murder had been shockingly brutal, with elements of torture so repellent that even the most jaded reporter tended to generalize about the details. The appeal died, the new trial was quick, the death penalty given, and the governor approved execution by lethal injection for the first time since Gary Heidnik was put down in 1999. Even the expected protests by human rights and prolife groups were listless. Nobody wanted Gibbon to live.

"So what *did* happen?" asked Trout.

"The remains were shipped to his family."

"Uh-uh. He didn't have any family. I did the background on Gibbon."

"I know, right? You wanted to do one of those bullshit human interest things. 'What's the cost to the family of the killer?' or 'The victims aren't the only victims.' Some crap like that."

"I'm so glad you respect my work."

"C'mon, Trout, let's be real here. I lock shit up and you shovel it onto the headlines. Neither of us is doing any great humanitarian good here. Best-case scenario for me is I make life hell for the baby-rapers while they're waiting for the system to put them back into the community; and maybe you write a piece once every ten years that has more genuine heart than exploitive bullshit. Tell me I'm wrong."

Trout was impressed. Schlunke was an insect but apparently not as stupid a creepy-crawly as previously thought. Trout filed that away.

"The family," he prompted, swinging back to that. "The court records said he had no family."

"Court records were wrong. Some old broad stepped up after the last appeal. Said that she was his aunt and apparently produced enough proof to convince the judge and the warden. Point is, she petitioned to claim the body for burial. All last minute, all hush-hush."

Trout was genuinely interested now. "An aunt, huh? How old?"

"'Bout two years older than dirt. She arranged to have his body shipped back and to have a mortician tidy Gibbon up before they put him in a pine box."

"What cemetery would allow—"

"No . . . She wanted to bury him on the family estate. Well . . . farm. Used to be an estate but there isn't much of it left. Few dozen acres that have been left to grow wild. There's a family cemetery behind the house, and she wants Homer Gibbon buried there."

"Why? She trying to ruin the property value?" asked Trout, but he was already seeing it. Old lady who's only relative is a serial murderer. Maybe she knew him as a kid and wants to honor the child he'd been rather than the man he'd become. Classic stuff. Or, maybe she really believed in the defense's theory that Gibbon suffered from a chemical imbalance. Was that the tether she used to cling to her self-respect and the family name?

"Are you even fucking listening to me?" growled Schlunke.

"Sure, sure," Trout lied, thinking that the story might actually have legs. Could be a feature piece. A heartbreaker. Might even be something that could be squeezed into a Lifetime movie if the aunt was a Betty White type. "You were saying . . . aunt, burial prep . . ."

"When she petitioned the judge to receive the body, she requested that the information not be released to the press. She was afraid that his grave would be desecrated by friends and family of Gibbon's victims, or by kids. Thrill seekers and stuff."

"Yeah, yeah," said Trout. He was casting the rest of the movie in his head. Maybe go with Kristen Bell as the waitress who gets killed. "But I need that address. Story's dead without it."

"I know. So . . . we're absolutely clear on the hundred-twenty-five percent?"

"You're on the wrong side of those bars, Schlunke."

"Yes or no?"

"Yes, yes, yes. Now where's the fucking aunt li—"

"Stebbins."

Trout missed a beat, then said, "What?"

"Stebbins. The aunt . . . She lives in Stebbins."

"But . . . I live in . . ."

"Yeah," said Schlunke, "the old broad lives in your town."

CHAPTER ELEVEN
HARTNUP'S TRANSITION ESTATE

"Find him!" bellowed Chief Goss. "Doc Hartnup's injured and prob-ably in shock."

"Going to rain soon," said one of the officers.

"Then hustle your ass. If he's hurt then he can't have gotten far."

"He's not injured, Chief, he's fucking dead. Somebody stole his body," Dez said, but her voice was small. JT looked at her and gave a small shake of his head.

Officers ran in all directions, plunging into the woods, banging open doors on the outbuildings, shining lights into corners and under parked cars. Goss called the news in for the officers already combing the woods for the killer. They were working the far side of the mortu-ary.

"Here!" yelled an officer from Nesbitt who had been working his way across the lawn toward the woods. Dez ran toward him. For a fat man, Goss could move fast, and he was only a step behind JT. The Nesbitt officer—a black-haired kid named Diviny who was one year out of the academy—knelt on the grass on the forest side of the prop-erty. He pointed at a scuff of blood on the pea gravel and the streaks of red on bent blades of grass. "Looks like he went into the woods."

JT bent and peered at the blood trail and then began following it, keeping to one side to protect the evidence. Dez flanked him on the other side of the trail. The smears of blood faded from bright wetness to faint touches to nothing forty yards from the wall of trees.

"Lost it," said Diviny, who was dogging JT and, Dez thought, clearly avoiding her. All of the cops were giving her strange looks.

Fuck 'em, she thought. Her nerves were still jangling and the skepticism of Goss and the other officers was doing nothing to take her blood pressure off the burner. If this had been a UFO sighting or if she'd seen Bigfoot poking through her garbage can, then maybe she'd give some weight to JT's unspoken assumption that her perceptions were still being filtered through a mix of Jack Daniels and Yuengling lager. But what happened back in the mortuary office was no visual hallucination, and it wasn't pink fucking elephants. The woman had been dead. And then she had gotten up and gone apeshit. That was fact. Dez could still feel the slack weight of the woman bearing her down to the ground and her cold fingers trying to grab Dez's hair.

She hunkered down and peered at the grass. "No . . . look at the grass."

Diviny and JT bent low and looked where she was pointing. The grass was short and springy, resistant to footfall impressions, but as the law of forensics goes, every contact leaves a trace. Some of the grass, though unbroken, was pushed down and was still in the process of standing up.

"Nice catch," said Goss, but there was a strong reserve in his voice. "Diviny, see if you can find this asshole. If you spot him, don't engage—call for backup." Goss gestured to an officer from Nesbitt. "Natalie—go with him, okay? No heroes."

They nodded and moved off toward the trees.

"Where do you want JT and me?" ask Dez.

Goss sucked his teeth for a moment. "I want you to go sit in your unit and write me up a report I can live with. No, don't look at me like that, it's not a request."

"Why?" asked JT. "This is an active crime scene and—"

"—and it appears that a victim of a violent attack got up and waltzed right out of your crime scene."

Dez cursed silently. She wanted to get away, go home.

"No way," insisted JT. "Doc Hartnup did not get up and walk away. No sir."

"Then pitch me another scenario, Officer Hammond." Goss pointed to the trail they had followed from the mortuary. "We followed shoe prints coming out of the building. That trail starts right where you said Doc was killed. I'll bet those shoe impressions are going to match those of the victim. Are you suggesting, officers, that someone entered the crime scene while you were engaged in your violent struggle with the cleaning woman, took the time to put the dead man's shoes on his own feet, then picked up the body and carried it into the woods? Take your time; think it through before you answer."

JT clamped his jaw shut so firmly Dez thought his teeth were going to crack.

The chief's eyes flicked back and forth between the two of them. "We called in for a shitload of backup. If Diviny and Natalie come up dry, we'll start a proper search of the woods, and our people are already checking the buildings."

Dez pointed to the gables of a whitewashed Victorian barely visible beyond the Grove. "At least let us check Doc's old house."

"I thought it was empty," said Goss.

"It's up for sale, yes, but it's not empty," corrected Dez. "Doc's sister, April, and her two little kids, Tommy and Gail, have been living there while her divorce is being finalized. Been there two weeks. We didn't get a chance to check on them, so let us—"

"No," Goss said firmly. "I'll send someone else. You go work on that report. Give me something that doesn't sound like science-fucking-fiction."

Dez turned away to keep the hurt she was feeling from showing. JT sighed heavily. They watched officers Ken Gunther and Dana Howard vanish into a path that wound through the Grove to the old Hartnup house. Without turning, Dez said, "This was a righteous shooting, Chief."

When the chief did not answer, Dez turned and locked eyes with him for several silent seconds. Gradually, the stern line of Goss's mouth softened a little and he sighed. "Christ, I hope so, Dez."

JT said, "Are we going to need a lawyer?"

Goss sighed. "Not with me. But the state's going to come in on this, no question about it. Talk to the union rep, get their lawyers on standby."

They turned suddenly as the forensic officer, Scott, came hurrying out of the mortuary, waving a clipboard at them. As he closed in on them he said, "JT, Dez . . . what happened to the third body?"

JT and Dez stared blankly at him.

"Which third body?" asked Goss.

"The dead one," said Scott.

"You trying to be funny?" barked JT.

"No," said Scott, "I mean the body from the morgue. The one that Doc Hartnup was here to work on. What happened to it?"

JT shook his head. "There were no bodies in the cold room or the prep room. Doc might have been here to do paperwork or—"

"No," Scott cut in, "there was definitely a body." He tapped the papers on the clipboard with a fingernail. "It was on the log. Came in a little over two hours ago. Doc signed for it himself."

"There were footprints of a third person," JT said slowly. "Somebody must have come in and moved the body."

"Footprints I saw were bare feet," said Scott. "That's kind of weird."

"Everything's kind of weird today," JT said under his breath. "Question is why someone—bare feet or not—would come in, kill Doc Hartnup, attack the cleaning lady, and then carry off a corpse."

Scott sucked his teeth. "Maybe this was all about stealing the body. Someone breaks in to do that and didn't know Doc was there. Might have been opportunistic."

"Doc's car's parked right outside," said Goss.

"Yeah, but Doc could have arrived after the perp was inside. Ditto for the cleaning lady."

"Which brings us back to why someone would want to steal a corpse," said JT. "And it might have been more than one person. Corpses are heavy as hell."

"Yeah, dead weight," joked Scott. No one laughed. He cleared his throat and said, "Seems like an obvious motive to me."

"Not to me," growled Goss.

"Are you kidding? Celebrity corpses are hot," Scott said, gesturing with the clipboard, "especially one like this?"

The word "celebrity" hung in the air for a moment, and then Dez snatched the clipboard out of Scott's hand. She scanned the form and gasped.

Goss and JT read over her shoulder. The top sheet was a standard mortuary receiving order for the transfer of a body from a prison to a local funeral home. However, it was attached to a signed and notarized confidentiality agreement from the warden of the State Correctional Institution at Rockview. It was couched in complex legalese that promised fines, loss of business license and criminal prosecution if Dr. Lee Hartnup broke the seal of secrecy to reveal the name of the deceased prisoner entrusted to his care.

Standing there under the harsh morning light, they read the name.

Dez was unable to speak. Goss just stared at the paper, mouthing the name silently.

JT whispered, "Holy mother of God . . ."

The name of the deceased was Homer Gibbon.

CHAPTER TWELVE
MAGIC MARTI IN THE MORNING
WNOW RADIO, MARYLAND

"This is Magic Marti at the mike with the latest on the storm. Despite heavy winds, the storm front is slowing down and looks like it's going to park right on the Maryland-Pennsylvania border, with Stebbins County taking the brunt of it. They're calling for torrential rains and strong winds, along with severe flooding. And here's a twist . . . even though this is a November storm, warm air masses from the south are bringing significant lightning, and so far there have been several serious strikes. Air traffic is being diverted around the storm. So, let's settle back and listen to some appropriate tunes. First up we have Bob Dylan with 'A Hard Rain's A-Gonna Fall.'"

CHAPTER THIRTEEN
OFFICES OF REGIONAL SATELLITE NEWS

Billy Trout was totally jazzed about the story. Or stories, as it would probably turn out. There was the short-term exclusive—Homer Gibbon, the killer comes home. That was gold, particularly since the only previous hometown for the serial killer had been a series of foster homes in the Pittsburgh metropolitan area. Nobody—no-fucking-body—knew about his connection to Stebbins. Nobody knew he had an Aunt Selma.

And, Trout thought as he gathered up his field gear into his laptop case, how cool was the name "Selma"? Selma Elsbeth Conroy. Aunt Selma. It was tailor-made for a news story, and perfect for Hollywood. Which was the second story. Trout had promised himself that if there was even a scrap of meat on this bone he'd turn it into a box office feast. Fuck Lifetime . . . He was going to pitch this to someone huge. Scorsese. De Palma. Maybe Sam Raimi. Get Helen Mirren to play Aunt Selma. Maybe work in a hint of incest and get Kate Winslett to play Selma as a younger woman.

The thing was writing itself.

For the first time in weeks he felt like getting up and coming to work had some purpose. He was so excited that he wished he could call Dez Fox and share the news with her, but . . . that would be a bad move. The last time they broke up, Dez had made it abundantly clear that she would rather be eaten by rats than hear from Trout again. It didn't matter that the breakup was her fault.

Trout understood it because he understood Dez. He understood it every time they broke up, and every time they got back together. Dez was damaged goods and probably always would be. She had a heart of gold—Trout knew that for certain—but it was surrounded by barbed wire and land mines.

He glanced at the pictures of her that were pinned to the inside walls of his cubicle. Dez in tight jeans and a halter, wildflowers in her hair, laughing at something Trout had said while he took her picture.

Dez graduating from the police academy. Dez sitting along on the dock behind Trout's house, her arms wrapped around her knees, her whole body silhouetted by the setting sun. Dez in a heart-stopping string bikini that was little more than tiny triangles of brightly colored cloth. Dez as a teenager with braces when he picked her up for the junior prom.

Dez, Dez, Dez . . .

The memory that burned the hottest in his mind was not their breakup, which was both a legendary clusterfuck and a seven-day wonder for the local gossip mill. Nor was it the argument that had lit a fuse to their explosive deconstruction as a couple. No, the one unshakable and unpolluted memory that Trout lived with day and night—especially nights—was their last evening together before it all went wrong. It had been perfect. They'd spent the day riding horses through the state forest, Dez on a spirited gelding and Trout lumbering beside her on a Clydesdale who was a retired Amish lumber horse. The forest had been filled with flowers and birdsong, and it seemed that all they did was laugh. Dez had a great laugh. She laughed with her whole body, her eyes squeezed shut, tears streaming down her cheeks.

Then they'd gone back to his place. On any other night Dez might have chided him for the corniness of the set-up he'd prepared. Chilled wine, candles faintly scented with lavender and lilac, pink and red roses, and new sheets on the bed. They danced in the middle of the floor to Sade and then stood there and kissed until they were both lightheaded. Then Dez and Trout slowly peeled off the layers of clothes that kept their fingers and mouths from each other's skin.

When they were naked, there was a strange and lovely moment when they simply stood there and looked at each other. Trout touched her as gently as if she were a phantom of mist, his fingertips ghosting across her lips and throat, trailing lines of heat down her chest to each full breast and each pink nipple. She took him by the hand and led him to his bed. Sex for them was always good but often quick, with Dez wanting to brush past foreplay and get "right to it." That night was different. They spent a long time with each other, playing games that coaxed each other to the edge and then backed off, only to start again in another way. Then he lay back and gently pulled her on top of him. They made love slowly, as if they had all the time in the world. And then they lay together afterward, their bodies pulsing with animal heat, sweat running down to soak the sheets, hearts pounding rhythms that each could feel beneath the other's skin.

It was the last time they made love. Maybe the last time they ever would. Within a day they were at war and both knew how to fire the rockets that shattered hearts and hopes.

Trout almost dug out his cell phone to call her. Maybe she wasn't angry anymore. Maybe she'd calmed down enough to regret what she'd done. Maybe she missed him.

He left the phone in his pocket and, through force of will, shifted his mind back to the moment. To something real and present and tangible. Something over which he had actual control.

Trout let the excitement of this new story pump through him like adrenaline. He got up and headed down the hall to the video room. A young man was slouched in a chair, tapping a message into Twitter. He looked up as Trout slid into the chair next to him.

"Goat!" said Trout brightly. "Just the man I was looking for. Grab your camera."

Gregory "Goat" Weinman was a tall, gangly collection of loose-jointed limbs, tangled black curls, and never-seen-the-sun white skin wrapped in nouveau Bohemian mismatched clothes. "Oooo, are we having a 'stop the presses' moment?" he said without inflection.

"As a matter of fact," said Trout. "Get your stuff."

Goat finished composing his tweet and hit "Enter." Trout read the comment, which was an scathing observation about the latest Woody Allen film. Goat was the cameraman, film editor, general engineer for the Regional Satellite News, and, Trout knew, a prima donna of legendary dimensions. Goat was a failed indie filmmaker with an MFA from Carnegie Mellon and a far too refined sense of artistic snobbery to give him a snowball's chance in Hollywood. He might as well have "auteur" tattooed on his forehead. Trout also knew that Goat hated every second of it here in the land of regional cable news, but in this economy and with that temperament, it was the only steady work he could get. On the other hand, Goat could take footage of Little League games, Tea Party rallies, Nascar races, or gun shows and turn it into compelling viewing. It would win awards if anyone ever watched their shitty news feed, which no one did.

"C'mon," urged Trout. "Chop-chop."

"Not going to happen."

"Why? Did you finally watch all of the porn on the Net?"

"Don't I wish, but no. I was editing film all night. The frigging mayor's speech and the soccer game. If it wasn't for soccer moms I'd kill myself. Anyway, I'm beat, I'm out of here, man."

"This is important—"

"What? The storm? If you think I'm going to stand out in a frigging hurricane while Gino reads the weather, then you need better drugs."

"Screw the storm. I have a lead on something that might actually *be* something."

"Something by whose scale? Town or county?"

Trout grinned. "Figure somewhere between Pulitzer and Oscar."

Goat blinked. "You shitting me?"

"I shit thee not." Trout dropped the story on Goat.

"Oh hell yes," said Goat. "That's *huge.*"

"I know, right?"

"This is going to give the whole Gibbon story some new legs. Let me tweet something."

Trout nodded. Like anyone who still planned to have a future as a paid reporter, he understood the value of social networking. Twitter and Facebook moved mountains in terms of PR and buzz. Goat managed the online accounts for their division of Regional Satellite News, and he'd goosed the buzz to the point where RSN had over eighty thousand followers. Ten times the number of people who lived in the county.

"How's this?" Goat typed in a short message: "Coming soon— RSN exclusive—Untold secrets of Homer Gibbon!"

"Perfect," said Trout. "Short, though. I thought Twitter let you write a hundred and forty words."

"A hundred forty characters," corrected Goat. "Brevity is God to the ADD crowd. This is fifty-seven. Makes it easier for people to retweet it while keeping their user names. Helps with spreading it out even more." He paused. "When we get back, I think I'll edit a Homer Gibbon "best of" reel. News headlines, footage of the FBI pulling that body from the Dumpster in Akron, stand-ups from the trial, the perp walk, all that, then upload it to YouTube. We can post the link on Twitter, see if we can goose it to go viral. Prime the pump for when we drop the real bomb."

"Works for me," said Trout.

Goat shut off the computer and began stuffing equipment into a reinforced duffle. When he stood, he loomed over Trout like a giant stick bug. "Let's roll."

Three minutes later they were in Trout's Ford Explorer, bucketing along Doll Factory Road toward Transition Estate.

CHAPTER FOURTEEN
HARTNUP'S TRANSITION ESTATE

Officer Andrew Diviny was twenty-three years old. He had graduated from the police academy one year and four days ago and planned to log another year on Nesbitt PD to establish a solid record and maybe a commendation or two, and then he was going to put in an application to the FBI and blow Small Town America so fast his résumé would have skid marks. That had been the plan since high school. No way was he going to loiter in a dead-end former coal town like Nesbitt, a town whose only claim to fame was that it was not as much of a shithole as Stebbins.

He knew he fit the FBI profile to a tee. Good GPA from school and college, with a degree in criminal justice and a minor in accounting. That had been a deliberate choice. He knew that the FBI was all about accounting. Follow the money, even now with the Bureau under the auspices of Homeland. Everything was money, and Diviny knew numbers. He even liked accounting. His dad and uncles were CPAs and his mother had a degree in economics from Pitt.

As he ran softly through the grass toward the woods, he cut covert glances at the officer sent to accompany him. Natalie Shanahan. She was north of thirty, carrying ten pounds more weight than her uniform had been cut for, and she ran with her face pointed forward as if this was a game of catch-up rather than an exercise in tracking. She wouldn't find anything, Diviny was sure of it. He would. He'd pick up the trail once they were in the woods, and he'd find the missing victim. He would make the save, so to speak. It would go in his jacket.

He pulled a little ahead as they reached the edge of the lawn, wanting to be the first one into the Grove.

"Slow down, kid," puffed Shanahan, but Diviny pretended not to hear her.

The forest was thick with tall, dense pines whose shaggy coats of needles meshed together so tightly they turned bright morning into dim twilight. Diviny made sure that he had his flashlight out and on before Shanahan. He'd find a way to mention that in his report, always being careful to appear to be praising his fellow officer while slanting the details in his favor.

In the poor light the grass thinned and faded to bare earth and moss. Diviny spotted the erratic line of shoe impressions almost at once, but he crossed over them and edged toward the right, knowing that Shanahan would follow. She did, and he steered her twenty yards away from the trail.

"Shit," she said, slowing to a walk, breathing hard under the Kevlar vest. "Lost it."

"I know," Diviny lied. He chewed his lip as if in thought. "Look, he's hurt, right? He's not going to want to climb any hills. There are two trails." He indicated two natural paths between the tree trunks. "That one goes downslope. Path of least resistance. Why don't you take that and I'll go uphill just in case?"

Shanahan never batted an eye. "Good call. Stay frosty, kid."

Christ, he thought, *which bad cop movie did you crib that from?*

"Absolutely," he said with a grin that showed a lot of teeth. He set off to the left, moving at an angle that was almost certain to intercept the line of footprints he saw. He cut a look to see Shanahan trundling down the slope toward a minor footnote in his after action report. When he reacquired the footprints he smiled.

He bent to study them. Man's shoe, probably size nine or ten. Ground was soft but the impressions weren't deep. Diviny knew that Doc Hartnup was five nine and slender. Maybe one sixty-five. A perfect fit.

The line of flight was erratic. A drunk would walk like that, or someone badly hurt. Maybe delirious with shock. That also fit.

He thought about what he had overheard back at the mortuary. JT

Hammond and Desdemona Fox had reputations as cops better suited to more challenging departments, and both had a bunch of commendations. Granted, Dez Fox had also racked up as many reprimands as honors. Use of foul language on the job. Destruction of public property and excessive force—she allegedly threw a wife-beating town selectman through the front window of the county assessor's office. Rumors of a couple of off-the-clock DUIs she was allowed to skate on because a lot of the local cops either liked her or wanted to get into her pants.

Diviny could appreciate that. Dez Fox was an überhottie. Built like Scarlett Johansson, with ice blue eyes, bee-stung lips, and a natural blonde if the rumors were true. If she hadn't had a personality that one mutual friend had described as "Genghis Khan with boobs," Diviny might even have considered asking her out. But her reputation might leave a stain on his record. No way, José.

He stopped. The ground was scuffed and he shone his light to read the scene. A confusion of footprints, palm prints, and knee-shaped dents. Doc Hartnup had clearly fallen down here. Diviny edged around the scene, careful to steer well clear of every trace of evidence. Then he paused. The footprints leading off from where the victim had fallen were no longer heading in the same direction. Instead of an erratic but straight line to the northeast, they curved around a thick tangle of wild rhododendron. That path would take Hartnup down toward Shanahan.

"Shit," Diviny said, and began moving fast. He had to head off the Doc before Shanahan saw him, otherwise he'd have to split the save.

He broke into a light jog, following a trail that he barely needed a flashlight to see. He kept his head down, body bent at the waist, and he was smiling in anticipation when he rounded a thick tree and ran headfirst into a silent figure.

Diviny rebounded from the impact and looked up, smiling in instant embarrassment and surprise.

The smile died on his face.

"Doc?"

Doc Hartnup's face was covered in blood. His eyes were dark and dead, his features slack. Except for his mouth, which opened wide as he lunged at the officer.

There was a wet crunch as white teeth closed around Officer Diviny's windpipe, and then a hydrostatic hiss as bright blood shot with fire-hose force into the air, splattering the grasping arms of the surrounding trees.

CHAPTER FIFTEEN
HARTNUP'S TRANSITION ESTATE

Dez, JT, and Chief Goss stared at the name on the clipboard for a shocked three seconds, and then they all turned and began hustling back through the field toward the mortuary building.

"How the hell did the body of a sick psycho like Homer Gibbon wind up here?" Dez grumbled as she racewalked along beside Goss. "Did you know about this, Chief?"

Goss's eyes shifted toward her and then away. "It was arranged last minute."

"And you didn't think that responding officers might need to know about it?"

"Keep your voice down," Goss snapped, his face coloring. "Why should I have told you or anyone about this? He's a stiff in a bag, and he's scheduled to go into the ground tomorrow. Besides, there was a court order forbidding anyone involved in the transfer from talking about it."

"Why?" Dez demanded.

Goss hedged, clearly uncertain whether the gag order was still in force under the circumstances. He walked several fast paces before he replied. "Okay, okay . . . Gibbon had a relative in town and she petitioned the court to be able to claim his remains and bury them on family property."

"Wait," said JT, holding up a hand, "Gibbon was from here?"

"No, but his aunt lives here. Selma Conroy."

JT looked at him. "Sexy Selma?"

"Who's 'Sexy Selma?' " asked Dez.

"Way before your time," said JT. "When I was still a rookie, Selma Conroy ran a hot-pillow joint on Route 381 for years. We busted the place a dozen times, though somehow Selma always skated. No major convictions. She retired years ago."

"And she's Homer Gibbon's aunt? Nice family." Dez looked at Goss. "Would have been nice to know that's what we were stepping into when we took this call."

"Hey," said Goss, "just about the only two things they told me were jack and shit. Besides, the gag order was imposed because of all the threats."

"What threats?" demanded JT.

"They got fifty kinds of threats during the trial. People wanted to drag Gibbon's body through the streets or string it up and use it as a piñata. A lot of people said they just wanted to piss on his grave."

"Might have done that myself," muttered Dez.

Goss ignored her. "And they also got letters from a couple of dark worship groups."

"Who?" asked Scott.

"Cultists. Bunch of assholes who worship freaks like Gibbon, or Satan, or Ozzy Osbourne, I don't know. Black Mass dickheads. They said they wanted his body as a holy relic."

"Oh, for the love of . . ." Dez couldn't finish it. It was all too absurd, and her nerves ware so raw that what she really wanted to say was "Fuck it!" and go back home, order a pizza, drink a six of Yuengling and watch *Die Hard* films until the day started making sense again.

They were almost to the mortuary now. Additional police units had arrived from other towns and the road was completely blocked.

JT cleared his throat. "Chief, in light of the threats and all," he began, keeping his tone in neutral, "don't you think it might have been prudent to give responding officers some kind of clue? We could have been walking into a real mess if there had been cultists or . . ."

Goss said nothing, but his eyes shifted away.

You never even thought about it, Dez thought angrily. *Shithead.*

"Ah," said JT. His disapproval hung in the air. Like Dez's it was unspoken. The chief's face went red and he quickened his pace.

"Well," said Goss, changing the subject, "at least there's no press yet."

"There's blood in the water," Dez said, "the sharks will be here."

They reentered the mortuary, moving carefully to avoid further contamination of the evidence. Scott went straight to the overturned gurney and the others gathered around it. Now that they were focusing on it—rather than the blood and death—they didn't need Scott to explain it. The gurney lay on a pile of stained white sheets and a black rubber body bag.

Goss turned to an officer who was using a digital camera to document the scene. "Barney, you do this stuff?"

"Yeah, Chief, go ahead."

Scott took a pair of polyethylene gloves from his pocket, pulled them on, and then carefully lifted one corner of the sheet to expose words that were stenciled on the border in faded blue ink. STATE CORRECTIONAL INSTITUTION AT ROCKVIEW.

The same name was stenciled in white on the body bag.

"Okay," said Dez, "so they really did bring Gibbon's body here. That's just fucking peachy. So . . . we could have a group of religious nuts, an actual mob with pitchforks and torches, or a Satanic cult willing to kill Doc Hartnup and who knows who else just to steal the body. I love this job."

CHAPTER SIXTEEN
HARTNUP'S TRANSITION ESTATE

He could feel everything.

Every. Single. Thing.

Jolts in his legs with each clumsy step. The protest of muscles as they fought the onset of rigor even as they lifted his arms and flexed his hands. The stretch of jaw muscles. The shuddering snap as his teeth clamped shut around the young police officer's throat.

And then the blood. Hot and salty and sickeningly sweet. Flooding his mouth, bathing his gums and tongue, gushing down his throat.

Lee Hartnup screamed. He screamed from the bottom of his soul as his mouth opened and closed again, and again. Biting, tearing. Chewing.

Devouring.

He screamed and screamed, but not with those lungs. Not with that voice. Those things, each physical part, no longer belonged to him.

They existed around him. He existed within. Disconnected from control but still connected to every single nerve and sensory organ. He felt it all. From the scrape of teeth on jawbone and vertebrae to the sluggish movement of half-chewed meat sliding down his throat. He felt it all. He was spared nothing.

His screams echoed in the empty darkness. If anything, any part of his cries, escaped, it was only as the faintest of whispers. Merely a low and plaintive moan.

Hartnup tried to pull back. He tried to throw away the ragged red thing that he held in his hands . . . and even though he could feel the flex of muscles in hand, wrist, biceps, shoulders, and chest, he could control nothing. He owned nothing except a terrible awareness.

God, he begged, *let me die.*

But his own voice whispered to him, *I'm already dead.*

The teeth bit and tore and chewed.

This is impossible. How can my body do these dreadful, disgusting things?

No voice, inside or out, offered an answer.

He hung trapped in darkness, an unwilling passenger, unable to move so much as a finger or a nostril. Nothing.

His body dropped to its knees, shaking its head to worry a chunk of flesh from the corpse.

I am in hell.

The body bent over its feast, biting and tearing.

I am a monster.

I am a hollow man.

In his sensate darkness, Doc Hartnup screamed and screamed.

CHAPTER SEVENTEEN
DOLL FACTORY ROAD
STEBBINS COUNTY, PENNSYLVANIA

"So, what's the plan?" asked Goat. "Do we just roll up on Doc Hartnup and say, 'Dude, we hear you got a dead serial killer in the fridge. Can we take his picture?'"

Trout snorted. "Ambush journalism? Sure."

"You serious?"

"No. We have to finesse him or he'll clam up, throw us the hell out, and call Aunt Selma to tell her to raise the drawbridge."

"So what's our evil master plan?"

"We hit him with a cover story. We tell him we're doing a story about the death business. You know, the coroner's office, old folks' homes, cemeteries, mortuaries, that sort of thing. We'll tell him it's going to be a series. Sober and compassionate stuff about the process of dying and the various stages of caregiving before and after death. Respect for life even in death, shit like that."

"Yeah," agreed Goat. "He's kind of New Agey. . . . He might buy it."

They drove for a few seconds.

"On any other day," Goat said, "it'd be an okay story, too."

"I know," agreed Trout. "I was thinking that while I was saying it."

"How's that get us to Gibbon and Aunt Selma?"

"Not sure yet. If the cover story gets us in the door then we work him a bit, try to get him on our side. Maybe even cut him in on it. Feed him the Hollywood angle. The best-seller angle, too. If he can't see the marketing advantages of that . . . then, well that leaves bribes and threats."

"Count me out of that, Billy."

Trout speeded up to pass a school bus. "I'm not talking about threatening to break his legs. If this is the same Selma Conroy from when I first landed out here, then she's an old hooker. We could play up some kind of connection between the Doc and the hooker. Doesn't matter if it isn't true, because he'd have to prove a negative, and you can never do that on social media. Twitter, as you well know, is mightier than the sword, and in this economy no business owner needs bad press."

Goat turned in his seat and stared at him. "You're kind of a dick. You know that, right?"

Trout drove for a few seconds before he responded. "And you're what? A saint?"

Goat sighed and shook his head. "You really know someone in Hollywood you could pitch this to?"

Trout nodded. "I have an agent, but so far I haven't had anything this juicy to send her. Nothing remotely this juicy. She'll know exactly where to go with this."

"What if Hartnup stonewalls us?"

"We do an end run and go to Aunt Selma. Her past gives us a lever. And if that doesn't work we write the story anyway and force it to break. Every story breaks, kid. Every one."

"You should put that on your business card. It's worlds better than 'Fishing for News with Billy Trout.'"

"Blow me."

Goat grinned as he fished out his iPhone and pulled up his Twitter account. "Hey, we're doing okay. We got three hundred retweets of the coming-soon post. Nice. Give me something else so this doesn't get cold."

Trout thought about it. "How about . . . 'Homer Gibbon: Does Witness X know where he buried the bodies?'"

"Lurid," said Goat, and he posted the message. "I like it."

They turned off of Doll Factory onto Transition Road. Trout immediately stamped on the brakes and the car skidded to a halt, slewing sideways and kicking up gravel.

The road was blocked with police cars and ambulances.

"What the fuck?" yelped Goat. "Oh, man . . . someone else found out about our story."

"No," murmured Trout, shaking his head slowly, "this is something else. But . . . it looks like we're the first press on the scene. I think we just got even luckier, kid."

Trout pulled the car onto the shoulder, turned off the engine and got out. As Goat unfolded himself from the passenger side, they saw two police officers staring at them. One of them, a woman, began walking toward the Explorer with the kind of determination that, in Trout's experience, never boded well. No surprise, either, because even at that distance he could tell who it was.

Trout gripped the wheel with white-knuckled fists.

Dez. They had avoided each other for months now, but here she was. Any foolish thought he might have entertained about being *over* her crumbled into dust. His heart hammered suddenly in his chest but he couldn't tell if it was excitement over seeing Dez or fear that she'd kneecap him the second he stepped out of the car.

"Brace yourself, kid," said Trout under his breath. "We're about to experience Hurricane Desdemona."

"Her? Is that the chick in those pictures in your cubicle? She's got a serious ass on her. Nice rack, too, and I—"

"Goat," said Trout quietly, "if you would like to continue having your nuts attached to your body, do not—absolutely DO NOT—let Dez hear you say that. She is not a tolerant woman at the best of times, and when I'm around she's a lot less tolerant than, say . . . Hitler at a bar mitzvah."

"Yeah? You got some real history?"

"Kind of."

Goat shrugged. "Who'd play her in the movie?"

"The shark from Jaws," muttered Trout.

Dez Fox stormed up to the Explorer and kicked the door shut. Trout had to do a fast sideways shuffle to keep from getting clipped by it.

"Jesus Christ, Dez," he barked, "you dented the whole—"

"What the fuck are you doing here?" Her tone was loaded with enough frost to start an ice age.

Trout winced but tried to turn it into a smile. "Hey, is that any way to treat me after—"

Dez got up in his face, her voice low and tight. "Bring up the past, Billy, and I'll tase you and stomp the shit out of you while you lay pissing in your khakis. Don't think I'm joking."

"Geez, Dez, let's have a little perspective here. I wasn't the one who—"

"You're a dickbag who should have been thrown out with the afterbirth."

Trout sighed and placed his hand over his heart. "You wound me, Desdemona."

"I'm about to."

"Whoa there, officer," interjected Goat, waving his hand between them. "Let's dial this down and—"

"Fuck off," Dez and Trout said at the same time.

"I . . ."

JT had been a few steps behind Dez and stepped in now to take Goat by the arm and pull him back. "Come on, son, best to stand at a minimum safe distance when those two are in gear."

Goat let himself be pulled to the other side of the road, watching as Dez and Trout bent toward each other, almost nose to nose, shouting at the top of their voices.

"What's with them?" Goat asked. "They have some bad blood between than or something?"

JT wore a tolerant smile. "You figured that out, did you? Good for you."

Goat turned to him, and he wasn't smiling. "Don't patronize me. I'm a freaking news cameraman, so how about a little respect?"

JT spread his hands. "Don't have a stroke, kid. It was a joke. I got you out of there before you got hurt. Even I don't try to get between Dez and Billy, and I'm armed."

Goat was hardly mollified and grunted something in Yiddish. JT chuckled.

Twenty feet away, Dez and Trout were still going at it.

"I didn't come here to start a fight, Desdemona," said Trout.

"Call me that again and I'll put a baton across your kneecaps. It's Dez or Officer Fox. Actually, for you it's only Officer Fox. Now tell me what you're doing here."

Trout bit back something he was going to say, and instead pointed at the crooked line of parked police units. "Chasing a story, Officer Fox. Why else would I be here?"

"There is no story. Thanks for coming. Have a nice day. Fuck off and die."

"No story? So why are half the cops in the county here? And . . . Christ . . . is that blood all over your shirt?" His guts knotted like a fist. "Damn it, Dez, are you hurt?"

Dez stepped back from him, and Trout could see shutters drop behind her eyes. She cut a look at JT, and when Trout followed the line of her gaze he caught Sergeant Hammond giving a tiny shake of his head.

Dez cleared her throat. "This is an active crime scene," she said in the uninflected tone cops are taught to use at the academy. "Should the situation require it, a formal statement will be made at the appropriate time."

She started to turn and Trout touched her arm. "Come on, Dez, don't run that shuck on me. I own the patent on bullshit in Stebbins County. There's something serious going down here and I want in."

Dez, in control now, stopped and looked pointedly at the hand and then at his face. "Please remove your hand, sir."

"'Sir'? Oh please . . . cut the shit, Dez," said Trout, though he took his hand back. "At least tell me if you're hurt."

It took Dez a while to reply to that, and Trout watched various emotions struggle to present themselves on her face, but the wooden cop face won out.

"Why?" she asked.

"Why do you think?" Trout forced a smile despite the hurt he was feeling. "Look . . . just because we have some issues—"

"'Issues,'" she echoed softly.

"—doesn't mean that I don't care about what happens to you."

Dez glanced down at the drying blood on her clothes and then looked up into Trout's eyes for a long three count.

"I'm not injured," she said, her tone and selection of words coldly formal.

Trout felt his stomach begin to unclench. "Then what happened?"

"Just go away, Billy," she said as she turned and began walking away.

Trout ground his teeth. *Ah . . . fuck it*, he thought, and then called after her, "Is this about Homer Gibbon?"

That stopped Dez in her tracks. Trout knew that she was too good a cop to do something as lame as whirl around in shock, but the sudden tension was there in every line of her body. She turned and walked back to Trout.

"Would you repeat that, please?" she said.

Trout licked his lips. "Does that mean that this *is* related to the Homer Gibbon case?"

"What do you know about that, Billy?"

Not "sir." Not "fuckhead." She used his actual name.

"I know that he's here," said Trout, nodding toward the mortuary.

Dez said nothing.

"Did something happen?" Trout asked. "There were some threats during the trial and before the execution. Did someone break in to desecrate the body?"

Nothing. Dez's eyes might as well have been made from cold blue stones.

"Did someone steal the body? There were threats about that, too."

There was a flicker in Dez's eyes that told Trout that he'd scored a point. *Holy rat shit*, he thought. Someone actually did steal Gibbon's body. If the execution was the third act, this is a solid gold epilogue.

He kept the triumphant smile off his face. "Any theories on who stole it?" he asked.

"I never said a goddamn thing about—" Dez began and then stopped as JT Hammond crossed the road and stood next to her. Goat followed silently in his wake.

"Do you have information to share with us, Billy?" asked JT, his voice as cool as Dez's.

"No, but I'd like to get some information from—"

"Then please get into your car, turn around, and go back to the road," said JT.

"You can't throw me out. This is news and—"

JT stepped close. Trout was tall at six feet, but JT was two inches taller and a great deal tougher. "This is a private road, Billy," said JT. "It's mortuary property all the way down to Doll Factory. You can wait down at the crossroads or up the road at the diner, but you cannot park here."

"Since when did you join the gestapo, JT?" Billy asked in a disappointed tone.

The skin around JT's eyes tightened. When he wanted to, JT's face could transform from the genial nerd Samuel Jackson from *Jurassic Park* to the far more predatory Samuel Jackson from *Pulp Fiction*. This was the first time the transformation was done for Trout's benefit. "You didn't have many friends when you arrived here, Billy . . . and you have fewer of them now. Now get in your car and drive out of here. I won't ask again."

Billy Trout tried to outstare JT Hammond, but he knew that it was a lost game before it started. He had no cards to play.

So, without another word, he turned around, gestured curtly for

Goat to get in the car, and within ten seconds he was driving down the road. Just to piss off the two cops he broke the speed limit all the way. It was a silly little victory and it made him feel about three inches tall.

CHAPTER EIGHTEEN
MAGIC MARTI IN THE MORNING
WNOW RADIO, MARYLAND

"This is Magic Marti at the mike with news from the exact middle of nowhere. If you're in a hurry this morning, steer clear of Doll Factory Road east of Mason Street. There's some police activity in the area and we're getting a rubbernecker slowdown."

Sound of canned thunder.

"Time for an update on that storm that's grinding its way here from Pittsburgh. Heavy winds have picked up, and we're seeing fifty-mile-per-hour sustained winds and gusts reported up to ninety miles per hour. The National Weather Service has classified it as a Category One hurricane, and there are reports of moderate damage to motor homes, billboards, and other light structures, as well as small to moderate stream flooding. It's expected to hit our area in two hours, so expect a list of school and business closings."

CHAPTER NINETEEN
HARTNUP'S TRANSITION ESTATE

"How the hell did he find out about this?" growled Dez as they watched Billy Trout's car vanish.

JT shrugged. "Maybe he was monitoring the police radio and heard the call."

"Doesn't explain how he knows about Gibbon."

JT shrugged. "He's a good reporter, Dez. He probably has sources. Maybe in the department, maybe with the courts, or even the prison.

Could have been anyone, and it's moot. He knows and now this circus is going to turn into a state fair. This will draw down the big media. CNN, Fox, and everyone else."

"Yeah."

JT looked at Dez, who was rubbing her temples and wincing. "Why are you so hard on that young man," he asked.

"Don't start."

"Dez—"

"Billy wants too much. He wants shit that I can't give."

"I know what he wants, Dez. I was there the last five or six hundred times you two broke up. What I can't understand is why you're always giving him such a hard time. I've seen you treat wife-beating meth addicts with more compassion. All the boy did was ask you—"

"What's it to *you* what he asked?"

JT pointed a finger at her. "Don't take that tone with me, girl."

Dez glared at him for a moment, then her eyes shifted away. "Sorry."

In a softer tone, JT said, "It matters a lot what happens to you, Dez. You've been a raging bitch since the last breakup. You were drinking too much before, and now—"

Dez's hands were clenched into fists. "Listen, Dr. Phil, I don't need you to tell me how fucked up my life is. The real news flash is that I'm doing okay with it. Fucked up is my comfort zone, so stop trying to be my mother."

"If I was your mother I'd send you to your room."

Dez stabbed a finger toward the mortuary. "Is this about what happened in there? You trying to build a case for diminished capacity or something? Poor Dez, she's so torn up with a broken heart that she's been pickling her brain in Jack Daniels. Can't trust a fucking word she says these days. Pink elephants and—"

"What's with you today, Dez? You keep thinking that I didn't back your play in there, but if you'd stop shouting at everyone for two minutes maybe you'll remember that I sure as hell backed you up."

"You sold me out in there. You didn't believe me and you didn't back me up."

"The hell I did. I had your back then and I have it now. All the way, and you damn well know it. I told the chief the only version of the story that makes sense, so stop trying to alienate everyone. I am not your enemy. Neither, by the way, is Billy Trout or the rest of the human race."

Her eyes blazed with icy blue challenge. "So, you're saying that you believe that the Russian broad attacked me?"

"How many ways would you like me to say it?"

She poked him hard in the chest with a stiffened finger. "Then why didn't you say so when we were inside?"

JT pushed her finger aside. "Because I was in shock, what the hell do you think? You were in shock, too. At that moment I didn't know what to think about anything. Can you stand there and tell me that everything that's happened today makes sense? That it's easy to swallow?"

Dez said nothing.

JT nodded. "What I thought. So, what would you have said if I'd told you that Doc Hartnup just got up and strolled off? You trying to tell me that you'd accept that without pause? Without question? No . . . you wouldn't because it doesn't make sense. But we know it happened. Just like we know the cleaning lady attacked you. None of this makes sense."

JT and Dez stood staring at each other for several silent seconds. Far to the west there was a low mumble of thunder. The sound broke the moment, and Dez's eyes flicked to the west and then down at the gravel.

"Shit," she said.

"It's okay," JT said softly, touching her arm. "We'll get it all sorted out." He didn't specify which issues would be resolved. The case, Billy, or the train wreck that was Dez's life. Even so, she nodded slowly.

There was a dull crackle behind the trees. Dez looked up at the clouds. The radio said that a bad storm was coming, but . . .

The crackle came again.

Not distant thunder.

It was gunfire.

That's when the screaming started.

CHAPTER TWENTY
GREEN GATES 55-PLUS COMMUNITY

Dr. Herman Volker nearly shot himself when the phone rang. His nerves were fiddle-string taut, his heart fluttered like nervous fingers on a tabletop, the old Makarov pistol rattling in his hand. His clothes smelled of body odor, Old Spice, cigarettes, and fear. He had the barrel pressed to his temple but had not yet slipped his finger inside the trigger guard. If he had, he would already be dead. Instead his finger jerked tight round the outside of the guard.

"God!" he gasped aloud. There was no one to hear him there in the brown shadows of his house. The single word banged off the walls and burst apart into silent dust.

The phone rang again. It was an old hotel model. Kitschy when he bought it, merely cumbersome now. And loud. The bell seemed to shriek at him.

Volker's entire body had jerked on the first ring and he could feel the tremulous echo still reverberating in his chest. The sensation grew worse with the second ring. Anxiety was a cold wire in his stomach.

Was it the police? Had his handler called them? Turned him in for what he'd done? Would the police call first or just burst in? Even after all these years working with prisons he didn't really know.

Ring!

Mr. Price—Volker's handler at the CIA—would call his cell rather than the home phone. So would the warden and the staff at Rockview.

The hand holding the pistol twitched like a dying fish. He slapped the pistol down on the table, jerking at the solid clunk the metal made against the hardwood. Then he jerked again a second later as . . .

Ring!

Volker knew that he was a dead man. Even if the police broke down the door and arrested him before he could pull the trigger, he was dead. A prison official in jail was marked. The convicts would tear him apart. Especially when what he did got out. Homer Gibbon was a legend at Rockview. A convict's convict. They called him the Angel of Death. Some of them had Gibbon's face tattooed on their arms.

When they learned what Volker had tried to do—had, in fact, done—they would . . . His mind refused to form any specific end to that thought.

Volker held his breath as he watched the phone ring two more times. Five in all. There was no answering machine attached to the phone. No voice mail. It would ring until the caller gave up. Or until Volker went mad.

Who was calling?

Then he abruptly lunged for it, snatching the receiver from the cradle before it could ring again, pressing the phone to his ear and mouth. And here he faltered once more, unable to speak a word.

A voice crackled down the line. "Hello?"

Volker closed his eyes in relief. A stranger's voice. Not his handler. Not the warden. Not the cool formality he imagined the police would use.

After a moment, the voice said, "Dr. Volker?"

The doctor swallowed a lump in his throat that felt as big as a fist. "Y-yes . . . ?"

"Oh, good," said the caller brightly. "Thought I'd misdialed."

"Who's calling?"

"Ooops, sorry. This is Billy Trout, Regional Satellite News. I was at the prison yesterday and—"

"Please," interrupted Volker, his irritation immediately overriding his fear, "I cannot comment on that event; and I would appreciate it if you—"

Trout cut him off. "This isn't about the execution. Not exactly . . ."

Volker said nothing. God! Did this man know about Lucifer 113? If so—how?

"I apologize for calling you at your home, doctor," Trout continued. "I tried your office and your cell."

"Then why are you calling me?"

"I'd like to talk with you about Aunt Selma."

"Who?" He knew it sounded like the lie it was.

"Selma Conroy," prompted Trout. "Homer Gibbon's aunt. The

one who claimed the body . . . ? It's my understanding that you released the body to her?"

"Yes," said Volker woodenly. Even to his own ears his voice sounded dead. He glanced at the pistol lying on the table. He closed his eyes. "How do you know about her, Mr. Trout? It was *my* understanding that such information was not to be released to the press. How did you find out?"

"Sorry, Dr. Volker. Confidential sources," said Trout.

Volker gave a disgusted grunt. "What do you want? My part in this is over. If you were at the prison as you say, then you know that."

"Ye-e-es," Trout said, stretching the word to imply other possible meanings.

"Then what do you want?" Volker asked again. Was the phone tapped? It would not surprise him if the CIA had kept this place tapped since they moved him in. He looked around as if he could see agents huddled over elaborate wiretapping equipment, but all that surrounded him were the empty shadows of his sterile home.

"I want an opinion, Doctor," said Trout. "As the prison's senior medical officer you would be in a unique position to know Homer Gibbon. On a personal level, I mean. People talk to their doctors."

"No," Volker said evasively. "I was the doctor for the whole facility. I had a large staff. I was not that man's therapist or caseworker."

"I understand that, but can we agree that you knew Homer Gibbon? I mean, at least as well as anyone on the medical staff?"

"I . . ." Volker said and let his voice trail off, not knowing which answer was safest.

"So," continued Trout as if Volker had given his agreement, "could you speculate, doctor, as to why someone might want to steal his body?"

"'Steal'?" Volker's chest heaved so sharply that he almost vomited onto the phone. He slammed down the receiver and backed away from the instrument as if it could bite him. "Oh, God," he said to the brown shadows that filled the room. "Oh, God. What have I done?"

CHAPTER TWENTY-ONE
FAIRVIEW SHOPPING CENTER PARKING LOT
STEBBINS COUNTY, PENNSYLVANIA

"Smooth," said Goat, grinning with a mouthful of Burger King french fries. "Watching you in action is like a crash course in investigative journalism. You really opened Dr. Volker up. Wow."

"Shut up," grumped Trout.

"No, really . . . I'll bet Anderson Cooper thinks you're a rock star. I mean, I was impressed with how you dealt with that lady cop, but when you do a phone interview people unburden their souls to you. Wish I had video of that to put on YouTube."

Trout gave him a withering stare. "You finished?"

Goat considered, shrugged. "Yeah. Unless there's a third act to this comedy."

Trout sighed.

"Speaking of the cop," Goat said, "what's with you and Lady Deathstrike?"

Trout chewed on it for a bit, then sighed. "We've been seeing each other off and on for a while. A long while. We mostly kept it off the radar—you know, cop and reporter. That sort of thing always looks hinky. But . . . things keep getting more serious, and we kind of hit a wall. You know how it is—one person wants to commit and the other wants to keep things 'open.' After a while all we were doing was fighting."

"Let me guess," Goat said with a grin, "you were the asshole who didn't want to commit. All those wild oats to sow."

Trout looked through the windshield as if it were a window into the past. He sighed again . . . deep and long. "No," he said, "I was the asshole who wanted to marry her."

That shut Goat up. He stared at Trout's profile for a while and then shook his head. He fished out his iPhone and began trolling Twitter.

Trout didn't bother filling in any details about the breakup. He didn't want to go any farther down that road. The breakup with Dez was six months old and it felt like yesterday. From what he'd heard, Dez had soothed her shattered heart by screwing anything that had two legs, testosterone, and a tolerance for boilermakers. And every one of them was probably the same type, too. Tall, blond or sandy hair, blue eyes, an outdoorsy face with laugh lines and a tan. That was Dez's type. It had been ever since high school and that sizzling junior year when they were dating for the first time. They'd broken into the school at night and lost their virginity together on the couch in the vice principal's office. The detention couch, no less.

On his good days, Trout believed that he was the template for Dez's subsequent conquests. Trout had blue eyes, blond hair, and a passable version of a weathered smile. On his bad days, he wondered if he simply fit the bill that had coalesced in her head during puberty. He knew that some people were like that; they fixate on a type and go hunting for it. Years ago, before he and Dez had become an item for the third time, a reporter friend had once remarked that "Dez would blow the captain of the Titanic all the way to the bottom of the Atlantic if he had blue eyes and a cowboy smile."

So far they had been an item five times, and between some of those times Trout had gotten married and divorced. It did not help his peace of mind any when that same reporter friend pointed out how much each of those women looked like Dez.

The last time they'd been involved, Trout had given Dez an ultimatum. He couldn't take the roller-coaster ride anymore. He wanted to make it permanent with Dez, despite the therapy bills and probable mutual murder that would almost certainly go along with that. Dez had told him she wanted to think about it.

The next day he went to her trailer with a ring, flowers, and plane tickets to Aruba. He let himself in with the key she'd given him, smiling like a kid and ready to put it all on the line—his heart, his career, his actual hopes and dreams. Dez was sprawled naked in the arms of a biker with jailhouse tats and long blond hair.

Trout lost it. He threw the flowers at Dez, dragged the biker out of bed by his hair, kicked him in the nuts, and threw him naked into the dirt outside. Then he called Dez a lot of names that he normally reserved for the lawyers who had represented his ex-wives.

Dez chased him out of the trailer and halfway down the road with a shotgun.

She was naked, and the shotgun, it turned out, was unloaded. It took JT Hammond and two pairs of handcuffs to quiet things down, but the magic seemed to have gone out of their relationship.

Ain't love grand? Trout mused as he drove.

"I posted another teaser on Twitter," Goat said, breaking into Trout's dismal reverie. "So, what's next?"

"Let's listen to the call again." Trout had recorded the call on his digital unit and played it back with the speakers on high. Even with the mild distortion, Volker's voice and inflection had been clear. "Okay, O mighty Goat . . . you're supposed to be the great filmmaker and director. . . . Give me notes on Volker's performance."

Goat stared up at the roof of the car, considering. "Well . . . he was upset."

Trout twirled his finger in a "keep going" gesture.

"Volker was either trying to keep his voice in neutral, and fucking it up," Goat said slowly, "or he was scared."

"Scared? I didn't get that."

"Sure, scared and maybe paranoid. His voice was stiff. He vacillated between guarded defensiveness and trying to figure out what you knew."

Trout was fascinated. "Explain."

"Well, think about it. You called this guy at his house. When you were dialing, you told me that he was probably going to hang up on you. Which he did, but not at the right time. He's a prison's senior medical guy and he just performed a lethal injection on a mass murderer. He's probably been dogged by everyone from the media to the Christian right. If his home number was public knowledge, then he'd be letting it go right to voice mail, or he'd yank the cord because he'd be getting a million calls, right?"

"Right."

"But it *wasn't* public knowledge. You had to call in favors to get that number. Volker isn't getting calls on that line, so yours must have been a genuine surprise."

Trout nodded, seeing the shape of it now. "So he should have been outraged at my call. He should have read me the riot act, threatened repercussions, yada yada."

"And he didn't. He didn't even press you to find out how you got the number. He wanted to know why you called. Anyone else in his position would already know why you were calling—an insider's view on Gibbon or the protests, or the issue of execution. That stuff. The sort of stuff you usually do. But Volker didn't do that. I think he was not only trying to figure out why you called but was afraid of what you'd say."

Trout grunted. "You're building a case for guilty knowledge."

"Hey," said Goat, tapping his own chest with a crooked french fry, "if I was building a guilty knowledge scene in a movie, this would be cookie-cutter."

Trout settled back and stared into the middle distance. Goat held out the cardboard sleeve of fries; Trout took one and munched it slowly, biting his way along its length with tiny, contemplative nips.

"What'd you get out of it?" asked Goat.

"Not that much. You're good, kid," said Trout. He picked up his cell and punched a speed dial number.

"Regional Satellite News," answered a voice that was as bright and flowery as a spring meadow.

"Dear Marcia," said Trout, "how would you like to earn some overtime cash?"

"As long as it doesn't involve a stripper's pole or popping out of a cake, I'm your girl."

Trout grinned. Marcia Sloane had the voice that promised the smile and curves of a twenty-something California blonde. Everyone who called the bureau fell in love with her. She was actually just north of forty and far north of two hundred pounds. Curvy to be sure, with a heart-shaped face, masses of curly black hair, and—she claimed—nineteen separate piercings. Billy Trout had seen eight of them and, despite the fact that she outweighed him by at least fifty pounds, was intrigued to one day discover the rest.

"Sadly, not this time," Trout said.

"Murray approve it?" she asked. Their editor, Murray Klein, was notorious for denying overtime for anything, expecting his staff to finish their work on their personal time. Trout didn't hate him for it, though. Regional Satellite News worked with a budget surplus that could barely finance two cups of diner coffee.

"Yes," Trout said, fudging the truth. Although Klein hadn't approved this, given the nature of the story, he would. "I need some of your research magic. You could find Jimmy Hoffa if there were any legs left to that story."

"Probably. What can I do for you, Billy?"

"I need everything you can dig up on two people. Deep background. I need what's on the Net and anything you can find from other sources. First is Selma Conroy. Don't know if that's her maiden or married name."

"Sexy Selma? God—don't tell me she's back in business. She went to school with my mom, and I'm pretty sure she was at least some part of my dear parents' complicated divorce."

"Look . . . this is for something really important. Major. You can't tell anyone. An-nee-one."

"Lips are sealed."

"I'm serious."

"So am I."

"Okay . . . this is tied to the Homer Gibbon case. And there is a strong possibility that Selma Conroy is Gibbon's aunt, and she filed to have his body brought here to Stebbins."

Marcia grunted.

Trout said, "That's it? I thought you'd be surprised."

"Actually . . . I'm not," she said, " 'cause now that you say it I can see a little resemblance."

"To Selma?"

"No . . . to her sister."

"There's a sister?"

"There was. She died a while back. Look, I'll put that stuff together. I know where to look for everything on the Conroys. Who's the other target?"

"Prison doctor from Rockview. Herman Volker. When I did a background on him for my story I got as far as him being from Europe. The name's German, but the accent isn't. Sounds Polish or something. Lived here a long time. Medical degree from Jefferson in Philly."

"Okay. I'll get what I can get. Anything else?"

"No, sweetie, but I need this ASAP."

"Is this tied with what's happening at Doc's?"

"I don't know. We stopped there and ran into Dez, and that could have gone better. She ran us off."

"Ouch," she said. "I'll see if I can find out what's going on out there. Lots of cops on that one and more coming in, and they just made a second call for ambulances."

"Who's hurt?"

"Unknown. They've switched to a tactical channel that we can't get."

Trout felt a momentary flash of panic in his chest. *Please don't let it be Dez*, he thought.

Marcia, insightful as ever, said, "I'll call Flower over at the station and see if I can pry anything out of her. Dez probably beat someone up because he looked like you."

"Nice."

"Seriously, Billy, I'm sure everything's copacetic," Marcia laughed.

"Thanks. You rock, Marcia."

"You have no idea," she said with a wicked laugh and hung up.

Goat was grinning as Trout put his phone away.

"What?" asked Trout.

"When are you going to tap that?"

"She's a coworker."

"Uh-huh. Not after hours and not between the sheets. She's a wild woman."

"How the hell would you know?" growled Trout.

Goat's grin broadened. "The only way there is to know."

Trout looked at him. "Is there anyone you haven't screwed?"

"In Stebbins?"

"In North America."

Goat considered. "I haven't screwed that cop with the tits."

Trout shook his head. "You're not her type."

"Why? 'Cause I'm Jewish?"

"No. 'Cause you're sane."

He turned the key and put the car in drive.

"Aunt Selma's?" Goat asked.

"Aunt Selma's."

Billy Trout cut through the parking lot, bullied his way into traffic, spun the wheel, and kicked the pedal down toward Selma Conroy's farm. He didn't care at all about the speed limit. All of the cops were busy.

CHAPTER TWENTY-TWO
HARTNUP'S TRANSITION ESTATE

The gunshot echoes bounced around under the low ceiling of storm clouds. Dez whirled, instinctively pushing JT out of the line of some imagined fire as she reached for her gun. It was all reflex and it was very fast.

A long, high piercing shriek ripped through the air, muffled by humidity and flattened by distance. There were two shots. Then three more. Then continuous fire until a second scream rose higher and sharper. The scream disintegrated into a wet gargle.

Then silence.

"There!" JT barked, pointing toward the tree line, but Dez was already running.

"Shanahan!" she yelled. "That was Natalie Shanahan. She went into the woods with that kid, Diviny."

JT caught up with her as they pelted along the path that lead past the mortuary. Officers came spilling out of the building, running in the same direction. Chief Goss waddled along in the center of the pack, but the fitter cops were outstripping him, racing toward the trees. Everyone had guns drawn, but Dez didn't like what she was seeing. Most of these guys were as inexperienced in combat as JT, and the academy training was far from enough and, for most of them, too long ago. Or too recent. They ran with panic on their faces. Someone was going to get shot, she thought, and it wasn't going to be the bad guy. It was going to be another cop, or maybe a civilian.

She poured on the steam and cut left to get ahead of the pack, waving one arm in an attempt to slow them to a safer pace. But those screams still seemed to echo in the air.

"JT . . . watch my back."

"Got it," he said. "Go."

Dez reached the tree line first and then slowed to a careful walk as she stepped from gray daylight to purple shadows. JT broke right and brought his gun up. They fanned their barrels back and forth in overlapping patterns. They saw nothing except tree limbs and bushes shifting in the breeze.

As the other officers reached the tree line, Dez stepped clearly into view and raised a fist. Most of them spotted it and skidded to a stop. Two officers collided and fell, but JT was there to help them up and warn them to silence.

Dez turned to look at the cops. Two from Stebbins and seven others. Three of them, she knew, were combat vets. Dez saw them watching her, and she hand-signaled them to advance in a wide line. She waved the others back.

"What do you need, Dez?" whispered JT, coming up on her flank.

"Keep them back. Line of sight with each other, but spread out. Make sure Simmons keeps his fucking finger out of the trigger guard. I'll take the others with me."

He nodded and faded back to close on Officer Simmons, the youngest officer in the county.

Dez checked left and right to see that the vets were formed up in a wide line but behind trees. Two of them—Schneider and Strauss—had pistols in two-handed grips, the third—Sheldon Higdon from Barnesville—carried a FN self-loading shotgun.

Dez pointed forward with a slow movement of her hand and she broke cover and began advancing at a quick walk-run from tree to tree, zigzagging to alternate her route and deter possible return fire. She heard the crunch of shoes on dry leaves as the others kept pace. After three hundred yards, Dez stopped to assess the terrain. She saw two sets of footprints and off to the left, a third. The third set was Doc Hartnup's, she was sure of that. One set of prints diverged to follow the Doc, and from the size she figured it for Andy Diviny. The smaller set was Natalie's, and they broke right to follow a downland path. That was odd. Why wouldn't she have accompanied the other officer to follow a clear trail?

She waved Mike Schneider over and showed him the upland trail.

Schneider got it and nodded, and he peeled off to follow that, jerking his head for Strauss to follow him. Dez flagged Sheldon and pointed downland. He nodded and as she began creeping forward, he followed along on her wide right flank, his gun steady, his eyes narrow and hard.

As they moved down the shadows grew deeper. There were boulders, left behind by a glacier thousands of years ago. Natalie Shanahan's trail was easy to follow through dirt or moss, but soon it vanished as the ground became rockier. After another hundred yards Dez lost it completely.

Two minutes later Sheldon gave a sharp, short whistle, and when Dez turned, he waved her over. She saw why before he even pointed it out. Natalie's trail reappeared in a different spot than Dez expected to see it. It looped around one of the big boulders and headed uphill in a straight line. The shoe impressions were deeper on the balls of the feet.

"She went running up that hill like a bat out of hell," murmured Sheldon.

Dez nodded. "I'll go up the hill. You go around and come up the east slope."

"On it," he said, and he was off, running low and fast. Dez watched him for a moment, nodding approval. Like her, Sheldon had dropped the veneer of "cop" and was back in the Big Sand.

The hill was too steep to climb without using both hands, so Dez holstered her gun, grabbed some roots, and pulled herself up. She was surprised Natalie managed to haul her ass up this way. Natalie was the queen of Weight Watchers but she snarfed down two Big Macs every lunch break.

As she reached the top of the hill, Dez took a firm left handhold and drew her pistol. She couldn't hear Sheldon, but she knew he would be coming up the slope. It was a longer route but easier, so they should be hitting the same spot at the same time.

Dez took a breath, pulled herself up, peered briefly over the edge, and then ducked down, letting her mind process what her eyes had seen in that flash look.

The green forest was red.

"Christ," Dez said aloud as the data splashed across her mental screen. Leaves and grass painted a dark crimson. Something lying there. Pale and streaked with dark lines of red. An arm. She was sure of it. Was there a figure standing there? No. It was a tree. She was sure of that, too.

Dez's heart was hammering as she tightened her grip on the root and the gun. Then, with a grunt and a curse, she was moving, her feet scrabbling and slipping on the mossy stones of the hill. Up, up and then she was over the edge, swinging her Glock around into both hands, fanning the barrel from point to point, checking everything, making sense of shapes, putting everything into order.

Except that it wasn't orderly. None of this was going to fit into a picture that would make sense. She knew that at once, and for a disjointed moment she couldn't even feel the gun in her hand.

Natalie Shanahan lay sprawled on the leaves and moss. Her eyes were open. So was her chest. The vest was torn open. Shirt and bra in rags. Ribs stood up jagged and white through the torn meat of her breasts. Her body was bathed in blood, her face was splattered with black mucus. The skin around the wound was ragged, the ends pulled and torn. Steam curled upward from the burst meat. Smoke curled from the barrel of the pistol that was still clutched in Natalie's hand; the slide was locked back. Brass cartridges lay scattered among the leaves and stones and dropped pieces of flesh.

Nothing else moved in the clearing. No perp. Nothing.

"Jesus God Almighty . . ."

Dez didn't even turn as Sheldon Higdon spoke. She couldn't. She was unable to move.

"Officer down!" yelled a voice. "Officer down!"

Dez looked up. Sheldon glanced at her and then they both turned and stared off to the east. The cries were coming from farther up the slope. She recognized the voice. One of the other two combat vet cops. And with a sinking dread, Dez knew that they had found Andy Diviny.

"God," she murmured. "God . . ."

CHAPTER TWENTY-THREE

"Jesus . . . ," breathed Sheldon. "Look at her!"

"I know," said Dez.

There were more shouts and then the hollow *pok-pok-pok* of pistol fire.

"Dez . . ." began Sheldon, but she cut him off.

"I *know*," she barked again, and that fast she was charging up the slope. Sheldon was right there with her.

"The fuck is happening?" grunted Sheldon as he ran.

Dez said nothing. The day was all wrong and it was spinning away out of her reach. Even as she ran forward she felt like she was shrinking back, retreating within her own mind. This was all impossible.

She tore the shoulder mike from its clip and yelled into it. "We have officers down, repeat, officers down. We need backup right fucking now!"

Then she and Sheldon broke through a screen of shrubs . . . and the day became even more impossible.

Officer Jeff Straus lay faceup on the grass at the far side of the clearing. His entire face was . . . gone. Torn away to reveal ragged red muscle and white bone. Blood oozed down the sides of his face. Strauss's pistol lay three inches from his hand.

Much closer, just a few yards away, Officer Mike Schneider stood with his back to Dez and Sheldon. Schneider's Glock was down at his side, clutched in a tight fist. Schneider's whole body twitched and he jerked the trigger. The blast was sharp and loud and the bullet punched a bloody groove through the side of Schneider's ankle bone before burying itself in the dirt. Then Schneider's legs buckled and he dropped full-weight onto his knees, the jolt knocking the gun from his twitching fingers. There was a hissing sound and Dez saw a geyser of bright red blood shoot outward from below Schneider's chin and splash the pale face of Andy Diviny. The blood struck him in the mouth and eyes and splattered the rubbery leaves of a big rhododendron. As Schneider canted sideways and fell, Diviny stared straight at Dez.

Purple lips peeled back from bloody teeth and Diviny hissed at her.

CHAPTER TWENTY-FOUR
HARTNUP'S TRANSITION ESTATE

"No . . ."

Dez heard the word, but she could not tell if she spoke it, or Sheldon. It could not have been Strauss. That much was obvious. He had no lips left with which to speak. His mouth and cheeks had been torn away, and his eyes stared in terminal astonishment up at the roof of green leaves.

The sounds of the forest were gone, washed out of the moment by another sound. That of Andy Diviny chewing a mouthful of flesh.

"No!"

This time it was Sheldon who spoke—who almost sobbed the word—and then his sob turned into snarl as he rushed forward and swung the stock of his shotgun at Diviny's jaw. Dez watched, unable to react. There was a terrific crack! Bone shattered, teeth flew, and the young cop's head whipped around so fast that his whole body was spun into an awkward pirouette. Diviny crashed into the rhododendron and fell almost out of sight except for his twitching legs.

Sheldon looked down at him and then jerked his head around to look at Schneider and Strauss; then he spun toward Dez. His eyes were huge and wild and he was breathing in and out with alarming rapidity.

"Fucking no!" screamed Sheldon.

Dez shook her head in mute agreement and denial.

There were sounds behind her. Yells, bodies crashing through the brush, and, as she turned, JT was there, and the others were right behind him. They hit the edge of the clearing and jerked to a stop as if there were a force field. It was impossible to them as well.

Three officers down. Two dead. One battered and twitching.

Everyone looked around wildly for the perps, for the maniacs who had done this; and gradually those eyes focused on Sheldon and Dez.

"It was Andy Diviny," said Dez woodenly. "When we got here Strauss was down and Andy was . . . biting Schneider. I don't . . . I don't . . ." She shook her head, unable to construct a logical end to that sentence.

JT stood blinking at the dead officers, his eyelids fluttering as if they could brush away the image that he was seeing. Then he took a tentative step in, and another, and then he ran the rest of the way to Dez. He took her by the arms and stared at her, his gaze flicking up and down, looking for injuries.

"Dez! Are you hurt?"

She half laughed. That was what he had asked her before. The answer was clear. The answer was yes.

She said, "No."

He suddenly pulled her to him and gave her a fierce hug. Like a father would. Like a brother in arms would.

Chief Goss came waddling into the clearing, his face bright red and his uniform damp at the chest and armpits with fresh sweat. Dez pulled free of JT's hug and turned toward him. She watched him as he tried to read the scene.

"It was Andy," said Sheldon in a hoarse voice. "Andy Diviny . . . He . . . he . . ." He shook his head. Like Dez, he did not possess a vocabulary for this.

"He did what?" shouted Goss. "What are you trying to say?"

"It's true," croaked Dez. "Diviny, he . . . when we got here he was . . ."

"Hey!" yelled JT. "Sheldon . . . watch . . . He's getting up?"

Everyone turned toward Diviny, who was struggling to get to his hands and knees in the dense tangle of the shrubbery. He snarled, exposing jagged rows of broken teeth. Then, with a savage growl, Sheldon Higdon stepped forward and grabbed him by the back of the belt and hauled him up, spun him violently around and then flung him face first onto the grass.

"Cuff that sick son of a bitch!"

The two closest officers hesitated. This was all so weird.

"Wait . . . what are you saying, Shel?" said the older of the two.

"You're all screwed up here. Andy got here the same time we did. He couldn't have attacked Doc and—"

"Open your eyes! He just killed Mike Schneider and Jeff Strauss, goddamn it. We saw him do it," yelled Sheldon, and he aimed a savage kick at Diviny's backside, knocking the young cop down as he tried to get up. "Throw some cuffs on that motherfucker before I pop a cap in—"

Diviny twisted around on the ground. His eyes were wide and dark and empty. His shattered chin was bearded with blood, and his throat was a junkyard of torn flesh. His mouth was a feral snarl. With another unnatural hiss, he threw himself at the older cop, but the officer jerked away, backpedaling ten feet. Every gun swiveled around and pointed at Diviny.

As Diviny rushed at Sheldon, Dez stuck a leg out and tripped him. The deranged young cop fell hard, but again he began climbing to his feet, showing no signs of pain or fear.

"What the hell's wrong with him?" demanded Goss.

Dez began moving around the edge of the circle of cops, waving them back. "I don't know. He just went crazy." She grabbed Goss's sleeve. "Chief, listen to me . . . Natalie Shanahan's down, too. I think Andy killed her, too."

"Holy Jesus."

Andy Diviny's body swayed and trembled. Black drool trickled from his mouth. Dez remembered that same ooze coming from the lips of the Russian cleaning lady. She didn't know what it was, but just the sight of it filled her with an atavistic dread.

"Be careful!" yelled Dez. "Don't let him spit on you."

Everyone was yelling at him. "Andy! Get down on the ground. Arms out to your sides. Do it now! Do it!"

If the young officer was able to understand the shouts there was no sign of it on his snarling face. He suddenly rushed at Chief Goss, reaching for him with clawlike fingers.

JT and Sheldon raised their shotguns and fired. The Mossbergs were loaded with small fabric pouches filled with #9 lead shot weighing about an ounce and a half. They were nonlethal but each one kicked like a mule and the rounds caught Diviny on both sides of his chest. He was plucked backward like he'd been pulled from behind by a chain and crashed to the ground. By all rights he should have been dazed, coughing, and nauseous; instead he immediately rolled onto his stomach and got up again.

"No fucking way . . ." breathed Chief Goss.

Someone yelled, "Pepper him!" But Dez already had her pepper spray in her hand. She slapped Diviny's reaching arm aside and blasted him in the eyes.

He did not cough or choke or even blink. Instead he tried to spit at her.

Dez hit him again and again, but now she was backpedaling away from those bloody fingers, away from that black mucus.

"Christ!" she cried. "Somebody drop this crazy son of a—"

Five officers fired their Glocks at once, the bullets punching into Diviny, slamming into the Kevlar and shattering bones beneath the vest, making the officer dance and judder like a puppet. The barrage sent him sprawling backward against a tree trunk, and he hit it with enough force to knock pinecones from the branches. But even as they rained down, Diviny rebounded from the trunk and made another run at Goss.

"Andy, for the love of God, stop!" cried JT, but the officer flew at the chief, bloody spit flying from his mouth. JT pointed his gun at Diviny's head.

"Hold your fire!" bellowed Dez. She threw down the pepper spray, whipped out her baton, stepped forward and smashed Diviny across the shins with it. The shock vibrated a line of hot needles up her arm, but the blow swept Diviny's legs out from under him and he crashed onto his chest. Before he could roll over, JT was there, dropping his knee down hard between Diviny's shoulder blades, and then six pairs of hands were at work, grabbing Diviny's hair to hold his head down and his snapping mouth toward the dirt, fishing for the flailing arms, twisting them behind the young man's back, snapping cuffs around the wrists. His weapons were removed and his utility belt unbuckled. JT kept his weight in place. They didn't have leg shackles.

"Christ, what's wrong with him?" Goss asked over and over again, but no one had an answer.

Dez looked around. "Anyone have a spit hood?"

"I got one," said an officer from Martinville. He opened a small pouch on his belt and removed a disposable spit sock hood. Dez shook it out and pulled it over Diviny's head. The elastic throat band would keep it in place but wouldn't choke the officer. There were better devices, including plastic bite masks, but none of them carried one on them or in their cars.

"Got to do something about that throat," advised JT. He fished in his pocket and produced an Izzy, tore open the plastic cover and handed it to Dez, who had the best angle to apply it.

She quickly wound the bandage around Diviny's throat. The dressing—formally called an Israeli bandage as a nod to where it was developed—had a built-in plastic tension bar that applied continuous pressure to a wound, allowing the bandage to act as a stand-alone field dressing. All soldiers carried them and they had become very common in domestic law enforcement. Diviny spit at Dez as she worked, but the spit hood caught the spray of black blood.

"Careful not to make it too tight," JT cautioned.

"Ought to strangle the cocksucker," muttered Sheldon.

They ignored him. Dez tested the tension and nodded.

"If he's going to live," said Dez, "that should hold him." Dez directed two officers to keep him pinned down.

The other officers stood in a ragged circle around Diviny. As Dez got to her feet, she studied their faces and saw each of them take quick, frightened looks over at what was left of Mike Schneider and Jeff Strauss.

"What the hell's going on?" someone asked in a hollow voice.

Dez realized with a sick jolt that the voice had been hers.

CHAPTER TWENTY-FIVE
OFFICE OF OSCAR PRICE
DEPARTMENT TEN, FEDERAL BUILDING
PITTSBURGH, PENNSYLVANIA

Oscar Price stared at his cell phone and considered what to do.

He was a cool, disciplined man, and he was in a climate controlled office and yet sweat was popping out along his forehead.

"Jesus Christ," he said softly. He was alone in the office but he looked around as if he expected someone—maybe even Jesus Himself—to step up and offer a solution. A few moments later he snarled, "Shit!"

Price sat back in his chair, trying to pretend a posture of calm nonchalance in the hope that it would trick his body into relaxing. He could feel a newborn migraine wailing at the edges of his consciousness.

Price was absolutely certain that if he and Dr. Herman Volker were alone in a quiet place, he would put the doctor on his knees and park two hollow points in the back of the stupid bastard's head.

Lucifer 113 was off the leash.

That was what Volker had called to tell him. Not exactly in those words, but close enough.

It was a protocol improbability bordering on impossibility. Everything about Project Lucifer was old news. Buried with the Cold War. Virtually forgotten, except by psychotic sons of bitches like Volker, and luckless schmucks like himself.

On the whole, Price had a fairly simple job, day in and day out. No stress, no dramatic moments. There were twenty-two low-profile "clients" in his caseload, and each of them was in some phase of career step-down. No longer integral to the research machine that was Department Ten. Most of them were years past their prime, naturalized foreigners who now lived in an age when "Cold War" was not even a phrase anymore. Old men and women, their genius spent, but still potentially useful enough as consultants—on works now long in progress—that they still merited a Level Two handler instead of a Three or Four. The Threes and Fours were also on career downslopes. Twos, like Price, were short-listed for steps up.

Except when things like this came along. That bothered Price, because he really wanted that step. Working for the Company wasn't a hobby. He wanted a regional directorship or a chief of station in a country that mattered. Japan, for instance, now that North Korea was a constant threat.

This matter with Herman Volker, however, could reverse that upward momentum and very quickly bury Price's career ten feet under an outhouse. Or . . . handled the right way, he mused, it could shine a bright, white light on him.

The question was . . . what was the right move?

Volker was a former CIA all-star. The information he'd taken with him when he'd defected was the political equivalent of a nuclear bomb. Reagan's diplomatic corps had used it to beat the shit out of the Soviets. It may not have actually torn down the Wall, but it sure as hell knocked out the first brick. Price still marveled at it. Fucking zombie parasites as bioweapons. Or, as it was called in the Project Lucifer documents: metabolically minimalized ambulatory organic hosts. A dreadful weapon that contravened every global and closed-door biological warfare agreement on the books. Should have called it Project Screw the Pooch. It truly did not matter that the Lucifer research had hit a dead end and was scheduled for termination by the Soviets, documents to be sealed. Volker got out of Dodge weeks before that was implemented, and by then Reagan and the Company had the goods.

The tricky thing was, Volker was not supposed to be working on anything related to Project Lucifer. The old fart was supposed to be indulging his damaged brain by messing with death row patients who, let's face it, thought Price, nobody gave a sloppy fuck about. Volker was not—by federal order and private agreement—supposed to be screwing around with anything even *remotely* related to Lucifer. Nothing. Nada.

And yet.

Price sucked his teeth as he thought about what to do.

It was not in his pay grade to know whether the US of A was doing anything with the project research. Price hoped they'd left it in a sealed box, ideally buried in a ten-foot cube of cement. But he was far from stupid, and never naïve. Somebody, somewhere had to be working on it. They'd had it for thirty years. Thirty years without outbreaks, he reminded himself, which suggested that they were at least being careful.

Volker, on the other hand . . .

Price drummed his fingers on the desktop hard enough to rattle the phone in its cradle. He knew that he had to call this in. Question was—who to call? Protocol demanded that he take it directly to his section chief, and though Tony Williams was no fool, he was very career minded. Would he, in turn, pass it along? Or would he use it to crush the young go-getter nipping at his heels? Price rather thought the latter. This could very easily be made into a blame game, with Price as the target.

People were dying, though, and the longer it went on, the higher the body count. Price did not lie to himself that his motivations stretched to cover the lives of a bunch of Pennsylvania redneck farmers with cow shit on their boots. But he had to be seen to care.

Which made the second option look tempting. Doing an end run around Williams and taking this directly to regional director Colleen Sykes. She was a classic ballbuster, but she was so tightly networked into D.C. and Langley that her career was virtually bulletproof. She could get something done on this ASAP, no question.

But, she was also pretty much by the book, so how would she view the end run? Would she see Price as a man on a mission who risked everything to protect the common good? Or would she seem him as a self-serving loose cannon who broke protocol?

Price didn't really see a clear path. Either way, this could kill him in the Company.

"Fuck it and fuck you," he said aloud. And then reached for the phone.

CHAPTER TWENTY-SIX
HARTNUP'S TRANSITION ESTATE

"What do we do now?" asked one of the greener officers in a voice tainted with panic. He wore a guilty, caged expression as if this was somehow their fault rather than something that had come out of nowhere and swept over all of them.

"We don't do a goddamn thing," barked Chief Goss. "This situation is way out of our control, so we're going to sit tight and wait for the staties. They'll be here any minute."

"Chief," said JT discreetly, "shouldn't we call this in?"

Goss pulled his walkie-talkie out of its holster and keyed it. "Dispatch . . . we have officers down, I repeat officers down."

"W-What?" exclaimed Flower. "Who's hurt—"

Goss cut her off. "I need paramedics and additional units. Expand the call out another tier. Send everyone you can get . . . and give me an ETA on the state police."

Flower stumbled over her words for a second before she could organize an answer. "State police are eight minutes out. Two units are—"

"I don't want to hear that shit, Flower. Tell them to roll *every* available unit because we're going to need roadblocks and a lot of feet on the ground. I want choppers, too. And get on the horn to the Zimmer boys—Carl and Luke. We need them and their dogs out here. And get me somebody to handle crowd control."

"What's happening?" Flower demanded, her voice rising to a screech.

"Just do it," Goss snapped, and turned off the walkie-talkie. He was sweating badly and there were starbursts of red on his cheeks. Damp winds blew up the slope and rifled his sweaty hair.

"Rain's coming," said JT, still pitching his voice to keep things in neutral. "And with these winds . . . I don't think we're going to be able to use helos or spotter planes."

"Rain and wind won't stop the dogs," said Sheldon. "The Zimmers have hounds that can track a weak fart in a hurricane."

Dez looked at the chief, whose expression was that of someone a short step away from screaming. Dez could understand it. Like most of these officers, Goss was a career cop in a town where there just wasn't any serious action. Bar fights and DUIs don't instill the same combat awareness that big city cops and veteran soldiers have. This was way beyond Goss's experience and he was losing control of the details. "Chief," she said, pitching her tone to match JT's, "we have people all over the place and we don't know if this is the end of this. Shouldn't we get a head count?"

Goss blinked at her for a few moments as if she had asked the question in Swahili. Then understanding flicked back into his eyes, and he nodded. "A head count. Good, good . . ." He looked around as if he expected everyone to be there ready to be counted.

Christ, thought Dez, *he's really losing it.*

She glanced at JT, whose brown face seemed to be carved from an inflexible hunk of mahogany though his eyes were bright and almost unblinking. He was trying to keep his game face in place, but he was at the edge, too. Even Sheldon, who had been in Afghanistan, was freaked.

Dez swallowed. *I guess we all are. All of us.*

Then Goss grabbed his walkie-talkie again and keyed it to the team channel. "All officers report in. Name, location, and status."

One by one the calls came back. Paul Scott, two paramedics, and another forensics collector were in the mortuary. Five officers—all from other towns—were here with Goss, JT, and Dez. That left two unaccounted for.

"Wait—who's missing?" asked JT.

Dez said, "Wait, who was it that went up to check on Doc's sister and her kids?"

Goss cursed and keyed the walkie-talkie again. "Hold the air. Officers Gunther and Howard, report your location and status."

Then there was sharp hiss of static and a voice spoke intermittently through the squelch.

"We're at the Hartnup place. Nothing to report. I thought I heard shots. I called Flower but she—"

Goss cut him off. "Did you tell April about her brother?"

"You said not to."

"Good, because he might not be dead."

Gunther paused. "Say again?"

"It's not confirmed, but be aware that Doc Hartnup's body is missing and there is a strong possibility that he is injured and in shock, maybe delirious, and somewhere in the Grove."

"How? Chief . . . I thought Dez and JT said he was—"

Goss cut him off. "Don't ask me how 'cause I don't know. Just keep your eyes open. Doc might be trying to head to his sister's place. I want one of you on the porch and the other inside with the family. Do not let April see her brother if you can avoid it, and definitely not the kids. You see him—or anyone—call it in right away."

"Yeah, okay, Chief."

Goss disconnected. If he was relieved by what Gunther had told him, it didn't show. Fresh beads of sweat glistened on his head. Dez was afraid he was going to stroke out if things didn't calm down. "The staties will be here soon," Goss repeated. He looked around, licking his lips with a nervous tongue tip. "We need to secure this crime scene and also where . . . um . . . Natalie was . . ."

One of the other officers said, "I got that." He tapped another cop from the same town and they set off down the slope, following Dez's directions.

"I want in on the manhunt," protested Dez. "We should be out there now so we can get a jump on—"

"On who?" snapped Goss. "Do you know what the hell's going on? 'Cause I sure as shit don't. We got a double homicide at the mortuary that turned out not to be a double homicide. One vic attacks you and the other goes for a stroll in the forest. We have an officer-involved shooting of one of those presumed homicide victims. We got an unknown person in bare feet leaving the scene of the crime; and we don't know how or if he was involved. We also have the theft of the body of a dead serial killer. And now we have three dead officers and one who's gone completely batshit nuts."

"Chief, I—"

"So you tell me, Officer Fox . . . exactly what crime scenario are we trying to get a jump on? If it wasn't for the fact that all of this is happening right here and right now, I couldn't build a reasonable argument that they're all part of the same goddamn case."

Dez clamped her mouth shut. She had no answers and it was clear that arguing with Goss was likely to end badly. She didn't like the man, but she didn't actually want to cause the big vein in his head to explode.

"Okay, Chief, we hear you," said JT gently. "If you had to make a horseback guess, what would you say is going on?"

Goss eyed him for a blistering moment. "How the fuck should I know?"

"Chief," said JT, moving closer, his voice ever quieter, "I think we should dial it down a few notches, what do you think?"

The chief took a deep breath that threatened to pop buttons on his shirt, then he exhaled slowly, nodding. "Christ. I don't need this shit. I really don't."

Dez couldn't argue with that.

"Maybe this isn't a murder scene," suggested Sheldon, who had also managed to regain control of his emotions. "Look, you got ordinary people suddenly doing some mighty weird shit. Inexplicable shit. Maybe this isn't people committing crimes . . . maybe this is something else. Something that's affecting people. Y'know, like a toxic spill, or something in the water . . ."

They all looked at each other and the idea changed the mood as abruptly as switching stations with a TV remote. Even Goss's posture relaxed as he stared into the middle distance, considering the question.

"I don't think it's in the water, Shel," said Dez slowly. "Andy got here after Doc and the Russian woman were attacked. And I didn't see him take a drink after he got here. Not tap water or anything."

"Whatever it was," JT said, "it must have hit Strauss or Schneider, too. I mean . . . look at Andy's throat. He didn't do that to himself."

Goss paled. "So, you're saying that we have another one out there?"

"Stands to reason," said Dez. "Could even be Doc, if this thing affects people. Or it could be whoever left the bare footprints that went out of the mortuary office."

"Maybe it's something you get from a bite," suggested Sheldon. "Somebody bit the cleaning lady and then she went apeshit on Dez, right? Maybe the same thing happened to Andy. He got bit, got sick, and freaked out."

"Isn't that awful fast for an infection to spread?" asked JT. "Doesn't that sort of thing take days?"

"I'm just saying that we need to look at it," Sheldon said.

"Could it be something in the air?" asked one of the officers who still knelt to keep Diviny pinned down.

"If so, we'd all have it," countered Dez.

"A virus," said JT. "Not everyone reacts the same way to diseases."

Sheldon nodded. "Allergens, too. Some weird plant the Doc brought in for a funeral. Or a chemical he uses. Maybe certain people are susceptible to it."

Suddenly everyone was throwing suggestions at him while, on the ground, Andy Diviny still writhed and tried to bite.

Finally Goss held up his hand. "This isn't getting us anywhere. If you have a theory, then we share it with the state police and the doctors." He pointed at Diviny. "Right now, though, we need to get him tested. Dez, JT . . . get him into an ambulance and get his ass over to

Wolverton Hospital. Call ahead, tell them that this is a potential bio-hazard situation."

"Okay, Chief," Dez said and then punched JT on the arm. "Come on, Hoss."

"Hey," said the chief. "Nobody here talks to the press. Nobody calls home and tells their family and nobody fucking puts this on Twitter. This is a family matter now, so let's keep it indoors until we know where we all stand."

They all looked at one another and slowly nodded. Even the younger cops.

Dez exhaled a ball of dead air that she'd been holding in her chest, and then nodded. She and JT grabbed hold of Diviny and half dragged, half carried him down the hill. The moment had become orderly, but the day was still impossible.

CHAPTER TWENTY-SEVEN
CENTRAL INTELLIGENCE AGENCY
LANGLEY, VIRGINIA

Lorne McMasters, director of the Central Intelligence Agency, looked at the name on his phone's screen display. He smiled as he picked up the receiver.

"Colleen," he said brightly, "how are you? How's Ted and the—"

"Lorne," interrupted Colleen Sykes, "this is a Livewire Protocol."

McMasters took a half beat on that, then punched the scramble on his phone. "Confirm. What's on the window sill?"

"Bluebird," she said, giving the first part of the day code.

"And in the tree?"

"Yellow kite."

"What's the other thing?"

"Foxhounds."

"Confirmed," said Lorne. "What's happening, Colleen?"

Colleen Sykes was deputy director of the CIA's Directorate of Science and Technology. Only once before in her career had she made a call of this kind. The first situation had been resolved quickly and with minimum fuss, and no trace of it had reached the news radar.

"I just received a report that the 'devil is out of the bag,'" she said.

McMasters opened a screen on his intranet browser and typed that in. The name Lucifer 113 popped up, followed by bullet points about the science, the dangers, the key players, and the in-place protocols. In the upper right corner of the screen was a coded threat status icon. Not the same color codes that Homeland used. Blue was the lowest level of threat, black was the highest. This file was coded black.

"Christ," he snarled. "Tell me."

Sykes told him what Oscar Price had told her.

"Has this entered the population yet?" demanded McMasters.

"We have no direct confirmation, but there is a suspicious incident developing at the mortuary where Gibbon's body was taken. We've gotten conflicting reports of a double homicide, but follow-up reports indicate that the 'victims' may not have been dead. One allegedly attacked a responding officer who was apparently compelled to use lethal force to defend herself. The other suspected victim is missing, having apparently left the scene of the crime under his own steam."

"I'm still a half-step behind you on this, Colleen. What does that mean? Dead people don't attack cops and they don't get up and walk away."

Sykes paused. "Actually, Lorne . . . if you open report sixty-three in the translations of the 'Soviet Strategic Implementations' folder you'll see that this is in keeping with predicted effects. It is, in point of fact, the primary reason that the entire research line was ultimately scrapped by the Russians."

McMasters read through the data. He could feel the blood draining from his cheeks. "This is . . . Good God, Colleen, are you telling me that we let someone *continue* this project?"

"No we didn't," Sykes said firmly. "Dr. Volker was under express orders not to go anywhere near this project, or anything remotely related to it."

"Then how did he gain access?"

"His handler believes that Volker did not so much gain access as 're-create' the research . . . and then take it forward an additional few steps. Volker is a brilliant scientist. At his request we set him up as a prison doctor, and unfortunately it looks like he played us. The security buffer we provide, plus the additional security at a secure correctional facility, made it harder for Price—or anyone, for that matter—to keep tabs on everything the doctor was doing. Lucifer 113 is not an expensive project, and many of the components are neither controlled substances or on watch lists. Volker took his time—decades, really—and he fooled everyone."

McMasters was seething. "If he's so fucking smart then how did he lose control of this thing? It's not like letting your dog off his leash so he can fuck the neighbors poodle, goddamn it."

"I know."

"Is Volker a terrorist?"

"Unknown, but unlikely." She told him what Oscar Price had told her about Volker's motivations.

"Sweet suffering Jesus," said McMasters. "I'm going to have to brief the president, and he'll need to contact the governors of Pennsylvania and Maryland."

"Possibly Ohio and West Virginia, too. Maybe even Virginia."

"Tell me you're joking, Colleen."

"I wish I could, Lorne."

"Okay, okay . . . give me some talking points for my call to the president. Where do we stand and how bad can this get?"

"Lorne . . . I'm not sure you looked closely enough at the Soviet strategy stuff. The only limit to the spread of this thing are natural barriers and direct sterilization."

McMasters closed his eyes.

"Mary, Mother of God," he whispered.

CHAPTER TWENTY-EIGHT
CONROY'S ACRES
STEBBINS COUNTY, PENNSYLVANIA

Billy Trout followed a crazy zigzag of back roads and side roads to find Selma Conroy's place. It was deep in the heart of the county's endless farm country. Though the town of Stebbins was small, the county was huge, composed mostly of a patchwork of enormous fields of wheat, barley, potatoes, apples, peaches, and corn. Cut between these were tracts of grazing land for cattle and sheep. Houses and farm buildings were scattered around, but the farmlands were so broad that each house looked like a lost island in a vast sea of waving green.

When Marcia called, Trout pulled onto the shoulder of the road and put her on speaker.

"What've you got?" he asked.

"Half the job," she said. "Dr. Volker's taking some time, but I think I got just about everything on Selma Conroy. You want all of it now?"

"E-mail me everything but for now give me the bullet points."

"Okay," said Marcia, and they could hear her tapping computer keys. "Selma Elsbeth Conroy is eighty-two years old, born in East Texas. Dinky little place called Red Lick near the Arkansas border. Moved to Stebbins in 1969, and even though she had family here in Pennsylvania, the move was apparently along the lines of being run out of town on a rail. Her mother was a similar paragon of virtue. Six kids, five fathers. Class. Want to guess what one of the father's names was?"

"If you say Gibbon I will kiss you."

"It is Gibbon and do I get to pick where that kiss lands?"

"We'll talk. Tell me about the Gibbon connection."

"Is Goat listening to this?"

"And enjoying it," said Goat.

"Well, you boys are going to love this. Homer is Selma's sister's only child. Want to guess what Homer's mom's first name is? Clarice!"

There was a two count as Trout looked at Goat. They burst out laughing.

"Are you shitting me?" Trout demanded. "The mother of a serial killer is named Clarice?"

"Hello, Clarice," Goat said in a passable Hannibal Lecter.

"I kid you not," Marcia assured them. "Is that life imitating art or something like that? Anyway, now here's a wrinkle. The family name is actually Gibbens. Clarice Gibbens. G-I-B-B-E-N-S. No idea where the spelling change started. Court and birth records are sketchy at best, but from what I could piece together, Clarice had a child out of wedlock and put it up for adoption within a few months. Whoever filled out the adoption intake form misspelled the name."

"How come nobody traced this back to Stebbins before?" Trout asked.

"No reason to. Clarice gave a cousin's address in Pittsburgh when she turned over the baby. There's no one in Stebbins with the name Gibbon or Gibbons, and Clarice only stayed here for a while. She was never an official resident. Besides, I was only able to piece this together when I added Selma Conroy's name to the search. Selma was given as next of kin for Clarice. Even then, though, it was Selma's East Texas address. The records are messed up six ways from Sunday."

"Intentionally?"

"Can't tell. Most of it was probably the result of some semiliterate white trash filling out hospital forms. And later maybe Homer Gibbon brushed out his own backtrail."

"What about the mother, Clarice? Where's she?"

"Off the radar, and probably dead. Last record of her was an arrest for possession in Harrisburg in 1993. My guy at Harrisburg PD looked in her jacket, and she had a dozen arrests for drugs and solicitation. Medical records say she had HIV and a bunch of other problems. She probably died in a crack house. Lots of junkies die in those places without ID, or their ID gets stolen after they OD."

"Dead end," Trout said. "Any other living relatives?"

"None of record. There's more background stuff but nothing else exciting. Copies of records, stuff like that. I'll dig in on Volker now."

"Okay, Marcia," said Trout. "You are the best."

"I know I am," she said with a bit of sauce, and disconnected.

Trout turned to Goat. The cameraman was grinning. "Oh yeah," he said, "Pulitzer for sure."

"Movie for sure," countered Trout. He restarted the car. "Now, let's go see Aunt Selma."

The GPS directed them onto smaller and smaller roads, until they thumped along a rutted dirt road that threatened to tear the undercarriage out of the Explorer. They turned onto a lane that was so small the GPS had no name for it.

"Is this even a road?" complained Goat as he bounced around in the passenger seat.

The road rounded a bend and passed under the reaching arms of a double line of twisted elms whose bark was mottled with blight and wrapped in hairy vines. Poison ivy lined both sides of the lane that twisted a crooked half mile toward a weathered, abused old farmhouse.

Trout rolled to a stop, his foot on the brake, the engine idling quietly.

"Jeez," breathed Goat, and Trout nodded. Not even the blaze of fall colors could lend this place a shred of grace. The reds and oranges melted together into a pattern like the skin of a burn victim. The house itself was shuttered against the coming storm. The walls had once been whitewashed, but the paint had peeled to reveal leprous gray wood beneath. A broad gallery porch surrounded the house, and a row of empty rocking chairs creaked in the stiff westerly breeze that came whipping off the overgrown cornfields. Those fields were withered and brown, the stalks sagging under the weight of unpicked ears.

"Get some footage of this place," said Trout. "This is gold."

"I know," Goat said, already fiddling with settings on a small high-definition digital unit. "Frickin' Addams Family farm. I've been to haunted hayrides that are cheerier. Be best if we can get flyover shots from a chopper."

"Who's going to pay for that?"

Goat smiled. "I'm just saying. If you want to put some real mood in this thing."

Trout rolled down his window and leaned out. Even the air was ripe with the sweet stink of vegetable decay.

"This place has all the mood we're going to need," he said as he eased off the brake and drove the rest of the way to the front of the house.

They parked in a roundabout next to a two-year-old Nissan Cube that was so clean and out of place that it looked Photoshopped into the landscape.

"Aunt Selma drives a Cube?" asked Goat, grinning at the thought.

Trout shook his head. "Got to be a visitor. She's old, so maybe it's a Meals-on-Wheels thing. I don't know. Car's clean. Nothing else out here is."

They got out of the car and began walking toward the porch steps. Goat had his full-size camera now and he hoisted it onto his shoulder, the tape already running.

As they approached the bottom step, the front door opened a cautious five inches. Trout stopped and touched Goat's arm. The face that peered out at them was that of a woman whose skin was so comprehensively wrinkled that she looked like an ancient mummy. The one eye they could see, however, was a startling and lambent green.

Before Trout could say anything, the woman demanded, "What?" Her voice was as sharp as a breaking stick.

"Pardon the intrusion, ma'am," said Billy Trout in his very best hat-in-hand, aw-shucks voice. For all that Pennsylvania was a nominally northern state, there was a lot of country out here in the farmlands. "I'm with Regional Satellite News. My name is—"

"I know who you are," she cut in. "I've seen the TV."

Swell, Trout thought, *this is my demographic?*

He kept his smile in place. "I'd like to ask you a few questions."

Selma Conroy studied him with that fierce green eye, then opened the door and stepped out onto the porch. She was thin and old, but Trout could see that beneath the wrinkles was a woman who was probably very beautiful before life and her own bad choices had chopped her down. She wore a faded blue frock under a thick gray bathrobe which she cinched tight as she came to the edge of the porch. "Questions about what?"

"About your nephew," Trout said. He didn't say the name and wanted to see how she would respond.

Selma's cold eyes went colder. "All my family's dead," she said.

"I understand you had a sister and she had a son."

She gave a brief, bitter shake of her head. "My sister's long dead. And I've got a ticket for the same train." She turned and spat off the porch into a row of withered roses.

Trout put a foot up on the bottom step of the porch.

"But you do know about your nephew."

Selma said nothing, but she cut a single brief look toward the car in the turnaround. Trout noted it but didn't know how to approach that subject.

"What about him?" Selma asked quietly.

"You arranged to have him brought here to Stebbins."

She said nothing.

"With," Trout continued, "the intention of having him buried here on the family farm."

"How do you know about that?" she demanded.

"Does it matter?"

"You're not supposed to know about that. No one's supposed to know. The judge and the prison guaranteed it."

"I don't think anyone knows but me," said Trout as he stepped up onto the first riser and put his foot on the second. Selma held her ground.

"That's a bullshit statement," she fired back. "You're here for a story and whether I say anything or not, you're going to tell the world. That's what you reporters do. You find people who have been hurt and you dig into their wounds. What's that expression? 'If it bleeds, it leads?'" She shook her head. "Why would I want to talk to someone like you?"

"Okay," said Trout, "fair enough. Reporters trade in pain. It sells papers. Everyone knows that. And this story will get out, no doubt about it." He stepped up so that he was almost eye level with her. "It's your call, though, as to whether it gets out with your voice and opinion included . . . or not."

"Is that a threat?"

Trout spread his hands. "It's journalism."

"You're a shit."

"And you're an ex-whore," Trout said flatly, dropping all pretense. "Let's start there and see if we can get somewhere interesting."

Aunt Selma folded her arms across her breasts and studied Trout with the frank coldness of a butcher appraising a side of beef. Then she smiled. It was small, just a curl of one corner of her mouth.

"Okay," she said. "Let's have a talk."

But before Trout's smile could blossom on his face, Selma pointed a sharp finger at Goat. "Not him, though. This doesn't go on the camera. I got about a spoonful of self-respect left and I can keep that intact if I can say that it's your word against mine. No pictures, no video, no tape recorder."

Trout thought about it, then nodded. He turned to Goat. "Wait in the car, okay?"

"Sure," said Goat. He turned and trudged down the lane and vanished behind the Explorer.

Trout turned back to Selma. "Shall we go inside and—"

"No," she said flatly. "There's a lady from church in there and she don't need to hear this."

Ah, thought Trout, *the Cube*.

Without another word, Selma walked down the steps and headed toward a rust-colored barn that stood by a creek sixty yards into the field. Trout put his hands into his pockets, used his left thumb to click the button on his digital tape recorder, and followed.

CHAPTER TWENTY-NINE
OFFICE OF THE PRESIDENT OF
THE UNITED STATES OF AMERICA
WASHINGTON, D.C.

The president went through the day-code ritual with Lorne McMasters, feeling his gut tightening as he did so.

"Go ahead, Lorne," he said when the protocols were completed and the secure line verified.

"Mr. President, there has been a deliberate but unauthorized release of one of a Class F biological in rural Pennsylvania."

"Terrorists?"

"No, Mr. President. One of our guests." McMasters quickly brought the president up to speed on Volker, Lucifer 113, Rockview, Homer Gibbon, and the real possibility of an outbreak in Stebbins. As he spoke, corresponding information filled the screen on the president's laptop.

"My God," breathed the president. "Where are we on containment?"

"Law enforcement agencies have been notified, Mr. President," said McMasters. "Local law in Stebbins may be compromised, but we're coordinating with the state police in Pennsylvania and Maryland. However, we're going to need the National Guard to lock down the entire area."

"I'll call Governor Harbison immediately. Stay on the line." The president punched a button. "Janine, please get Governor Harbison on the line. Code One emergency. Also, get the national security director and the secretaries of defense and state in here. Now."

His secretary had the governor of Pennsylvania on the phone in under a minute.

"Mr. President," began Harbison, "what a pleasure. What can I—"

The president cut him off. "Teddy, I need you to listen to me. Time is critical."

He hit Harbison with both barrels.

CHAPTER THIRTY
CONROY'S ACRES

Goat peered around the Explorer and saw Selma and Trout walking down a crooked lane toward a barn, their backs to him. Goat opened the hatch, set his heavy camera inside and took out a smaller unit. He checked to make sure the coast was clear, then sprinted to the near side of the house.

He moved along the side of the gallery, then, when he was sure it was safe, he climbed onto the porch using the side steps. There were three windows on the side and he moved to the first one, where he knelt and peered in through the bottom corner of the window. The glass was smoked gray with grime but still clear enough for him to see the living room. Couple of big armchairs that looked like they were a thousand years old; mismatched sofa. Various tables and cabinets filled with all kinds of collectible crap. Decorative spoons, plates with Disney characters, a collection of porcelain bunnies. Bunnies? He loved it. Juxtaposition always worked in stories like this. Hooker with a soft side. Or, maybe hooker who'd become a sad, lonely old lady surrounded by cheap tchotchkes. Sweet.

He raised the camera and shot the room from various zoom levels.

The second window revealed a dining room with a table with one end piled high with stacks of mail and piles of old magazines. The other half of the table was set out for tea. China pot, two mismatched cups, sugar bowl that was a souvenir from Atlantic City, opened pint carton of half-and-half, and a plate of cookies. As he had walked away

Goat had overheard Aunt Selma tell Trout that she had company. A lady from church. No sign of her, though, so Goat moved on. As he swung the camera across the window he thought he saw a piece of shadow detach itself and moved toward an open interior door. Goat shifted around to the rear window of the kitchen to try and get a better view, but the figure was gone.

It had been a figure, too. A person. The church lady? Probably, he thought, though it had seemed too large.

There was nothing else to see downstairs so he moved to the yard, which was as dreary as the front of the house—diseased elm trees supporting a threadbare hammock filled with last year's rotted leaves, a picnic table with one missing leg that sat unevenly on cinder blocks. Junk that made a statement about a life spiraling downward, so he shot it all. This was all background footage. There was nothing actually happening here, so he clicked off the camera and trudged back to the Explorer to kill time plugging the story on Twitter.

Goat did not see the shadow that moved slowly from window to window, watching him go.

CHAPTER THIRTY-ONE
HARTNUP'S TRANSITION ESTATE

"Give a hand!" Dez called, and two paramedics erupted from the back of their ambulance and sprinted to meet them. Dez knew them—Don and Joan. A male and female team who looked like they could have been siblings: they were both tattooed and muscular, neither had much of a neck, and they looked like they had bulldog genes somewhere in their DNA.

"Is that a throat wound?" Joan asked. She reached for Diviny, but Dez batted her hand away.

"Careful," Dez warned, "he's a biter . . . and he's spitting some nasty black shit."

"Get the gurney," Don said, and Joan peeled off back toward their vehicle. She pulled it out and began loading equipment onto it. JT and Dez held onto the squirming Andy as Don bent forward as close as he dared and lifted the edges of the Izzy to try to see the wound.

"What's the nature of the wound?" demanded Don.

"Bite," said Dez.

Don flicked a look at her. "What kind of bite?"

"Human."

"Christ. Looks ragged as hell. But he hasn't bled through the dressing, so I'm going to leave it in place. We need to get him to an ER stat."

"That's the plan," Dez said between her teeth.

"Why's he cuffed?" Don asked.

"He went crazy," JT said. "Reason unknown. Killed at least two other officers, possibly three."

The paramedic gaped at JT. "Bullshit! I know Andy and—"

"You ever known him to eat anyone?" Dez said sourly.

"You're out of your mind, Dez, Dez . . ."

"Really? Take off the spit mask and bend a little closer," she said. "After he's done eating your face we can have this conversation again."

Joan returned with the gurney and collapsed it down. "What've we got?" she asked Don.

"They said Andy lost it and started attacking people."

"Killing people," JT corrected. "Jeff Strauss, Mike Schneider, and maybe Natalie Shanahan."

Joan's face went white. "Oh my God!"

"I'm telling you," insisted Don, "that's impossi—"

Diviny surged forward so unexpectedly that Dez and JT almost lost their grip on him. The young officer's teeth bit the air inches from Don's nose.

"Holy rat fuck shit!" Don screamed as he fell backward against the gurney.

"Stop screwing around and get the backboard," JT yelled as he and Dez wrestled Andy back down.

The paramedics were stunned for a moment. Dez saw the spark of disbelief flare in their eyes and knew exactly how they felt. Impossible. Every damn thing was impossible. Then they snapped back into the moment and went to work.

The backboard was a body-length piece of heavy-gauge plastic with holes along the edges that served as handholds or places where a patient could be secured. It took the four of them three minutes of sweating and cursing to force Andy Diviny onto the board, cuff his wrists to the sides, and secure his legs with duct tape. Better equipped departments had expensive strapping for these kinds of situations, but out here in the sticks duct tape was quick and durable and always available. Joan wrapped the tape around and around each shin. Then she repeated this around his midthighs and chest.

"You have a plastic bite mask?" asked Dez as she forced Diviny's head down for the twentieth time.

"Philadelphia collar's better," said Don and he pulled one out of an equipment case. The device was a two-piece foam plastic cervical collar that fit together with Velcro and had an opening to allow access to the throat. It effectively kept Diviny from opening his jaws wide enough to bite, and nicely immobilized his head. They reinforced this by winding another turn of duct tape around his forehead, securing it to the backboard. Dez grabbed the tape from Joan and put a final loop around Diviny's chest and shoulders.

Then Dez and JT sat back, drained and sweating. Don and Joan wavered with indecision.

"Is he safe?" JT asked.

Diviny moaned and snarled and thrashed.

"Can you give him something?" asked JT as he wiped sweat from his eyes. "Don't you have some kind of chemical restraint? Valium or something?"

"We use Midazolam—Versed—these days," Joan said, fishing in the trauma kit. She produced a hypodermic, removed the safety cap, shot a little into the air to remove bubbles. But she hesitated. "With him thrashing like that I could get this wrong, and I sure as hell don't want to nail myself with an accidental needle stick."

"Go intranasally," suggested Don. "Doesn't kick in as fast, but it's a lot safer."

Joan handed him the equipment and Don fitted a port into one of Diviny's nostrils and attached the syringe to that. Once in place he pushed the plunger and the filter converted the liquid stream into a mist.

"Let's get his vitals," Don said, "and then get him the hell out of here."

Joan clipped an oximetry monitor to the tip of Diviny's right index finger while Don wrapped a pressure cuff around Diviny's arm and began pumping the rubber bulb.

Joan keyed the portable radio and called the hospital. When an ER doctor came online she said, "We have a police officer down with trauma to the throat. Other officers think that it's from a human bite. They applied an Izzy and the patient has been administered intranasal Midazolam. Taking vitals now. Patient's skin is cold." She took a digital thermometer and placed the tip in Diviny's ear. "Whoa . . . temperature is eighty-eight point four. Pupils nonreactive. Not getting any pulse with the oximeter." She dug her fingers into Diviny's wrist, made an irritated face, tried again in a different spot. Tried again. Into the radio she said, "Doctor, I still can't find a pulse. He's in serious shock and—"

"BP is nonpalp. Zero over zero," said Don as he began pumping the pressure cuff again. And again. "Damn cuff's broken."

"Forget this shit and let's go!" urged Dez.

Don ignored her. He looped his stethoscope from around his neck and pressed the chestpiece against Diviny's ribs. His face went from confused to blank. "No respiration. We need to intubate him."

Diviny snapped and bared his teeth.

"Can't intubate a biter," Joan said.

"We're losing him," Don yelled, "he's crashing . . ."

His words trailed off. Diviny wasn't crashing. He continued to snarl and writhe and fight against the restraints.

"This doesn't make sense," he said.

"What doesn't?" asked Dez.

Dez could hear the doctor yelling for information and clarification, and Joan picked up the mike. "We are unable to get reliable vitals at this time."

She listened for a moment and then disconnected.

"He wants us to start an EKG as soon as we get him into the ambulance. And take a blood glucose reading. He's prepping a room."

The four of them stared at each other for a moment, and then looked down at Diviny.

"I don't understand this," said Joan in a distant voice. "He has no blood pressure, no pulse. He's not breathing . . ."

"What are you saying?" asked Dez.

Joan almost said it, but didn't. What she said was, "We can't get any vitals from this patient."

"It's not the equipment," added Don quietly. "We just . . . can't get any vitals. He's . . . he's . . ." He shook his head.

Neither of them said the word.

Dez looked at JT, who was sweating as badly as if he stood next to an open fire.

"Let's get him to the hospital," Dez said quietly. "And I mean right fucking now."

Without another word they hoisted the gurney into the back of the ambulance. Joan climbed in back but she sat on a metal fold-down stool as far away from Diviny as she could. JT climbed in with her and Don got behind the wheel. Dez ran to her unit, fired it up, and led the way through the maze of haphazardly parked vehicles. Another Bordentown unit was parked down by the road and the officer was erecting sawhorse barriers. Beyond his unit were a dozen cars and vans. The press had arrived, and once the true nature of this got out there would soon be more reporters than cops. Rubberneckers were walking along the highway and cutting through the woods, their cars parked on the shoulders of Doll Factory Road for half a mile in either direction.

As soon as they reached the blacktop Dez hit lights and sirens and kicked the pedal all the way down. The cruiser shot out onto the road and went screaming away from that place of death and mystery. The ambulance, carrying its own mysteries, followed.

CHAPTER THIRTY-TWO
HARTNUP'S TRANSITION ESTATE

Chief Goss stared down at the madness that lay sprawled in shades of red and green before him. Two officers here. Another down the slope. Not his officers, but that didn't matter. The towns in this part of the county always shared work; their cases always overlapped. They were all a family.

Three dead.

One completely out of his mind.

The clearing was still. No one moved. Shock danced in every set of eyes; it beat wildly in their chests.

He stared at the bodies. Mike Schneider, Jeff Strauss. Not only dead but torn apart. What the hell was Andy doing to them? Eating them?

Goss felt the contents of his stomach turn to greasy sludge. He wanted to throw up. He wanted to go the hell home. He turned to Sheldon.

"Shel," he said softly, "what happened here?"

Sheldon shook his head. Then he took a breath, licked his lips, and explained things exactly as he'd seen them. Goss was shaking his head throughout. Not to suggest that Sheldon was lying, but because it was all so weird. So wrong.

"Any sign of Doc Hartnup?"

He carefully lowered his bulk to one knee a few inches from Strauss. Goss knew him better than Schneider. Their kids were in the same grade, they played on the same Little League team. Strauss's son was the shortstop, his own Mikey was the catcher.

This was going to have to be a closed casket. The whole lower half of Strauss's face was gone. Pieces of it were stuck to the dead man's uniform, to the grass, to his hair. The rest was . . .

He couldn't allow himself to frame the thought.

"Ah, Jeff . . . damn it to hell."

Goss had never been beside the body of a fallen friend. Everyone he knew had died in bed or in the hospital, and accident victims were usually strangers. He wondered if he should close Strauss's eyelids. That's what they always did in movies. Close the eyelids. Kind of like closing a door, or pulling up a sheet. It meant something, he supposed. A show of respect. A gesture to restore some little bit of dignity.

Would it matter to the forensics guys?

He thought about that, lips pursed, heart heavy.

"Yeah," he murmured to himself, "it's only right."

He reached his hand out, his fingers trembling with adrenalin and shock. And revulsion. It was hard to look at that torn face. Goss felt the greasy sludge in his stomach bubble and churn.

His fingertips brushed the half-closed lids.

Suddenly Jeff Strauss's lipless mouth lunged forward and those naked teeth clamped down around Chief Goss's fingers.

CHAPTER THIRTY-THREE
PENNSYLVANIA ARMY NATIONAL GUARD
COMPANY D, 1-103RD ARMOR
108 WASHINGTON AVE.
CONNELLSVILLE, PENNSYLVANIA

Sergeant Teddy Polk stood in the rain, waving his men forward and pushing them up into the back of the troop truck. A line of troop transport trucks stood idling in the downpour.

One of the soldiers, a corporal named Nick Wyckoff, from Pine Deep, the same small town as Polk, nodded at the convoy. "What's the op? Sandbagging streams and shit?"

Polk shook his head. "Nobody's saying nothing, Nickie."

Wyckoff nodded and reached for the strap to pull himself up into the truck, but Polk tapped his shoulder and Wyckoff bent close. "Couple weird things about this, man."

"Yeah? Like what?"

Polk spoke as quietly as he could given the roar of the rain. "We were told to handpick single men. No one with family in the area, no one with kids. Married guys are to be used for flood control and emergency evac only. None of them roll with us."

"What's the—"

"No, wait," said Polk, "it gets weirder. . . . I saw them loading some crates into a couple of the trucks."

"Crates of what?"

Polk licked his lips. "Hazmat suits."

"Oh . . . shit, man," murmured Wyckoff.

"Yeah."

A few minutes later the trucks were rolling through the gate.

Major General Simeon Zetter stood at the window in his office, hands clasped behind his back, face impassive, eyes fixed on the line of vehicles heading into the storm. He was alone in his office. All of his senior officers had gone with the convoy. This wasn't an operation that could be trusted to lieutenants.

The rain troubled him. It was like a thick gray veil and even from where his office was set it was hard to see the line of trucks. With these winds his Apaches and Black Hawks were grounded. That was bad. If there was ever something that was a perfect operation for the air cav, this was it.

Ground troops? Stebbins County was sparsely populated, but it covered a huge amount of ground. Fields and forests and barns. So much natural cover. In any other situation he could rely on thermal scans for target acquisition, but during the conference call with the governor, the president, and the national security advisor, he had been told something that still echoed in his head. Something that screamed in his head.

"Hostiles may display variable heat signatures," said Blair, the national security advisor.

"Sir?" Zetter had asked.

"We have to prepare for the possibility that a fair number of the infected may not be trackable by body temperature."

"How so? Are they using thermal suppressors or—"

"No," said Blair, "these are civilians."

"Then I don't—"

"Their body temperatures are dropping. On average, one degree per hour. Faster in this cold."

"Is . . . is this a symptom of the disease, sir?"

Blair said, "No, General Zetter, it is proof of the absence of life."

PART TWO

DEATH'S OTHER KINGDOM

We are each our own devil, and we make this world our hell.

—Oscar Wilde, *The Duchess of Padua*

CHAPTER THIRTY-FOUR
MAGIC MARTI IN THE MORNING
WNOW RADIO, MARYLAND

"This is Magic Marti at the mike with an update on the storm that's currently chowing down on our area. A hurricane warning is in effect for Stebbins and Fayette Counties. Take my advice: if you don't have to go out, don't. I have an updated list of school and business closings . . ."

CHAPTER THIRTY-FIVE
TOWN OF STEBBINS

The radio crackled while Dez was still two miles from the hospital. She snatched up the mike.

"Unit Two."

"Dez? What the heck's going on out there?" blurted Flower. "They've upgraded the storm again and they want to start moving the kids to the elementary school. All the stores in town are closing at noon, and I can't get the chief on the radio."

The elementary and middle schools in Stebbins were regional, pulling in busloads of kids from all over. Early closings meant long delays as parents had to scramble to get out of work and drive to pick up their kids. That meant that the kids were usually kept in the school auditoriums or lunchrooms for hours. But with a storm coming, only the elementary school was rated as an official shelter. It was on high ground at the end of Schoolhouse Lane. All of the middle school kids had to be bussed there, and all of the parents rerouted. It was a logistical nightmare under good conditions. Today it would be insane.

"I can't help with that, Flower. Things are pretty crazy right now. You're going to have to bring in the volunteers to handle bussing the kids over to the Little School."

"Are you at the hospital yet?"

"Almost."

"Well . . . what should I do with the lieutenant from the state police?"

"Say again?"

"Lieutenant Hardy's on the other line. He keeps asking to talk to the chief, but—"

"Patch him through, Flower," said Dez, "I'll bring him up to speed."

"Thanks! Meet him on channel eight," Flower said, sounding greatly relieved.

Dez dialed over to eight, which was one of the secure lines. There was a burst of squelch and then a strong male voice spoke.

"With whom am I speaking?"

"This is Officer Desdemona Fox, Stebbins County PD."

"Officer Fox, good. This is Lieutenant William Henry Hardy, State Police, Troop B. Are you with Chief Goss?"

"No, sir. He's at a crime scene—"

"The Hartnup scene?" interrupted Hardy.

"Yes sir."

"He isn't answering his radio." Hardy said in a tone that seemed to suggest that he was deeply offended that a police chief from a one stoplight town would dare to dodge his call. "I can't seem to make contact with him."

"He had a radio when I left him, Loot. Maybe fifteen minutes ago. Aren't your boys on site yet?"

Just as she said that, three state police cruisers rounded the corner and shot past her, lights flashing, sirens blaring. She'd have heard them if it hadn't been for the wail of the ambulance.

"Correction, Loot . . . three units just passed me en route to the scene."

"Very well. I'll get a full report from them," said Hardy, sounding only slightly mollified. "In the short term, what can you tell me?"

Dez was expecting this and she made sure she phrased it as blandly as possible. She gave him straight facts without any speculation or color. Hardy listened without comment until she was finished.

"My condolences on the loss of your colleagues, Officer Fox," he said. The comment lacked any real emotion, but Dez gave him a couple of points for good manners. "The officer who was overcome—was there any indication of erratic behavior beforehand?"

"None," Dez said.

"Very well. I'll be in touch." Hardy disconnected without another word.

"Dick," she grumbled. The hospital was four blocks away. Maybe she'd get some answers there.

The radio buzzed again and Flower was back on the line.

"Dez," said Flower, "we have a regular police call, too, and I don't have any other units. It's a carjacking. Guy said a naked man rushed him when he braked for a light. Beat him up, took his pants, and drove off in the car. Can you believe that? Took his actual pants. And get this . . . the guy who attacked him bit him!"

Dez nearly drove into a telephone pole. "Say again?" she demanded.

"That's what I said. The guy bit him, and it's pretty bad, too. Hospital doesn't have any ambulances to send. They're all at Doc's place. So, I need you to take his statement at the hospital."

Christ, thought Dez, *another bite*?

Then she thought about the set of bare footprints that led out of Hartnup's.

"What's the location?"

"The victim is at the diner. Murph is going to take him to the hospital."

"Okay, we'll try to get his statement there."

Half a block away the façade of the hospital loomed out of the gloom.

CHAPTER THIRTY-SIX
CONROY'S ACRES

Trout walked side by side with Selma, and neither of them spoke until they stood in the lee of the sagging barn. Crows lined the pitched roof and thirty kinds of birds flew in and out of holes in the rust-colored wood. There were no animal sounds from inside, and Trout suspected the barn had been in total disuse for at least twenty years.

"Okay," Trout said, "we're officially out in the sticks. Let's talk."

Selma fished in the pocket of her robe and produced a pack of unfiltered Camels and a lighter with the logo of a Pennsylvania casino. Mohegan Sun at Pocono Downs. Selma kissed a cigarette out of the pack, lit it, and stuck out the corner of her lower lip to blow smoke up and over her face.

"Ask your questions," she said.

"Are you Homer Gibbon's aunt?"

"Sure. Why not?"

"How well did you know him?"

"Seen him once in a while. Mostly when he was like seventeen and older. After he ran away from foster care the last time."

"When was the last time you saw him?"

Selma puffed, shrugged.

"Could you be a bit more specific?" Trout asked.

"I don't know. Maybe back in ninety, ninety-one."

"That was after he had committed several murders."

"Alleged murders," she corrected. "He was never convicted for anything back then."

"Alleged," Trout conceded. No reason to argue that point. "Did you know about his . . . um . . . activities?"

She made a face. "Ever heard the expression 'country don't mean dumb'?"

"Sure."

"You're asking a question that you'd ask a stupid hayseed who didn't know shit from Shinola. Is that how this is going to run? You going to treat me like I'm poor unedumacated white trash." She leaned on the deliberately mispronounced word, giving it a heavy rural twist. "If I say I knew what he was up to then I'm an accessory. I look old, but do I look stupid?"

Trout grinned, unapologetically. "No, ma'am," he said, "you don't."

"Show some respect."

Trout found he suddenly liked Aunt Selma. "Sorry."

She nodded and took a long drag.

"Did you have any contact with Homer Gibbon after he was arrested for murder?"

"No."

"No letters? E-mails? Christmas card?"

"Homer strike you as the kind of guy who buys Christmas cards?" she asked, smiling.

"Actually," Trout said, "he tried to send valentines to the jury during his first trial."

"Publicity stunt. Probably cooked up by his lawyer to make him look crazy."

Probably true, Trout thought.

"So, you had no contact with him after his first arrest?"

"No."

"At all?"

"No."

"Then why did you place the request to have his body brought here to Stebbins for burial?"

She shrugged. "Family."

"Sorry, Selma," said Trout, "but that's thin. Not to offend, but it doesn't look like you have two dimes to rub together. Between the fees, transportation, mortuary costs, and a crew to dig a grave, you have to be shelling out five, six grand."

"Four and change."

"Still a lot of money."

"Only if I was interested in saving it." Selma picked a fleck of tobacco from her tongue and flicked it into the wind. "You have any family?"

"A sister in Scranton," he said. "Distant cousins somewhere in upstate New York."

"When's the last time you saw your sister?"

Trout had to think about that. He and Meghan had never been close. They swapped cards at the holidays, but the last time he'd actually seen her?

"Couple of years ago."

She arched an eyebrow. "A couple?"

"Okay, four years ago."

"So, you're not close. If she died, would you go to her funeral?"

"Sure."

"You say that without thinking about it. Why?"

"She's my sister."

Selma nodded, and Trout got it.

"Well, yeah, okay," he said, "but she's a nurse and a mother. She's not a serial killer."

"Neither was Homer last time I saw him. He was a scared, lost young man who hadn't gotten much of a break or a kind word from anyone. His mom gave him up when he was just born—and let me tell you, that leaves a mark—and he was in and out of foster care until he ran away. You ever do a story on foster care, Mr. Trout?"

Trout said nothing.

"Yeah, I bet you have. So, you know what kind of meat grinders they are. Half the foster parents are in it just for the paychecks and they don't give a flying fuck about the kids. The other half are pedophiles who shouldn't be around kids. You think Homer got to be the way he was because he had bad wiring?" She tapped her skull. "Fuck no. He was made to be what he was. The system screwed him every bit as much as those baby-raping sonsabitches they call foster parents. Don't try to tell me different because then you'd be lying."

"No," he said. "I know what those places are like. A lot of kids get torn up in there and that makes them victims of the predators and victims of the system."

"And it turns them into predators themselves," observed Aunt Selma.

"Not all of them," said Trout. "Not even most of them."

"Enough of them. Enough so that people became used to them being killers and when that happened it stopped being an aber . . . aber . . . what's the word I'm thinking of?"

"Aberration?" Trout supplied.

"Yes. And then they say that since most people don't turn bad then those that do have done so because of choice." She threw her cigarette into the cold dirt and ground it under her heel. Trout noticed that she wore bedroom slippers with little hummingbirds on them. A touch of innocence? Or a memory of innocence lost? Either way it made Trout feel sad for her. He wondered how much of her life was forced on her and how much was choice? And that made him wonder if a person who is forced into bad situations over and over again when they're too weak or helpless to do anything about it will eventually make bad choices of their own simply because they've become habituated to them.

He'd have to talk to a psychologist about that. It would make a great motif to string through the whole story, be it a book or a screenplay.

"Are you saying that none of what Homer did was his fault?"

Selma did not answer that right away. She took out her Camels and lit another and puffed for a while, one arm wrapped around her ribs, the elbow of the other arm propped on it, wrist limp so that the hand fell backward like someone considering a piece of art in a gallery. Only this wasn't an affectation, he was sure of that. She was really thinking about his question. Or, he thought a moment later, carefully constructing the content of her reply. On the roof of the barn one crow lifted its voice and sliced the air with a plaintive cry that was disturbingly like that of a child in pain.

"No," she said at length, "that wouldn't be the truth and we both know it. Homer may have been pushed in the wrong direction, but over time . . . yeah, I think he got a taste for it."

"And yet you wanted to have him buried here."

Selma nodded. "Yes."

"Why?" Trout asked.

"You asked that already."

"You never actually answered the question."

"He's family."

"Okay, but it's not like this is your ancestral home. You were born in Texas. Homer was born in Pittsburgh. Why here?"

"It's the family place now."

"Is there more of the family around?"

She shook her head. "I don't expect you'd understand, Mr. Trout."

"I'd like to." He intended it as a lie, but he surprised himself by meaning it.

She smoked her cigarette and stared at the line of gray clouds that had begun to creep over the far tree line.

"I've got cancer," she said.

Her comment startled Trout. "What? I mean . . . God, I'm sorry. Is it very . . . advanced?"

"I'm a corpse," she said. "I'll be dead by Christmas." She waggled the cigarette between her fingers. "Three packs a day for forty years."

"I'm . . . sorry."

"Fuck it. The warnings are right there on the side of every pack. I knew what I was getting myself into. Slow suicide. Knowing that these coffin nails would kill me one day made them taste a little better."

Trout said nothing.

Selma cocked her head and looked up at him. "I won't pretend that I'm anything but what I am, Mr. Trout, and being a whore and a madam is far from the worst things I've done. I've lived down in the gutter since the day I was born. Shoved into the life but chose to stay there. My choice. I make no apologies and I'd spit on anyone who said they felt sorry for me. This is my life, and I had some good times, too." A tear glittered in the corner of one eye and she wiped it away irritably. "I can't fix anything I ever done. Most of the people I wronged are long dead, so there's no way to make any kind of amends, even if I wanted to. I don't regret most of it, but there's one thing . . . one single thing that I wish I hadn't done. Or, maybe it's a thing that I wish I had done."

"What's that, Selma?" Trout asked softly.

"When my sister Clarice got knocked up, she came to me and asked if I'd take the baby. She was really far gone, even then. Her hurt went so deep that she lost herself in her own darkness and she knew—like anyone else knew—that she was never going to find her way out."

"Who was the father? Where was he in all of this?"

Selma gave a bitter laugh. "He was any one of a hundred ten-dollar tricks. Even if she knew his name there was no way he'd ever do the right thing because nobody ever does the right fucking thing."

"So she asked you to take the baby?"

Another tear formed and this fell down her cheek, rolling and stuttering over the thousands of seams in her skin. "I had a place and I had a little bit of money. I was running ten whores, and I could have made them take care of the kid in shifts. I could have done that and it wouldn't have been no skin off my nose. It would have been nothing to me." Two lines of tears fell together. "But it might have been everything to Homer. Nobody would have laid a hand on him. None of those foster parent fucks would have stuck their dicks in him. No one would have whipped him with electrical cords or burned him with cigarettes or made him kneel on pebbles." Selma suddenly grabbed Trout's sleeve. "Homer might have had a chance, you see?"

"Yeah," he said thickly. "I see."

"And all the hurt he did to other people. All those killings. The bad things he did to women and little kids. He might not have done any of that . . ."

"You don't know that, Selma. He might have had this in him from birth."

She pulled her hand away from his sleeve and gave a derisive shake of her head. "A bad seed? Bullshit. I don't believe in that. Babies don't carry sin."

"I'm talking a chemical imbalance or—"

She shook her head again. "No. It was the system that made him into a monster. It's their fault. Theirs and mine."

They stood in the cold wind, watching the sunny day grow gradually darker.

"So," Trout began slowly, "bringing him back here . . . ?"

"Homer never had a home," she repeated. "I didn't give him anything before. Now . . . at least I could do that much. A home . . . and maybe some peace."

Trout had a hundred other questions he wanted to ask, but he left them all unsaid. They tumbled into the dirt like broken birds as he looked into those lambent green eyes. Windows of the soul, and hers looked in on an interior landscape that was ravaged by storms and blighted beyond reclamation.

He said, "I'm sorry."

She nodded. Tears streamed down her face, but she set her jaw. Trout watched as she stubbed out her second cigarette and lit the third.

Without another word he turned and walked slowly back along the road to the Explorer. This story was solid gold, no question about it, but he knew with absolute certainty that it was going to break his heart to write it.

CHAPTER THIRTY-SEVEN
WOLVERTON REGIONAL HOSPITAL
STEBBINS COUNTY, PENNSYLVANIA

Dez braked hard and jolted to a stop in front of the emergency room entrance and was out of the car before the ambulance passed her and pulled into the turnaround. Orderlies, nurses, and a doctor were running in a pack and converged with Dez as the back door of the ambulance opened and JT jumped out.

They brought the stretcher down, dropped the wheels, and then the swarm turned and ran with it into the hospital amid a flurry of technical medical jargon neither JT nor Dez understood.

Instead of taking Diviny to a regular curtained bay in the emergency department, they wheeled him into the trauma bay, which was a large semi-operating room intended for a single patient. Dez and JT stood in the open doorway, not wanting to enter but needing to know something—anything—that would make some sense of this.

An argument broke out between the doctor and paramedics over the vitals, and the doctor—an Indian man whose name tag read Sengupta—was loud and condescending. He ordered the nurses to "take a proper set of vitals, goddamn it."

They did. Or, at least they tried. They cut through Diviny's clothes and stuck EKG leads onto his chest. They tried taking his temperature by the ear and later rectally. They put him on an automatic blood pressure machine and clipped another oximeter to his fingers. They used a Doppler device to try to take a pulse.

Sengupta was soon yelling again.

"Check the damn machines!" he snarled.

They did. Then he went and checked for himself. New blood pressure machines were wheeled in. New thermometers were used. Half a dozen stethoscopes were pressed against Diviny's chest and abdomen.

And then the noise and confusion in the room suddenly melted down into a hushed silence as the medical professionals stood around the table. Some stared at Diviny; the rest looked to each other for confirmation or explanations. No one said anything for at least half a minute.

Oh, shit, thought Dez; and she realized how much hope she was placing on a proper medical examination.

Then the doctor began firing a new set of orders. "I want a CHEM-7 panel. Electrolytes and renal function tests. Do a liver function test, ABG, CBC with diff . . . serum-urine tox screen. Check for everything: alcohol, Tylenol, aspirin, cocaine, heroin, any other narcotics, amphetamines, marijuana, barbiturates, benzodiazepines. Get me a UA culture and sensitivity, as well as blood cultures, cardiac enzymes. And let's get a chest X-ray and a CT scan. Get IVs going."

He turned to the paramedic. "Who brought him in?"

Don pointed to Dez and JT, and the doctor stepped away from the table and headed toward them, herding them outside with wide arms, like a shepherd herding goats. They backed out into the hall.

Sengupta had a dark, scowling face and very intense eyes. He loomed over them, taller even than JT's six one. "What happened to this man?"

"I don't know—" began Dez, but he cut her off.

"Then tell me what you do know."

She nodded and launched in. Sengupta interrupted constantly, digging into the story for little bits of information. Dez could see him becoming more and more frustrated because even though they had a lot of details, none of them seemed to want to assemble into a reasonable picture of any kind.

Sengupta drained them dry and then stood silent, looking from them to the swinging vinyl doors that separated the hallway from the trauma room.

"Doc," asked Dez, "what's wrong with him?"

The doctor didn't answer. Instead he asked, "Did you see anything unusual? Containers of chemicals? Unusual poisons? Anything like that?"

"Just the stuff Doc Hartnup keeps in the mortuary," said JT. "Don't really know what he has in there."

"Is there a landfill near the mortuary? Anyplace where a toxic leak might—"

Dez shook her head. "Nothing like that."

"Did Officer Diviny drink or eat anything while he was there?"

"No," they both said.

"I don't think he was even inside the mortuary building," said Dez.

"Okay, okay . . ." The doctor chewed his lip. "I'm going to call Poison Control and have them get some people out there. I would like you to contact Chief Goss and ask if anyone else has become sick, or is acting strangely. Anything, even small symptoms."

"Is that what this is?" JT asked. "A toxic spill?"

Again the doctor didn't answer.

"Could it be a disease of some kind? Or an insect bite?"

"We . . . should wait until we get some test results."

Sengupta started to turn away, but Dez touched his arm. "Doc . . . what about the vitals? The paramedics couldn't get any and I didn't see your team get any. What's that about?"

The doctor's eyes were hooded and he repeated, "We need to see the test results. Now please, officer . . ."

Dez sighed and stepped aside. Sengupta went back inside the trauma room and the vinyl doors swung shut in Dez's face. She tried to peer through the window, but it was virtually opaque. All she could see were figures milling around.

She stepped back and turned to JT.

"This is some shit, Hoss."

"I need to sit down," he said, and he staggered over to a row of ugly plastic chairs and collapsed onto one. Now that the urgency of the moment was over, exhaustion hit them like body blows. JT bent forward with his elbows on his knees and buried his face in his palms. Dez stood and watched him, afraid for a moment that he was crying. He wasn't. After a moment he rubbed his palms over his face, rubbed his eyes with his fists, and sat up.

"This is definitely some shit," he said.

"I know," she said, "and it's not over. While we were en route Flower called to say that they were bringing in a bite victim. We'd better go find him and get a statement."

JT stared at her, his brown eyes filled with fear and confusion. "What's going on?"

Dez looked down the hall toward the nurses' station, and instead of checking on the bite victim she sat down next to JT. There was a clock on the wall across from them and the second hand chopped its way through a minute of silence. It seemed to take an hour.

"You want to talk about this?" she asked, her voice idle, the question loaded.

He shook his head. "Not now or ever."

They watched the second hand.

Then JT said, "It doesn't make sense."

"No, it damn well doesn't," Dez agreed. It felt as if there was a war going on inside her body. She could feel the shakes wanting to kick in, trembling there at the edge of her self-control; and deeper inside was an anger that was unlike anything she'd felt since Afghanistan. When your friends roll over a land mine and a sudden blast scatters them and their vehicle over a hundred yards of the landscape, the same feeling begins to burn. There's never a signature; you have no one specific to hate. It's hard to hate an ideology or concept with any degree of satisfaction. Hate is a personal thing, a reaction to attack. Here . . . Dez didn't know if this was a person somehow spreading a toxin, or a bug that escaped from a lab somewhere, or a microscopic bug kicked out by Mother Nature. She wanted a cause, a culprit. Someone to go after. Someone to hurt as a way of reducing her own hurt.

JT kept shaking his head. "Doc Hartnup was dead. I mean . . . you saw it, right? He was dead. He was way past dead."

"Yup. So was the Russian broad."

The silence that followed that remark was filled with all kinds of ugly thoughts. After a few moments, JT looked sideways at her. He licked his lips. "About that . . . I'm sorry, kid."

"Fuck it."

"No . . . you were right earlier. I doubted you in there. Not for long, but there it is, and that makes me an asshole and a bad partner. I'm really sorry."

They stared at each other for a few seconds. Dez smiled. "Make me a pot of your ass-burning chili and put a six of Sam Adams on ice and we're square."

He grinned. "You asking me out on a date, girl?"

"Gak! Don't be a disgusting old fuck."

"Good, 'cause I don't date white girls."

Dez snorted. "What I was saying, old man, is that we eat some chili and drink some brew and forget today ever happened."

He nodded. They pretended to smile. Time passed with infinite slowness.

"So . . ." she said slowly, "where the hell are we?"

JT shook his head again. "At a guess, I'd say the Twilight Zone. Damn murder victims coming back from the dead. Cops killing cops. Cops *eating* cops. How does that make sense? I mean . . . even if this is a toxic spill or something."

"I know," she said.

"I'm going to either become a serious drunk or I'll be in therapy the rest of my life."

"Fuck therapy. I'm going to get drunk and stay there. It's safer. The pink elephants and polka-dotted lobsters don't try to eat you."

A nurse burst out of the trauma room and ran past them.

"Hey!" Dez called as she jumped to her feet, but the nurse never even turned her head. Dez looked at JT for a moment, then without saying a word they both moved to the big vinyl doors and bent close to listen. More medical chatter, but they only caught slices of that between shouts and yells and the constant snarls of Andy Diviny.

The sound of footsteps made them turn and they saw the nurse hurrying back down the hall with an armful of folded hazmat suits. She didn't want to stop, but JT stepped into her path and blocked the hall.

"Excuse me . . . nurse? We brought Officer Diviny in. What's his status?"

The nurse gave him a single haunted look and then a fierce shake of her head. "You'll have to talk to Dr. Sengupta."

She shouldered past him and pushed into the trauma room.

Dez and JT stared at the door.

"That can't be good," JT muttered.

Dez sniffed and turned away.

"Hey," said JT gently, "are you okay?"

She shook her head but said nothing.

"Talk to me, kid."

Dez took in a long breath and sighed it out, blowing out her cheeks. When she turned back to him her eyes were rimmed with red and wet with unshed tears. "I'm really scared here, Hoss." She pointed at the trauma room. "You saw the paramedics try to take Andy's vitals. He had no blood pressure, no pulse, and he wasn't breathing. I don't watch *Grey's Anatomy* but I'm pretty sure what that means."

JT was shaking his head. "Can't be, Dez. Absolutely cannot be. Boy was moving and fighting the whole time."

"Yeah? Well that Russian bitch was pretty damn spry, too. And neither of us believe that someone came in and carried off Doc Hartnup."

JT said nothing.

"Doc and the cleaning lady were both dead," Dez growled. "So was Andy. And then they . . . they . . ." She waved around as if she'd snatch the right words out of the air.

"And then they were not dead," JT supplied. "Come on, Dez . . . if you're going to try and sell me on some bullshit that they're vampires or ghosts or something, then I really am going home to get drunk."

She wiped angrily at the tears. "Did I say anything about vampires? Andy wasn't Vlad the motherfucking Impaler. He was Andy and he was dead and he was trying to bite people."

"Okay, so what does that make him?"

She chewed her lip. "I don't know. I guess it makes him fucked up."

They both nodded.

"We'd better see about that other bite victim," Dez said. JT nodded and they hurried off. But the nurse in the ER informed them that the man was in surgery under a general anesthesia. JT suggested that the nurse talk with Dr. Sengupta who was dealing with a similar bite wound. The nurse nodded and headed off to do that.

Dez and JT walked back to the row of chairs.

"It's hard to believe they're all gone," said JT as he sat back down. "Doc, Jeff Strauss, Mike Schneider, Natalie Shanahan. Andy, too, I guess. Five people that I've known for years." He snapped his fingers. "Gone just like that."

Dez nodded.

JT cleared his throat. "Is this what it was like in Afghanistan?"

Dez shook her head. "Yes and no. The shock and the grief . . . yeah, they were the same. But the fear was different."

"Different how?"

"Over there," she said, "it was just bullets and bombs. But this . . ."

She shivered. "I don't know how to be afraid of this. The right way, I mean. You know what I'm trying to say?"

"Sadly, I do."

The door to the trauma room opened and the tall Indian doctor came out. It took a moment for them to recognize him because he was covered head to toe in a white hazmat suit. He came toward them but stopped ten feet away and held up a hand to keep them from coming closer to him. His hazmat suit was splattered with betadine and other chemicals.

"Doc," barked Dez, jumping to her feet, "what can you tell us?"

"We are taking Officer Diviny to quarantine."

"What's wrong with him?"

"We . . . still need more information." He considered them. "Since you were in direct contact with the patient, we should consider admitting you both for observation . . ."

"Not a fucking chance, doc," growled Dez. "Storm's hitting any minute."

Sengupta nodded. "Then at least I would like to have a nurse draw blood from both of you. Urine samples, too."

They didn't ask why. They agreed.

"I've been on the phone with Poison Control and with several of my colleagues. We have specialists on their way here and I requested a hazmat team for the crime scene."

"What specialists?" JT asked.

"Toxicology, epidemiology . . . others. This is a very . . . unusual . . . matter. I . . . may put a call into the Centers for Disease Control in Atlanta."

"The CDC?" JT frowned. "Then you do think it's a disease."

"As I said, this is very unusual. We don't know anything yet."

The vinyl doors opened and the team, all of them in hazmats, wheeled the gurney out and hurried away down the hall. A metal frame had been erected over the bed and it was draped with heavy protective sheeting.

Dr. Sengupta directed a nurse to get samples from JT and Dez, and then he hurried down the hall after the gurney.

CHAPTER THIRTY-EIGHT
STEBBINS COUNTY

Billy Trout climbed back in the Explorer and drove away from Selma's place, a frown etched deeply onto his face.

"What'd she say?" asked Goat.

Trout fished in his pocket and removed the digital recorder, thumbed back the rewind, dialed the volume up, and pressed play. The recorder had excellent pickup and the playback was only slightly muddied by the cloth of Trout's trousers. They listened to it twice.

Goat said, "Interesting stuff."

"Isn't it, though?" replied Trout.

"She really got to you, didn't she?"

"I'm not afraid to admit it." Trout cut him a sideways look. "What's your take on her?"

Goat fished a York Peppermint Pattie out of his jacket pocket, opened it, broke it in half, and handed one piece to Trout.

"She's really something," Goat said, then nibbled the edge of his candy. "She was maybe twenty, twenty-five years younger, I'd have tapped that shit."

"Really? You listen to that tape and the only thing you can say is that you'd throw her a pity fuck?"

"I ain't talking a pity fuck. She looks like she was hot stuff, and not that long ago. I could really see Helen Mirren playing her, 'cause I'd tap Mirren in a heartbeat."

"You worry me at times, Goat."

"Why? 'Cause I'm on the prowl instead of pining for a redneck lady cop who'd like to see your nuts on her key chain?"

"Don't," warned Trout.

"Don't what? You telling me you're not still hung up on Officer Boobs?"

"I've interviewed twenty serial killers over the years, Goat. I know everything there is to know about how to hide a body where it'll never be found."

"Truth hurt?"

"I'm talking dismemberment and multiple burial sites . . ."

"Okay, okay. Subject closed."

"Selma," Trout prompted. "Give me your *professional* opinion."

Goat shrugged. "The theater lost a major player when she decided to fuck for a living."

"Meaning?"

"She's incredibly controlled. I could barely tell where she was lying and where she was telling the truth."

"Whoa . . . barely? So, you could tell some of the times she was lying?"

"Well, sure."

Trout glanced at him in the rearview mirror. "Like where?"

Goat played part of the tape back. "Here. Listen to this."

Ask your questions.

Are you Homer Gibbon's aunt?

Sure. Why not?

How well did you know him?

Seen him once in a while. Mostly when he was like seventeen and older. After he ran away from foster care the last time.

When was the last time you saw him?

A pause.

Could you be a bit more specific?

I don't know. Maybe back in ninety, ninety-one.

Goat hit the pause button. "See?"

"No," admitted Trout.

"The pauses. First when you asked her if she was Homer Gibbon's aunt. She lost about half a second answering."

"So?"

"So . . . why the hesitation? She knew that you were going to ask that, and yet she still stumbles over her answer. And then again when you asked when she saw him last."

"She shrugged."

"Okay, she shrugged. She should have had that answer on the tip of her tongue."

"Damn, kid, she's dying of cancer and her only nephew was just executed yesterday. How smooth can a person be after all that?"

Goat spread his hands. "I'm just saying. In film, pauses mean something, they convey meaning. Same thing happens in conversation. Maybe not always as calculated as theater, but people uses pauses to convey a message or allow a person to stall in order to write a script for a specific message."

"And people call me cynical."

"You asked."

"No, keep going. What else?"

Goat played another fragment.

That was after he had committed several murders.
Alleged murders. He was never convicted for anything back then.

"See? She not only threw 'alleged' at you, she got kinda pissed that you didn't use it."

"She's related to him."

"No doubt," said Goat. "But I don't think that's why she got pissed."

"Why, then? You think she thinks he's innocent?"

"No . . . I don't think she cares. That's a family thing. Especially families on the edge like this. Kind of the 'my country right or wrong' mentality distilled down to a single family. People can fuck up and do all manner of harm, but at the end of the day if their name and your name are spelled the same, then there's going to be some kind of . . . I don't know . . . acceptance? Forgiveness? Maybe even allowance?"

"So . . . what's your bottom line here?" asked Trout. "Why's she being so dodgy?"

"How should I know? I read performance; you're the writer . . . You build the story."

Trout grunted. He rounded a turn too fast and his BlackBerry slid out of the little tray below the dash. Goat picked it up.

"You got mail," said Goat, showing Trout the flashing red light. "You got your ringer turned off?"

"Usually. I have two ex-wives and they have aggressive lawyers. I'll subject myself to that shit later."

Goat grunted. "Looks like you have a zillion missed calls and one e-mail."

"That'll be from Marcia. Probably the Volker stuff. We'll be at Volker's place in ten minutes, so read it for me."

Goat punched the keys and peered at the lines of text. "This is an hour old. Mmm . . . looks like a bunch of biographical stuff first. She says that Dr. Herman Volker was born in someplace called Panevėžys. No idea how to pronounce it. In Lithuania."

"That fits. I thought he sounded more Slavic than German."

"Father was German, but he was raised in Lithuania. Always into medicine. Worked as a lab tech as a teenager, went to medical school. Did residencies in psychiatry and epidemiology. Went into the Soviet army as a doctor. Then he's off the radar for a while, but get this . . . he surfaces again as a field surgeon with the Russian forces in Afghanistan, and while he's there, he defects to U.S. personnel."

"What kind of personnel?"

"Doesn't say."

"But it's inside Afghanistan?"

"Seems so."

"CIA," said Trout. "Has to be."

"Yeah. That works. Eleven months later he's working at a good hospital in Virginia. The notes mention that he has a wife and daughter, but Marcia says that she can't find any records of them after he went into the army. Divorced, maybe?" Goat scrolled through the notes. "A lot of this is dry background stuff. He moved several times. Worked at several hospitals in Virginia, Maryland, and then Pennsylvania, and ten years ago he took a job as a doctor in the corrections system. Federal first, and then a few transfers. Another interesting thing . . . he got the job as senior medical officer at Rockview ahead of six other doctors with more seniority in the prison system."

Trout nodded. "So he still has some federal juice. Someone's making sure he gets what he wants. Wonder why."

"That's about it," said Goat. "The rest is straight employment info, a few tax records Marcia could scrounge, and references to employee evaluations, all of which gave him top marks for everything."

"More federal juice. If you're sucking on the CIA's tit, they watch out for you. I'd hate to be a traffic cop who tried to give him a speeding ticket."

"Or a professional rival," suggested Goat as he handed the phone back. Trout stuffed it in his pocket without turning the ringer back on or checking his voice mail. The Volker information was so compelling that he plain forgot.

They chewed on the information as they drove.

"If he has federal juice, then why is afraid of anything?" asked Goat. "I mean, someone fucks with him and he's one phone call away from calling down the wrath of God."

"Yep," agreed Trout "which means that if he was being harassed about having performed the lethal injection, then he could call in ten kinds of support."

"And here we are," mused Goat, "driving right to his door to try and bully him into giving us a story. How smart are we?"

Trout didn't answer. Overhead the storm was darkening the sky to the color of a fresh bruise.

CHAPTER THIRTY-NINE
HART COTTAGE
STEBBINS COUNTY, PENNSYLVANIA

Officer Ken Gunther stood on the porch and sipped coffee from a mug that had HARTNUP'S TRANSITION ESTATE in fancy script on one side and a quote on the other: "Death is Momentary—Life is Eternal."

"Bullshit," he said. He sipped the coffee. April, Doc's sister, was not only smoking hot by Gunther's finicky standards, she could brew a pot of damn good coffee. No lattes or macchiatos. No hazelnut or Irish-fucking-cream. Good old-fashioned American coffee from Colombia. Black and bitter. Hot, too, which was a blessing because he was freezing his nuts off. He still wore a lightweight summer uniform under a nylon Windbreaker, which was dumb because all he had to do was turn on the TV to see what the temperature was. Even the plastic cover for his hat was in the trunk of his cruiser, and the storm clouds were so thick and black they looked ready to explode.

He sipped and stared out at the trees.

The Hartnup place was called a cottage but it was really a big split-level. Roomy, tidy, and remote. He could see himself living in a place like this. Maybe even with April. She was divorcing that ass pirate Virgil, who, despite having fathered two kids, had finally realized that he was gay. Wow, Gunther thought. What a news flash. Everyone had known that since the fifth grade. He wondered how April didn't know it. She seemed pretty smart, but then again a lot of people are dumb when it comes to love.

Gunther drank some more coffee and set the cup on the porch rail. He needed to pee but he did not want to go inside. If he did, then he'd get stuck in there while Dana Howard would escape out here. On the upside, he'd get to spend some time with April; but on the downside he'd have to spend time with the kids. Gunther was not a fan of children.

He looked at the front door, which was closed, then cautiously peered in through the window. Dana was standing with her back to him in the doorway between the living room and the playroom. April was changing a diaper.

Now was a good time.

Moving quietly so as not to squeak any of the porch floorboards, he crossed to the steps, went down, and then cut around to the side of the house where there was a row of thick holly bushes. He looked up and down the side yard, saw no one, unzipped, and began pissing on April Hartnup's autumn sunflowers.

When he heard the crunch of a foot on dried leaves he jumped sideways, trying to stop his stream, cover his penis, and grab his zipper all at the same time.

"Dana, I—" he began.

But it wasn't Dana Howard.

It was a white-faced thing that came out of the shadows between two massive willow trees. It had eyes as black and empty as bullet holes, fingers the color of old wax, and a mouth that was filled with bloody teeth.

Gunther got one word out before those teeth tore into him.

He said, "Doc—"

And then the world was red and black and, ultimately, empty of all color and sense.

CHAPTER FORTY
CONROY'S ACRES

Selma sat with Homer on the dining room floor. His head was buried in her lap, his arms around her waist, Mildred Potts's blood soaking through the fabric of Selma's bathrobe. She stroked his hair and hummed disjointed fragments of nursery rhymes to him as he wept.

"It's okay," she said every once in a while. "It's okay."

Except that it wasn't. She knew it. The truth screamed in her mind. He knew it, too. How could he not?

It took a long time for his body to stop trembling. For a long time his sobs were so deep that they threatened to break apart the shadows of the room. They were terrible sobs, torn from some deep place that Selma was sure Homer had not accessed in years. They were the broken sobs of a tortured child, magnified by the mass and muscle of a grown man.

She used the flap of her robe to wipe the blood off his face. His lips were pale, his skin was like wax except for small bursts of red around his eyes.

"Selma," he whispered, looking up at her the way a confused toddler might.

"Yes, honey, what is it?"

"Did I . . . die?"

She closed her eyes for a moment, trying not to wince at the question even though it dug under her skin like a fish hook.

"Please . . ." he begged.

She stroked his cheek. "What do you remember?"

He closed his eyes, too. "I remember the prison. I remember being there. I was there for a long time, wasn't I?"

"Yes."

"I remember them coming for me. They gave me some food and I ate everything on my plate."

"Like a good boy," she purred.

"I wasn't even hungry. I was sick to my stomach . . . but I wanted to eat it all. To make it last."

"I know."

"But they still came for me. Four of them. In the movies there's a preacher, but he didn't come to my cell." He sniffed. His nose sounded dry, almost dusty. "They took me to the place. Like a doctor's office, but it wasn't Dr. Volker's office. It wasn't the infirmary. It was the other place."

"Yes."

"They made me lie down. I . . . almost didn't. I thought about it. I wanted to fight. I wanted to make them force me down, y'know . . . make a stand? Show them that I was tougher than them, that they hadn't beaten me, not in the end. But . . . I was afraid they'd think I was a coward—yknow, trying to pussy out at the end. I think they must have put something in my food. I wanted to fight . . . but I couldn't. I was so out of it. When they pushed me down on the gurney . . . I just let them. It was weird . . . I could feel myself wanting to fight. That Black Eye was opening inside my head like it always does. I could feel my hands ready to go. My whole body was ready to go. I was going to tear into them. Take at least one or two of them with me and ugly up some of the others. That'd be an exit, wouldn't it? Rip off some faces and pop some eyes. The eye was open but the Red Mouth didn't whisper to me. It didn't . . . give me permission."

Selma squeezed her eyes shut, not wanting to sob. Or scream. She knew all about the Black Eye and the Red Mouth. It was on page after page of the trial testimony. There were photos of a black eye from thirty crime scenes. Photos of red mouths cut into the chests of so many people. Men, women. Children.

In court, Homer had never spoken those words. He had never admitted that they were part of his . . . Selma fought for the word. Method? His style? And yet here he was telling her about them.

God, she thought, *oh God, oh God, oh God . . .*

Not that Selma ever doubted that Homer had done these things. But hearing him say it was somehow more real. She could turn off the

TV, refuse to read the newspapers. But these were words spoken to her. She owned them now, and there was no way to turn away from them.

Dead by Christmas.

Maybe sooner, if there was a kind God somewhere up there.

Homer shifted his head so that it rested against her breasts. He pressed his ear to her sternum as if listening to her heart. The way he had done as a baby. The way he had done when Selma had held him while Clarice drove them to the shelter in Pittsburgh. Clarice never held him except to hand him to someone else. To Selma, to the intake nurse. Clarice winced every time she put her hands on the child.

Selma had wanted to lock her arms around him and never let him go.

Why had she? God . . . why had she done that?

Homer was speaking again, fishing for the thread of his fractured memory.

"They spoke to each other in a weird way. The guards. The doctors and all. Like a church thing. Like a litany. It was strange, everybody saying out loud what they were doing and the others in the room saying that they saw it. Or agreed. So weird." He sniffed again. "They put two IVs in. I asked why they needed two, but I had to ask three times before Dr. Volker told me. He said that one was a backup in case the other line failed. I thought that was funny. Going to all that trouble just to kill a man. Killing is easy as snuffing a match. The state never understood how to do it right. They should let the other convicts do it. Even some of the new fish can do a man faster than a wink, and do it clean, without fuss. Even without much pain. Those prison fucks . . . they think it's rocket science."

Homer laughed and Selma tensed. The laugh was an older laugh. Less of the lost child. More of the man who had gone to prison.

"They ran one of the IV lines into the next room. But . . . you know what's really funny? I mean really fucking funny, Aunt Selma?"

"Tell me," she said, and her throat was so dry that her voice cracked.

"Before they put the IVs in . . . they swabbed my arm with alcohol. How stupid is that? I mean . . ."

He burst out laughing, his body trembling against hers.

"They're stupid people," said Selma, trying to soothe him.

"Yeah. That was rich. That was really something. Afraid I'd get an infection."

"There's was a chance you'd get a stay of execution," she said.

"Yeah, yeah, I know. It was all about my comfort and protection." He chuckled again. It was older still. A small, dark laugh. Even so, he still lay on the floor with his arms around her. His voice was still soft.

"What happened then?" she asked, not knowing what else to say.

"They started a heart monitor. That's part of the show, I guess. Watching to see the blips. He's alive, he's alive, he's alive . . . ooooooh, he's dead." He gave her body a squeeze. "The other convicts told me how it works. They give me a shot of sodium somethingorother to put me out. Some kind of barbiturate. Then some kind of muscle relaxant that paralyzes everything. And then something else to stop the heart. They say it takes about an hour, but the dope is supposed to drop you under right at the start. But they don't do it right then. No, they open the curtains and start the show. Other side of the glass is a big room filled with all kinds of people. I recognized a lot of them from court. Family members of the people the Red Mouth took. The Black Eye saw and marked each one. They were there to see me go, and they'd probably been working up to it, eating their hate, convincing themselves they had the juice to do this, to see me strapped down and pumped full of death. The Black Eye looked into each one of them, and there was nobody—no-fucking-body who was carrying enough hate to get them through this. The Red Mouth was laughing inside me, 'cause we knew that this was going to fuck them up six ways from Sunday. They were all going to take a little bit of me home inside their heads, and I was going to be standing by their bedsides when they went to sleep, and I'd be pulling on their sheets every night until they died. That's one of the things the Red Mouth gives me. I'm inside their heads, and I always will be. And when they looked at me through the glass, they saw someone so much more powerful than them that they could see they were just specks of bird shit floating in the universe."

Selma said nothing. She continued to stroke his hair, though now the effort required deliberate effort. This was not the Homer she had cuddled as a baby, or the teenage boy on the cusp of manhood that she had held when he cried in the night. This was the one who was in the newspapers, and she did not know how to speak with him. So, she stroked his lank hair and listened as the monster told his tale.

"The reporters were different. There were a few of them there. I heard they had to win a lottery to get in, so they probably felt lucky as shit. They're a lot different. They're not afraid of the Black Eye or the Red Mouth. They love them. Almost like I do, but in a different way. Like Baptists and Presbyterians. Same religion, different churches. Without the Black Eye, they'd be lost. Just like me. Without the Red Mouth, they'd be reporting on car shows and hog contests. I didn't mind them there. I could see the Black Eye on their foreheads. I felt like I was Jesus looking down and seeing Peter and John and Simon."

Homer was quiet for a moment, and Selma tried to predict where his mind had gone. The old house creaked in the cold wind. She hoped that it would cave in and bury them both. Right here, right now. With Homer in her arms.

Dead by Christmas. That was too far away.

"Then things got weird. The other convicts said that doctors didn't usually give the injections. Something about some oath they took. Or some law. I'm not sure. But Dr. Volker was running the whole show . . . and Volker . . . now there is one motherfucker who knows everything about the Black Eye. I saw it on his forehead the first time I went into the infirmary. Fucking Angel of Death got nothing on that prick."

"What do you mean?" asked Selma.

"A lot of people tried to get me to open up, to admit shit. Like I was that stupid. Not him, though. He knew. From the first time I met him, he knew who I was. He never said so, but I know that he knew about the Black Eye and the Red Mouth."

"Was he . . . was he like . . . ?"

"Like me?" Homer thought about that for a long time. "Yeah. Not really, but yeah. It was there in his eyes. The Red Mouth had whispered its secrets to him, and probably a long time ago. He had that lived-in look, like someone who was at peace with the voice. It's crazy . . . but I kind of admired him. Prison doctor and all. Getting paid to stick the needle. Everybody watching. Biggest audience you can imagine. Papers and TV. Witnesses there to see him perform."

Perform.

The word hung in the air, impossibly ugly.

"He only opened up to me once," said Homer. "Just once. It was the only time I was alone with him. After that spic shanked me in the yard and I had to get stitches. Wish I'd killed that spic. Ah, well . . . Anyway, I'm cuffed wrists and ankles, face down on his table, and Volker's stitching me up. Then he bends forward and says, 'I know.' Just like that. Two words, but man, they said everything."

"Was that all he said?"

"No . . . but that was enough. I got it. He was telling me that he could hear what the Red Mouth said. What else could it mean?" Homer pulled away from her and sat up, resting his bare back against the door frame. The blood on his chest was clotted and dark and he scratched at it with a fingernail. His eyes were hidden by the shadows cast down from his heavy brow, but Selma could feel them on her. Boring into her like slow drills.

Selma licked her lips. "What else did he say?"

"Just one more thing. He said, 'After you go, you won't be gone. You'll be with us forever. You'll know forever.'" Homer shook his head. "I wanted to thank him. It was the only nice thing anyone's said to me since they busted me."

"Are you sure he meant—" She stopped herself.

Homer nodded. "I know what he meant. He hears the Red Mouth. He knows what it means to live forever in the sight of the Black Eye. He was telling me you know, you see. That was decent of him. I thanked him and told him I'd like to shake his hand. But someone else came in the room, so that was that. We were never alone again after that." He paused. "Except for a split second in the execution chamber. Doc Volker bent down to check the IV, and he shifted so that I could see his face. He mouthed the same words: 'You'll know forever.' Then the warden gave the signal for the circus to start. I . . . don't remember much after that."

Selma looked down at the bloodstains on her robe. She tried not to flick a glance toward the cellar door, but failed. Homer caught it and his face tightened for a split second. Was it humor? Annoyance? Shame? She had no way to judge.

"Is that what happened?" she asked. "Did the doctor . . . rig things? Did he fake your death so he could get you out?"

Homer chewed his lip. Or so Selma thought until she realized with sick horror that he was sucking up some drops of dried blood.

"Has to be," he said. "I don't know how . . . but somehow he pulled a Gypsy switch and next thing I know I'm waking up in a fucking body bag in a funeral home. Scared the living shit out of the guy who unzipped me. He was chewing gum and listening to some lame-ass Celtic music shit when he pulled down the zipper and there I was. Eyes open, grinning at him. At least I think I was grinning."

A look of confusion crossed Homer's face and Selma waited it out. The walls shuddered under a cold blast and the windows rattled like false teeth.

"I remember being hungry. So . . . insanely hungry. I've never been that hungry before. Not until . . . not until . . ." He ran his fingers across his bloody abdomen.

"What did you do?"

He leaned forward into a slanting beam of dusty light. Now his face was completely Homer Gibbon. The newspaper Homer. There was no trace of the child or the young man.

"The Black Eye opened," he said softly. "The Red Mouth told me what to do. And it was clearer . . . God . . . it was clearer than ever." As he spoke these last words his eyes drifted shut. The way a connoisseur's would when savoring the delicate flavors of a piece of perfectly prepared lamb. The garlic and rosemary, the tarragon vinegar, the mint. The blood.

"Did you kill Doc Hartnup?" Selma asked, and it cost her a lot to ask it. Her hands were shaking so badly that she had to ball them into fists around the flaps of her robe. "Did the, um . . . Red Mouth . . . tell you to do that?"

"Yes," he said, soft as a whisper.

"God." Her voice was softer still. Tiny. Almost not there.

"And the woman."

"Woman?"

"I think she was Russian. Came to clean the place. Came just in time."

"Oh, Homer . . ."

"I had to." He opened his eyes. "The Red Mouth was screaming at me. Not whispering. Not talking. It was screaming!"

"And Mildred Potts?"

"Who? Oh . . . her." He nodded. "I never . . . in the past . . . I never heard the Red Mouth speak so soon after. But I got hungry."

"'Hungry'?" She echoed the word, almost fainting at what it now meant.

"I was full . . . stuffed from. . . ." He let his voice trail off, and looked away with a half smile. "I was full and I was still hungry. You wouldn't understand."

The phone rang.

It was so sudden, so loud, that Selma Conroy screamed. She recoiled from the sound as if it had tried to bite her.

Homer smiled at that. He looked from the phone to Selma and back again. The phone was on the counter in the kitchen. It rang a second time.

"You going to get that?" he asked calmly.

"No."

"You should. It could be that reporter again. Don't want to make them suspicious."

Selma stared at him as the phone rang a third time.

"Go ahead," Homer prompted.

Selma reached out for the wooden chair that stood in the corner. She pulled herself up slowly, her joints creaking and popping.

"You got old," Homer said.

She said nothing, grunting with the effort. The phone rang again and again before she tottered into the kitchen and picked it up.

"Hello?"

There was no sound behind her, nothing to let her know that Homer had also gotten up, but suddenly he was there, his body pressing against her. When he was a baby his skin was always furnace hot. Now he was cold. So cold.

"I would like to speak with Selma Conroy," said a voice. A stranger's voice. Male, accented. And hesitant.

"This is she," murmured Selma, her voice still small. "Who's calling, please?"

Homer bent close to listen. Selma could barely feel his breath, but what little there was stank of corruption. It was like the open mouth of a sewer.

The caller said, "My name is Dr. Herman Volker from the State Correctional Institution at Rockview."

The breath caught in Selma's throat.

"I would like to speak with you about Homer Gibbon."

The breath in Selma's throat wanted to burst out of her as a scream. God, how she needed to scream.

CHAPTER FORTY-ONE
ON THE ROAD
STEBBINS COUNTY

Trout called Marcia to get an update on the Volker research and put the call on speaker.

"Marcia, we got what you sent but—"

She cut him off. "Where are you idiots?"

"Heading to Dr. Volker's place. Why, what's up?"

"I don't know but all hell seems to be breaking loose around here. I called you a dozen times. Murray's been on my ass about you. The police are keeping it off the regular channels, but all I hear are sirens, and Nell over at the diner says that about a dozen state police cars and half as many ambulances have gone by in the last fifteen minutes."

"Heading where?"

"Doc Hartnup's. Whatever's going on there is getting worse."

"I know," Trout said. "I can try going back there, but Dez will just run me off again."

"Mm," grunted Marcia. "I still can't understand what you see in that piece of trailer trash. I mean, sure, she's got the body and the face, but she is seriously damaged goods. You'd need to win the lottery just to pay her therapy bills. Providing she ever got her head out of her ass long enough to go to therapy."

"Jealousy is an ugly thing, Marcia."

Marcia snorted and hung up.

A line of National Guard troop trucks passed them, heading south. Trout counted thirty of them.

"Lot of men for flood control," said Goat.

"No shit," agreed Trout. He said nothing for a few seconds, then he punched in another number. He did not put this call on speaker. It rang three times, and he was rehearsing what he was going to leave on the voice mail when a voice answered.

"Hello?"

"Dez . . . ?"

A pause. "I don't have time for this, Billy."

"No, don't hang up. Listen, Marcia's been telling me that some weird stuff's been happening at Doc's. Or at least in town somewhere."

"That's none of your—"

"Stop," he said. "I'm not calling for a story. I . . . just wanted to see if you're all right. She said there were ambulances and all."

A much longer pause.

"Dez?"

"Why?" she asked.

"Come on, Dez . . . don't be like that."

"I'm working here, Billy."

"I know . . . that's the point. You're on the job and something bad is happening. I need to know you're okay."

This time the pause was so long that Trout had to check the screen display to make sure the call was still connected.

Dez said, "I'm . . . not injured."

It was the same thing she'd said earlier and it was a funny way to phrase it. It felt awkward and evasive to Trout.

"You sure?"

"I'm fine, Billy," she snapped, then she took a breath and said it again. This time it was a softer voice than he'd heard her use in months. "Really, Billy. I'm okay."

Trout relaxed by half a degree. "JT?"

"We're both good," she said, and before Trout could say another word, Dez hung up.

Trout held the phone in his palm, weighing it, wondering if he could throw it all the way through the windshield. Beside him, Goat was studying him and for once he wasn't wearing a joker's smile.

"Everything cool?" Goat asked.

Trout shook his head. "No," he said, "I don't think it is."

Raindrops began spattering on the windshield as they made a

right and drove under a stone arch that read GREEN GATES 55-PLUS COM-
MUNITY.

Below that, in painted script, it read LEAVE ALL YOUR TROUBLES BE-
HIND.

CHAPTER FORTY-TWO
HART COTTAGE

Lee Hartnup stood in the shadows of his family house and watched
the officer die.

Because he did not need to breathe, he was able to scream con-
tinually the whole time, from first bite until the thing that was his body
turned away from the lifeless meat.

He did not understand that.

The thing fed on anything it could catch. People, animals, insects
crawling on trees. It fed, tearing each living being apart, drinking the
blood, eating the flesh, gnawing bones. And then it stopped. Floating
in the inner darkness but still connected to every nerve and sensation, he could tell that it was not a feeling of satiation that compelled
the monster to stop feeding. The hunger that lived inside this hollow
man was insatiable, vast and eternal. And yet it stopped.

Why?

His body let the policeman's corpse slide down the side of the
house and sprawl in an ungainly tangle of limbs.

Why discard it? Why stop eating when there was so much meat left?

And at that thought—at the fact that this thought came from his
own mind—the screaming started again.

The body moved. It shambled toward the front porch steps, moving awkwardly as rigor mortis took a greater hold over each joint.

Please, he begged, *let it stop me completely.* That was his only hope
now, that the death stiffness would freeze his body and stop it from doing these terrible things. He had no way of telling time, but he knew
that rigor began setting in about three hours after death. Rigor was
growing in him quickly. But it would take up to twelve hours for it to
reach its peak, and then it would last for three days.

Three days.

Surely if rigor made this lumbering monster fall and lie stiffly in the grass someone would find him within three days. Find him, and do what was necessary to stop this. Bury him. Dissect him. Burn him.

Please . . . anything!

He would welcome any death, any true death, no matter how painful or protracted, as long as it stopped this.

At the bottom step the thing's feet hit the wooden riser and rebounded. Hartnup tried to listen inside that darkness for some trace of a mind, of a presence. If something was there, if there was some consciousness or spirit—even that of a ghost or demon or whatever had done this to him—then perhaps he could reason with it. Bargain with it.

The right leg bent at the knee and the foot rose over the riser and thumped down on the bottom step.

Hartnup felt it happen but nowhere in this vast darkness could he detect the slightest trace of a directing intelligence.

What was making the legs move? What allowed this thing to encounter the problem of an obstacle like stairs and come up with the solution of stepping up? Even a newborn baby could not do that. This thing has less consciousness than an infant, so how—how—HOW—was it doing this?

His rational mind tore itself to pieces trying to solve that.

The dead thing took a second step, a third, and then it was on the porch, facing the front door.

With a burst of terror more profound than anything he had so far experienced, Hartnup knew what door this was. Just as he knew what unbearable horror lay behind it.

Through the closed window he heard the sound of voices. Two women. One was a stranger. The other.

April.

His sister.

And the laughter of children.

The thing raised a hand and pounded on the door. It was limp, almost completely slack, but it was loud.

"Hey, Ken—did you lock yourself out?"

The other woman's voice, coming close, a trace of laughter in her words.

The creature pounded again. And again.

And then the door opened.

Hartnup begged God to let him die for real and for good and to not have to be a witness to this.

His loudest cry was as silent as death, and not even God heard him.

Hartnup tried to scream loud enough to drown out the other screams that now filled the air. He tried.

He tried.

He tried.

CHAPTER FORTY-THREE
GREEN GATES 55-PLUS COMMUNITY

Dr. Volker surprised them by answering the door after the first knock. He pulled it open abruptly as if he intended to spring out at them, but then he froze, his eyes narrowed and suspicious.

"Who are you?"

Trout smiled. "We spoke on the phone earlier, doctor. I'm Billy Trout, Regional Satellite News."

Volker was in his late sixties. Beyond retirement age. His sharp German features were softened by age, his blond hair thinned to a pale rime. He wore a thick velour bathrobe and one hand was buried to the wrist in one deep pocket. The pocket sagged under a heavy weight, and Trout suddenly felt his testicles climb up inside his pelvis.

Gun, he thought. *Christ, he has a gun.*

"How did you get this address?"

"Does it matter?" asked Trout.

"Yes," snapped Volker, "it does. How did you—"

"DMV. The address on your license . . ."

"You shouldn't have access to that kind of information."

Trout spread his hands. Behind him, Goat shifted nervously and Volker's pale eyes shifted toward him.

"Who is this?" Volker demanded.

"My cameraman. Gregory Weinman."

"Weinman," Volker repeated, his lip curling slightly into a sneer.

Great, thought Trout, *he probably hates Jews. This is going to be so much fun.*

"Doctor," Trout said, "we would like to ask you a few questions. About Selma Conroy and Homer Gibbon."

Volker gave him a flat reptilian stare, and Trout was already fishing for something to say to try to convince the doctor to let them in, when Volker suddenly stepped back. "Very well," he said. He turned and walked into his house, leaving the door open.

Trout and Goat looked at each other. Goat raised his eyebrows in a "well, this is what you wanted" look.

They followed the doctor inside and closed the door.

The house was depressing and dry. The pictures on the wall were the kind you bought at Ikea. The living room was almost certainly picked without passion from a catalog and it was set up to match that page. It was technically attractive, but it lacked warmth and human-ity. No magazines on the coffee table. No novels or even technical books. Nothing. It was a place, not a home. Volker waved them to chairs. Trout and Goat sat on opposite ends of the couch.

Volker surprised them again. "Do you want coffee?"

"Um . . . yes," said Trout. "Thanks."

"It's instant."

"Instant's fine."

"I don't have milk or sugar."

Of course you don't, you sour old fuck. "Black works for me," Trout said aloud.

"Me, too," said Goat hastily, even though he was an eight packs of sugar and a quarter cup of half-and-half coffee drinker.

Volker set a tray with three steaming mugs on the coffee table. Two of the mugs had the logo of Rockview Correctional Institution on them. Very cheerful for home entertaining, mused Trout. The third had "Happy Birthday!" written in bright red cartoon letters. Trout took that one.

Volker lowered himself onto the La-Z-Boy across from the couch. He perched on the edge, elbows on his knees, holding the coffee cup between his palms. The vapor from the cup steamed his glasses.

"Before you ask your questions," he said, "I want to explain something to you. When you called this afternoon it got me to thinking that I ought to record this. I was going to write it down, but now that you're here I can see that this is probably a tale best told to real people. That way you can ask questions. I don't want any mistakes, and there won't be a chance later to get the facts."

"Why not?" asked Trout as he set his small recorder on the coffee table.

"Because," said Dr. Volker as he peered through the steam, "as soon as we're done here I'm going to kill myself."

CHAPTER FORTY-FOUR
WOLVERTON REGIONAL HOSPITAL

Dez and JT were climbing into her car when the radio buzzed. JT took it.

"Unit Two."

Flower screamed at them. "JT! Jesus Christ . . . get back to Doc's. Oh my god! The state police are there. They said . . . they said . . . oh my god!"

"Flower! Calm down and tell me what happened."

"It's the chief!" Flower wailed, her voice phlegmy with tears and shrill with panic. "Oh my god . . . the chief!"

Dez slammed the car in gear and stamped down on the gas so hard the cruiser shot away from the curb like a missile, burying JT and Dez deep into the backrests. She cut across the oncoming traffic, siren wailing, swung into the fast lane, and was doing ninety before they'd gone two blocks.

"Flower," JT said, speaking as calmly as he could. "Tell me what happened."

But he already knew. They both knew.

Flower said it anyway.

"He's dead! They called it in. The chief's dead! Oh my god, JT, what's happening?"

What's happening? Dez thought as she rocketed past cars that veered desperately out of her way. That's the question everyone's asking. What the holy fuck is happening?

She knew with perfect clarity that she absolutely did not want an answer to that question. And, with equal clarity she knew that she was racing toward that answer at over a hundred miles an hour.

CHAPTER FORTY-FIVE
GREEN GATES 55-PLUS COMMUNITY

Volker's living room was deadly still. Trout and Goat sat staring at the old doctor as motes of dust drifted like tiny planets through the air.

"Okay," said Trout as reasonably as he could, "*why* do you want to kill yourself?"

"Want to?" echoed the doctor. "I don't *want* to die. I would prefer to live out my remaining years somewhere quiet where I can spend my afternoons fishing and my evenings listening to Wagner. But as the saying goes, 'that ship has sailed.'" He smiled. He had surprisingly bad teeth for a medical man. "However . . . I don't care to spend the rest of my life in jail."

Trout leaned forward. "Why would you go to jail?"

Instead of answering, Volker said, "And, there needs to be a record of this. For . . . after."

"After . . . ?"

Volker shrugged. "If there is an 'after.'" He said it more to himself than Trout, but the words hung in the air.

"Okay, Doc," said Trout, "if you're fishing for the award for Best Cryptic Speech you're a shoo-in."

There was no trace of a smile on the old doctor's mouth, but he nodded. "Very well. But I suppose I need to give you a little of my history so that you'll understand the context of what I need to tell you." He sipped his coffee. "I am not a very nice man. I am deserving of no compassion. I have done many questionable things in my life, and I make no excuses for them. All I can do is provide a reason."

Trout nudged the recorder an inch closer. A passive gesture with just a touch of "hurry the fuck up" in it.

"I never wanted to be a prison doctor," Volker said. "That is a side effect. I detest criminals and I have a special hatred for a certain kind of criminal. Serial murderers, especially those who prey on families. I have a . . . personal connection to that kind of person. My sister and her two children were the . . . targets . . . of such a person. This was in East Berlin, years ago. During the Cold War. Your news services always concentrated on the politics of that era, but there were other stories, other . . . horrors. The restrictive and oppressive nature of life under the Soviet heel tended to cultivate the worst qualities in people. Paranoia, of course, but hatred, suspicion, ruthlessness, lack of sentimentality, avarice, and a kind of anger fueled by such deep resentment that it struck to the core of who we were. Many people, even those who appeared to live a normal life since the destruction of the Wall harbor the fruits of those emotions. The incidence of spousal abuse, child abuse, and sexual deviance is shockingly high, even today. Back then . . . back when crimes were committed wholesale but never—never—admitted to the non-Soviet world . . . we were breeding monsters. So many monsters.

"Here in the United States you create a media circus around serial murderers. They are celebrities. They get book deals. There are people who collect their possessions. Murderabilia, it's called. In your cinema, they are presented as charming and charismatic. Hannibal Lecter." He shook his head in disgust. "In East Germany, when a serial murderer was caught, he disappeared forever. Sometimes it was a family member, perhaps a war veteran who understood how to kill, who hunted the monster down and did what was necessary. More often it was the police who removed the person. Justice was swift but it was unpleasant. And it was inconsistent. However, Justice was not always served. Many times a skillful and practiced murderer was taken to prison and then recruited into the secret police or the Red Army. There was always a need for a skilled killer in both. And don't cock an eyebrow at me," Volker said, directing the comment to Goat, "I was there, you were not. How old were you when the Berlin Wall fell? Six? Eight? I was already a medical doctor and a major in the army. By then I had seen death in every imaginable form, and I had become familiar with every possible permutation of human and institutional corruption. The Soviet machine ran on corruption."

Goat held up his hands. "Didn't mean any offense, Doc."

Volker grunted.

"You were talking about your sister," prompted Trout. "She was killed?"

Volker's eyes swiveled toward him in a way that reminded Trout of the dead eyes of a crocodile. It was a strange blend of hostile potential and bland disinterest.

"Killed," Volker said, tasting the word. "Yes. She was killed. And believe me when I tell you that 'killed' is so pale a word, so inadequate a description of what was done to her. She was destroyed. Her humanity was stolen from her, torn from her. Dear Kofryna. My only sister. My last blood relative, except for Danukas and Audra, her twins. Three years old. Babies. Too young to grasp politics or even the concepts of good and evil. All three of them . . . destroyed."

"I'm sorry," said Trout.

Volker's lip curled in a sneer. "This was forty years ago. I was a young man then. A doctor, newly transferred from my hometown of Panevėžys in Lithuania. A medical officer stationed in East Berlin. Idealistic, a dedicated communist. A dedicated doctor."

"And then your family was taken from you," Trout said quietly.

"Yes. His name was Wolfgang Henker. You will not have heard of him. He was a sergeant in the Nationale Volksarmee. I did not know it at the time—how could I ?—but Henker was one of those monsters who had been arrested for heinous crimes and given over to the military as an asset. A tool. A weapon." Volker shook his head. "Even after all these years, even after all that I know of the world, it still amazes me."

"I get that," said Goat, and when Volker cut him a sharp look, the cameraman explained. "After World War Two, after the Allies dismantled the death camps, they found tens of thousands of pages of research material culled from the experiments performed on Jews and Gypsies and other prisoners. You'd think that we'd just chuck all that shit right into the fire. You'd think that we wouldn't want anything that came from that, um . . . process, but that's not what happened. Our government . . . and everyone else's, I guess; Russia, England . . . they took the research on the basis that, despite its source, it was valuable to the overall body of medical research."

"Yes," agreed Volker, his stern demeanor toward Goat softening by a few small degrees. "That decision is frequently defended at medical conferences and in papers, because there is strong statistical proof that it has since saved many lives and advanced medical science as a whole."

"End justifies the means," said Goat.

"That is the logic."

"But you disagree with that?" Trout prompted.

"Of course. Or . . . I did," said Volker. "It's confusing, because I have made some questionable choices of my own in order to accomplish my goal."

"And what is that goal, doctor?"

Volker smiled thinly. "To punish the monsters."

"How?" asked Trout.

"It became clear that I could not get to Henker. He was very much a prized soldier, and I was a simple army doctor. He was much more important than I was. His specialty was interrogation. Imagine it, gentlemen. Being strapped to a table so that you are entirely at the mercy of a monster such as this. A person who delights in your pain. A person to whom your screams are more delicious than a lover's whisper. A creature who knows how to keep you alive while he skillfully and meticulously deconstructs those things that define you as human?"

Trout swallowed. As Volker spoke he found that he could imagine it, and it was horrifying. He was one of the people who collected murderabilia. His desk chair once belonged to a mass murderer. He had followed the Homer Gibbon case more out of fascination with the man than empathy for his victims. Now, another window in his mind opened up and he looked through it into the horror Volker described.

"Christ," he said softly.

"Indeed." Volker took a breath. "Naturally I did not know that Henker was the killer. Not at first. No . . . after the police abruptly stopped investigating the case, I continued to look into it. I was very circumspect about it. I am a meticulous man, you see. I followed clues and compiled data until I built a picture of what had happened. I interviewed people—always under some unrelated pretense—and because I was a doctor and a member of the army, people were always willing to cooperate. I used, you see, the atmosphere of paranoia to investigate those murders. I won't go into every detail. Over the last few months I have written it all down." He stopped and waved his hand toward a cupboard. "There are several flash drives in there, in a sugar bowl. They lay it all out, and you may have them. You have me saying so right there on your recorder in case there is any dispute."

"Thank you, Doctor," said Trout without enthusiasm. The story was amazing but it was turning his stomach.

"In order to try and get within reach of Henker," Volker continued, "I volunteered for special services with the Red Army medical corps. I have both the aptitude and patience for research, and I am not a weak-hearted person. I knew that there were special divisions that would require nerve. Every time I thought that I might falter, I held in my mind the crime-scene photos of my sister. It was . . . very effective. I was accepted. My obvious willingness and my apparent cold detachment served me well in moving up through the ranks and deeper into the inner circles of classified medical research. Soon I was working in one of the more arcane areas of interrogation."

"With Henker?"

"Not at first. I was sent on research missions to various places around the globe. I spent time in Cuba and was part of a multinational expedition to Haiti. The cover story was that we were studying medicinal qualities of the flora and fauna."

"Cover story?"

"The truth is that we were looking for a new generation of psychotropic drugs upon which we could build drug combinations useful in interrogation. You would be surprised what nature provides in such areas. I led three expeditions into the Amazon and various parts of the Brazilian rainforests, which are treasure troves for pharmacologists. I became skilled in ethnobotany and related sciences. It amused my superiors that in the course of searching for drugs of warfare we also stumbled on compounds that have contributed significant treatments for a variety of diseases. And there is little government interference in such countries. The biologically rich countries in the tropics are poor in money, thus the rainforests are ripe for exploitation." Volker spread his hands. "On the books I was a field surgeon, but in truth I was part of the medical team that offered support and protocols for the interrogators. And . . . from there it was a short step to biological warfare."

Trout nodded. "You're here in the states and you have a high security job at a supermax prison. Somewhere up the line the feds have to know your history. Our background checks show that you defected. Why?"

If Volker was impressed by Trout's knowledge, he did not show it. "I did not defect per se. I was recruited. The CIA had spies peppered all through the Red Army, just as we had spies in the American military. Nature of the game. There is an expression in covert work that a 'prospect is cultivated.' It means that there is a process of contacts used to establish trust and look for chinks in one's political loyalty. I am not political at all. My focus is entirely built around punishment. When my CIA handler finally recognized that, he made me an offer than I quite simply could not turn down. I defected at a pre-arranged time and shortly became an American citizen."

"I'll bet the CIA was happy to tap you for information."

"Very. And it is a scorched place on my soul that the information I shared has almost certainly been put to terrible use. I am well past the point of idealistic trust where I believe that governments only target bad people. That view is absurdly naïve. They drained me of everything I knew. I was offered various positions within the covert scientific community here in the States, but I chose to work in the prison systems. They arranged that for me, with some encouragement to continue my research."

Trout and Goat shared a look.

Here it comes, Trout thought.

"I was accorded far more freedom than is typical with a prison doctor. My staff was handpicked by my real employers. That was necessary because otherwise there would be too many obvious irregularities . . . and in truth very little of what I did in the corrections system was regular." He sighed and rubbed his eyes. "And that's what brings me to this moment."

"Homer Gibbon," urged Trout.

"Yes. Another monster like Henker. But a monster I could get close to."

"What happened to Henker?" asked Goat.

Volker gave a short, cold laugh. "He died of prostate cancer. I never laid a hand on him. I never, in fact, met him."

"Damn . . ."

"Yes."

"Gibbon," said Trout.

"One last bit of history," said Volker. "But it's crucial and I guarantee you that it will be worth your time to hear me out."

Trout nodded.

"Among the projects in which I participated was one intended to create a mind-control drug. I know, it sounds melodramatic, but it's a common research theme in biological warfare. The goal is to create a compound or pathogen-borne virus that can be introduced into an enemy population and affect brain chemistry. Much of what we know of the therapeutic uses for ethanol, scopolamine, 3-quinuclidinyl benzilate, temazepam, and barbiturates like sodium thiopental and sodium amytal have come from bioweapons and interrogation chemistry research."

"Okay."

"Our trips to Cuba and Haiti were intended to deepen that research by using combinations of those drugs along with various neurotoxins, particularly tetrodotoxin, which is found in certain species of puffer fish common to that area. At near-lethal doses tetrodotoxin can leave a person in a state of 'apparent' death for several days, while the person continues to be conscious. It was our task to create a bioweapon that would render an enemy population inert but alive."

"I heard about that stuff," said Goat. "There was a movie about a guy who went down to Haiti to study it."

"Yes," said Volker. "Dr. Wade Davis, another ethonobotanist, though not one of ours. He was the first person to determine that it was tetrodotoxin, along with a few other substances, that was used to put a person into a deathlike trance. So deathlike, in fact, that victims were often declared dead by trained physicians and buried, only to be later 'raised' from the grave. It's cloaked in cultural mumbo jumbo, but I assure you that it is very hard science. Science that we developed to a very high degree of effectiveness. Science I brought with me to the United States and shared with your government. Our government, I suppose. And . . . science I continued to explore as a doctor in the prison system." He rubbed his eyes again. "Science that I now fear has slipped the leash . . . science that may endanger us all."

Trout stared at him. "Wait a goddamn minute . . . Wade Davis? Te-trodotoxin? Jesus Christ, Doc, you're talking about fucking zombies."

A cold tear broke from the corner of Dr. Volker's eye. "Yes," he said in a hollow voice. "God help me, but yes . . . I am talking about zombies."

CHAPTER FORTY-SIX
STEBBINS COUNTY LINE

Lieutenant Colonel Macklin Dietrich turned to his aides. "Give me a minute."

The two junior officers saluted and stepped outside to stand in the rain. When the door was closed, Dietrich tapped his headset.

"I'm clear, sir," he said.

Major General Simeon Zetter sounded tired. "I was just on the horn to the president, Mack. This is bad and they're looking to us to keep it from turning into a complete clusterfuck."

"Seems to me this was a clusterfuck from the jump."

Zetter and Dietrich were old friends who had served together through three wars and had transferred from regular army to the Guard as career moves, taking the promotions and taking to heart their orders to bring the Pennsylvania Guard up to a level of combat readiness second to none. They'd done that, despite having equipment that was mostly post-Iraq hand-me-down crap. The whole line of two-and-a-half-ton troop trucks was ancient, and there was not one of their gunships that would pass a civilian flight safety inspection. The troops were top notch though, and they would need these men to be sharp as knives for what they were about to face. Not just physically tough but emotionally and psychologically tough.

"My teams are in position," said Dietrich.

"You're going to need to keep a tight hand on them, Mack."

Dietrich looked through the streaked windshield as sergeants handed white hazmat suits out of the back of a pair of trucks. Other NCOs walked among the soldiers, overseeing the process of transforming a thousand men in camouflaged BDUs into the cast of a big-budget science fiction movie. Hazmat suits looked scary enough at the best of times; but when the wearer is slinging an M16 and has fragmentation grenades jiggling on his belts, it became dangerously surreal.

"They're professional soldiers," said Dietrich, "they'll do their part."

"Don't bullshit a bullshitter. This isn't their 'part.' None of them signed on for something like this."

"Well, hell, Simeon . . . neither did we."

Zetter snorted. "And, you'll love this . . . the governor wants our assurance that we can guarantee a secure perimeter around Stebbins County."

"With a thousand troops?" laughed Dietrich. "During a hurricane?"

"I told him that. He authorized me to pull as many men as I needed away from flood control."

Dietrich was silent for a moment. "That'll mean married men, too."

"I know."

"The press is watching this storm, Simeon. They'll want to know why."

"I told the governor that. His people are preparing a story and a statement. Viral outbreak of a type and source unknown. It's a stalling tactic until they build a prettier pile of bullshit."

Dietrich grunted sourly.

Zetter said, "And, Mack . . . the governor's going to pull the state police out and turn the county completely over to us. That order is being cut right now."

"We could use the extra boots on the ground—"

"Not for this," said Zetter tiredly. "A lot of these troopers are local boys. They know the people here."

"Ah," said Dietrich. He kept watching the process of transformation that was making spacemen of all of his troops. "So, how do they want us to play this? Containment is problematic under these circumstances and—"

"Mack," said Zetter, and there was a note of deep sadness in his tone, "we've been authorized to go weapons hot. The Q-zone is a no-cross line. No exceptions."

Mack Dietrich closed his eyes. He knew that this had been a possibility, but it was still absurd on American soil. Obscene.

"God almighty," he said.

CHAPTER FORTY-SEVEN

Desdemona Fox stood at the edge of the lawn and watched hell itself unfold before her. She knew that the impossibility of the day had now become its defining characteristic, and that all hopes of normalcy had been consumed in a red banquet of unnatural hunger.

"God . . ." she breathed. A soft whisper, not a prayer.

The state police cars were scattered around, parked on the lawn and in the roundabout, interspersed with county cruisers, emergency apparatus, and unmarked cars. Thirty, forty vehicles. Three news vans. Two of the vehicles were burning, the smashed windows coughing black oil smoke into the still air. Most of the vehicles were pocked with bullet holes or peppered by shotgun pellets.

There was blood everywhere.

On the lawn, splashed high on the front wall of the mortuary, glistening on the driveway gravel. Everywhere.

"They're dead," murmured JT in a voice every bit as wooden and lifeless as hers. "They're all . . . dead."

Dez could only nod.

They were all dead.

She knew, though, that JT did not mean the bodies that lay scattered around, their eyes wide, skulls punched in by small arms fire, or skulls smashed by shotgun stocks. He was not speaking about those lifeless corpses molded into the crimson landscape.

No, JT spoke of the others—the black-mouthed, empty-eyed, shambling hulks who had all stopped what they were doing and turned toward them as JT and Dez had gotten out of their car. Their mouths opened and closed like gasping fish, or as if they were practicing chewing a meal that was not yet theirs.

They were on all sides of them, the closest about twenty yards away. Dez recognized that one. Not a statie. Paul Scott, the forensics officer. He only had one eye and patches of his scalp had been torn away. Over to his right, standing half-obscured by the smoke of a burning cruiser was Natalie Shanahan, her Kevlar vest hanging open, her blouse torn, and gaping holes where her breasts should have been. There were others. Sheldon Higdon stood by the open mortuary door, his chest marked with a line of bullet holes. There were four people—a civilian, two cops, and a trooper—with their hands cuffed behind their backs, but their faces were just as empty and pale as the others.

A sound made Dez turn and, closer than all of them, moving slowly out from behind an ambulance, was Chief Goss. One half of his face was gone, exposing the sharp angles of bare white bone and stringy muscle laced with yellow fat. The chief reached for her and she could see that most of the fingers were missing from his right hand. Bitten off, leaving a palm and one fat pinkie.

"Dead," echoed JT.

Dez felt her arm move and she looked down to see her right hand rise. She was not aware of any conscious choice or deliberate intent. The hand rose, and the arm with it. The gun was a thousand-pound weight in her fist.

I could end it now, she thought. *Under the chin, against the temple, or maybe just suck on the barrel and go meet Jesus. Ask that fucker for an explanation. Say good-bye to this shit. This isn't right. This isn't how the world's supposed to be. I can't live in a world like this.*

The chief was ten feet away. Three shuffling steps and he would have her.

I can't.

The gun rose.

Goss stepped closer. She could smell him. Open bowels and an outhouse stench.

Just do it! screamed her inner voice. Just one trigger pull and a wake up in the big hereafter. If they weren't lying in Sunday school then it was a ticket to heaven. Mom and Dad would be there. If it was all a lie, then there was nothing at all. Even that option was better than this shit.

The chief's half of a face wrinkled in a snarl of predatory lust. Hunger flickered like matchstick flames in his eyes as he stepped so close that he could touch her. The fingerless hand pawed at her, leaving smears of red on her vest. The other hand scrabbled to grab her shoulder, to pull her close as his mouth opened wide.

Chin, temple, or mouth. Do it!

She chose the temple.

The barrel pressed in against the skin until it stopped against the hardness of bone.

"Daddy," she whispered. "Help me . . ."

And pulled the trigger.

The blast was huge. The bullet punched a big red hole through two walls of bone and blew brain matter twenty feet across the lawn. Chief Goss fell.

And Dez Fox became alive again.

"JT!" she screamed as she spun and aimed, firing at Gunther, hitting him square in the center of the chest. A certain kill shot. He went back and down to one knee. Then he climbed to his feet and kept coming forward. She fired again, a double tap, one to the sternum—which only slowed him—and one to the bridge of the nose. Gunther's whole body rocked back, paused for a moment as if he was going to recover and keep coming, and then fell.

The other things around them moaned and hissed and snarled as they came. They all came.

Dez turned and fired at Natalie and blew away most of her throat.

Natalie kept coming, red drool dripping from her lips.

"Fuck!" Dez yelled and fired again, and again, the bullets hammering into Natalie's body. "Fucking die, you ugly cow!"

Natalie kept coming.

Dez took the gun in two hands and aimed. Her next shot blew out the light of Natalie's left eye and blew off the back of her head. Natalie's next step was meaningless and she collapsed down, making no attempt to catch her fall.

Dez whirled toward JT, who was still frozen and immobile. Dez shifted her gun to her left and with her right slapped him as hard as she could across the face. Again and again, forehand and back.

JT staggered back, his lips exploding with blood.

She saw the precise moment when the vacant space behind his eyes suddenly filled again. Just as the gunshot had brought Dez back from her brink, her slaps had dragged JT back from his.

"Watch!" he barked and shoved her aside as he brought the shotgun up and fired a blast at Paul Scott. The beanbag round hit Scott in the chest and spun him in a full circle, but Scott bared his teeth and lunged again.

The second beanbag caught him on the bridge of the nose and his head snapped back so fast and so far that Dez knew that his neck was broken. Scott fell backward and sprawled like a rag doll. He did not move again.

The others were coming now.

They were not fast, but they kept coming. Lumbering, some of them limping on damaged legs, a few—those with head injuries—staggering more awkwardly. Dez fired into them, hitting everything she aimed at. Punching hollow-points through hearts and stomachs and thigh bones and groins.

"Why won't they go down?" she bellowed.

As they came closer she raised her gun, tried for the more difficult head shots. She caught a state trooper on the cheek, tearing a huge chunk of his face away, but he kept coming. She shot him again, right over the right eyebrow and he abruptly crumpled.

She fired two more shots and the slide of her pistol locked back. She began backpedaling as she swapped out the magazines, letting the spent one fall—against all training and instinct—and slapping the fresh one in. The new mag was heavy with bullets. Reassuring.

She fired.

JT was back to back with her, firing at the things she could not see. Dez had seen the beanbag round drop Scott, but that had been a neck-breaker. JT tended to go for body shots with the shotgun. Dumb, she thought. Dumb, dumb, dumb.

She heard JT mumbling something over and over again.

"Holy Mary, Mother of God, pray for us sinners, now and at the hour of our death."

He fired and fired.

And fired the gun dry.

"I'm out," he said, as if surprised that a gun could commit such a heinous act of betrayal in so obvious a time of need.

"Get to the car! I've got a box of buckshot under the seat," Dez said, turning, shoving him, and then they were running.

Dez did not even remember walking this far from the cruiser, but it was a dozen yards away. Some of them were in the way. All of them were closing in, some moving much faster than the others. Distantly Dez wondered if they were the more recently dead.

Another part of her mind wanted to laugh at that thought.

And still another part was whispering her three choices. Chin, temple, mouth.

JT used the shotgun like a club. An EMT grabbed at his sleeve and JT hit him in the eyes. The blow was savage and the sheer force of it pitched the EMT onto his back, but the young man immediately started struggling to get up. Another state trooper lunged at JT and clamped his teeth down on his shoulder. Even through the Kevlar the pain was immediate and excruciating, but JT channeled it into his rage as he swung the shotgun stock up under the trooper's chin so hard that it snapped his neck. The thing fell backward, colliding with two others who had been reaching to grab.

That gave JT a tiny window and he leaped for the car door, opened it, threw the shotgun in, and pulled his Glock. "Dez, get in! I'll cover you."

He began firing spaced shots at the creatures that had been closing in on Dez. He dropped a few—a bullet through the forehead or sideways through an ear. Most of them merely staggered but still came on. It created a window for Dez and she jerked open the driver's door, dove in, and slammed it shut. They rolled up the windows.

"Get us the fuck out of here!" JT bellowed as he fished under the seat for the box of shotgun shells.

Dez jammed the key into the ignition and turned it so hard that it fired the car and began stripping the starter. She released it, threw it into drive, and stamped on the gas. The road was filled with shambling bodies and the car went four feet before it slammed into two of them. Even with the windows closed they could hear leg bones break. The car rocked to a stop, lacking the momentum to roll over the two bodies that now tried to crawl out from under.

She threw it into reverse and slammed backward, crushing others. Sheldon Higdon tried to claw open the door, but he could not master the mechanics of the door handle. He pulled the gun out of his holster and used it like a club. There was enough intelligence left in him for that, and the heavy pistol smashed through the rear driver's side window. JT pivoted around in his seat and fired at Sheldon, but the bullet merely punched through his chest. Dez cried out at the blast—it felt like someone was smashing her head with hammers.

A dozen of the creatures began pounding on the car, some with empty hands, some with stones or sticks. The rear window dissolved into a lace pattern of cracks.

Dez threw the car into drive again and kicked the pedal to the floor. There was a ten-foot lead in front of them, and she gave the car all it could take. It surged forward, the big engine howling. As the front wheels hit the crippled dead, the car bucked and lifted and crashed down—but it did so on the backs of the creatures. The wheels spun and the car thumped down over them. As the back wheels dropped onto the gravel, Dez kicked the gas again and the cruiser shot forward toward a line of the dead. At the last second she cut hard to the right, clipping a dead reporter on the hip and sending him flying into the air.

The mass of dead behind her were still coming. Some were trying awkwardly to run. Some could only crawl. But all of them kept coming.

"Go . . . *go!*" yelled JT as he fed shells into his shotgun.

She swerved around parked cars and smashed through hedges. She hit two more of the things and then angled down for the service road. There was a thump and when she looked in the rearview mirror she saw that she had just run over the bumper and part of the grille. The whole front of the car was torn apart and the steering alignment was shot. She had to fight the wheel to keep it under control.

She rounded the buildings and angled down toward the exit road.

And slammed on the brakes.

The cruiser skidded thirty feet, kicking up plumes of dust and sending gravel flying into the nearby trees. The road ahead was completely blocked. Two cruisers had been parked nose to nose to keep the press and civilians out, and beyond that were dozens of cars and trucks. There had to be three hundred people there. Most of them were still alive. Most were trying to flee. But at least sixty or seventy of those things were seeded through the crowd. It was a madhouse of struggle and red carnage. Screams filled the air, but there were few gunshots. Unlike the police, who had been the first to be overwhelmed, these people had no way of fighting back except with hands and feet and whatever they could pick up.

"Dez," said JT.

"I know," she said.

"We can't help them."

"I know."

"They're coming!"

She turned and saw the mass of troopers and county cops coming around the side of the building. There was no clear exit.

"Dez . . ."

"I *know*," she said again.

And floored it.

The cruiser was up to eighty miles an hour when it hit the two parked cars, and the impact flung the cars apart. It also rocked Dez and JT back and forth in their seat belts so hard that pain exploded in their necks and backs and the air was driven from their lungs. Both front-side windows shattered.

Dez kept pressing the gas.

The car rolled forward now, barely moving at twenty miles an hour. Smoke curled up from the engine. All the dashboard service lights were lit. People tried to jump on the car, desperate for a way out; but the creatures reached for them, biting and clawing at them, dragging them down. Dez steered with her right hand and fired her Glock with her left through the ragged window. JT filled the interior of the car with thunder and smoke as he worked the shotgun.

The cruiser crept forward and finally caught the edge of Doll Factory Road. The road curved into a long slope down to the crossroads, and Dez steered into the arms of gravity. The dying car picked up speed. One man, his leg bleeding from a bad bite, held on to the roof of the car, his fingers grasping tightly and his mouth open in a continuous scream. When the car crossed the train tracks at Mason Street, the man fell off and went crashing down on the rails.

Behind them, dwindling in size, at least thirty of the dead things continued to follow. The man who had fallen off was trying to get to his feet, but his bitten leg buckled under him. Before he could crawl away, the creatures swarmed over him.

The car rolled down and down and around a curve. Big pines blocked the road behind them, but Dez knew that they were still coming.

Then the engine coughed and died, but Dez kept steering until it rolled all the way down to the crossroads by Turk's Getty. She turned the wheel and the car drifted to a stop in the exit lane.

Dez and JT piled out of the car and stared up the hill. The curve and screen of pines was four hundred yards away. So far they could not see any of the dead.

Were they all clustered around a red thing that no longer screamed? Or were they still coming?

God, Dez cried, her voice a shriek inside her own head, *are they still coming?*

CHAPTER FORTY-EIGHT
MAGIC MARTI IN THE MORNING
WNOW RADIO, MARYLAND

"This is Magic Marti at the mike with new tidbits for travelers. Okay, kids, the storm is here. Batten down the hatches and make your peace with Jesus, 'cause this one's a doozy. National Guard units are being deployed to those areas where high floodwaters are anticipated, and we're already getting reports of small stream flooding in Fayette and low-lying towns to the north and west of Stebbins. If you live near a stream or river and still haven't gotten to high ground, you better do it now or wave at Aunt Marti as you go swimming by."

CHAPTER FORTY-NINE
GREEN GATES 55-PLUS COMMUNITY

"Zombies?" Trout whispered. The word was so strange. It didn't fit into his mouth. Zombies were movie stuff. Bela Lugosi and Hal Leighton. Old black-and-white late night stuff. *The Ghost Breakers* with Bob Hope. *I Walked with a Zombie.*

Zombies did not belong in the real world. Maybe in a National Geographic article. Not here in Pennsylvania. This was a serial killer story. This was Silence of the goddamn Lambs, not King of the goddamn Zombies.

"Wait, wait . . . you're saying you guys were dabbling in black magic?"

"No, no, of course not," said Volker, wiping the tear from his cheek. "There is nothing supernatural about this. Though, by your standards, it is perhaps *un*natural. Neither the devil or Mother Nature had a hand in what we were doing." He paused. "In what *I* did."

"What did you do?" Trout and Goat asked at the same time.

Volker said, "Homer Gibbon."

"Oh, man . . ." breathed Goat.

Trout licked his lips. "Okay . . . tell us."

"As I said earlier, I have committed my fair share of sins. Not sins in the same way as Gibbon, but sins nonetheless. Ethical sins, not religious. I have no faith. It died with my family. And that is how I came to make the decision I made." He drank the rest of his coffee but still held onto the empty cup. "My handlers did not place me at Rockview by chance. It was one of several prisons in states where capital punishment was technically still on the books. I would have preferred a less liberal state . . . say, Texas, but they use the electric chair. That did not fit my needs."

"Needs?" echoed Trout.

"Death by lethal injection. I thought you were following me in this." Volker sniffed. "I wanted to be in a position where I could oversee the execution of a monster like Henker. Homer Gibbon was a perfect substitute. His crimes are every bit as heinous as those perpetrated by Henker. Gibbon has destroyed so many lives . . . and not just those of his victims. Their families are destroyed, ruined by what he did. If there was a God then divine justice would dictate that Gibbon burn in eternal torment. The thought that he would sit in a prison cell with television and a library and more comforts than millions of innocent people have . . ."

"Death row's hardly the good life," said Goat, but Volker turned an acid stare on him.

"Oh really? And when was the last time you visited the ghettos of West Baltimore or North Philadelphia? Have you seen the squalor and rampant destitution in Louisiana and rural Mississippi? Have you seen three or four families crowded into a rat-infested single room in Gary, Indiana or Birmingham, Alabama? No? Then please keep your privileged opinion to yourself."

Goat flushed a deep red and sank into his seat.

"I've made a point to visit these places," said Volker. "Just as I've made it a point to visit women's shelters, and child protection services offices, and support group meetings for families of victims of violent crime. My whole life . . . or, perhaps it would be fair and truthful to say 'my obsession,' has been to find a way to provide punishment for men such as Gibbon and Henker. Death row is inconvenient. It is not a punishment that fits the crime." His voice was as sharp as broken glass. "But I found a more appropriate punishment."

"Which is . . . ?" asked Trout, and his heart was split between the reporter's desire to get this story and the man's dread of what Volker could say. Everything so far had been bizarre. Red Army, covert bio-weapons research. Zombies.

Volker said, "Even ordinary execution is an escape for these killers. We tranquilize them first. They feel nothing, or at worst they feel a little discomfort and some fear in the days leading up to the execution. But, I ask you gentlemen—measure that against what their victims felt and what the victims' families feel every single day for the rest of their lives." He shook his head fiercely. "No. That is a sin. That is immoral. That is fundamentally wrong and a crime against justice."

"What did you *do*?" asked Trout.

"I devised a way for these monsters to suffer. Not just during the execution . . . but afterward. Long, long afterward."

"That doesn't make sense," murmured Goat.

"It does if you've been paying attention. I have spent years seeking and developing compounds that control consciousness. Tetrodotoxin and the other elements from *Bufo marinus*, a species of cane toad; and an irritant produced by *Osteopilus dominicensis*, the hyla tree frog. Half a dozen others, all combined into what the witch doctors of Haiti, the *bokor*, call *coupe poudre*. You see, the religion of vodou makes a critical distinction between the physical body, the *corps cadavre*, the animating principle, or *gwo bon anj*, and the consciousness and memory, the *ti bon anj*. Correctly mixed and administered, the *coupe poudre* brings the physical body to the very edge of death—so close that only the most sophisticated electrical monitoring equipment will be able to detect respiration and heartbeat. The consciousness becomes separated, much as it does with certain hallucinogenic drugs, or during the spiritual exercise of astral projection. There is a disconnect between higher mind and physical body. The consciousness has no control at all over the body, and yet the subconscious mind can be manipulated by suggestion."

Trout was breathless. "Are you actually saying that you turned Homer Gibbon into a zombie?"

"Yes," agreed Volker with a sober nod. "That is precisely what I did. Or . . . a species of zombie. A variation, however you want to put it. Instead of the standard chemicals used for lethal injection, I injected him with my own version of the *coupe poudre*. It was an extension of something my team began many years ago, a project code-named 'Lucifer.' This compound is Lucifer 113."

"How is that punishment?" demanded Trout.

Volker sighed. "Gibbon had no known family, correct? As a result, his remains are the responsibility of the state, so he was scheduled for burial shortly after the execution. Had his aunt not showed up at the last minute, Gibbon's body would have been sealed in a cheap coffin and he would have been buried in a numbered grave in the potter's field behind the prison. No one except the warden and the judge would know where he was buried, and there he would remain forever."

"Again . . . how is that punishment?"

"No, no, wait . . ." said Goat. "Oh man . . . no, I get this. This Lucifer 113 stuff put him in . . . what? A kind of trance? A fake death state?"

"In so many words," said Volker.

"But not really dead?"

"No."

"And his consciousness . . . that was still there, just detached, am I right?"

"Yes. The many *bokor* I interviewed in Haiti and Cuba confirmed this. And our own bioweapons research bore it out. The consciousness remains. Fully aware, still connected in a passive way to every nerve ending, but totally unable to exert the slightest control over the physical body Not a twitch of a finger or a blink of an eye."

Trout felt the blood drain from his face. *"In the grave?"*

Volker nodded, his eyes filled with dark light. "In the grave. Can you think of a more fitting punishment for a serial murderer than to be awake and aware in a coffin while his body slowly rots?"

Trout slumped back in his chair. "Jesus Christ . . . that's horrible."

"Is it?" asked Volker coldly.

Goat shook his head. "No, no . . . there's something wrong here. Even if Gibbon were in a trance state, he would still need oxygen, right? I mean, how long would he last in a sealed coffin before his brain got oxygen starved and he just shut down?"

Dr. Volker made a face that Trout could not identify as a smile or a wince. "That would normally be correct."

"'Normally'?" Trout said. "Oh fuck. What's the rest?"

"Well . . . as you say, the body needs oxygen, even in a reduced metabolic state. However the precise needs of that oxygen can be modified." Volker sat down with a grunt. He looked very old and tired. "One of the principal areas of bioweapons research conducted by the Soviet Union was what people loosely call germ warfare. Project Lucifer was built around an exploration of select combinations of disease pathogens and parasites. I took it several steps further by applying transgenics to those parasites, tailoring them to my needs."

"Parasites?" Trout asked.

"Nature is so clever, so subtle. People have no idea how many parasites are all around them. Everywhere. They have been found in the hypersanitized interiors of NASA spacecraft. They are everywhere. It's a conservative estimate that half the world's population is contaminated with toxoplasmic parasites, either in the body or the brain. *Toxoplasma gondii* is a very common parasite found in the guts of cats. Its eggs are shed in cat urine and picked up by other animals and by many home owners who are cleaning cat boxes. The eggs become cysts in the stomachs of rats, and the parasites exert control over the rat's brain function. Normal rats will avoid areas that have been doused with cat urine; however, rats infected with toxoplasma actually seek out the cat-urine-marked areas again and again. This is the deliberate work of the parasite. In humans, scientists have noticed a definite link between toxoplasma and humans with schizophrenia. This potential for schizophrenia will cross the placental barriers and present in newborns."

"Why include that in what you gave to Gibbon?" asked Trout.

"Schizophrenia heightens fear and increased psychological distress."

"Jesus God."

"The toxoplasma is only one of several parasites introduced into the mix. We have re-engineered the DNA of flukes *Dicrocoelium dendriticum* and *Euhaplorchis californiensis* to work in harmony with toxoplasma. Each of these flukes affords a measure of predictable control over the behavior of the host body. The key player, however, is the green jewel wasp, which normally targets cockroaches. It injects a venom that blocks the neurotransmitter octopamine, which is associated with alertness and movement. This subjugates the actions of the host body. We greatly accelerated the life cycle of the wasp. Where it normally takes weeks for its larvae to mature, now it happens in a matter of minutes. Unfortunately the total lifespan is accordingly diminished. In order for the parasite to stay active and in control, it needs a constant source of protein. It therefore feeds on the host body . . . and that, too, is a desired goal. Lucifer 113 has transformed Homer Gibbon from a man to a parasitic factory whose sole output is suffering. Gibbon was supposed to be not only awake and aware in his coffin, it was my intention that he feel himself being consumed!"

Trout and Goat stared in absolute horror at the doctor.

Trout abruptly stood up and walked back and forth across the living room. He felt like he wanted a bath so hot that it would boil even the memory of this conversation off his skin. His skin itched and he stared at the backs of his wrists as if expecting to see parasites moving beneath the skin. Finally he wheeled on Volker, forcing control and a faux calm into his voice.

"Doc, I can appreciate you wanting revenge on bastards like Gibbon and the man who killed your sister and her kids. That's normal. If you told me you took a gun and shot him, I'd be 'hey, no harm, no foul.' If you told me you went all Dexter on him and carved him up into deli meat, I'm good with that, too. But this . . . this is fucking crazy. This is actual mad scientist stuff here. This is . . ."

He fished for the word, but Volker supplied it, "Sinful?"

Trout nodded as he ran his fingers through his thick blond hair. "Homer Gibbon wasn't fucking buried in a numbered grave. He's in a mortuary in Stebbins County. Now you have to tell me how bad this is. Can those parasites get out? Do we need to call someone?"

Volker's face was unreadable. "It's already too late for that, Mr. Trout. I called the Centers for Disease Control before you arrived. They did not believe me. I called the warden, and I called my CIA handler. He *did* believe me, and it is up to him to get the government machinery working to contain this situation."

"Wait . . . so the authorities already know about this?"

"Yes. But, there is one more . . . wrinkle."

Volker's eyes were jumpy. Trout thought the man was half wacko when they arrived, but now he was sure Volker was a short twitch away from going totally batshit.

"Then tell me," demanded Trout.

"Minutes before you arrived I placed another call," Volker said, his voice slow and dry. "To Selma Conroy."

"Why? To warn her?"

"To have her warn everyone. Gibbon was supposed to take the parasites with him into the ground. Into a sealed coffin. With their reduced life cycle they would consume all of the host matter in a few weeks and then die. End of Gibbon and the end of them. Clean and tidy. These parasites were never intended to be allowed to enter the general biosphere. Even when we were working on them in East Berlin we knew that Project Lucifer was likely to produce a bioweapon that was too unstable to use, even when deployed in remote spots."

"Did Selma call anyone? Is she out there raising the alarm?"

A drop of drool dripped from the corner of Volker's mouth and ran down his chin. He did nothing to wipe it away.

"No," he said, and in a voice that was almost too soft for Trout to hear, he added, "No . . . after I told her some of what I told you, Mrs. Conroy cursed me and damned me . . . and then she put Homer Gibbon on the phone."

CHAPTER FIFTY
HART COTTAGE

Lee Hartnup stood in the middle of the living room, his body sway-ing with mindless indecision as the immediate need leeched away to be replaced by a deeper and inexplicable need. The front door was open and the wet fingers of the storm reached in to touch everything. The walls, the furniture, the curtains, the bodies.

The smell of blood was even stronger than the wet-earth smell of the rain. Even floating formless within his stolen body, Hartnup could smell it. And it drove him to madness that the smell made him feel hungry. Or, rather . . . it made him completely aware of the hungers that drove this thing, this shell.

Worse than the hunger, though, was the grief. It was so vast a thing that it should have split this infected husk apart and sent his soul screaming into the wind.

April.

Tommy.

Gail.

Oh God . . . please let me die.

His stolen eyes were not looking in that direction, so for the mo-ment Hartnup was spared the horrors of seeing what had become of his sister and her children. Even so, the last image of them hung burn-ing in front of him, there in the vast inner darkness. April in a sprawl, dying as she tried to run with a savaged throat. Her blood painted in broad arterial splashes onto wall and ceiling. And the two smaller bod-ies who lay under her, still wrapped in her limp arms as if she could protect them in death more effectively than she did in life.

Tommy and Gail. Small bodies. So little of them left. So much of them in him, in his own stomach.

Please let me die and not see this . . . let me not know this . . .

There was a wet sound behind him and his body turned, a clumsy, lumbering act, triggered by an awareness of movement. He saw the policeman. Was this the second policeman he had killed, or the third? *Gunther*, Hartnup thought, *his name is Ken Gunther.*

The policeman rose slowly from the cooling body that was bent backward over the arm of the couch. Hartnup stared at the sprawled corpse, wishing he could weep for her. For all of them. But he did not own even as small a thing as his own tear ducts, and so no tears fell for officer Dana Howard. Her eyes and mouth were open. So was her stomach. Steam rose from the red drama of that gaping hole.

As Gunther moved sluggishly toward the door, his shoulder collided with Hartnup's and the impact staggered them both. There was no reaction other than for each to right himself. No growls, no exchange of words. Like insects, Hartnup thought.

On the couch, Dana Howard suddenly sat up, and the motion forced air out through the torn tissue of her throat. A hollow sound for a hollow person. She slowly clambered to her feet, indifferent to the intestines that sloshed out of the ragged hole in her stomach and slapped onto the carpet. Dana tottered two crooked steps forward, her head slowly turning left and right but her expression remaining vacant. Absent.

Hartnup wondered if the real Dana was still in there. As he was in here, a hijacked soul in a hollow body. He wanted to step close, to look into her eyes, to see if there was still some sign, however small, that the soul or personality of Dana Howard still remained.

And if it did, what then? What would it change? Would it make him feel less alone, knowing that he was part of some larger, shared catastrophe? Or would it build another layer of impotent sadness and grief atop what he already felt? Which was better? Which hell burned less intensely?

There was another moan. More truly a moan than the sound Dana had made. Hartnup's body turned and he cursed God as it did so, because he knew what horrors lay behind him.

No. Not lay. Stood.

April.

Somehow her face was untouched, though every other part of her was crumpled and torn and slashed by teeth and nails.

April. With her dead eyes. Holding small, squirming, hissing, moaning things in each arm.

The Hollow Man turned away and shambled toward the door, moving away from this place because there was nothing left here to hunt. The ache, the deep hunger, was waking once more in his stolen body. Within shuffling steps, he followed his sister and the police officers out into the howling wind.

CHAPTER FIFTY-ONE
INTERSECTION OF DOLL
FACTORY ROAD AND MASON STREET
STEBBINS COUNTY, PENNSYLVANIA

When Dez and JT got to the gas station it was deserted, the doors locked and the staff gone.

"Turk's gone," JT said as he peered in through the grimy office window.

Dez rubbed a clean spot on the window of the roll-down garage door. "Yeah, both of his wreckers are gone. Must be out cruising the roads between the schools."

Turk and his son made money every time there was a heavy rain, pulling cars out of the mud. Dez slammed her fist on the door and turned back to their car. It was a smoking wreck and getting to the gas station took all that it had left.

JT ran over and crouched behind a corner mailbox, squinting through the gloom up Doll Factory Road. Dez opened the cruiser door and grabbed the mike, but all she got was static. Her cell phone was lost and she had no idea where. Maybe at Hartnup's, maybe at the hospital.

"Talk to me, Hoss," she called over her shoulder. "Are they coming?"

JT reloaded his shotgun and shoved the remaining shells into his pants pocket. "I can't see them," he called in a loud whisper. "They must be over the rise. Did you get Flower on the line?"

"Trying . . ."

Dez tried again, but there was only white noise. She threw down the mike and hurried over to kneel down next to JT.

"What are we into here?" she asked. "I mean . . . Jesus, JT, this thing is spreading out of control."

He licked his lips. "Those people . . . they're dead?"

It was maybe the tenth time he'd said it since they got out of the car.

"Yes, they're fucking dead," she said through gritted teeth.

He glanced at her. "No . . . no . . . I mean . . ." He shook his head, tried again. "We shot the shit out of them, Dez, and they kept coming."

"Except some of them," she corrected.

"Right, that's my point. Some of them went down. Some of them are *dead* dead, you know? Not running around dead. God—could this make less frigging sense?"

Dez touched his shoulder. "I know, Hoss . . . I know. The chief . . . a few of the others. I shot them and they didn't go down, and then I shot them and they did. It doesn't make any sense."

"When you . . . killed the chief," he asked slowly, "where'd you hit him?"

Dez thought about it. "In the forehead."

JT let out a breath, almost a sigh of relief. "Same thing happened when you shot the EMT. And I hit Paul Scott in the head and that broke his neck."

"And the cleaning lady back at Doc's?"

"I shot her in the cheek and she—"

"No," he said, "where'd you put your last shot?"

Dez paused. "Right above the eye."

"Head shot," said JT. "That's it, then. It's the head. The brain, probably. Definitely the spine. That's how to put them down for good."

"Are you sure?"

JT said, "Think . . . did any of them get up after you shot them in the skull?"

Dez thought about it. "No," she said. "Not one."

"Head shots," he said again. "We need to get them in the head."

She shook her head. "I'm a good shot, but I can't guarantee a head shot unless those fuckers are right on top of us. Maybe if I had a hunting rifle with a scope. No . . . we need SWAT. We need snipers firing from elevated positions."

"Try the radio again, Dez. Maybe we can stop this if we get those snipers in here."

She nodded. "Or enough people with guns to create a shooting line. Most rounds slow them. Double tap the fuckers back to wherever they came from."

JT gave her a troubled look. "Dez . . . they came from here. That was Chief Goss and Sheldon and Paul . . ."

"You know what I mean," Dez snapped, though in truth she didn't know what she meant. She turned and hurried back to the cruiser and tried to call the station again. Nothing. Dez threw down the mike in disgust and just as the handset bounced off the seat she heard a voice.

". . . *report your* . . ."

Not Flower.

Dez lunged for the handset and clicked the button.

"Unit Two to dispatch, do you copy?"

The response was immediate. "Unit Two, identify."

She recognized the voice. The state police lieutenant, William Henry Hardy.

"Lieutenant Hardy, this is Officer Fox."

There was considerable static, but Dez got every word. "Officer Fox, please state your location and status."

"My unit is wrecked at the corner of Doll Factory Road and Mason Street. Turk's Getty. Requesting immediate backup. We have officers down. I repeat, we have multiple officers down. Estimate thirty plus. County and troopers. We have civilian casualties. Estimate fifty plus."

"Say again."

Dez repeated it. The enormity of it was like a fist against her head.

"Backup is already rolling," said Hardy. "What is the nature of the emergency?"

"I . . . don't know."

There was a moment of crackle.

"Officer, please repeat. What is the nature of the—"

"People are going crazy down here, Lieutenant. Everyone's attacking everyone. People are fucking eating people. Cops, too."

"Officer Fox, did you make contact with Chief Goss?"

She took a breath. "Chief Goss is dead." Tears boiled out of her eyes and fell down her cheeks. "Christ . . . they're all dead." A sob hitched inside her chest and suddenly she was crying. She leaned against the side of the cruiser and slid down to the ground, the sobs wracking her, the pain in her soul doubling her over. She buried her face against her knees and banged the microphone against her head. Over and over again.

"They're coming!" JT yelled and she jerked her head up to see him rising to lay the shotgun atop the mailbox.

"Christ," Dez said, and realized that she was still holding the radio send button. "Lieutenant . . . with the storm the emergency evacuation center is the elementary school. There's going to be hundreds of kids in there. Old folks, too. It's only a couple of miles from here. Please . . . get some people over there. You can't let any of the infected in there . . . those kids . . ."

With sudden horror Dez realized that she was yelling into a dead mike. She clicked the button, jiggled the handset, and this time she could not even raise a whisper of static.

"Shit!"

Her mind was filled with a terrible image of all those kids crouched in the cavernous old school as the storm pounded on the walls and the hungry dead clawed at the doors to get in.

She threw the microphone down and pulled her piece. She had eight bullets left and one extra magazine. JT had the loaded shotgun, nine extra shells, and two full magazines—one in his Glock, the other on his belt. Dez used her bloody sleeve to wipe away the tears.

She was not going to let the infection reach the school. No way. If she had to kill every one of those monsters . . . if she had to break their necks with her bare hands, she was not going to abandon those kids. Not the little ones. Dez knew what it was like to feel abandoned. To feel like the people who were supposed to be there just left you in the dark. With the boogeyman. With the monsters.

Despite what Billy had said on the phone, Dez knew the shape of her own damage. It wasn't particularly obscure, and she even understood how it warped her. Big deal. She could see it right there every time she looked in the mirror. That was a couple of grand saved on therapy, and it didn't provide a magic pill any more than it gave her a road map to a brighter future. To hell with that Dr. Phil shit.

The simple truth was that parents let down their kids. It was a fact of life. It happened all the damn time. But there was no way that she would become another statistic in that drama. She was going to get to those kids. End of story.

Dez Fox was not a religious woman. She lost a chunk of it in second grade when her father was killed by friendly fire in the first Gulf War and the rest when her mother died of cancer a few weeks later. She believed in God, but hated Him for His cruel indifference. However, as she racked the slide on her Glock, she murmured a small and almost silent prayer.

"God help us," she whispered.

She kept listening, hoping to hear sirens, but all she heard on the breeze was the faint moans of the dead and the splats as the first fat raindrops fell from the leaden sky.

"God help us all."

CHAPTER FIFTY-TWO
HARTNUP'S TRANSITION ESTATE

Everything should have looked familiar. The Grove, the wide green lawn, and tall trees were the same. The main funeral house and the mortuary work building, all the same. But nothing was familiar. Cars and emergency vehicles were parked haphazardly on the roads and the lawn. The grass around the mortuary was splashed with wild swatches of red and puddles of black in which larvae squirmed and writhed.

And everywhere were the Hollow Men.

Dozens of them. In uniforms, in ordinary clothes, in farm clothes, and work clothes. Several of them had cameras hung around their necks and plastic press credentials clipped to their jackets. Two of them were twins, girls of about seventeen, unique now because of the individuality of their wounds. This wasn't like the crowds who gathered for funerals. There were no tears, no suppressed laughter, no broken sobs, no whispered conversation. Their shoes whispered across the soft, wet grass.

The hollow ones milled, bumping into one another or against the fenders of cars. One of them tripped over something and Hartnup saw that it was the fat body of Marty Goss. The chief lay sprawled and silent, a big black hole punched through his forehead. His white fingers did not twitch, he did not try to get up. He looked . . . dead.

Dead.

Hartnup felt suddenly and irrationally jealous of the dead man. How could a fat putz like Marty Goss deserve an actual death when Hartnup had to go on and on, floating like a dust mote inside a stolen body? It was wretchedly unfair.

How did Goss die? A lot of the creatures here had gunshot wounds. What was different about Marty?

Hartnup's body kept shuffling forward. Hartnup screamed for it to stop. He wanted to examine the body, determine the answer to this mystery. From the blood smears on Goss's face it was clear that he had reanimated and become what Hartnup still was. So . . . how had that curse been broken for the chief?

His body moved on and on, shambling toward the road, just as some of the others were turning that way. There was a sound coming from around the bend. A car was coming.

More flesh for this feast.

God, no!

As his body moved toward the noise, it passed another body that lay unmoving in the mud. The whole top of its head was missing. Blown away by a shotgun blast.

And then Lee Hartnup understood. It was the brain.

Yes . . . yes . . . yes . . . yes . . . yes . . . whispered his own inner voice.

It did not answer the questions of why and what, but it gave Hartnup a shred of insight. The brain. The motor cortex and the nerve conduction of the spinal cord. Even a stolen body needed that much. Maybe only that much. Rudimentary control and nerve signals. To stand, to walk. To grab and bite. To chew.

Destroy the brain and you stop the monster.

That would be perfect. Not merely hollow . . . but empty.

God, he pleaded, *let someone shoot me! Please, God, let someone blow my head off and kill me!*

It was the strangest thought that had ever flown through his brain, but also the sanest. And it was his truest prayer.

Unless.

Unless . . .

What if destroying the body did *not* turn off all of his own lights? What if he remained, lost in the darkness of a dead and decaying body?

Would that be worse?

No, he told himself. *If my body is dead I can't hurt anyone else.*

The car rounded the bend. State troopers.

The crowd of things moaned almost as one, their cries rising in intensity now, louder than the downpour. The cruiser slewed sideways as the driver kicked down on the brakes; gravel and mud showered the dead things that staggered toward it. None of them fell, none of them stopped.

The doors opened and two troopers stepped out, guns in their hands, their faces almost as blank as the things that approached them.

Hartnup heard one of them yell. "What the Christ—"

And then the creatures were upon them.

The troopers yelled warnings. Over and over again. They leveled their weapons. Hartnup waited for the shots, needing to see the bullets punch through skull and brain, needing to see one of the monsters fall. His own body moved forward on stiff legs, hands reaching for the distant flesh; hunger swelling like a scream inside his body.

Then the troopers were gone beneath a mountain of white limbs and red mouths.

Please . . . no! Hartnup pleaded. *Please, for the love of God, no! You haven't killed me yet.*

CHAPTER FIFTY-THREE
GREEN GATES 55-PLUS COMMUNITY

"Wait," said Trout as he leapt to his feet. "*What?* Homer Gibbon is alive?"

Tears rolled down Dr. Volker's face as he nodded. He pulled a handkerchief and pressed it against his eyes. His body trembled with quiet sobs.

Goat sat in open-mouthed shock.

"No, no, no, goddamn it," Trout shouted as he strode over to the doctor, looming above him with balled fists. "You fucking tell me what you mean? How the hell did Homer Gibbon speak to you on the goddamn phone? He's dead! I saw him die. I saw you pump that shit into his veins and I saw the machines flatline. I watched you *execute* him, for Christ's sake."

When Volker only shook his head, Trout snarled, "You gave him that stuff, didn't you? Didn't you?"

"Yes." Volker's voice was tiny.

Goat whispered, "Oh . . . holy mother of shit . . ."

"Are you saying that Gibbon is free?" Trout demanded.

"Free?" echoed Volker. "No . . ."

Trout started to relax, but then the doctor added, "It's much, much worse than his being free."

With a snarl, Trout grabbed Volker, hauled him halfway out of the chair and did a fast pat-down to find the pistol he knew Volker carried. It was a heavy nine millimeter, and he tore the pocket open to retrieve it and flung the doctor back down. Volker made a swipe for the pistol, but Trout slapped his hand away and retreated a step. He stared down at Volker with contempt.

"So the plan was to dump this shit in our laps and then eat your gun? You fucking coward."

"No," Volker protested, "I told you . . . I called my handler. The authorities already know about this. They are taking care of it."

"Taking care of it? Really? A serial killer infected with—Christ, what do I even call this thing? A zombie parasite?—is free in my home town and you think a call to your bosses and a confession to a couple of reporters is enough to balance the scales here?"

"No, I . . ."

Goat leaned forward. "Doc . . . if this gets out, if Gibbon is out there among people . . . what's the risk of infection?"

"I thought I made that clear."

Trout racked the slide and put the barrel against Volker's kneecap. "Make it clearer."

Volker's eyes flared with terror. "Please . . . the parasites were re-engineered for survival and proliferation. Outside of a containment unit such as a coffin, they will drive the host to find and infect other hosts."

"Why?" demanded Goat. "Why would you engineer it to do that?"

"Understand," said the doctor, mopping tears from his cheeks, "when the Lucifer research was active, it was intended as a bioweapon. Something that could be introduced into an enemy population—a military base or some isolated encampment—and then we would sit back and let the parasites do their work. It would spread through host aggression, and the vastly accelerated life cycle would make each newly infected person a disease vector within minutes. Then military in protective suits could clean up the infected with flame units and acquire the physical assets."

Trout narrowed his eyes. "What do you mean by 'host aggression'?"

Volker's hands gripped the arms of the chair so fiercely that the doctor's fingernails tore scratches in the fabric. "This is a serum transfer pathogen," he said in a ghostly voice. "It lives in any body fluid. Blood and sputum would be rife with newly hatched larvae. The logic inherent in parasites would cause the host to transfer the larvae through the most efficient possible means. Spitting into the eyes, nose, or mouth of a target host would work well. The parasites would be absorbed through the mucus membranes. But the most efficient and direct way to guarantee infection would be to forcibly introduce the parasites directly into the bloodstream."

"'Forcibly,'" echoed Goat.

Volker nodded. "Through a bite."

Trout backed away like he'd been slapped. "Goat . . . oh, shit!"

"What?" asked Goat.

"This morning . . . at the mortuary. The cops were there . . ." He pointed the gun at Volker. "What time did you talk to Gibbon?"

Volker flinched. "Half an hour ago."

"Fuck. So the cops were there putting that sick son of a bitch in cuffs."

"No," admitted Volker. "Gibbon had already . . . left . . . the mortuary."

"Whoa," cut in Goat. "What's that supposed to mean? That pause. What happened *at* the mortuary? What did Gibbon tell you?"

Volker sniffed and clutched his handkerchief in one bony fist. "He told me that he . . . woke up . . . at the mortuary in Stebbins."

Woke up. The two words hung in the air, throbbing with ugly meaning.

"What about the mortician? Lee Hartnup?" asked Trout, lowering the gun.

Volker shook his head. "I don't know."

"What *do* you know? What did Gibbon say?"

"He . . . thanked me." Saying it seemed to cause physical pain for the doctor. He winced and touched his chest. "God help me . . ."

"Thanked you?" Trout felt the moment slipping away from him. "Thanked you for what? I thought this was supposed to be a punishment. Are you telling me that this was something else? Are you saying you helped this asshole escape?"

"No! God in heaven . . . no. I injected Gibbon with Lucifer 113 because I wanted him to suffer. I wanted him in his coffin screaming in torment as the parasites kept him alive just so they could feed on him. He deserved it. They all deserve it."

"Then why did he thank you?"

"Because he thinks I helped him escape," cried Volker. "That maniac thinks that we had some sort of agreement, that all of this is part of some plan I had to free him. He said that he knew it back when he first came to me in the infirmary."

"Why would he think that?" asked Goat suspiciously.

Volker shook his head, but he said, "Once, months ago, when I was briefly alone with the prisoner, I made some kind of veiled threat to him. I said something like . . . 'After you go, you won't be gone. You'll be with us forever. You'll know forever.' Something like that. It was a threat. I wanted him to fear what would happen to him when the execution day finally arrived. I didn't want him to have a single night's peaceful sleep."

"But he didn't take it that way?" said Trout as he sat back down. He nodded to himself. "Yeah, I can see it. Twisted mind like his."

Volker gave another shake of his head. "On the phone . . . I told him the truth. I told him everything that I had planned to do to him. I told him that it was still going to consume him. I told him that he was still going to be punished for what he did."

"How did he react," asked Trout.

"Gibbon laughed at me. Then he said that he would be coming for me. A hollow threat . . . he has no idea where I live. And, I suspect, he doesn't have your resources for finding out."

Trout sneered. "But you were going to shoot yourself anyway. Just in case?"

The doctor said nothing.

Goat was shaking his head "Homer Gibbon never died? He's alive . . . ?"

Volker cleared his throat. "In a manner of speaking. Homer Gibbon *did* die. He was clinically and legally dead."

"But it was a dodge," suggested Goat.

"No. He was dead. His body was dead. His mind was . . ." Volker shrugged. "Even in Project Lucifer we had no word for it. 'Elsewhere' is as good as anything."

"But what about oxygen starvation?" demanded Goat. "That destroys brain cells, right?"

"It does in every case except this. The parasites use their own larvae—a network of them linked through mucus—very much like a charged plasma. It's fascinating and—"

"Seriously, Doc?" asked Trout, jiggling the pistol. "You want to brag? Now?"

Volker colored. "Sorry."

"So," Goat said, "these parasites, these wasp thingies, kept Gibbon's brain alive?"

"No." Volker looked frustrated. "Gentlemen, in order to discuss this, and to have you understand it, we have to step outside of our normal scientific lexicon. We are not discussing life or death as we have always known it. Those have always been the only two states of existence. However the activity of these parasites, and the unique way in which they protect and maintain their host, has no parallel in nature. This is a third state of existence. Something entirely new, though hinted at in the religion of vodou. This is, to give it a name, a 'living death.' Homer Gibbon did die. That is a fact. But the parasites maintained a key few functions within his body so that, instead of dying, Gibbon transitioned into the state of living death. His body is certifiably dead. Right now his skin is putrefying, and he is almost certainly far along in the process of rigor mortis. He is dead. However, the parasites require that certain motor functions remain intact. When I spoke to him on the phone, he was a . . . reduced . . . personality. Less keenly intelligent, and yet still capable of accessing his memories, still able to speak and reason."

"That's horrible . . ." murmured Trout. "And you wanted him to be like that in his grave?"

"It was a punishment, damn it!" bellowed Volker. "You were at his execution, Mr. Trout. You know the scope and nature of his crimes. Do I need to remind you of what he did to children? To babies?"

Trout said nothing.

The doctor pounded his fist on the arm of the chair. "I have no regrets for what I had planned for Gibbon. Even with the amount of suffering he would endure . . . weeks, perhaps months before he truly died . . . I think he is getting off more lightly than his crimes deserve. Tell me I am wrong."

Trout looked inside his mind and saw no counterarguments there. Instead he played one tired old card. "You're not God, Doc."

Volker snorted. "Neither is any member of the jury that convicted him or the judge who ordered his execution."

"Guys," interrupted Goat, "a little focus here. I don't give a rat's ass about how appropriate the punishment is or isn't. What has my balls in a vise is the fact that this son of a bitch is still alive. Or . . . whatever. Living dead." He shook his head in frustration. "He's *out* there."

"By now . . . others may have been infected," said Volker, cutting a wary look at the pistol in Trout's hand. "I explained this to my handler. Anyone infected by Gibbon will be entirely overwhelmed by the parasite. Gibbon, however, seems to be an unusual case. He was narcotized using the Haitian zombie *coupe poudre* before the parasites were introduced. When I spoke to him on the phone, he was lucid. That's not in keeping with the profiles we worked up during Project Lucifer. The parasites invade the brain and essentially disconnect the higher functions in favor of their own needs and directives. Consciousness remains but intelligent control is gone. Except . . . that's not what happened with Gibbon. For some reason he is still in control of his body. Mind and body are still connected even though he is infected. I would need to . . ." he paused and licked his lips, "to 'study' him to understand this variation on the ideal model."

Trout's hand tightened around the pistol. He wanted to whip the barrel across this old maniac's face. He wanted to brutalize him for this. "How do we stop it?" he asked hollowly. "What's the cure?"

"Cure?" Volker repeated as if the word was unknown to him.

"How do we treat the infected? How do we save them?"

Volker was already shaking his head. "You can't save them. There is no cure, no treatment, nothing. The parasites are hermaphroditic, so there's no queen to find and kill. Each parasite is born pregnant. They begin laying eggs seconds after they hatch. They stay perpetually in the larval state, producing and laying eggs. The only way to stop that cycle is to destroy the host. That was the *point*." He paused, perhaps aware of how he sounded. In a calmer voice he said, "However . . . if no other human goes near the corpse, then within a few weeks the larva inside the host will have consumed it. Without food, no new larvae will be born. The old larvae die off within days. Three, four weeks and the corpse is inert. But if you want to stop the ambulatory hosts, then you can do that by destroying the motor cortex or the brain stem. And then incinerate the body."

Trout stared at him, needing all of this to be untrue, to be a lie told by a sick and delusional old man.

"I'm losing my cool here, Doc," he said, gesturing with the gun. "I need you to tell me what you're going to do about this."

Volker's face wore an expression of profound confusion. "Do? Haven't you been listening to me? There is nothing I can do. There's nothing you can do, either. I doubt at this point that there's anything that the government can do. We are not sitting here discussing a response protocol. You and your friend are here as witnesses to these events. You are the historians who will tell the truth of this story. But you are witnesses only from a distance. Go back to Stebbins and you become part of the infestation. Stay here, or at least away from town and you will be able to report what I've told you." He nodded toward the door as if that was a clear line to the town. "Don't worry about Homer Gibbon. The parasites are consuming him even as we speak—"

"He could spread it across the whole goddamn country," interrupted Goat.

"No. As I said, I told my handlers. There are people in the government who know the full potential of the Lucifer program. I'm sure all appropriate steps are being taken."

"What do you mean by 'appropriate'?"

The old doctor's eyes glittered with new tears. "Exactly what you would expect that word to mean."

CHAPTER FIFTY-FOUR
WOLVERTON REGIONAL HOSPITAL

Dr. Raja Sengupta stared through the reinforced plastic window of the hazmat suit. Inside the suit the figure of Officer Andy Diviny still writhed and thrashed against the four-point restraints and canvas strapping. There was no way he could break free, but even so Sengupta was not willing to go back inside that room.

Not now. Not after the test results had come back. There was a pulse, but it beat less than once per minute. There was respiration, but so shallow that it was impossible to detect without machines. So shallow that it had to be destroying brain cells. Sengupta had seen hypoxia at a hundred different degrees of intensity, but nothing like this. There was so little blood and oxygen going to the brain that it bordered on anoxia; cellular respiration was nonfunctioning at any detectable level. Without cellular energy, tissue all over the man's body was becoming apoptotic, turning necrotic. He was rotting like a corpse even while he growled and fought to get up.

None of which was possible. Not even with the worst coma patients.

Even that wasn't the worst thing. That wasn't what frightened Dr. Sengupta on the deepest levels. The blood and saliva tests were nightmarish.

His fingers trembled so badly it took him four tries to punch in the number for the Centers for Disease Control in Atlanta.

CHAPTER FIFTY-FIVE
THE Q-ZONE, NORTHERN PERIMETER
STEBBINS COUNTY, PENNSYLVANIA

Lt. Colonel Macklin Dietrich bent over a plastic-coated map of Stebbins County. Three other officers and several aides were clustered around the table. A portable communications table had been set up against the far wall of the plastic shelter that had been erected to serve as field HQ for this operation.

He tapped the map with a forefinger. "This is the funeral home where Gibbon was taken. We've lost communication with the local and state police at the scene, so we can assume that it's been compromised. However, a second wave of state troopers arrived a few minutes before we secured the perimeter. They're on cleanup for this."

"Sir, what do the local police know?" asked a captain.

"Nothing," said Dietrich, "and we're going to keep it that way."

A major asked, "Can't we use them as local assets?"

"No. This is not a joint operation. We do not want any bonds formed between our people and the infected."

"May I ask why not, sir?" asked the major.

"Because we are to regard anyone inside the Q-zone as potentially and indeed probably infected." Dietrich sighed. "I know how you must all feel. I feel the same. These are American citizens and they didn't ask for this. This is a goddamn tragedy. Our sympathies and the sympathies of the men under our command are going to naturally be with these people."

The major shook his head. "We've been trained to help the civilian population, not stand aside and watch them die."

"This isn't something anyone's been trained for, Major," said Dietrich. "This is a worst-case scenario that should not have happened. But it *has* happened and it's up to us to contain this inside the Stebbins County line. We drop the ball and we're going to need a mass grave the size of the Grand Canyon to bury the dead."

The officers glanced at one another in horrified silence.

"What are the safety regs on this?" asked the captain.

Dietrich said, "Containment and sterilization are the only options they gave us to work with. We're running without safety measures, and they tell me we don't have a viable treatment. These parasites make ebola look like a weak dose of the clap. We're talking about something that is one hundred percent infectious and one hundred percent terminal." He looked around and watched the truth and its implications bury spikes in each of the officers. "So, the hard news is that everyone who is infected is not only terminal, they are a very real and substantial threat to the rest of the country."

The major made a disgusted face. "So—they want us to go in there, lock it all down, and flush it? Seven thousand people?"

Dietrich leaned on the table and stared hard into the major's eyes. "Yes. No exceptions. You see your own mother in town and she's infected, you put a bullet in her goddamn brain."

"What if she's not infected, sir?" asked the captain.

Dietrich's eyes were bleak. "Everyone in Stebbins is infected."

CHAPTER FIFTY-SIX
MASON STREET NEAR DOLL FACTORY ROAD

"God," whispered JT in a sick voice, "they're coming."

Dez crept up beside him and peered around the corner of the mailbox. A hundred and fifty yards up the long slope of Doll Factory Road, emerging like ghosts from the gathering mist, came the creatures. Even from here, even without seeing their dead eyes or the wounds that had killed them, it was clear they were not people. Not anymore. They lumbered like animated scarecrows, their limbs stiff and awkward. It hurt Dez's heart to accept that these things existed at all. They were nightmare creatures; they didn't belong in the waking world. It hurt her worse that she knew so many of them, and would have to kill as many as she could.

She sniffed back tears. Beside her, JT banged his head on the cold metal of the mailbox. Once, again, and again. He stopped when a sob hitched in his chest.

Dez wrapped her arm around him and hugged him and for a moment they squatted there, foreheads pressed together, refugees in a world that no longer belonged to them.

"What *are* they?" he begged. "Are they people?"

She shook her head. "I don't know, Hoss. God, I really don't know."

The wind blew down the hill toward them and Dez watched it whip an empty plastic grocery bag past them. She followed it with her eyes and saw the lights of the diner. There were at least a dozen cars in the lot.

"We got a problem," she murmured and JT followed the line of her gaze.

"What?"

Dez chewed her lip, looking around. The intersection was on the very edge of town. There were a few decaying factories from the town's more prosperous era, including the crumbling remains of the factory that gave the road its name. There were other stores and businesses beyond the diner. If the creatures went that way it would be a slaughter. The southern end of the cross street, Mason, led only to a corn farm, and the farmhouse was two miles away. Six hundred yards to the north, right at a bend in the road, was Bell's Tools and Hardware. Even at this distance they could see half a dozen cars and pickup trucks in the lot, too.

"Talk to me, kid," said JT. The shambling mass of the dead was halfway down the hill.

"We can't let those things get to the diner," said Dez. "We have to stop them here until the staties get here."

"We can't," said JT. "We don't have the ammunition for that."

"Then we have to draw them away." She nudged him and nodded toward Bell's.

"There are people down there, too."

"Yeah, but Bell's is a blockhouse, solid as a rock. Not much past it, either. Just farms and no one's going to be planting seeds with this storm coming."

The rain was still only a drizzle and through the noise they could hear moans. Even with the slow gait of the creatures, the distance was closing fast. Not all of the dead were slow . . . a few loped along at an awkward run.

JT studied her for a moment. He flicked a glance at the shambling dead—still hundreds of yards away—and then at Bell's. Dez was right about the hardware store—it was a squat cinder block building with roll-down steel shutters. They could hold off the legions of hell in there.

"I don't want to die out here, Dez," JT said indecisively. "We have backup coming and we're not trained for this."

Dez said, "Give me a better plan."

He closed his eyes. "Fuck me."

Dez stood up from behind the mailbox. For a moment she stood there, waiting to be seen, but when the dead did not visibly react to her, she began waving her arms over her head. They kept coming. Maybe they had seen the two officers all along, or maybe it was that they could not show emotion, but there was no appreciable change in their speed.

"Fuck 'em," JT said again as he rose, laid the shotgun over the curved hump of the mailbox, and fired. At that distance the pellets did no harm, but instantly each of the dead swiveled their heads toward him.

"Yeah . . . that did it," said Dez.

The creatures began moving faster. Some could only stagger along on crippled limbs, but others—perhaps the more recently risen among them—began loping down the hill at a sloppy run.

"Oh . . . *shit!*"

Dez and JT said it at the same time, and then they were running north on Mason Street.

Dez was younger and could run like a gazelle. JT was fit for his age, but he was a lot older and heavier and had one knee that was a few years shy of needing a replacement. The rain was intensifying and brought with it a cloying, choking cold. JT was breathing hard before they covered the length of a football field. Dez had to slow down to let him keep place.

"The backup will be here soon," she said. "I want to draw these crazy fuckers into an isolated area so the staties can set up a proper kill zone."

"Jesus, Dez," JT puffed, "those are still people."

"You didn't seem to think so when you were putting buckshot into them, Hoss."

"That was different. That was self-defense."

Dez wiped rainwater out of her eyes. "The hell do you think this is?"

JT said nothing. Sweat and rainwater poured down his cheeks, and under his natural brown skin tone a furious red was blossoming. Dez noticed that he was slowing down, too. She turned and looked back.

The crowd of dead things was falling farther behind them. Some of them had not even rounded the corner from Doll Factory, and as the rain thickened it was harder to see them. They were still coming, though, Dez was sure of that. Whatever drove them was as powerful now as it was when they first attacked them at Doc Hartnup's.

"Thank God they're slow," she said.

JT nodded, unable to speak and run at the same time.

One of the cars pulled out of Bell's parking lot and turned their way. Dez and JT were running up the middle of the street, so the car slowed. Dez began waving her arms.

"Turn around!" she yelled. "Turn around!"

The driver pulled close and lowered her window, using a flat hand to shield her eyes from the stinging rain. It was Bid McGee, the woman who owned the craft shop in the center of town.

"Bid! Turn around and get the hell out of here. Go! Go!"

"Good lord, Desdemona Fox, what happened to you? Are you all right, dear?"

Dez gave her fender a savage kick. "Are you frigging deaf? I said turn the frigging car around and go the other frigging way, Bid, or I'll drag you out of there and beat the stupid off of your skinny ass."

Bid went white with shock and then purple with outrage, but turned her car around and then laid down thirty feet of rubber going the other way.

"Stupid cow," Dez snarled.

Despite everything, JT smiled. "You have a real way with people, Dez. Charm and poise and—"

"We're one half sentence away from me kneecapping you and leaving you here for those dead fuckers to eat."

"Point taken," he said, and they kept running. They didn't speak again until they reached Bell's parking lot. The rain was hammering them now and in the distance they could hear the angry growl of thunder. JT collapsed against the tailgate of a black Ford F-150. "I'll . . . I'll wait here. Keep an eye out . . ." He flapped a hand toward the door.

Dez lingered for a moment, "When did you go and get old on me, Hoss?"

He tried to grin, but it was a ghastly attempt.

Dez burst through the door and stopped inside. The store was bright with fluorescents and country music was playing on bad speakers mounted high on the wall. Thom Bell was behind the counter ringing up a purchase of black pipe for a construction worker. He and the customer both stared at her in surprise.

"Thom!" Dez snapped. "Listen to me. We have a problem. There's been some kind of outbreak. Very, very bad stuff. A bunch of infected people are on their way here and whatever they have is making them act all schizo. Help is on the way, but we need to keep everyone in here and lock this place down, and I mean right now."

Thom Bell asked only one question. "Is this some kind of terrorist thing?"

"Yes," lied Dez. "Now come on, I need you to—"

Bell was already in motion. He reached beneath the counter and flipped a switch to kill the music, and hit another to turn on the public address system. He told everyone in the store almost word for word what Dez had told him. One woman screamed, but the rest merely ran to the front of the store and started asking questions.

"Okay!" yelled Bell, "Now everyone listen up. We have a situation here. A terrorist situation. Officer Fox just told me that we need to secure this place and that's what we're going to do. I want all of the customers to go into the back. There's a staff locker room there with some chairs. You all just go in and sit down, and we'll secure the building. Nothing or no one is going to get into here, I can promise you that."

He spoke with absolute command; Dez knew that he had been a two-tour sergeant during the first Gulf War. He was a big man with a wind-raw face and calm eyes beneath the brim of his Snap-on Tools cap. A man to be taken seriously.

Dez watched the faces of the patrons and staff as Bell spoke. She saw the shock, the first wave of surprise and doubt, saw their eyes flick toward the door, but she also saw how Bell's commanding voice held them in place and, at least for the moment, emotionally in check.

"Chip," Bell said to one of the clerks, "you show everyone where to go. Scott, make sure the back door's locked. Drop the bar, too." Bell clapped his hands with the sound of a gunshot. Everyone jumped. "Let's go, let's go."

And they went, just like that. Bell told another employee to roll down the shutters.

"Thanks, Thom," said Dez, closing on him and lowering her voice.

He nodded, but his eyes probed hers. "Is help really on its way?"

"Yeah, and JT's outside."

Bell looked her up and down. "You're covered in blood, girl."

"I know—" she began, but he cut her off.

"No . . . I mean, is that infected blood?"

Dez opened and closed her mouth. "I . . ."

"Maybe you shouldn't get too close to anyone." To emphasize this he took a step back. "Now . . . tell me what's really happening?"

She shook her head. "I really don't know."

"Tell me what you do know."

She did, moving through it in quick, clipped sentences. As she laid it out, the whole thing sounded impossible to her and she'd lived through it. She watched for, and saw, the doubt grow in Bell's eyes.

There was a moment of pursed-lipped silence as he considered it. He went to the door and called out in a hushed voice. "JT . . . what's happening out there?"

Dez heard JT say, "Still coming. I can't see them but I can hear them."

"Better get inside," suggested Bell, and he held the door as JT hobbled inside, limping on his bad knee, and Bell closed the door behind him. The door was steel with only a small wire-mesh window the size of a piece of loose-leaf paper. The lock was a heavy dead bolt. Bell pounded his fist against the door to show how solid it was.

"Nothing short of a tank will get in here."

The clerks came up the aisles to assure Bell that the place was locked down. They wore identical expressions that were a mixture of fear and excitement.

"Okay," Bell said. "You boys go wait down with the customers. Keep everyone calm. Let them have whatever they want from the machines. Go on now."

Bell turned back to Dez and JT. "I have to say," he began slowly, "if it was just you telling me a story like this, Dez, I'd think you were on the sauce. No offense, but I've seen you at the bar enough to know that you don't mind knocking a few back."

Dez said nothing.

"But you, JT," Bell continued, "we've known each other for too many years, and I know that you're a serious man."

Being a "serious" person was a mark of distinction with Bell. Everyone knew it, and it was a label he only grudgingly awarded.

JT glanced at Dez. "You told him?"

"All of it," she agreed.

"Hell of a story," Bell said. "People turning into . . . into what? Some kind of ghouls? Eating each other? Marty Goss? Paul Scott?"

"The proof's on its way here, Thom," said Dez. "Want to go outside and see what they have to say?"

"Don't smart off at me, Dez," said Bell sternly. "This is my store and you brought this here to me. I did what you asked and secured the perimeter, but I have a right to ask questions."

Dez flushed. When the pressure was on it took effort for her not to be a smart-ass, and Bell wasn't the kind to accept it.

"Sorry," she said meekly.

"I know how crazy this sounds," said JT.

"Crazy about covers it," agreed Bell.

Dez said, "Why not take a look outside and you tell us what you think. I'm not joking, Thom."

Bell studied her for a few seconds. Before he did, he reached beneath the counter and removed a big .45 Colt Commander. "I have a permit," he said, though at the moment Dez wouldn't have cared if he'd produced a shoulder mounted antitank weapon. Bell quietly opened the small grilled window and peered out. Rain slashed at the door in waves.

He stared for several seconds. "Now that's disturbing," he said softly.

"That's what we've been telling you," said JT tightly.

Bell turned and gave them both a quizzical look, then he unlocked the door.

"What the hell are you *doing?*" demanded Dez, taking a step toward him.

Bell gave her a sad, disapproving shake of his head as he stepped back, raising both arms, holding the .45 with two fingers out and away from his body as a dozen men in black BDUs and helmets with ballistic shields came swarming into the store. They carried M16s and shotguns and nine millimeters and they were all yelling.

They took Thom Bell's gun away from him and pushed him to the floor.

A SWAT officer pointed a shotgun at Dez's face. "Officer Fox, you are under arrest. Hold your arms out from your side . . . do it now!"

"What the fuck are you assholes doing! We're police officers, goddamn it—"

Two officers closed on her, spinning her, taking her weapons, forcing her to the ground. JT bellowed like a bull, but he hit the deck next to her.

Dez knew every dirty trick in the book. She twisted as they forced her down and pulled one leg free and used it to kick one of her attackers in the shin. He crashed to the ground next to her, and suddenly there were six pairs of rough hands on her, slamming her chest-down onto the linoleum floor. Dez screamed and fought and cursed them to hell and back.

"Officer Fox," growled the SWAT sergeant, "I need you to shut up and stop resisting or I will tase you."

"Fuck you, you faggot! I'll shove that Taser right up your—"

She felt a sudden sting and then a prolonged, searing burn. Her whole body went rigid and then shuddered with convulsions as thirty thousand volts flooded through her.

The world went blood red and then velvet black. Dez tried to scream, she tried to fight, but all she could do was fall.

She heard JT calling her name from a million miles away.

She heard someone yell, "Catch her!"

She heard her own twisted scream.

She felt her head hit something. The counter, the floor—she couldn't tell—but it opened a big dark hole in the world and Dez Fox fell into it.

CHAPTER FIFTY-SEVEN

Trout shoved the pistol into the waistband of his jeans. He stood in front of Volker, looking down at the doctor with undisguised contempt. "Listen to me you piece of shit. We're going back to Stebbins. If one person is infected, if one single person dies because of what you did, I'll make sure every newspaper in the world runs this story with you as the villain."

Volker leaned back from Trout's intensity, but there was some defiance in his blue eyes. "You were there to report on a man being killed by pumping poison into his veins, Mr. Trout. You profit from such stories. The public loves to read of such things. Should I believe that you're naïve enough to think that we are not all monsters? Each in our own way."

"Save that crap for a jury, asshole."

"Or is it that you're so arrogant," Volker continued, "that you believe that your moral worldview supersedes all others? Can you tell me that you would not have executed Homer Gibbon, or even tortured him a little, knowing what you know of the horrors he inflicted on women and children?"

"Yeah, sure, I might have even enjoyed waterboarding the fucker," snarled Trout. "That's not the point. I wouldn't have risked using radioactive water to do it, though. There's revenge, and there's primal satisfaction, and then there's risking the health and wellbeing of others just to satisfy your own bloodlust. Don't try to put me on the same playing field as you, Volker. As far as I see it, with the destructive potential of what you shot in Gibbon, you are every bit as bad as Gibbon. You're every inch the monster he is."

Trout's blood roared in his ears.

Volker shook his head and turned away.

"I hope you rot in hell," Trout whispered.

Then he turned and ran for the door. Goat lingered a moment longer, staring at Volker but unable to express the horrors that screamed in his head. He spat on the floor in front of the doctor, then followed Trout.

The Explorer roared down the lane, burning through the rainwater to leave skid marks on the asphalt. Trout and Goat both had their cell phones out, punching numbers as fast as they could.

In the wreck of a Stebbins County police cruiser, lost under a seat amid a jumble of spent shell casings, Dez Fox's cell phone began ringing. The ringtone was from a Dwight Yoakum tune. The phone rang four times and then went to voice mail.

Dez's message was: "You got the machine. Leave a message and a number. If I don't call back, your message wasn't interesting."

When Trout heard the call go to voice mail, his heart juddered in his chest. "Come on, Dez . . . come on."

At the beep, he said, "Dez, I need you to call me back right away." He paused, trying to word a message that she wouldn't immediately delete. "I got a reliable tip that someone infected with a dangerous disease is in town. Call me now!"

He clicked off and tried JT. Straight to voice mail. He left a similar message, hung up, and called Marcia.

The phone rang three times. Four . . . and then she answered.

"Marcia!"

"Oh . . . Christ . . . Billy . . ." she said. Her voice was weak and she was breathing too fast and too hard. It sounded like she was having sex. "Billy . . . God . . ."

"Marcia, what's wrong? What's going on there?"

"Billy . . . I tried calling 9-1-1. They . . . they didn't answer . . ."

"*Marcia!*"

"It hurts, Billy . . . oh my god . . . it hurts so bad. I can't stop the bleeding . . ."

The line abruptly went dead.

Trout screamed into the phone. Nothing. He redialed, and got nothing. No voice mail. Not even a ring.

"What was that?" demanded Goat, his eyes filled with fear.

"Marcia. She was hurt. She said she was bleeding and then the line went dead." He looked at the phone display. "Says the number is unavailable."

"Oh shit. I called my roommate," said Goat. "He started to say something about hearing sirens and some gunshots, then nothing. You think the storm knocked the lines down? Or . . . ?"

Trout cut him a brief, savage look. "Try the police."

Goat hit 9-1-1 and got the regional dispatcher. He put it on speaker and asked to be patched through to Stebbins County. He expected to hear Flower's voice. Instead a stern male voice said, "Sir, what is the nature of your emergency?"

Instead of asking about the nature of the emergency, the operator asked for his location. Trout hung up.

"What'd you do that for?" asked Goat.

"That was the military," said Trout. "I'd bet my ass on it. They're intercepting all the calls to Stebbins police."

"Oh, shit," said Goat softly. "Oh shit."

Trout cut in and out of traffic. Cars blared horns at him but he didn't even slow down long enough to give the finger. His heart was racing faster than the engine.

Goat licked his lips. "The military . . . that's good, right? I mean . . . ?" His voice trailed off. A moment later he said, "We're in deep shit."

"I know," said Trout, and he stepped down harder on the gas.

CHAPTER FIFTY-EIGHT
WOLVERTON REGIONAL HOSPITAL

"Where is he?"

Irene Compton, the desk nurse, looked up at the intern, who looked about a year younger than her daughter. "Pardon?" asked the nurse with a half smile.

The intern, a petite redhead who could not possibly be out of high school let alone a medical student, was not smiling. "Patient in Sixteen. Chart says he presented with a bite?"

"Oh, that's Mr. Wieland. One of the farmers picked him up at a gas station and brought him in. We took vitals and put him in . . . um. . . ." She punched a few keys on the computer. "Yup . . . in sixteen."

The intern, whose name tag read Slattery, narrowed her eyes. "No, he's not in sixteen. I just came from sixteen. There's no one there."

Nurse Compton kept her smile in place. She was well aware that she looked matronly and these interns usually started thinking of her as a mom figure. "Maybe he went to the bathroom."

Dr. Slattery turned and stalked away. No thanks, no nothing. Nurse Compton watched her slim figure retreat down the hall. "Bitch," she said quietly.

Dr. Gail Slattery pushed through the double doors leading to the emergency unit. There were two central nurses stations surrounded by rows of curtained bays. Each bay was marked with a number that was painted on the floor and stamped onto a bright plastic disk mounted on the ceiling just outside the curtain tracks. She stomped past bays eleven through fifteen. Most of them were unoccupied. Fourteen had a broken hip, fifteen had a seventeen-year-old skateboarder. Sixteen was supposed to be the bite victim, but wasn't. The room was a mess, too. Bloodstains on the sheets, pillow on the floor. Open suture kit sitting on a chair.

She snorted and kept going, peering into bay seventeen, also empty, and eighteen, probable torn ACL. The last bay, nineteen, was next to the bathroom. The patient in nineteen was one that Slattery had already seen. Mona Greene. A geriatric with chest pains. Woman was ninety-three, a smoker, and had a history of angina, emphysema, and congestive heart failure dating back to the Clinton presidency. It was a wonder she was alive, let alone able to drive herself here about once every three months for "chest pressure."

The curtains were drawn, and Dr. Slattery parted them for a quick peek.

She was about to say something, but she froze, her lips parted.

Mrs. Greene was there, sure enough . . . but so was Mr. Wieland. He was bent over the old woman, and for an odd moment Gail Slattery thought that the man was kissing her. Or whispering something in her ear.

He wasn't.

Dr. Slattery gasped.

Mr. Wieland heard the small sound and his head jerked up, eyes darting toward the part in the curtains. His roved over the curtains, not lingering for even a moment on the narrow part. Those eyes were completely empty.

His mouth, however, was full.

Red bubbled on his lips and ran in lines down his cheeks and over his chin and splashed on the ivy pattern of the Wolverton Hospital patient gowns. Mr. Wieland's mouth worked and worked, and even across the twelve feet that separated them, Dr. Slattery could hear the sucking, smacking sounds as his teeth chewed on what he had taken from old Mona Greene.

Dr. Slattery should have backed quietly away. She should have cleared the area and called security. She should have called the police. She did none of those things. Instead, Gail Slattery did the one thing that she should not have done.

She screamed.

Mr. Wieland's eyes snapped back toward her and now he did see the narrow part. And the eye that looked through it. His lips curled back from his teeth and he dropped the remains of the sticklike arm he'd held.

With a howl of insatiable hunger, a hunger not at all satisfied by all that he had consumed, Mr. Wieland rushed around the bed straight toward Dr. Slattery. She screamed and screamed. She screamed as long as she could. As long as she was able.

CHAPTER FIFTY-NINE
MAGIC MARTI IN THE MORNING
WNOW RADIO, MARYLAND

"This is Magic Marti at the mike with new tidbits for travelers. Well, it's official, campers . . . the cow manure has hit the fan. We got a major storm clamped down over the region. Airports and bus terminals are shut down. Schools are closed and all nonessential activities have been canceled all across our listening area. And there's still some police activity on Doll Factory Road in Stebbins. And we have uncon-firmed reports of an incident at Wolverton Hospital on the Stebbins-Bordentown border. No details yet except that state police are on the scene. And . . . one more thing, kids. I know that big storms are kind of fun in a haunted house, roller-coaster ride sort of way, but this is serious business. Folks are out there dealing with this. Police, fire, and rescue units are going to be pushed to the limit, so please . . . no more of the crank calls about monsters eating people. Aunt Marti likes a good prank as much as the next gal, but c'mon guys . . . now's not the time."

CHAPTER SIXTY
THE FOREST
STEBBINS COUNTY, PENNSYLVANIA

Hartnup moved through the woods a dozen yards from the road, par-alleling Doll Factory, heading toward Mason Street. He had no con-trol over where his body went, just as he had no idea where it was going. There were more like him in the woods. Some close enough to see, others merely gray shapes in the rain. Some headed in the same direction, drawn by some force beyond Hartnup's perception; others walked across his path, going north or south or east, drawn by other needs, other calls.

The body around him moved stiffly, and he could still feel it. The hoped-for rigor mortis was upon him now, slowing him, making his limbs move like stilts . . . but they kept moving. It hurt, too. No hu-man before could ever appreciate the terrible, ceaseless pain of rigor. He knew the science and that was no comfort. The pain was going to get worse and worse. It was a process that starts as soon as respiration ceases. Muscles begin an inevitable and irreversible contraction. It was worse than a charley horse, worse than stomach cramps. It was everywhere at once and each jarring step sent nerve flashes through the dying muscles.

Hartnup's world was pain. He tried screaming to endure it, but there was no way to escape this hell. All he could do was experience it.

This is hell, he thought, *I've died and now I'm in hell.*

His body moved like a badly managed puppet, and there, beneath the pain, was something far worse. Something that burst through the cracks of agony in each contracting muscle.

Hunger.

That hunger was so big that Hartnup could not grasp its dimensions. It was the god of this thing.

The hunger was all.

And all was hunger.

The dead body in which he floated staggered on, heading down a slope, away from the road, heading into the farmland. To where the food was.

CHAPTER SIXTY-ONE
MASON STREET NEAR DOLL FACTORY ROAD

Dez woke up in the backseat of the state police cruiser. She was alone, JT was nowhere to be seen. Her hands were cuffed and her head hurt like she'd been kicked by a horse. She had been slumped over as far as the seat belt would allow, now she straightened, and just that little bit of movement sent a wave of nausea sloshing through her head and guts.

"What the hell happened?" she growled.

The windshield wipers slapped back and forth. The trooper in the front ignored her.

Dez kicked the back of the seat. "Yo! Fuckface! I asked you a question."

Without turning, the trooper said, "I can pull over to the side of the road and tase you again, Officer Fox. Or you can behave yourself and wait until we get to your station."

"Is that where you're taking me?"

"Yes."

"Why the hell didn't you just say so? Whatever happened to professional courtesy?"

He made a sound. She thought it was a snort of laughter. She kicked the seat again.

"Hey!" he barked.

"Why did you ass-monkeys tase me in the first place? And who hit me in the head?"

"You struck your head on the counter when you fell. An accident . . . and I'm sorry about that. Doesn't look serious though."

"Feels pretty goddamn serious," she snarled. Dez considered throwing up on the screen. That would make her stomach feel better and would really piss this guy off. But she didn't. Instead, she asked, "What the shit is going on here?"

"You've been arrested, Officer Fox. I'd have thought that was clear. Even to you."

"What the hell is that supposed to mean?"

He didn't answer. Dez looked at her cuffed wrists. For most prisoners the chain of the cuffs would be threaded through a D ring on the floor, but they had given her the smallest slice of courtesy by cuffing her hands in front of her without attaching her to the ring. Even so, the rear doors were reinforced and could not be opened from inside. The wire mesh cage separating front from rear seat was heavy grade, and she wasn't going to kick her way through it.

Dez looked out the rain-slick window. They were halfway across the county from the hardware store, just a couple of miles from the center of town. Stebbins was a tiny community on a massive piece of land. The "town" proper was one traffic light long. Three blocks in one direction, two in the other, and all of it clustered around a Baptist church and the public safety office—which served as the police station, post office, fire station, municipal offices, mayor's office, and various other one-person offices. The next biggest building in town was a Bean-O's coffee shop, a greasy spoon with aspirations of Starbuckshood.

Even on its best days Stebbins was a ghost town. The only thing that kept Stebbins from drying up and blowing away was some state and federal money for a regional elementary school that occupied the northwest corner of the township and a slightly smaller regional middle school a few miles away from the town proper—and the county hospital whose campus shared real estate with Bordentown.

They stopped at a crossroads to allow four yellow school buses to pass, heading from the middle school toward the shelter of Stebbins Little School. Dez craned her neck to look at the buses, at the pale, frightened faces pressed to each window. One of the kids, a little girl with yellow curls, waved to her. Dez waved back, needing to lift both hands to do it. Then the buses turned onto Schoolhouse Lane and were gone into the swirling gray wind.

"Where's my partner?" Dez asked.

"You'll see him at the station," said the trooper.

"What's going on? We're the frigging police, or were you too busy looking at my tits to read the wording on my badge?"

"Don't flatter yourself."

"Fuck you and answer the question. Why arrest us?"

"You'll have to discuss that with Lieutenant Hardy."

"How about you stop being a total prick and tell me. What happened back there? Did you stop them?"

Nothing.

"Did you fucking stop them?"

"Stop whom?"

"What the Christ do you mean, 'stop whom'? There were fifty of those things in the middle of the street. You had to have driven right through them."

"I think we should get to the station and you should listen to your Miranda rights before you say anything, Officer Fox. And that *is* professional courtesy."

"What?"

"I don't like seeing another cop in cuffs, and I don't know what happened out there or why you did what you did," he said, "but you need to have a lawyer in the room and your rights on record. That's me talking here, cop to cop."

Dez stared at the back of his head. The impossibility of the day had slid sideways into the surreal and she sputtered, trying to find a route of logic that would take her back onto firmer ground. She suddenly stiffened.

"You didn't even *see* them . . . did you?"

"See who?" he demanded again.

"Christ." Dez tried to think it through. JT said that they were coming up the road, but he'd been hunkered down behind the pickup truck, and everyone else was in the store. The rain was getting heavy and it was dark as the devil's asshole out there. Maybe that was it, she thought. Maybe those things lacked the brain power or imagination to seek out prey unless they saw it or heard it. Or smelled it. Walking uphill toward an empty road in a downpour, they might not have had anything to go on.

So . . . where did they go?

There was forest on both sides of Mason. Forest with farmland beyond it. She tried to remember if you could smell the farm animals from Mason. Probably. You could always smell cow shit.

"Did anyone go to the crime scene at Hartnup's?"

The trooper shook his head. "You really don't want to do this now."

"Yes, I fucking well do, because you have me cuffed in the back of your cruiser when I should be out there. Somebody's made a big goddamn mistake and we'd better do something before it bites us all in the ass . . . and that is not a frigging joke. Now pull over, undo these cuffs, and put me on the radio with someone who doesn't have his own dick in his ear."

The trooper sighed. "I'm sorry," he said.

"For what?"

"For whatever happened to you. For whatever's wrong with you. I heard you were a fuckup off the job, but I always heard that you were pretty good on the clock. What happened? No . . . wait. Save that for when we're doing this right. I don't think I want to hear it."

Dez leaned as far forward as the cuffs would allow. "What's your name?" she asked.

There was no need for him to stonewall her on that, so he answered, "Trooper Brian Saunders."

"Trooper Saunders. Good. Brian. I've seen you around. People call me Dez."

"I know."

"I don't know how or why they think that I'm responsible for anything that's happened today, but I want you to hear me on this. I was protecting the public at all times. I was defending myself at all times. I am not irrational, and I have committed no crimes."

"Okay." His tone was neither encouraging nor dismissive. Merely an acknowledgement that he heard her.

"There are people out there who *are* acting irrationally. They're sick, possibly as a result of a chemical agent or some kind of toxin. It might be a disease. I don't know. Whatever it is, it hits hard and it hits fast. I saw it hit one of the locals. Kid named Diviny from Bordentown PD. Diviny went apeshit and attacked fellow officers. We restrained him and my partner, Sergeant JT Hammond, and I transported him to the hospital. This is a matter of record. Check with the hospital. Immediately after that we received a call from dispatch to return to the Hartnup crime scene. Dispatch said that people were killing each other. Understand that? Killing each other. Whatever this thing is, it must have spread. That dispatch call is also a matter of record. Call the station. Talk to Flower, she's the dispatcher. Let her play the tape."

Saunders said nothing. The sound of the windshield wipers seemed unnaturally loud.

"When my partner and I arrived at the scene we were attacked by the infected. Some of those infected were police officers, including state troopers. We tried everything—verbal control, beanbag rounds—and then the situation forced us up a rung on the force continuum, so we defended ourselves to the best of our abilities and training. As any cops would. As you would, Brian."

Saunders was shaking his head, but he didn't say anything.

"Brian . . ." Dez pleaded. "Please. Just check."

"They are checking," said Saunders with exasperation. "They did check, and that's not how we're reading the scene. We didn't find any 'infected.' All we found was evidence that two officers went batshit and began killing people. Killing cops. We found Chief Goss with half his head blown off. Burn marks around the wound look like the barrel was right against his flesh. His own gun was still in its holster. How would a cop let someone get that close unless he knew the person?"

"He was infected!"

"Uh-huh."

"What about the hospital? Have your people talked to them? Dr. Sengupta?"

"I don't know anything about that."

"At least let me talk to—"

"Hey! Watch out!" Saunders suddenly yelled and turned the wheel violently to the right as a pregnant woman stepped out from behind a farmworker bus that was parked on the shoulder of the road. The fender of the cruiser missed her by an inch and Dez screamed in the back seat, sure that the woman was going to be smashed.

"God*damn*!" Saunders stamped down on the brakes and the cruiser slewed sideways on the wet asphalt, kicking up a wave of dirty rainwater. Dez was thrown forward as the car rocked to a jarring stop. Saunders jerked open the door handle. "Stupid bitch."

"Don't!" cried Dez, but Saunders ignored her as he got out. Rain chopped in through the open door. Dez twisted around in the seat to see what was happening. The pregnant woman was looking the wrong way, but she had stopped in the middle of the road; her hair hung in wet rattails and her clothing was disheveled.

Saunders crammed his Smokey the Bear hat on his head, hunched his shoulders against the cold rain, and stomped toward her, his back rigid with anger and stress, one stiffened finger jabbing the air as he yelled at her.

Dez knew this was all wrong even before the woman turned.

It was wrong because the day was wrong. Because the world was wrong. Because everything was wrong.

"Don't . . ." she said, her voice much smaller. She knew that the moment was already rolling downhill.

The woman turned just as Saunders reached her. Her body was heavy with a late-term pregnancy. Her dress was a pretty farm country frock with a cornflower pattern. She was young, maybe twenty-five, with long blond hair. She had dark eyes and nearly every scrap of meat had been torn from her face and mouth.

Saunders juddered to a stop. Frozen by what he was seeing. By the impossibility of someone so badly injured still standing.

Through the open front driver's door Dez could hear the patter of raindrops on the wide brim of his hat. She heard him begin to say, "Jesus Christ. Lady, are you—"

"Don't!" Dez's shriek bounced off the closed windows of the cruiser.

And then the woman was on him. She lunged at him with small, pale hands. Her lipless mouth opened wide and white teeth streaked with black blood snapped forward.

Dez screamed.

A geyser of blood shot ten feet above Brian Saunders's head.

Dez screamed and screamed. She kicked the screen; she threw her shoulder against the door.

Saunders's legs buckled and he dropped to his knees as the woman bent over him, her teeth locked on the side of his throat.

There was movement on the bus. Beside the bus. Behind the bus.

More of them.

A busload of them.

They converged on the trooper and dragged him to the asphalt.

Dez screamed one more time. And then she tried to stop it, realizing far too late what that scream would do.

Several of the things looked up from their unspeakable feast. Looked in the direction of the scream. Looked at her.

"Don't . . ." Dez whispered softly as one by one a dozen of the monsters rose from the thrashing body and shambled toward the cruiser. The front driver door was open. Dez was in cuffs. She twisted around and popped the catch on her seat belt, but there was no way out of that car. She was trapped.

No . . . she was preserved. Meat in a locker.

"Don't . . ." Dez begged, even though Saunders was long past hearing her. "Don't leave me . . ."

They shuffled toward her.

There was no need for silence now.

Dez screamed again, and again.

CHAPTER SIXTY-TWO
AROUND STEBBINS COUNTY

"What scares you?"

The waitress working the counter at Murphy's Diner looked up from the coffee she was pouring. This wasn't the first odd question this customer had asked. He was a thriller writer and he had been round annoying other customers with questions for the last couple of days. Today he was the only one crazy enough to brave the storm.

"Slow days and bad tippers," she said.

The writer smiled. He was a blocky man with white hair and a gray mustache that was at odds with a youthful face. He wore an expensive leather jacket over a sweatshirt that had the emblem for the Northern Illinois Huskies college football team.

"Serious question," persisted the writer. He fished in his pocket and laid a business card on the counter and pushed it toward the waitress. The card read SHANE GERICKE. The waitress, who wore a white plastic name tag with SHIRL on it, picked up the card and flipped it over. On the back was a full-color picture of his latest novel.

"*Torn Apart*," she read, then set the card down. "I don't read horror novels."

"It's not a horror novel," said Gericke as he poured cream into his coffee. "I write thrillers."

"What's the difference?"

"No monsters."

"Then who's tearing who apart?"

"Serial killers, mass murderers. No vampires, no werewolves, nothing like that."

The waitress made one of those faces that suggested that she wasn't likely to be interested in anything this guy wrote about. At least, not until she saw how well he tipped. If he dropped twenty percent or better, then she'd be a lot more interested next time. She knew a couple of writers. They were always broke. Only people who tipped worse were college students.

"You ready to order?" she asked, setting the pot down and pulling her order pad from her apron.

"If I do, will you answer the question?"

"You taking a poll?"

"I'm researching a book. The lead character in my novels is out here from Illinois to participate in a multistate manhunt for a killer. I'm trying to get a sense of what people are like here. Moods, politics, relationships, personalities."

"Why not just make it up?"

He shrugged, blew across his coffee cup, sipped, and set it down. "Better to draw on real life."

"Small-town color," she said, "is that it? Make sure the hicks are properly redneck and uneducated?"

Gericke laughed. "I grew up in the burbs outside of Chicago. Not exactly 'big town.' And, no, I'm not profiling everyone as a redneck. It takes all kinds of people to make a town. There's no one 'type.'" He ticked his head toward the street outside. "I've met some interesting people so far. Chief Goss, a reporter named Trout, and—"

"Billy Trout? You met him?" Shirl managed a smile for that. Without the smile she looked north of fifty and off the radar for personality vitality, but the smile dropped fifteen years from her and chipped away a lot of the gray clay that seemed to have been built around her.

"You know him?"

Shirl gave him the kind of laugh that said that she not only "knew" Billy Trout, but could tell you stories.

"He comes in here every now and then," she said with a wonderfully coquettish slant of her eyes that made Gericke smile. He'd already planned to base a character on Trout, but he was starting to sniff a juicy subplot about the seedy newsman with a soul and the lonely but still sexy diner waitress. Maybe she pines for the guy, or maybe she's the one that got away. Something like that. Gericke knew he could take that and run with it. Put some desperate sweat-in-the-dark sex into the book.

"I'm planning on writing him into the novel," said Gericke. "Not under his name, of course, but a character based on him."

Shirl laughed. "Well, that wouldn't be a stretch, mister, 'cause Billy is a character."

At the other end of the diner the door opened and a man in a rain-soaked hoodie stepped inside.

"Damn, Sonny, close the door!" yelled Shirl, then she dropped her voice and in a confidential tone said to Gericke, "Speaking of characters. This one never did have enough brain cells to know when to come in out of the rain."

Gericke hid a smile behind his coffee cup as he turned to look at the man. He couldn't see Sonny's face, but he was still standing in the doorway, his foot propping the door open. Rain was already pooling on the red tile floor.

"Come on, Sonny," barked Shirl in a voice used to yelling out orders during packed lunch crowds of truckers. "In or out. Jeez . . . were you born in a damn barn?"

Sonny took a step forward, and Gericke frowned. The man moved heavily, awkwardly. Drunk, this early in the day? He figured he could get some mileage out of a character like that, too.

The door swung shut as Sonny took another couple of steps into the diner. He turned right and left as if uncertain of where he was.

"Come on and sit down," said Shirl, affection tempering her annoyance. "Get some hot coffee into you before you catch your . . . *death*?" Her last word came out crooked and weak because at that moment Sonny lifted his head and the fluorescents washed away the shadows inside his hood. Gericke froze. The face inside the hood was two-toned: wax white and dark red. The skin was bloodless, but blood poured down from a ruin of a mouth and between broken teeth.

"Holy Christ!" yelled Shirl. She grabbed a clean towel and hurried down the counter as she yelled over her shoulder for Gericke to call the police. "Sonny . . . good lord, what happened to you? Were you in an accident?"

She came around the end of the counter, raising the hand with the towel, her face showing both a clear revulsion and a take-charge strength. Sonny staggered toward her, reaching out as if to accept the towel. Or a hug. Or . . .

"No . . ." said Gericke. The word escaped his mouth before he knew why he said it. A visceral, instinctive reaction. Then he said it louder as he came off his stool. "No!"

Shirl flicked a confused look at him.

Sonny leaped at her, slamming her back against the counter, his fingers tangling in her hair, pulling her head back, stretching her throat wide and pale. There was a scream, a deep moan, and then a flash of bright red that shot all the way to the overhead lights.

By then Gericke was moving, running down the length of the empty diner. He had no weapon, he was not a fighter, but none of that mattered. He dove at Sonny like a defensive tackle, knocking the man sideways, breaking the ugly contact between him and Shirl. Hot blood sprayed the side of his face and as he bore Sonny to the ground, Gericke heard the wet, choking, burbling sound as Shirl tried to speak. In a weirdly disjointed and detached part of his brain, Gericke wondered what the dying waitress needed to say so badly that she would try and force the words out through a torn windpipe. He would like to have put that in his next book.

He and Sonny crashed to the floor and suddenly all thoughts of writing and dialogue and curious characters were swept away. The only thing on Gericke's mind then was keeping those red-smeared teeth away from his own throat.

He never heard the door open. Did not hear the wind and rain whip in, or the slap of slow, shuffling feet on the soaked red tiles of the diner.

Nick Pulsipher hated the place. The motel had been seedy when it was built back in the seventies and it had lost ground since. On the best nights he got a couple of decent family types looking to break up a long drive in a cheap room. Once in a while there were some bikers worth talking to. Sometimes even somebody from his home state of Nevada—people who had actually heard of Henderson, where he grew up. Though never anyone from Caliente, where he'd lived before moving east to this place. Nick thought that it might be an upward move, going from desk clerk to manager in the same chain of roach motels; but after three years here it was his opinion that if Caliente was the absolute asshole of America, then Stebbins was the "taint." As career moves go, this one wasn't going into the history books.

At least the motel office had cable, if the storm didn't knock that out. The lights had already flickered and he wouldn't have bet a torn dollar bill on making it through the night with lights, power, and cable all intact.

The rain was like a constant animal roar. The customers in the six rented rooms might as well have been on the moon. He hoped none of them needed anything from him. Nick did not want to go out in this shit. Winds like that, you don't hold on to something, next thing you know you're wearing ruby slippers and skipping down a yellow brick road.

He went around the counter and peered out through the window. The awning kept the rain from hitting the glass, but even with that it was hard to see all the way across the parking lot. The Crescent Motel was actually built like a blocky letter *C*, and Nick could see lights glowing in a few windows. And one doorway. Nick bent closer. Yep, the door to Unit 18 at the far end was wide open, and the damn wind was blowing that way.

"Son of a bitch," he muttered. The carpet would be soaked, and when it dried it would smell like old underwear. He saw three people run in through the open door, but with the failing light and the rain it was hard to make out who they were. 18 was rented by a woman traveling with her grown daughter, heading to Washington, D.C., for some political thing. At least that's what they told Nick during check-in. One-nighters. All well and good, but not if that one night left him with a soaked carpet and a mother of a cleanup job.

He saw two more people come out of the rain and enter the unit. Then another. And another.

"What the hell are they doing over there?"

What was it? Some kind of party to celebrate the storm? Ditzy broads.

The carpet was going to be ruined. That came out of his maintenance budget. His bonuses were based on a percentage of the budget leftover at the end of the month. Replacing carpets for a whole unit was going to cut that down to chicken shit.

Nick debated what to do. Call them or go the hell over there?

He called.

The phone rang and rang. He slammed down the phone, looked up their cell number on the register card, and called that. It rang three times and went right to voice mail.

"Shit." He grabbed his raincoat off the peg behind the counter and pulled it on, then crammed a Pirates baseball cap down hard on his head. Even with that he knew he was going to get soaked, but he was so mad that he didn't care.

He pushed the door open and had to force it closed against the claws of the wind; then he hunched his shoulders and bent into the blow, trudging through the rain like a man walking through mud. The gale winds were intense and the rain was numbingly cold. By the time he was halfway across the parking lot he was drenched, with lines of water running down inside his clothes. Rain pelted his face with the stinging force of hail, and runoff dripped from the tips of his long chin beard. Through squinted eyes he could see the crowd of people gathered at the open door, some of them inside Unit 18, some outside.

None of them had umbrellas or rain hats. They stood in the rain like they didn't give a shit and Nick was twenty yards away from then when that fact started to bother him.

He was ten yards away when he realized that everyone was chewing. They stood with their hands cupped and held to their mouths, each one totally absorbed in whatever they were eating.

"The hell—"

What was this? Some kind of crazy storm tailgate party? Beer and ribs and . . . ?

He was five yards away when he realized that he was wrong. About the nature of the gathering. About the menu. About everything. The people closest to him raised their faces from their meals and stared at him with eyes that were far too dark and mouths that were far too red.

Nick was three yards away when he stopped walking and turned to run.

That was two yards too late.

Jillian Weiner felt the darkness closing in. The calm-down drugs were taking her below the level of pain and stress, and soon the big, dark, soft wave of anesthesia would roll over her and she would go down into a sweet nothingness. She wouldn't feel the scalpel as the doctors went in and removed her appendix. Who needs an appendix anyway? She knew that there would be pain when she woke up, and more pain during the recovery, but for now . . . it felt like rolling down a hill that was lined with silk and covered with pillows.

Sounds were becoming muted, distorted, softened so that they made little sense other than as background noise. She could hear the doctor and the nurses speaking, and even understand snatches of what they said, but if it made any sense to Jillian, she was too deep to care.

". . . the hell's going on out there . . . ?"

". . . someone's hurt out in the hall . . ."

". . . oh my God . . . my God!"

". . . please . . . oh, sweet Jesus . . . please, don't let it in here . . ."

The screams became the cries of seagulls over a lazy beach. Even when blood splashed her, it was nothing more than salt spray from the summer waves.

It's nice down here, she thought. So sweet, so soft . . .

Jillian felt hands on her. Nurses? Doctors? Who cared?

She couldn't exactly remember what a doctor was.

Or why she was here.

The darkness was flowing around her, filling up the room. The figures that moved around her were painted in tones of mint green and bright red. Then the colors swirled as she went deeper, and deeper.

She felt the others hands, the colder hands, on her. But she didn't care.

She felt the dull pinch of teeth. That registered as pain, but as far away, on a shelf, over there, somewhere else.

As Jillian's eyes closed, as the anesthesia took her all the way down, she had one last glimpse of the room. A doctor with an Indian face and eyes filled with blood, bending toward her stomach. Another pinch, another bite.

The anesthesia pulled her under and she was smiling as Dr. Sengupta, the nurses, and several patients gathered around her gurney and devoured her.

CHAPTER SIXTY-THREE
MASON STREET NEAR DOLL FACTORY ROAD

The dead moved toward the cruiser. Trooper Saunders had stopped screaming by now. Dez's screams died slowly in her throat as she stared through the rain-smeared window at the monsters. Most of them were clustered around the body, but the rest were coming her way.

Oh God, oh God, oh God, oh God . . .

There was no way out.

The rain was getting heavier by the moment, obscuring the window, making it hard to see what they were doing.

"Shit," Dez breathed and immediately slid down off the seat, crammed herself into the footwell and tried to disappear. The rain was so loud she could not even hear the moans of the dead.

Please please please . . .

Then she heard the driver's door creak against its hinge. She dared not look. Above her, around her, there were soft sounds. Hands touching. Bodies bumping without force against the skin of the cruiser.

Dez held her breath.

They can't see me down here. Not through the rain on the windows.

The thin hiss of fingernails on wet glass and dripping metal.

They can't smell me. The rain stinks of earth and manure and ozone.

The vehicle rocked as someone . . . something entered it.

Please, God . . . they don't know I'm here.

The rain was so loud. It drowned everything out. Dez willed it to drown her out. The air began to burn in her lungs.

JT . . . where are you?

Outside there was a whishing sound as another vehicle drove by, and then a change in sound as it slowed.

"Hey!" called a voice. "Are you . . . oh, Jesus Christ!"

The scream of tires. Turning, turning, burning as the water on the blacktop evaporated and the rubber smoked. A higher shriek as the tires found purchase, the roar of the engine as the car accelerated away.

Then nothing but the rain. So much. So heavy.

It fell and fell. A steady thunder on the roof and the rear windshield. Cold and wet breeze coming in through the open door.

But beneath the rain . . . nothing.

Dez had to let the breath out. It was a fireball behind her sternum.

She let it out open mouthed. Slow, forcing her throat open wide. No stricture, no sound. Exhale it all out. Hold. Wait. Inhale. Silent.

God . . . don't let them hear me.

She waited for the dead-limp hands to start beating on the glass. She turned her head an inch and peered up, wanting to see and terrified to see the worm-white fingers poke through the grille.

Waited. Watched.

Dez breathed as silent as a ghost while she waited for the dead to come for her, to take her, to devour her.

She didn't have her gun. Saunders had taken it. If they got to her, if they infected her, there was not going to be a way out. No exit strategy. No fast ride on the night train. She would die, and be consumed, and . . .

. . . God, please don't let me be a monster.

God, please.

Please.

Please.

Mommy, please . . .

. . . Daddy . . .

Please . . .

The rain hammered down and the wind blew.

And she waited to die.

CHAPTER SIXTY-FOUR
MAGIC MARTI IN THE MORNING
WNOW RADIO, MARYLAND

"This is Magic Marti at the mike and we are in a world of hurt out there. The storm is parked over Stebbins County and we're seeing torrential rains and gale-force winds. Small and moderate streams are flooding, and we're getting reports of road washouts. Telephone and cell lines are taking a beating from the storm, which seems to have knocked out communication with local police and fire. That's the bad news, and I wish I had some good news to throw at you, campers. If you can hear my voice, then get to high ground, lock your doors, and we'll ride this out together."

CHAPTER SIXTY-FIVE
CONROY'S ACRES

Selma Conroy said nothing as Homer Gibbon paced back and forth across the dining room floor. He was agitated, his eyes jumpy, his fingers twitching. Every step was an awkward lurch as he fought the increasing stiffness in his muscles.

"He lied to me," Homer snarled. "He lied to me. To *me*."

He turned and swept his arm across the table, knocking dishes and stacks of magazines and a week's worth of mail onto the floor with a crash. Homer slammed his fists down on the tabletop and leaned on them, shaking his head slowly back and forth.

"I thought he understood."

Selma said nothing. Magazines and unpaid bills littered the floor around her like fallen leaves.

Homer stopped moving and looked down at his hands. They were caked with blood. They were cold hands, pale and . . .

. . . dead.

That's what Volker had told him.

You are a dead, damned thing. The doctor's words down the phone line. Venomous and filled with betrayal. Not the voice of the Red Mouth at all.

He held his right hand up to his eye, studying it. The flesh did not look right. Even apart from the scratches and blood, it looked wrong. On a deeper, more troubling level.

Wrong.

His skin . . . *moved.* Like the way flesh crawls when it contracts in the cold. Or when there is so much fear the skin wants to retreat from it.

Like that. Only . . . not like that at all.

It rippled. As if something were moving just below the surface.

He could barely feel it, though. His arms and legs were stiff and sore. Everything hurt. It was all he could do not to scream with each step.

You are dead.

Dead.

A damned thing.

The doctor had done something to him. Volker had admitted it. He'd thrown some scientific bullshit at him. Parasites and crap like that. The doctor had actually tried to hit with some shit about vodou.

Dead.

Homer pressed his left forefinger to the back of his right hand. The flesh trembled with a sensation like squirming.

"Oh God fuck me," whispered Homer. "What the fuck did you do to me?"

I damned you, Mr. Gibbon. I damned you to suffering so that you'll understand.

"Yeah, well fuck that, Doc." Homer's voice was hoarse. "I already know. I've known all my life. The Black Eye shows me everything. The Red Mouth tells me everything I need to know. Maybe you fooled it, you cocksucker, but the Red Mouth will whisper to you. Oh, hell yes and no doubt about it. Ain't that right, Auntie?"

Selma said nothing.

"But what did you do to me, you Frankenstein fuck?"

He pressed thumbnail against his skin. Below the surface it felt like something popped. Something wet and small. Setting his teeth in a grin that was wired in place by pain and hatred, Homer pressed his nail into the skin, rubbing it back and forth until it made a pale groove. Not a red welt, but a pale trench. That only made him madder. He pressed the thumbnail in, finding a cracked section and using that like a plow to cut the flesh, constantly rubbing back and forth, squeezing his fist to force the blood out.

Only it wasn't blood. It was a black muck, thicker than oil and filled with white threads. No, not threads. Worms. Or maggots. They wriggled and twisted in each black drop that rolled outward from the cut.

Homer Gibbon stared at the goo . . . and what swarmed and thrived inside of it. Inside of him.

"No," whispered Homer. The truth of it—what Volker had told him over the phone and the proof crawling from his veins—staggered him. He backpedaled drunkenly until his back crunched into the wall. He slid down to the floor, his mouth opening and closing as a scream kept leaping up from inside his chest to rip loose and break the world.

"Auntie?"

That word, small and plaintive, was the only sound he made. It was faint, nearly a child's voice. A lost voice.

Aunt Selma did not answer.

She could not.

She had no mouth with which to speak. No lips. No tongue.

She sat amid the debris from the table, her robe soaked scarlet from the blood that flowed from all the red mouths Homer Gibbon had opened on her skin.

Homer stared blankly at her, and it took him almost a minute to understand what he was seeing. There were black spots in his mind, obscuring memories both recent and old. But not Dr. Volker's words. No, each and every one of them were as clear as if he were crouched behind Homer and whispering in his ear, but Selma . . . ?

Homer knew what had happened to her.

He could feel the weight of meat in his stomach. He understood what that meant. It's just that he had no memory at all of having done it.

Homer had not wanted to do this. Not to Selma. Not to her.

He sat and stared and tried to weep. He strained to force out a single tear.

"Come on, you fucker," he yelled, as if Volker was right there in the room. "Give me that much. Let me still be human enough for that."

He felt a tingle at the corner of his eye, and with great relief he touched his fingers there, needing to see the ordinary glistening wetness of that tear. The world began spinning around him. The drop of liquid on his fingertips was as black as the Black Eye. Tiny worms wriggled in it.

Homer Gibbon screamed. And this time the scream was real, full and charged with all of the power of his hate and rage.

He screamed and screamed. He jumped to his feet and raged through the house, tearing it apart. Be damned to the pain in his muscles; he took that pain and fed it in like fuel to his fury. He shattered windows and threw chairs across the rooms. His hands swept pictures from the walls and his feet kicked side tables to kindling. He overturned the sofa and slashed at the curtains with fingernails and teeth and then with knives from the kitchen.

And then he stopped dead in his tracks.

Aunt Selma stood in the doorway to the dining room. Her face was a death mask of exposed bone and empty eye sockets. Her clothes hung in stained tatters exposing wrinkled, bloodless skin. Some of her fingers were broken and bitten.

"Auntie?"

Selma raised her hands toward him and moaned. A deep, aching moan of blind and unbearable hunger. Homer stared at her, watching as she shuffled toward him. Even from ten feet away he could see the black goo leaking from between the exposed teeth, and inside the goo . . . the worms.

It was then, in a grand leap of understanding, that everything Volker had told him about Project Lucifer, the *coupe poudre*, and the parasites coalesced into a shared body of knowledge with the things the Black Eye had witnessed all of Homer's life, and which the Red Mouth whispered incessantly in his ears. Homer looked at the ripped skin on Aunt Selma and touched his own mouth, making intuitive leaps. Making connections.

Over the years, in the service of the Red Mouth, Homer had used every kind of tool. Knives, saws, drills, pliers, hatchets, clubs, forks, and even dentist tools. Each of them had opened red mouths in the people whom he sacrificed to his inner gods. But now . . .

He ran his fingers over his teeth, feeling each one. Shape and size and sharpness. Ordinary teeth, but not really. Not anymore. He could feel the worms wriggling beneath the flesh of his gums and within the meat of his tongue and the walls of his mouth.

Yes, whispered the Red Mouth.

There was a soft thump from the cellar and a low moan, and Homer knew that the church lady was trying to climb the stairs. He knew that without having to look. It all made sense now. Everything was clear.

The state had captured him and chained him; Doctor Volker had tried to transform him into the living embodiment of suffering. But a higher, grander purpose was at work in Homer's life; and now he understood the purpose of that power. Like a grub that turns into a wasp, it was all about transformation.

Just as Aunt Selma had transformed from living meat to a servant of the Red Mouth, Homer Gibbon understood that he was no longer Homer Gibbon.

He *was* the Red Mouth.

"God!" he said aloud, meaning himself.

He felt the hunger inside. In the same instant he felt all doubt and confusion decay and die.

He opened the door and let Aunt Selma stagger out into the rain.

Then he looked through the debris until he found the keys to the church lady's car. With them in hand he stepped out onto the porch, smiling. Filled with purpose.

He remembered a snatch of an old poem that one of the older cons in Rockview used to repeat. Standing on the top step, he said it aloud.

"This is how the world ends," he whispered to the rain.
"This is how the world ends," he said to the wind.
"This is how the world ends," he shouted to the storm.
Not with a bang.
But a bite.

PART THREE

THE DEAD LAND

No one who, like me, conjures up the most evil of those
half-tamed demons that inhabit the human breast, and
seeks to wrestle with them, can expect to come through
the struggle unscathed.

—Sigmund Freud, *Dora: An Analysis of a Case of Hysteria*

CHAPTER SIXTY-SIX
MAGIC MARTI IN THE MORNING
WNOW RADIO, MARYLAND

"This is Magic Marti at the mike and we've been informed that Pennsylvania Governor Harbison is going to make an announcement. Okay, we're going live to the state capitol in Harrisburg."

"My fellow citizens of the Commonwealth of Pennsylvania," said the governor in a deep, somber voice, "as of seven p.m. tonight, I am declaring a state of emergency for Stebbins County and a state of high alert for the following counties: Beaver, Allegheny, Washington, Greene, Armstrong, Indiana, Westmoreland, Fayette, Somerset, and Cambria. We have been offered—and I have accepted—assistance from the federal government and FEMA. I have mobilized the National Guard to shore up flood-affected areas and to assist with evacuations and other rescue operations."

A pause.

"However, the storm is not our only concern. With police, rescue, and fire departments taxed to their limits, we have been receiving a number of accounts of looting and violence. So far most of this has been concentrated in Stebbins County, which is also being hit hardest by the storm. For that reason I have authorized the National Guard to place Stebbins under temporary martial law. A curfew has been imposed and Guardsmen will work with local law enforcement to restore order.

"It is a sad thing when a corrupt few take advantage of the many, especially during a time of crisis. We saw similar acts of cowardly opportunism during Hurricane Katrina and in the wake of the earthquakes in Haiti.

"However I am convinced—and will remain convinced—that the overwhelming majority of the people of this glorious commonwealth are working shoulder to shoulder with their neighbors to save lives, protect property, and do what is necessary for everyone to survive. The many will not be tainted by the heinous acts of the few, and I can promise that order will be restored in a timely and efficient manner.

"If you are in one of the affected areas, please follow the instructions provided by the police, emergency agencies, and the news services. Stay at home, stay safe, and pray for those in peril. Together we will weather this crisis and see our way to the other end of this storm. Thank you and God bless the people of the Commonwealth of Pennsylvania."

CHAPTER SIXTY-SEVEN
MASON STREET NEAR DOLL FACTORY ROAD

She was a huddled ball down in the footwell of the backseat, her entire body clutched as tightly as a fist. The state police cruiser was still and cold. Outside, the wind was a tireless howling monster.

Dez had no idea how long she lay there. Thirty minutes? More? Probably more. She knew that, despite everything, despite all need and logic, she had fallen asleep. There had been no other direction in which she could flee.

In her sleep she thought she heard the chatter of automatic gunfire, the screams of men and women, and the roar of truck engines. But now that she was awake she heard none of those sounds.

Every muscle ached from the tension of remaining perfectly still. Her head hurt horribly where she had struck it when they'd hit her with the Taser. Her chest hurt from the strain of keeping silent even while the sobs tore their way out of her.

And she was cold. God . . . so cold. The November wind blowing in through the open door cut her like knives. Frigid rainwater dripped from the wire cage and pooled under her. There was no escape from the cold. Rain soaked into the tight knot of her French braid and burned like drops of boiling water on her scalp, especially over the bruise she'd gotten when falling. It crept down the collar of her shirt and the waistband of her pants, soaking her underwear, pooling inside her clothes as she lay shivering.

He left me.

Those three words hung in her mind like an echo frozen in time. She knew that the thought was illogical, but what did logic have to do with her world anymore? Logic had been consumed back at Doc Hartnup's. Logic was torn flesh and gnawed bones. Logic was dead.

He left me.

She'd warned him. Goddamn it if she hadn't warned him. She told him not to get out of the car. He hadn't listened. They never do. That was a lesson Dez had learned when she had begged her daddy— begged him on her knees as she clung to his legs—not to go when they wanted to send him to Kuwait. She'd soaked the knees of his pants with her tears, and Daddy had been forced to peel her off of him. He'd been so frustrated that he'd yelled at her. Told her to grow up.

Dez had known that it was wrong for him to go. There were monsters out there in the darkness. There always were, hiding in the shadows, right beyond the corner of your eye, waiting to take you.

Daddy had gone anyway

On the last day—on that terrible morning at the airport—he'd tried to make it all right with her. He'd knelt down and stroked her blond hair and kissed her nose. He'd said, "Don't worry, Pumpkin, you know I'll come back for you."

That's what he'd said.

Not come back *to* you.

Come back *for* you.

Then he left. Six weeks later he was gone forever, his helicopter blown out of the Arabian skies by a rocket-propelled grenade fired by someone in his own platoon. Friendly fire, they called it.

Mommy was dying already when they got the news. She was leaving Dez one ragged breath at a time as cancer gnawed at her with relentless hunger. When the man from the army read the letter, Mommy had simply closed her eyes and looked away. A single, silver tear rolled down to the pillow. She never spoke a word after that. Not to the army man, not to anyone. In three weeks Mommy was gone. She went away from Dez, too. First into her own grief and then into the darkness and finally into the ground.

Dez was in the second grade. Too young to understand the mysteries of death, but too old not to grasp the concept that anyone could leave at any time. For any reason. Daddy had proved that. So had Mommy.

So had everyone.

Even this trooper. This young guy named Saunders.

Left her.

Alone.

In the cold rain.

With the monsters.

So, why not sleep?

Why not fall into the deepest, darkest hole that opened up in her mind? It was so much safer down there, because you're all alone. No one can leave you when you're all alone.

She lay there in the footwell and listened to the rattle of the rain on the roof. Fighting the shivers. Trying to ignore the cold. Trying to block out the pain in her cramped muscles.

Wondering, though, why she was alive. Why hadn't the monsters taken her? She couldn't run. She was cuffed, battered, helpless. Meat in a fridge for those fuckers.

Dez listened for the sound of moans threaded into the wind and the rain. Listened. Listened. She heard absolutely nothing except the storm.

Why?

She lay there, waiting—aching, needing—for JT to come. Not as a rescue. She did not see it that way, not even now. Dez did not need anyone to come and rescue her ass. Not even JT, who was the only man who had never let her down, the only man who didn't have his head shoved all the way up his ass. Backup, though . . . that would be great. Cop to cop . . . and now would be a good time.

"Come on, Hoss," she whispered. "L'il help here."

But JT did not come. No matter how many times she asked.

Dez even thought about Billy Trout. God, what a pansy-ass jerk. Even so, she wished that he were here. Dez could make a long, long list of Billy's faults—too much emotion for one thing, that was top of the list—but if he opened that car door right now, she'd drag his ass to the nearest chapel. If Billy could figure out how to pick the lock on a pair of cuffs, she'd bang him blind, maybe even squeeze out a kid or two, just like he wanted. She promised it to Jesus and the saints as she lay there in the wet and cold.

She closed her eyes and remembered how warm he always was.

His skin always felt like sunlight was shining on it, even when they made love in the dead of winter. Dez remembered doing that. Clinging naked to him as snow fell outside, her arms and legs wrapped around Billy's suntanned limbs, the heat of their breath as they gasped and panted into each other's mouths. The heat at the core of her as Billy moved his hips and she moved hers, creating a friction as old as the world and as fragile as a snowflake. She remembered the heat as he came inside of her, crying out her name as if it was the single word that would buy his way into heaven. And the heat after, as he held her close, stroking her hair, whispering promises to her deep into the night as all around them the world froze into perfect whiteness.

Then she remembered the heat in his eyes on that last day. When he'd come into her trailer with the flowers and the ring, and Big Ted was there. Billy's eyes had filled with blue fire, and Dez imagined that she could feel the flare of heat as the furnace of his heart burst apart.

Billy. He was the last heat in the world that she could remember.

"Billy," Dez called out, her lips tasting the shape of his name. "Billy . . . I'm so sorry."

But Billy Trout did not come either.

"Damn you," Dez said to the storm, pretending that her tears were rainwater.

No one came for her. No one at all. Not JT, not Billy. Not the state police.

But . . .

Dez's eyes snapped open.

Why?

Why had no one come?

Why had the dead not come?

She wanted to move, needed to move, but Dez needed to understand that even more. Saunders had left her and they had torn him to pieces. Dez had screamed, and the dead had come shambling toward the car. Toward her.

Only . . . they hadn't done that. The front door of the car was wide open.

Dez took the risk. She knew before she moved that it was the most dangerous thing she had ever done. The most foolish, which was saying a lot.

She straightened her left leg.

The muscles began to cry out in a long, slow voice of pain as she flexed her thigh and straightened her knee. Then she froze as a new and awful terror struck her.

Her right leg was dead. She couldn't even feel it.

Oh God! Her thoughts rang inside her head like a scream. They did get me. I'm dead . . . like them. I'm dying.

These thoughts collided and cracked apart like billiard balls, all logic gone. She rocked sideways, trying insanely to get away from the dead side of her body.

Then there was a sudden and intense flare of pain all along the dead leg and hip—and that fast she realized that panic was making her stupid. Nerve endings burst awake with scattershot pins and needles as blood flowed into muscles that had been crushed to numbness by a hour laying on her side in the cold.

"You stupid bitch," she told herself, keeping her voice almost silent but loading it with enough scorn and venom to strip the bluing off a gun barrel. "You stupid pussy-ass fucking idiot."

Scorn was a good lash for Dez. It made her angry, and for her, anger was the only thing that could outfight fear. Anger was an old friend. An ally since she was in the second grade. It made her want to hurt something. Herself, or the first thing she could find that would scream.

Even so, she moved cautiously. Slowly. Unfolding her cramped limbs, even smiling with the rictus grin athletes often wear during physical therapy. Loving the pain. Hating the weakness. Forcing strength back into the body. At the same time listening for changes in the ambient noise. Listening for the moans.

Nothing.

She sat up. It took five minutes. Her wrists were bruised and raw from the cuffs, but she thanked God that Saunders had been compassionate enough not to have cuffed her behind her back. That would be a death sentence. In front . . . there was at least a chance.

She could not see out of the window. She was too short and the window was fogged with condensation. That meant that she had to get up onto the bench seat.

"Come on, you lazy cow."

She reached up and threaded her fingers through the mesh of the wire cage that separated the front seat from the back. Her fingers ached from the cold, but Dez fed that pain to the furnace of anger that she was stoking in the center of her chest. She set her teeth and pulled, pushing with both legs. It felt like hauling a transmission out of a pickup truck, but her body moved.

Then she was on the seat.

She immediately lay back down, stretching herself on the seat as she listened for moans. Listened for anything that might be reacting to the noise of her movement.

The wind and the rain did not change in pitch or tone.

Dez slowly sat up again.

She leaned and tried to look out through the open driver's door, but the angle was bad. All she could see was a bit of blacktop and tiny waves of runoff cascading toward the shoulder.

She shimmied over to the left-hand rear window and used her sleeve to wipe away the condensation. Everything outside was still a blur, the shapes smeared by the constant rainfall. Even so . . . those shapes were constants. Unmoving.

What had happened to the damn dead?

It didn't make sense.

Until it did.

The hammering of the rain on the roof was half the answer. Noise. And the smell of the rain—charged with ozone and rich with earthy odors from the flowing mud—was the other half. The dead could not hear or see her. Not in that downpour. Not hidden in the back of the cruiser, not through those same smeared windows.

"Well fuck me blind," Dez said out loud.

She grinned. A real grin this time.

Then she looked down at the footwell. At where she had been. At what she had been down there. Small. Broken. Weak. Abandoned.

Her head abruptly rose and snapped around like a spaniel, her eyes focused to the east as if she could see through car and storm and buildings all the way to the elementary school.

Where the kids were. Where the old folks had been taken.

Were they trapped there? Abandoned by parents who could not get through the storm to pick them up? Or, by parents who had encountered some other problem? Like Saunders had.

"Christ," growled Dez. She patted her pockets in the vain hope that Saunders had somehow overlooked her handcuff key. Not a chance.

Damn.

The cage was heavy-gauge wire and she was never going to kick that out of its frame. The doors had no handles inside.

But the windows.

Dez sneered at the glass. She'd knocked in her fair share of car windows in her time. With her baton and the end of her flashlight. With a standing kick more than once. And even with the head of Rufus Sterko after Dez had busted him for beating his wife with an electrical cord. Side windows weren't that tough. Safety glass was made to shatter under the right kind of impact.

The problem was going to be one of angle and resistance. She couldn't stand up, and that was the best angle. And lying down meant that there was nothing to really brace against. This was going to have to be all muscle and speed. Snapping speed.

She turned and lay down on the seat and scooched down so that she could place her heels on the window with her knees bent. Then she wrapped her cuffed hands in the nylon seat-belt strap, took a deep breath, and kicked.

Her heels hit the glass and rebounded and Dez knee-punched herself in the mouth, smashing her lower lip against her teeth. She tasted blood as pain flared along the inside of her lip. The glass remained unbroken.

"Motherfucker!" she snarled, her anger stoked all the way up to white-hot rage and she kicked out again. And again.

And again.

There was a sharp crystalline pop, and then her heels shot through the disintegrating window out into the rain; however, the jagged teeth of the window raked her ankles and calves.

Dez jerked her legs back into the car, her chest heaving in anger and pain. Hot blood trickled down the back of each calf, but cold rain slanted through the window, driven by stiff wind.

She froze and listened once more to the sound of the storm.

Still no moans. No scuffling feet on the wet blacktop.

Dez leaned forward and cautiously stuck her head out the window, looked left and right.

The bus was still there, but that was it. None of them. Not even the remains of Saunders. Had they totally consumed him, flesh, bone, and clothes? No, that was stupid.

He was one of them now. Dez knew that for sure. The way you know bad things when the shit is really coming down around you. Saunders was out there somewhere, half torn apart but walking. Hunting for food.

Her stomach did a sickening spin.

Stop mooning around, you cow, screeched Dez. *Get out of the car. Get out . . . get OUT.*

Dez reached her hands through the shattered window and fumbled for the door handle, found it, hooked her cold fingers in it, clumsied it up, and felt the lock pop open. She shoved the door with her knee, and then she was out of the car, moving as fast as she could, and then dropping into a low crouch, studying the road.

Nothing moved but the wind-blown rain.

Dez crabbed sideways down the car to the open driver's door, found the trunk release, jerked it. Then she duckwalked to the back of the car, making maximum use of cover, peered around, and saw that the coast was still clear. She straightened and pushed the trunk hood all the way up.

And smiled.

Her hat was there. As was her gun belt, her Glock, and her ring of keys.

Dez grabbed for the keys, fumbled the small cuff key out and worked it into the lock. When they clicked open she turned and threw them as far away as she could, her face twisted into a mask of disgust.

Then she wrapped the belt around her hips and cinched it tight. She'd used up her pepper spray on Andy. Didn't matter, the shit didn't work on those dead sons of bitches anyway. She dropped the magazine in her Glock. Nine bullets left and one in the chamber. That was the bad news. The good news was the shotgun attached by aluminum clips to the underside of the trunk lid. It had beanbag rounds, though. Good for knocking them down; no good at all for killing them.

The keys to the cruiser were—where?

She went back to the driver's side, but the ignition slot was empty.

Saunders had been a dutiful little trooper and had taken the keys with him. Shit.

Dez turned and surveyed the road, hoping to see the keys glinting on the asphalt. No such luck.

She knew in theory how to boost a car, but she needed a screwdriver or some tools, and her fingers were so numb with cold that she wasn't even sure she could pull a trigger.

Dez looked around, considering her options. Her car was parked at the station, four blocks from here. But her car keys were in her briefcase in her own cruiser, and that was back at Turks's. Miles away.

And, if the staties thought she was a mad psycho killer—if the actual truth of what was happening hadn't yet come to bite them on the ass—then going to the station was a quick way to get arrested again. Dez knew that she wouldn't let that happen, even if it meant kneecapping a couple of troopers.

Would she kill one of them if she had to?

She weighed the shotgun in her hand. Beanbag rounds might be a way to muscle through them.

Or, just avoid that whole can of worms and figure something else out.

She looked up the road. The elementary school was two miles from here. A long, cold run in this rain. Her trailer home was the same distance but off to the southwest.

It was way out of her way, but she could feel the old place pulling at her. There was a locked trunk in her bedroom. In it, Dez had two hunting rifles, a shotgun, a Sig Sauer nine, a Raven Arms .25, and enough boxes of bullets to start a goddamn war.

Her landlord, Rempel, had a big Toyota Tundra, too. That thing could drive through a brick wall. If Rempel wouldn't lend it to her, then Dez had no problem at all knocking him on his ass and taking it. Or kneecapping him, if it came to that. He really was a prick.

She could change into warm clothes, grab her leather jacket and riot gear, put all the guns and ammo into the Tundra and then smash her way right up to the doors of the elementary school. She chewed her lip. That wasn't a great plan—it wasted time—but it was the only plan that sounded like it ended with her alive. And the kids alive, too.

The wind howled and the street remained empty.

Where the fuck is everyone?

For that matter, where was JT? Was he in lockup, sweating this out in a cage? Or had his driver stopped, too?

"Damn it, Hoss," she said to the wind, "don't you leave me, too."

There was a catch in her voice as she said it. And it made her mad.

"Fuck it," she told the storm. "It's only rock 'n' roll."

Dez turned and ran down the road toward her home. Toward her guns.

CHAPTER SIXTY-EIGHT

BIXBY ROAD
STEBBINS COUNTY, PENNSYLVANIA

Homer Gibbon drove the back roads away from Aunt Selma's house. He had no idea where Selma was. Homer had dropped her off on a neighbor's porch, rang the bell, and was a quarter mile down the road when the screams began. He dropped the church lady outside the church. Seemed fitting. He was laughing as he drove away.

The church lady's ugly little car bounced and rattled along the rutted roads and nearly got stuck twice in mud. Homer took it in stride. He had the radio tuned to WNOW, listening to Magic Marti talk about the storm and then hearing her voice change as she began reading news reports about outbreaks of violence in Stebbins County.

That confused him for almost a full minute, and then he got it.

As he drove, he tried to put it all together, to connect the chain of events that stretched from the execution chamber at the prison to this moment in the church lady's car. He remembered the needle and he remembered going to sleep.

Then he remembered waking up and seeing the man at the mortuary. And the ugly Russian lady. Homer remembered fighting with them. Biting them.

That had been the first real taste.

It wasn't really his first taste of human flesh—he'd bitten parts off a diner waitress once—but it was the first time he'd tasted it out of need rather than curiosity.

And, oh, how he had *needed* it.

Waking up in that bag—that fucking body bag!—had been awful. Dark and terrifying, like being inside a womb or a coffin. Worse still had been the hunger. It was so deep, so massive that he almost bit his own skin, and he would have, too, if the mortician hadn't unzipped the bag and bent close. Deliciously close.

He wondered if the mortician and the Russian lady had come back. Like Aunt Selma and the church lady.

Yes, he decided, they had. They'd come back as slaves of the Black Eye, and now they were probably out there somewhere, spreading the truth of the Red Mouth.

That was . . . He fished for a word that was grand enough, glorious enough.

That was *perfect*.

It was delicious. And it was fun.

He hit the button to roll the window down, leaned his head out of the Cube as the rain stung him, and screamed at the storm, "Fuck you, Volker!"

Homer laughed for the next five minutes. The old fuck doctor at the prison hadn't punished him, or damned him, or any such bullshit. Volker had given Homer the keys to the goddamn kingdom. He had empowered him.

Homer liked the word "empowered." He'd learned it from a Dr. Phil episode.

"Empowered." It tasted good to say it.

The only thing that bothered Homer was the fact that Aunt Selma and the church lady seemed a little—again he fished for a word. The only thing that seemed to fit was "dumb as shit."

He thought about it some more, not liking that. It seemed disrespectful. Not dumb. Empty. Like a hollowed-out gourd. Nothing inside except the hunger. Auntie didn't even seem to know her name. Granted, without a face she couldn't speak, but she didn't even respond to her name. Church lady still had a face, but she couldn't talk, either. They just "were."

Would that be how all of them were? He was pondering that when a figure staggered out of the brush and walked right into the middle of the road. Homer stamped on the brakes and had to steer like a madman to keep the Cube from spinning and crashing into the rainswept trees.

"You stupid fuck!" Homer yelled. But then he stopped and peered through the windshield as the wipers slapped back and forth. He knew this man, and Homer grinned. "Holy shit . . ."

The man turned toward the car, staring with eyes that were dark and empty of everything except hunger. He wore the remains of a blue smock over street clothes. The smock, the clothes, and the man were covered with so much dried blood that even rain this heavy could not wash it away. The face that peered through the windshield at Homer was the same one that had bent to peer at him when the body bag had been unzipped. The mortician. Homer got out of the car and the man suddenly staggered toward him, taking two quick steps as if preparing to attack.

Homer knew that he wanted to attack. He was hungry, after all— Home knew that on a gut level.

Then the man stopped and stood in the rain, looking lost. Looking . . . empty.

"Guess I'm not your Happy Meal, sport," said Homer.

The dead mortician lifted his head at the sound of Homer's voice and the barest shadow of perplexity flicked across his dead features. Then he turned and began staggering in the same direction he'd been going before Homer stopped. On the other side of the road was a farm field, and beyond that . . . a farmhouse.

"Nice," Homer said with approval. There was more movement up the road, and he saw a cop step out of the woods. His shirt and throat were ripped away, his eyes dark and dead. The cop crossed the road and headed in the same direction as the mortician. "Very nice."

Homer got back into the car. He felt satisfied. He'd wanted an answer to his question, and the universe had given it to him, no muss, no fuss.

The empty ones, like Aunt Selma and the mortician, were no different than the worms under his skin. They did what they did but there was no one at the wheel except the will of the Red Mouth.

"Kind of perfect," he said, nodding to himself. "That's right on the fucking money." He pounded the side of his fist on the steering wheel. Then he rolled up the window, put the car in gear, and kept driving. A mile down the road he came to a crossroads. Turn left and the road would take him into the town of Stebbins. Turn right and he could pick up Route 381, heading to the county line.

In the rearview mirror a military-style Humvee materialized ghostlike out of the rain, and a moment later a troop truck appeared. And another.

Homer waited for the Red Mouth to tell him, but there was silence inside his head. Then he remembered that he was the Red Mouth now.

Beneath his skin the larvae wriggled and in his stomach the hunger howled.

The crossroads waited. Left or right?

Smiling, he made his turn. He even used his turn signal, just for the hell of it.

CHAPTER SIXTY-NINE
MAIN STREET
TOWN OF STEBBINS

Dez Fox ran along the side of the road. Main Street was empty and on any other day Dez would have blamed the storm. Today, though, she could no longer take anything for granted.

The downpour reduced visibility to a dozen yards. Everything beyond that was a confusion of gray. Threatening shapes seemed to materialize out of nowhere and Dez suddenly tensed, bringing the shotgun up, finger slipping inside the trigger guard, only to take two more steps to reveal them as mailboxes, a stand of corn stalks left over from Halloween, a sheet-metal cutout of a smiling car salesman outside of Dollar Bill's Used Cars. Nothing. None of *them*.

A mile and a half from her trailer park, she found three dead bodies lying in the middle of the road. Two men and a woman. Civilians. Each of the bodies had been virtually torn to pieces by automatic gunfire. Multiple head wounds.

The ground was littered with brass. 5.56 x 45mm NATO rounds. M16s.

Dez looked around and saw muddy impressions from truck tires and boot marks from at least a dozen men.

The National Guard. Had to be. Hope flared in her chest. If the Guard was here, then someone was using their head. Someone asked for some serious backup and the Guard had come in here to kick ass and take names.

She kept moving and as she ran questions filled her head. How much did the government know? Did the government know anything? The Guardsmen could have been here to sandbag the riverbanks or evacuate the townsfolk. They might have fired as a response to an attack. If so . . . did the Guard take any injuries? Were any of them bitten and possibly infected?

That was the ugliest thought of all, because they went everywhere in the state. It would be a real bitch if the good guys riding to the rescue were the ones to spread this.

She realized with a sinking stomach that she had already seen that. That's what happened to Andy Diviny and the others. And Chief Goss. Probably Trooper Saunders, too.

Somebody had to warn them.

"Oh, shit," she growled and increased her pace. Running hurt her head, but she didn't care. She slogged through the mud as fast as her weary legs would carry her.

She got answers to some of her questions a quarter mile down the road. She saw the smoke first and as she rounded a curve in the road she saw the burning car. It was a Toyota RAV4. The vehicle was completely gutted by fire, the tires melted, the windows gone, bullet holes everywhere. Spent brass all over the muddy road.

There were six bodies there. Two of them were still inside the Toyota, both strapped into car seats in the back, burned to charred lumps.

"God, *no.*"

She turned away in grief and horror. The bodies on the road were all adults. Two women and two men. Dez knew the women. Katie Gunderson and her sister, Jeanne. Both of them were married, both had kids in preschool.

Had.

"God . . ."

Lying partly under Jeanne was a man Dez vaguely recognized from town events. A farmworker. She had no idea what his name was. The three of them were riddled with bullet holes. The farmworker was clearly one of the infected. His face and throat had ragged bite marks; but Dez couldn't see any trace of bites or the black goo on the women.

The last body was a real puzzle, and again it made Dez's heart sink.

It was a National Guardsman in a torn white hazmat suit. Dez squatted down and gingerly lifted his gas mask to reveal a young face, maybe twenty. He had a bite on his left hand, but it wasn't the disease that had killed him. Someone had put three rounds through his forehead.

But . . . why hadn't they taken the injured man into quarantine, given him some kind of treatment? Why leave his body here? Even if he'd died as a result of the bite, or if they'd killed him because they were terrified of the disease, why leave his body? Leaving a soldier behind is against everything soldiers are taught. They didn't even take his dog tags. They blew his head off and left.

That made no kind of sense.

Unless . . .

"Oh . . . shit," she said and she could hear the panic in her own tone.

It made no sense unless the Guardsmen were that afraid of the plague. Unless the plague was so desperately dangerous that even the respect for a fallen soldier had to be prohibited.

Dez licked rainwater off her lips. How bad was this thing? She looked at the bodies and then down at the dead soldier.

Do I have it?

The dead kept their secrets, but their silence seemed to mock her, to promise awful things.

Then she heard a squawking sound. At first she couldn't understand what or where it was, and then she heard it again, and she knew. It was squelch from a walkie-talkie.

Dez found it under the man's hip. Dez tore off a handful of leaves from a roadside bush and wiped the device clean of blood and mud. She began fiddling with it as she jogged down the road toward her trailer park. When she found a channel where there was some chatter she slowed to a walk and pressed the device to her ear, sticking a finger in her other ear to block out the sound of the storm. There were a lot of voices, lots of overlapping chatter, a lot of emotions running high. The result was a jumble from which Dez could only harvest a few scraps.

". . . last of state cops are in the holding pen . . . primary shooting line with a fallback at twenty yards . . . helos grounded . . . two cars of farmers tried to run the south barricade . . . CDC Wildfire team delayed by storm . . ."

Only bits and pieces, but it was enough for Dez. And more than enough to convince her not to say anything into the walkie-talkie. If they shot their own and shot civilians . . .

She heard the phrase "Q-zone" at least a dozen times. Quarantine zone. Had to be. That was both good and bad. Good for the rest of the state, or maybe the rest of the country. Bad as shit for her and her fellow citizens in Stebbins County. It wasn't a surprise, but it confirmed her worst fears.

Almost her worst. There was another phrase that was peppered through the chatter. Three words. Three terrible words.

. . . *shoot on sight* . . .

Dez stuffed the walkie-talkie into her jacket pocket and began running again. Faster.

A few cars and trucks appeared in the gloom, but each time they were ordinary. Parked where they should be parked, no sign of further violence.

Until she found the second state police cruiser.

It was smashed into a telephone pole half a block from the road that led to her trailer park. The front end was wrapped like a cruller around the shattered stump of the pole. Wires lay across the road like broken spider webs. Chunks of safety glass sparkled as raindrops struck them.

Dez raised the shotgun as she approached the vehicle from a quarter angle. The windshield was spiderwebbed out from a black impact hole. The driver, seat belt notwithstanding, had hit the windshield hard. From the degree of damage, and the lack of skid marks, it looked to Dez as if the driver had been driving at high speed and never touched the brakes.

There were multiple lines of bullet holes stitched along the passenger side of the cruiser. The brass in the middle of the road were from M16s. All four doors were open.

She darted forward and aimed her gun inside.

The front seat was torn and slashed, and there was an inch-deep puddle of bloody rainwater sloshing around the puddles. Standing like bleak islands in the puddle were small lumps of meat and a man's left thumb.

Dez's mind cruelly supplied a name for what she was seeing.

Leftovers.

She swallowed a throatful of acid and checked the backseat. Blood there, too.

Whose blood? The thumb had been from a white man, not from JT.

"C'mon, Hoss," Dez murmured. "Give me a happy ending here."

But there was no more to this story.

She moved around to the back of the vehicle. The trunk hood was bent and had popped out of the lock. The shotgun was gone. She tried on a smile, hoping that JT had been the one to cowboy up and blast his way out of there. The backseat was bloody, though.

"No . . . ," she breathed, and hearing the word drove a spike of doubt and fear into her heart. "C'mon . . . no . . ."

The rain was so loud that she never heard the wet footsteps behind her, but suddenly icy fingers clamped around her arms and dragged her backward.

CHAPTER SEVENTY
STEBBINS COUNTY LINE

Billy Trout suddenly swerved the Explorer off the road and pulled behind a billboard for a year-round Christmas store.

"What'd you do that for?" demanded Goat.

"Look!" Trout said, pointing.

Goat peered through the storm. A hundred yards ahead, almost invisible in the relentless rain, a line of military vehicles was barreling along Hank Davis Pike, the road that cut across the county line and went directly into Stebbins. There were at least a dozen troop trucks and two Humvees with top-mounted machine guns. They were bucketing along, and when they hit the crossroads they didn't even slow down, burning straight through the red light. Only the last vehicle slowed to a stop, slopping through mud onto the shoulder. Immediately soldiers piled out and began removing sawhorse barriers from the back of the truck. They erected them across the road that led into town. The guards were dressed in rain ponchos, but their M16s were visible on slings.

The soldiers were dressed in white hazmat suits.

"Oh man," said Goat. "This shit must be totally out of the box."

"Yeah," murmured Trout dryly. "God, this story has to get out. Damn . . . I wish the phones worked. Fucking storm . . ."

"Screw the storm, Billy. Our calls were going nowhere before the rain even started. Those goons cut the lines and jammed the cell towers and you know it. We'd need a satellite phone or the broadcast uplink to get the word out."

"Don't suppose you brought that stuff?" Trout asked hopefully.

"Pretty sure I'd be fucking using it right about now if I had." Goat stared at the Guardsmen down the road. "We're screwed, Billy. We'll never get in."

"Maybe, maybe. Let me think." Trout turned and looked the way they'd come, and then looked farther up the road, chewing his lip in thought. "Okay, they've got this road blocked, and there are four other significant roads that lead to town. Hank Davis becomes Doll Factory once you pass the reservoir. Then there's Sawmill Road at the west end, Brayer Bridge Road at the southeast corner, and Sandoval Road that crosses into Maryland. They're going to block those, no doubt about it. How many other roads does that leave?"

"Including farm roads?" asked Goat. "About a million."

"Right. So, if they're just now blocking the big roads, we can still get in on a farm road. What's close? Forest Lane . . . or that crappy little utility road by the Miller place."

Goat looked uncertain. "Wait, man, let's think this through. Why exactly are we trying to get *into* town."

"Are you serious?"

"As a heart attack. Think about it, man. Doc Volker infected a psycho serial killer with a bunch of parasites that are probably going to make him even more of a murderous whack job than he already was, and which are likely to spread like wildfire. He said that the infected would be—what's the word he used?—*suborned* by the parasite's need to replicate and feed. We're talking full-on zombies running around, maybe biting people, maybe doing who knows what to spread the parasite."

"Exactly," agreed Trout.

"Then why in the wide blue fuck are we even thinking about going in there?"

"We're reporters—"

"Yeah? Save that shit for the rubes, Billy."

Trout turned in his seat. "Okay, then all bullshit aside. Everyone knew that this storm was coming, so by now they would have evacuated the middle school and bussed all those kids over to the elementary school. That's the town shelter point. They'll probably be bringing in the old folks from Sunrise Home, and anyone who lives in areas likely to flood. That's—what? Two thousand people? More than half of them kids."

"Most of the kids' parents will have picked them up already?"

"Maybe from east and north, but anyone coming from west and south will have been flooded out. Or, maybe stopped by the military. No matter how you spin it, Goat, there are going to be hundreds of kids and maybe as many old folks and townies who have nowhere else to go. They're going to be inside that shelter."

"Okay. So?"

"So, if they don't know what they're facing, then they're going to take in anyone who comes to the shelter doors. That includes wounded people. People who might have been bitten. You heard what Volker said, this thing is completely infectious. If even one wounded person shows up and they let him in, then Lucifer 113 is going to sweep like wildfire through the shelter. Everyone is going to get sick and die, Goat. And I have a pretty bad feeling that the military is going to let them."

Goat turned away. "They can't just let everyone die."

"Yes they can," Trout said. "*We* can't let them. We can't let Stebbins be erased."

Goat shook his head. "Jeez, what are you? Captain Avenger? You don't even have family in Stebbins anymore."

"It's still my town, Goat. My friends are there."

"Dez Fox is there, too, right?" When Trout didn't answer, Goat nodded to himself. "You're going to get yourself eaten by zombies or gunned down by the National Guard over some chick who wouldn't piss on you if you were on fire."

Trout said nothing.

"Billy, if you go in there, then whatever happens to everyone else is going to happen to you."

"Maybe," Trout snapped. "Or, maybe I get to Dez or JT or someone and they get everyone over to the school and lock it up and we ride this out."

"What about the infected?"

"We check for anyone with a bite. Anyone who looks sick."

"And do what? Shoot them?"

"Christ, kid, who do you think I am? No, we lock them up. There's plenty of rooms in the school. . . . We take all the infected, anyone who even might be infected, and lock them up until this settles down. Then the feds can figure out a way to help them and rescue us."

Goat stared at him for a long time. "Damn, I wish I had your optimism. I'd blow my entire paycheck on scratch-off tickets." He shook his head. "Look, you can play Captain Avenger, but count me out. I—"

"Don't worry, Goat, I'm not saying you should come with me. In fact, I'd rather you didn't. I want you to get out of here. Hitch a ride to Bordentown or someplace. Get someplace where you're safe."

Goat narrowed his eyes. "Why?"

"Because you're going to take this stuff with you." He fished Volker's flash drives and his own small recorder out of his pockets. "If things go bad then make sure the truth comes out."

Goat made no move to get out. "Billy . . . this is nuts."

"Yeah, well we left 'sane and normal' behind the first time Volker said 'zombie.' "

"Look," said Goat, taking the evidence from Trout, "do this for me, okay? Before you do anything else, go to the station and get that little portable satellite uplink we use for field reports. It's in my office. There's an old sat phone, too. The army can cut off the phones and the Net, but they're not going to knock down a satellite."

"I can contact you with that?" Trout asked.

"Sure." Goat explained how the device worked. "You can reach me on Skype. The sat phone will give you audio but no video, so we can at least talk. Use it to let me know when you're going to upload a video file. Get one of my small digital cameras. Shoot everything. The zombies, the soldiers. Dead people in the streets, kids hiding in the school. Anything that will make news. Hell . . . it's *all* news."

"Good," said Trout. "That's exactly what we need. We have to get the news out."

Goat looked out the window, nodding toward the rainswept fields. "Bordentown's about four miles that way." He glanced at his heavy satchel with the cameras and laptop. It was going to be a bastard of a slog through the mud, but he merely sighed. Then he turned back to Trout. "Tell me something, Billy. If you were in charge of the military for this shit . . . what would you do? Would you like, I dunno—*nuke* the whole place?"

Trout gave him a cynical laugh. "No. But I guess I'd build a big freaking wall around Stebbins. But, no . . . I wouldn't nuke the whole frigging place, and I don't think they will, either."

"That's good—"

"They'll probably drop a couple fuel-air bombs," Trout continued. "Incinerate the whole place. Less risk, more efficient."

Goat stared at him. "Jesus Christ, Billy . . . you're building a case for the military to kill every man, woman, and child in town. In the town you are about to return to. That's insane."

"What Volker did was insane," said Trout. "What the CIA did in allowing Lucifer 113 into the country was insane. Burning this place down to save the entire country, maybe the whole world? It's harsh, but it's practical. No, don't look at me like that, I'm not saying they *should*, I think they *will*."

"Oh, man . . ." Goat held out his hand. "Take care of yourself, Billy."

"You, too, kid. See you on the other side."

Goat shook his head as he got out. He stood in the wind, rainwater running in lines down his face as the Explorer pulled back onto the road. Then he set his shoulders against the cold and began walking as fast as the storm and mud would permit.

CHAPTER SEVENTY-ONE
MAIN STREET

Dez shrieked as the cold hands pulled her backward, then she stepped back harder than the pull, jammed one foot flat on the ground and used the leverage to spin her body as hard as she could. As she turned, she whipped the shotgun stock at head level, smashing the hardwood into the cheekbone of a tall man in mechanic's coveralls, shattering the bones in his face and sending shock waves up Dez's arms.

The man staggered back and for a horrible second Dez thought that she had just hit an infected survivor, but then he caught his balance and turned back to face her. One eye was half-closed, the other stared at her from a red pit from which all of the flesh had been torn away. The rest of his face hung in tatters.

A crooked little laugh of relief escaped her throat. It was only one of the dead.

Or a ghoul.

More laughter bubbled out of her throat as she raised the gun and fired. She thought it was loaded with beanbag rounds but a load of double-ought buckshot blew off the top of the creature's head. It crumpled awkwardly to the wet ground.

"Yeah, fucking A," she cried aloud. "Booyah! Kill 'em all, mother-fucker!"

Dez stood over the fallen ghoul, feet wide and knees braced, chest heaving, the shotgun clutched so hard that her knuckles were white as bones; she could feel the fastenings that held her sanity in place popping one by one. Part of her even wanted to go crazy. Running batshit nuts through the street, shooting everything that moved until she fired all her guns dry, then running straight into a crowd of them.

Kicking, punching, biting, going down dirty and mean and in style. A warrior's death. Like a lion pulled down by jackals. It was every drill instructor's dream—to die in combat, wading through a sea of your enemies' blood as they choked on yours.

She recognized the man. Fred Wortz. Corn farmer whose spread ran alongside the trailer park. As she watched, a piece of Fred's skull fell away with a *plop*. It was a grotesque sight but Dez suddenly laughed out loud, and the laugh rose and rose until it was a piercing shriek like a gull's cry and then the laugh disintegrated into a sob that almost brought her to her knees.

Stop it! Screamed her inner voice. *Stopstopstopstopstop* . . .

The sobs fractured and fell apart into a choking cough. No more laughter boiled out of her.

"Fuck you!" she yelled at the rain and the storm and all the cold things that moved within it. *"Fuck you!"*

The words were so loud they burned her throat, but the storm swallowed them whole, eating each echo before it could roll back to her.

It hurt her that this was Fred. She'd had beers with him, sitting in lawn chairs outside of her trailer. Talking football and Monday-morning quarterbacking the war in Afghanistan. It was so *wrong* that she had simply killed him. Even though she knew that he was already dead. How could that matter on a day like this? What mattered was that this was a guy she knew. A drinking buddy. A friend. And now he was gone. Just as Trooper Saunders was gone. And Chief Goss, and Sheldon Higdon, and Doc Hartnup . . . and all the others. Everyone she knew was dying. Everyone she knew was leaving her. Everyone.

Her stomach bubbled and Dez turned away and vomited into the mud.

Then she heard something in the storm, behind the waving sheets of rain.

Moans.

Not just one voice.

Many.

So many.

She stared into the rain with mad eyes.

"Come on, you pussies!" Dez jammed the shotgun stock against her shoulder and fired into the wind. Again, and again. She turned and fired, turned and fired. The buckshot was wasted on the storm, but she didn't care. "Come on you . . . you . . ."

Her words disintegrated into sobs and Dez sagged to her knees. She shook her head as the moans floated toward her through the rain.

"I can't," she blubbered as tears and snot mixed with rainwater on her face. "I can't do this . . ." Not with JT gone. Probably Billy, too, the bastard. And the chief, and Flower . . . and everyone. All gone. How the fuck was she supposed to go on without any of them still left?

She let the shotgun fall to the asphalt as she collapsed forward onto her palms, head hanging down between her heaving shoulders. Voices—a thousand variations on her own voice—spoke inside her head. Telling her to get up. Telling her to give up. Telling her to just let go. Telling her that it was okay, that she didn't have to be afraid anymore. Telling her that this was all just a dream. A dream and Daddy will come and tuck her in and kiss her good night and make everything better. Nothing but a dream. Only that.

The moans changed into a hummed lullaby. A dozen voices humming in her daddy's voice.

No matter what happens, pumpkin, I'll always come back for you.

Come back *for* you.

She looked up, her eyes wide and desperate as if she expected to see her father come lurching out of the rain, his body twisted and torn by the explosion that had killed him. Daddy, coming for her. To take her. To consume her, the way these monsters wanted to consume her.

"PLEASE!" she screamed.

The moans were louder now. Dez closed her eyes. If it hurts, so what? It won't hurt for long.

It won't hurt for long. And then . . .

And then what?

The voices muttered and yelled and whispered, but none of them had an answer.

And then what?

Death? Sure . . . that was certain.

And then what?

Dez heard a sound. A soft scuff, and she raised her head an inch, opening her eyes to a squint as if afraid of a bright light. Raindrops swung pendulously from her eyelashes.

She saw a foot. Small, with a bright red sneaker. White tights.

Dez looked up. White tights and a plaid skirt and above that . . . ? Blood.

The face that came out of the rain could have been her own, years and years ago. Big blue eyes, corn yellow hair. Round cheeks. A pretty little girl.

A . . .

. . . little . . .

. . . . girl . . .

The little girl reached out her hands, a soft and plaintive gesture. A child wanting warmth, craving the safety of strong arms to hold her and keep her safe from the boogeyman.

The little girl could have been her.

Only it wasn't.

"Please . . ." whispered the little girl.

That's what Dez's mind tried to tell her, that's the lie her inner need created. *Please.* But it was a lie, and Dez knew it. Some fragment of her still understood that much. The voices in her head yelled the lie, but some deeper part of Dez was whispering back. No.

The little girl had not spoken at all.

She could not.

All she could do was moan. An empty plea to satisfy a hunger that was vast and endless. Dez looked into the little girl's eyes. She had seen the eyes of the other ghouls. Chief Goss . . . others. In their eyes all she had seen was nothing. But here, for a fragment of a moment, Dez thought that she caught the flicker of something else; it was as if she looked through the grimy glass of a haunted house and saw the pale, pleading face of a ghost. In the second before the thing lunged at her, Dez saw the shadow of the little girl screaming at her from the endless darkness.

It was the single most terrible moment of her entire life. Worse than the lingering death of her mother as cancer carved her down to a skeletal parody of who she had been. Worse than the imagined ghost of her father come shambling into her bedroom months after he had been buried in a sealed coffin. Worse than all the intervening years of drinking to shut down her mind and fucking to try to feel something. Worse than all of the things that had happened today.

The screaming face of the little girl, trapped inside the mindless thing that had been her, was worse than anything. Worse even than all the voices screaming inside Desdemona Fox's head.

So, Dez screamed, too.

And with a movement as fluid and fast as if she had been practicing her whole life for this single moment, Dez drew her Glock and pointed and fired straight and true and blew out the lights in the haunted house. The little girl pitched backward and fell onto the asphalt. Dez crawled over to her and looked down into the dark eyes. She bent close, staring, staring. All that she saw, however, was her own pale reflection in the black pupils and fading blue irises. The ghost was gone.

The screams in Dez's head . . . *stopped.* Just like that. Blown to silence by the blast of her gun. Falling empty on the ground like spent brass.

Dez Fox raised her head. There were other moans in the storm, coming closer. Slow shapes with dark bodies and pale faces were emerging from the shadows of the downpour. Dez lingered for one moment longer, looking at the victim of the small murder she had committed. However, Dez offered no apology. This was not her crime.

She had *saved* this little girl.

She turned toward the side road. Her trailer was less than a mile away now. Go there. Get the guns. Get Rempel's truck. Then get over to the elementary school. The Stebbins Little School at the end of Schoolhouse Lane. A gym for peewee league basketball. An assembly hall for meetings and Christmas pageants. And a basement designated as a shelter for all civil emergencies and natural disasters.

A safe haven . . . or a well-stocked larder, depending on who was in charge.

All the children of Stebbins County. All of the little boys and little girls.

Needing help.

Needing *her* help.

The ghouls were going to slaughter them all. And if not the ghouls, then the National Guard. Teeth or bullets or a fucking fuel-air bomb. Either way, no one was left to protect them. Everyone else had run away or died.

Except Dez.

"No," she said to the storm and the moans and to her own pain. "No!"

Dez holstered her pistol and ran.

CHAPTER SEVENTY-TWO
STEBBINS COUNTY LINE

As soon as he rounded the bend, Billy Trout cut sharply off the road and crashed through a screen of brush onto a deer path that snaked between two farms. The brush closed behind him, and if some of the bracken was crushed and twisted, Trout figured that anyone would blame it on the storm. There were trees falling, who cared about some brush?

Branches and shrubs scratched along the sides of the Explorer, and mud splashed as high as the windows as he bumped and thumped over ruts and roots.

This path wound around the Miller and Rubino farms and then crossed a paved road that would take him right into the back of the Regional Satellite News parking lot. With any luck the whole staff would be there, reporting the storm and manning the journalistic bastions. They'd help him get word out to whatever cops were left in town and definitely to the authorities. Some public appeal might coax the feds into considering other choices.

Of course, getting the word out would put his neck on the federal chopping block. Prison was a real possibility, First Amendment notwithstanding. They could beat him to death with the Patriot Act, disappear him to some hellhole for a few decades, and call it "interests of national security." It was no joke, and Trout wasn't laughing.

"What the hell are you doing, Billy Trout?" he asked himself.

Even though the heater was only set for defrost, he was sweating badly and his mouth was as dry as old cloth. It wasn't simply the threat of government retaliation for what he had planned. Things were much, much worse than that.

Trout was still in his thirties, but he'd seen his share of life's awful moments as a reporter—first in Pittsburgh after college and then here in Stebbins. Nothing he'd seen, however, ever filled him with anything approaching the fear that was screaming in his head. He had always considered "terror" to be more of an abstract political concept rather than an actual state of human experience. That was before Volker and Lucifer 113. Now he was truly and completely terrified. He wanted to pull off the road, curl up in the back, and pull his coat over his head. Or drive to Pittsburgh and buy a ticket for the first flight out of the state. Maybe out of the country. For once that wasn't a joke.

What if he ran into Homer Gibbon?

That thought made Trout want to scream.

It was one thing seeing that maniac in leg and waist chains in a courtroom or strapped to the execution table behind reinforced glass. It was something totally different thinking about meeting him out here. Meeting a Homer Gibbon who was free, insane, and infected. A Homer Gibbon who was a zombie.

Zombie.

The word was still so unreal.

Suddenly something broke from the foliage on his left and ran across the road. Trout stamped on the brakes and skidded through mud, fishtailing as he rocked to a stop.

He flicked on his brights and stared.

The lane was empty. Whatever it was had cut into the woods on the right.

And then the same shape moved back into the road, standing there in the glow of the lights, head swiveling in fear and panic.

A deer. Only a damn deer. On a deer path. Who'd have thought? Trout began to smile, but then he bent close to the windshield and took a closer look at the animal, and his smile bled away.

The deer was covered with open wounds that bled sluggishly in the rain.

Not bullet wounds.

Bites.

Clearly . . . bites.

The deer kept looking from one side of the road to the other, ignoring the car completely. It was a doe, maybe two or three years old. Lean and strong, but dying on its feet, its sides heaving with exertion or panic.

Trout put it all together. It wasn't hard. Everything Volker had said was burning in his mind like words written in fire.

"No," Trout said. "Come on . . . no."

Then a figure stepped out of the woods and stopped in the middle of the road, ten feet from the hood of the Explorer, thirty feet from the doe. A woman. Raven black hair, pale skin. Ample curves in a velvet and lace dress and spiderweb pattern stockings. The heart-shaped face stared at him, ruby red lips parted in a soft "oh." A Goth look. Heavyset but sexy.

And heartbreakingly familiar.

"Oh . . . no," whispered Trout, and the ache in his chest became ten times worse.

The woman's face was totally unmarked. The rest of her was not. Her arms and legs, her generous breasts and stomach . . . every other part of her was torn.

Bitten.

"No."

Trout knew every line and curve of the woman's face, from her liquid green eyes to her full-lipped mouth. Eyes that always twinkled with wicked fun; a mouth on which a thousand variations of a saucy smile flickered. Now those eyes were as empty as green glass; that mouth slack. Her expression was a total blank. No pain. No fear. Not even the wry, self-aware humor that perpetually defined her. There was nothing.

"God," said Trout as tears broke from his eyes. "Marcia. . . ."

Another figure stepped out into the lane. A young man in mechanic's coveralls and a baseball cap twisted sideways on his head. A stranger. His lower face and throat had been savaged, and even with the rain the whole front of his coveralls was dark with blood. He shambled into the path, turned awkwardly toward the headlights for a moment, and then wheeled around toward the deer. Without hesitation he lunged at the animal, but the deer pelted away down the road, uttering the strangest cry Trout had ever heard a deer make. The mechanic lurched after her.

Marcia, however, stood her ground, her head tilting first to one side and then the other as if she were trying to see past the high beams; but as she did that her expression maintained its bland vacuity. It was as unnerving as it was grotesque. This was the secondary infection that Volker described. Bodies totally enslaved to the parasites. Hosts without conscious control.

But where was the consciousness? Volker had intended for Gibbon to retain consciousness while in the grave. Unable to move, but able to feel and experience. Was that what he was seeing here? Was Marcia trapped in there?

It was the most horrible thing Trout could imagine. Her body hijacked by mindless insects that functioned on a purely instinctive level, and her mind—Marcia's beautiful, clever, cheeky, delicious mind—trapped and unable to control what the parasite made her body do. Like a ghost haunting a house that once belonged to it in life.

He wished he'd killed Volker. God, he wished he'd taken that gun and beat that fucking maniac to death with it.

Or, better yet, he wished he'd made Volker come with him. So he could see firsthand what horrors he'd wrought. Then he'd kick the son of a bitch out into the rain and let Marcia have her way with him.

He gagged and almost vomited on the dashboard.

Marcia was a monster. An actual monster.

Trout knew that if he stepped out of the car she would attack him. Or . . . rather, her body would. Marcia would have no control over it. She would have no choice. She would have to watch her body commit murder and cannibalism.

"Jesus Christ," Trout said.

How widespread was this? How many people had been infected? Where was Dez?

That thought ignited like a flare in his mind. Where the hell was Desdemona Fox? Was she alive or dead? And, if she was dead . . . what kind of dead was she?

Tears brimmed in his eyes again. He had the pistol, but Trout had no idea how to use it. He'd never fired a gun in his life. Even if he knew how, he was sure he couldn't bring himself to use it on Marcia. Or Dez.

Maybe on himself, though. That thought was whispered constantly in the back of his mind. If Dez was infected, if she was truly lost to him forever, then he would use Volker's gun and give her peace . . . and then he would join her. If he could not have her in life, then he would follow her into death.

Tears ran down his face and he wiped his eyes on his sleeve.

Screw this. Dez was probably already as dead as Marcia. Maybe everyone in town was. Say good-night, folks, and thanks for coming. So long.

Marcia took a small step toward the Explorer.

"Marcia," Trout said softly. "I'm so sorry."

She took another step. Trout tried flicking the lights at her. Her lips curled in a brief snarl, but then settled back to rubbery slackness.

Trout took his foot gingerly off the brake, allowing the engine idle to move the SUV forward a few feet.

Marcia did not move. He stepped down on the brake pedal.

"Come on, Marcia . . . please," Trout said, sniffing at the tears. "Cut me a break here." The pistol was on the seat beside him. Even a bonehead like him could suck on the barrel and pull the trigger.

He thought about Goat and what they had planned to do about this.

There were hundreds of kids at the shelter. Maybe more. If they'd gotten there when the storm started, then there was a good chance they were still alive, still safe within the blocky walls of the elementary school.

And Dez was out there somewhere.

"Fuck!" He yelled it.

Outside, Marcia heard him and took a more definite step toward the car.

Inside, a clock was ticking in Billy Trout's head.

He eased his foot off the brakes again and the car moved forward once more, slowly closing the distance between the Explorer's grille and Marcia. She didn't move out of the way. She reached for the hood, and Trout watched her red nails scratch long lines in the paint. One of her nails bent slowly backward and then broke, tearing away a flap of skin. Trout yelped in imagined pain; Marcia did not.

The Explorer moved against her, bumping into her with a soft, heavy sound that made Trout clench his teeth. Marcia leaned into the car, pushing and clawing at it as if she could tear through it to get to . . .

A fresh wave of sickness washed over Trout as he realized with perfect clarity what Marcia intended to do. It was something he had known all along but not quite accepted. Until now.

"Please," he begged. He hit the horn.

She clawed at the hood.

He tapped the brakes to try and jolt her away. The lane was far too narrow to go around, and there was no side road.

But she would not, could not, be deterred. She knew that he was in there. And she wanted him. Even though her eyes were dead, her mouth worked constantly, snapping at the air.

"Please," he said again, but even as he said so, he touched the gas. Just a tap, but it made the Explorer surge five feet forward. Marcia was flattened against the grille and hood for a moment, her feet sliding in the mud. Then she slipped. Just a few inches, her weight pulling her down as her feet lost their support.

Trout touched the gas again, just a whisper of extra power. The Explorer lurched forward again, and Marcia slipped farther down.

"I'm sorry," Trout said and then a sob broke in his chest as he pressed down on the gas, driving the car forward and watching Marcia slide slowly backward off the hood and sink down, inch by inch, in front of the car. In front, and under. Her arms were stretched forward, nails scratching and scrabbling at the wet metal. Rain pounded her, dancing along the white skin of her hands and arms.

Another few feet forward, another few inches down.

She was disappearing in horrible slow motion, sinking into the mud as the weight and mass of the Explorer pushed her down. Trout stared into her empty green eyes as they peered at him over the very edge of the hood . . . and then they were gone as she slid down. Her hands slid away from him, and they, too, were gone.

There was a moment when the car seemed to stall, but then Trout realized with even greater horror that it was because the wheels were trying to climb over an obstacle.

A second, deeper sob tore itself from Trout's chest as he fed the car more gas and the four-wheel drive found purchase. The Explorer rocked sideways as it climbed awkwardly over the obstruction. Wheel by wheel it thumped back into the mud, and the vehicle rolled forward without further hindrance.

Trout kicked the brake pedal to the floor and bent forward as if in physical pain. His forehead rested on the knobbed arc of the steering wheel. He let go of the wheel and punched it, and punched the dash and punched his own head. Trout screamed as loud as all the pain in the world.

When he finally began driving, he dared not look in the rearview mirror. It would kill him to see Marcia lying broken in the mud. It would kill him to see her getting to her feet.

"Oh, Christ," he said through his tears. "Dez . . ."

He gunned the motor and kept driving.

CHAPTER SEVENTY-THREE
AROUND STEBBINS COUNTY

"Where is everyone?" asked Jimmy Hobbs as he and his girlfriend, Elizabeth Donald, stepped into the foyer of the offices of Regional Satellite News. He was five years younger than Elizabeth and was the company gofer, doing everything from chauffeuring camera crews to replacing broken toilet seats. With his shocking red hair and freckles he looked like Archie from the comics. Elizabeth had curly black hair and dark eyes and a Goth style she modeled after Marcia's, minus all the piercings.

"Where's Marcia?" asked Elizabeth as she shrugged out of her wet coat. She was not smiling. A faint frown tugged at the corners of her mouth.

The receptionist's chair was pushed back against the wall and her Styrofoam Dunkin' Donuts coffee cup was on its side, still dripping into the pool that was spread under the desk.

"Maybe she went to get the mop," suggested Jimmy. "I'll go see."

Without another word he pushed through the batwing saloon doors that led into the newsroom. Elizabeth bent over to shake droplets from her hair. From that angle she could look under the edges of the flapping saloon doors and for a moment she didn't understand what she was seeing.

Jimmy seemed to be dancing with Murray Klein's secretary, Connie.

Dancing?

Even as she saw this, Elizabeth knew that it was wrong, that her perception was skewed, and not merely because she was bent over. The picture she saw would not fit into her mind.

She straightened slowly and peered over the top of the doors.

Jimmy was not dancing. Of course he wasn't dancing. That was crazy.

What he was doing, however, was crazier by far.

Connie and Jimmy were locked in a fierce embrace and it seemed to Elizabeth that Connie was forcibly trying to kiss Jimmy.

No. Not kiss.

Bite?

Jimmy was twice the secretary's size, but shock and the ferocity of the attack was crippling him. In a moment it would kill him, unless . . .

Elizabeth burst through the doors and into the newsroom.

She stopped, momentarily forgetting even the weird and absurd gavotte being performed in front of her. The newsroom was in shambles. Desks were overturned, papers thrown onto the floor. Computer monitors had been smashed and some still leaked smoke; and someone had splashed bright red paint everywhere.

Once more Elizabeth's mind rewound that thought and edited it with new words. Not paint. Blood. Pints of it. Gallons. Walls, floor, and even some on the ceiling.

Bodies lay scattered around. The rest of the afternoon staff. The weatherman, Gino Torelli, was spread-eagled over a desk with his crotch and the inside of both thighs simply . . . gone. Torn away. Elizabeth could see torn muscles and white bone, but worse than that someone had rammed a letter opener into one of his eye sockets, angling it to drive all the way into his brain.

"Oh . . . ," murmured Elizabeth.

The other secretary, Wilma, was slumped in her chair as if she was trying to awaken from a terrible dream. There were others, too. Two reporters, an engineer, a copy editor, and a man dressed like a state trooper. The engineer was lying face down on the floor; the others knelt around him like picnickers, pulling red pieces out of him.

Elizabeth uttered a single, sharp, high yelp. A sound with no meaning beyond an expression of horror so profound that adjectives for it did not exist.

Their white faces turned toward the sound; toward her.

Jimmy, still wrestling with Connie, yelled, "They've all gone crazy! Get out!"

She almost did. She almost turned and ran right then.

But Elizabeth liked Jimmy. A whole lot. She'd been waiting for a decent guy like him for years. And, irrational as it may have been, she felt her disgust and horror suddenly drain away to be replaced with a towering indignation. She did not know what kind of madness was unfurling around her, but she was goddamn well not going to let anyone take Jimmy away from her.

With a growl that was as inarticulate as her yelp but filled with much greater purpose, Elizabeth strode over to the wrangling couple, grabbed Connie by the back of the hair and yanked her away from Jimmy with such ferocity that Connie's feet momentarily left the ground. The smaller woman lost her grip on Jimmy and landed with her heels in a puddle of blood. Possibly her own blood. Elizabeth didn't care. She spun Connie around and belted her across the face with every ounce of strength she possessed.

Connie's head whipped to one side and she staggered several steps away.

The things that were crouched around the engineer dropped the pieces of meat they held and began to get to their feet.

Which is when Elizabeth's brief rage slammed into the wall of reality.

"Oh . . . fuck," she said.

"W—what the hell's going on?" demanded Jimmy. His eyes were glazed and, sweetheart though he might be, he was clearly not capable of handling this.

"Get out, Jimmy!" Elizabeth bellowed. "Run!"

He stared at her, clearly unwilling to leave her, but then the state trooper spat a mouthful of black mucus at Jimmy, who backpedaled to avoid it. His body, once in motion, apparently wanted to keep moving, and he turned and crashed through the saloon doors and then out through the vestibule and into the rain. The monsters—Elizabeth couldn't think of any better word for them—began to lumber after him, drawn by the sound and movement of his departure.

"No fucking way!" snarled Elizabeth. She hooked a foot around the leg of a wheeled chair and kicked it into their path. The state trooper fell over it, and the others fell over him. Elizabeth laughed by reflex even though the moment possessed not one ounce of comedy. Even to her own ears her short laugh had an hysterical note.

Connie turned toward her. Her lips writhed back from cracked white teeth.

"Shit," said Elizabeth, and then she was running. Not after Jimmy. She had the presence of mind to go another way, to give him a chance. Instead she shoved Connie out of the way and ran between her and the other monsters, barreled down the corridor past the editing rooms, and hit the crash bar on the back door with both hands.

She ran into the rain and darkness. Behind her she heard the crash bar strike again and again as the monsters followed her outside. Elizabeth was not a fast runner and the monsters seemed awkward and slow, but every time she looked back . . . they were closer. She realized with even greater horror that a few of them could move fast. Not as fast as Jimmy but faster than her.

I'm going to die! Jesus God, I'm going to die.

As she ran, she knew with completely certainty, that she was right about that.

But it wasn't the dead who killed her.

She cut across the parking lot and out into the street and never saw the National Guard troop truck that came bucketing down Main Street.

"What the hell was that?" yelped Corporal Nick Wyckoff as he fought to control the troop truck after the impact.

Sergeant Teddy Polk was in the passenger seat. He cranked down the window and craned his head to look down the road. "Nice one, Nick. You got one of those fuckers."

His voice was cocky, but his eyes were filled with terror.

Wyckoff licked his lips. "Are you sure? You sure it was one of the infected?"

"Has to be," said Polk. Despite the cold, he was sweating inside the hazmat hood. "You heard what the captain told us. Everyone in this damn town is already dead."

"Dead," echoed Wyckoff. He crossed himself and touched the medal of Mary beneath his clothes.

The truck raced along a side road, kicking up plumes of mud behind it.

A figure suddenly appeared in the headlights, running along the shoulder of the road.

"Christ, there's another one," said Wyckoff. In the pale glow of the dashboard the sergeant looked ten years old.

"Get her," urged Polk.

"Are you nuts?"

"Hey—the captain said that we can't let any of them out of here—"

"I know, Teddy, but she's just a—"

"Run her the fuck down, Nick!"

However, when the driver swerved to clip the figure, it was gone, vanished into the woods beside the road.

Wyckoff did not stop. He kicked down on the gas and headed toward the center of town.

As the truck's taillights dwindled into the distance, the figure stepped out of the woods. She was panting, drenched, bedraggled, and furious. She held her Glock in a two-handed grip and her lips were curled back from gritted teeth.

"Fuckers," growled Dez Fox. Then she lowered her gun, asking herself if she would have fired on them if they'd stopped and gotten out of the truck. Could she have drawn down on soldiers who were out here doing their jobs? Even if that job was the systematic extermination of everyone in town?

Could Dez even be sure that she didn't have the plague? She wasn't sick, but she knew that people could carry diseases that didn't make them sick. Typhoid Mary.

She touched the walkie-talkie in her jacket pocket. If she called them and tried to explain things to them . . . would they even listen?

At some point she was going to have to find out.

She checked the road for more vehicles, but there was nothing.

Dez holstered her pistol and kept running. She was almost there.

CHAPTER SEVENTY-FOUR
REGIONAL SATELLITE NEWS

Billy Trout sat in his Explorer and watched most of the people he knew and worked with at RSN close in around the office gopher, Jimmy, and drag him kicking and screaming into the shelter of a parked news van. Trout almost got out of the car to try to help, but as he reached for the door handle he could see that Jimmy was already pretty far gone. The actual killing was over quickly. So quickly that it left Trout breathless.

They grabbed Jimmy from all sides. The weatherman, Gino, had his teeth buried in Jimmy's cheek. Wilma had both arms wrapped around Jimmy's waist and was tearing at his thigh with bloody teeth. The young man's screams were as high and shrill as a girl's.

There wasn't a goddamn thing Trout could do about it, and, as he watched, the scene collapsed down into a feeding frenzy more savage than a pack of hyenas around a downed zebra. Trout reeled back from the sight, squeezing his eyes shut and wincing as if he could feel the pain of those bites. How had it spread so far so fast? His mind kept replaying the image of Marcia falling slowly under the wheels of his Explorer.

Come on, you idiot, growled his inner voice, *you're wasting time.*

He opened his eyes and studied the building. From where he was parked he could see in through the open front door, through the glass vestibule, and into the reception area. There was no movement inside.

Trout licked his lips. Volker's pistol was a cold weight on his thigh, and Trout touched it with trembling fingers. He expected the solidity of it to comfort him, but it did not. To kill these things—to really kill them—Volker said that you had to destroy the motor cortex or the brain stem. Trout didn't like his chances with a head shot. He'd be lucky to hit the body let alone a target as small as the motor cortex. Not unless he was almost face-to-face with them, and that thought was unbearable.

He got out of the car very carefully. The zombies did not look up from their meal. None of them appeared to notice the dome light come on in the Explorer. The rain was still an effective screen. Even so, every sloshing footfall, every ragged breath seemed insanely loud to him as he crept from the side of his car to the side of the building. It felt so strange to carry a gun and, despite everything, Trout felt vaguely foolish, like a kid playing cops and robbers.

He paused at the entrance, looked inside and looked back, and cursed himself. That quick look into the lighted building spoiled his night vision. Taking the pistol in both hands, Trout sidled in through the vestibule and hip-checked the door so that it swung shut.

The reception area was empty, and he cautiously crept into the newsroom. Trout bit down on a cry of horror. The station engineer, a gray-haired man named Jock Spooner, lay on the floor. The dead had been at him. The man was like a scarecrow with all the stuffing removed. His arms and legs were spread like a starfish and were strangely intact . . . but the rest of him—chest, stomach, organs, and meat—had been torn away. And eaten. Trout was sure of that.

The devastation to the man was appalling. It was dehumanizing on a level that Trout had never witnessed . . . but it wasn't the worst part of the grisly spectacle. Not by a million miles was it the worst.

The man's eyes were open.

His mouth was moving.

Not trying to speak. Trying to *bite*. Destroyed as he was, the engineer was trying to raise his head and bite.

Trout stared down at Jock. "Oh . . . God, no."

Jock's teeth clacked together. His arms and legs were attached by a few strings of meat. Compelled by a twisted fascination, Trout leaned as close as he dared and stared into the engineer's eyes.

Jock snapped the air causing Trout to flinch.

"Shit . . . um . . . Jock? Hey, buddy . . . are you still in there? Can you hear me?"

The dead eyes stared at him without expression. Trout bent closer still to examine the wounds, trying to make sense of animation and apparent life in the presence of so much physical destruction. He caught movement along the lines of torn flesh, and when he realized what it was he recoiled in terror. Jock's blood had coagulated to a dark jellylike substance, and it was teeming with tiny worms. They looked like maggots, though much smaller and thinner.

He looked at the blood splashed on the floor. Some of it was bright red, some was as dark as Jock's blood. All of the dark blood was pulsing with larvae. But where the black blood and the red blood intermingled he could see waves of even smaller larvae and tiny spots of white. Eggs and hatchlings. Had to be. But it was so fast. Insanely fast.

"Volker, you sick bastard."

Trout backed away, looking frantically round the office, but, aside from Jock, the place was empty. He turned and ran down the hall to Goat's editing room. Trout was moderately tech savvy from being around the equipment for so long, and he gathered up what he needed and shoved it into one of Goat's big canvas rucksacks. Then he tiptoed to the door and ran through the rain to his car. The zombies raised their heads as the engine roared to life, but by the time they lumbered to their feet, Trout was back on Doll Factory Road, rolling hot and fast toward the school.

CHAPTER SEVENTY-FIVE
SWEET PARADISE TRAILER PARK

Byron Rempel sat on the floor next to the woman who killed him.

Fifteen minutes ago, Rempel was alive and so was the woman. She was Mrs. O'Grady, who had a modest trailer three pads down from the double-wide that served as Rempel's office and home. Mrs. O'Grady was a quiet old lady who paid her rent on time and more often than not preferred to live with something broken rather than bother Rempel for a repair job. That made Rempel like her. Or at least tolerate her. Rempel didn't like any of the residents of Sweet Paradise. They were all white trash losers as far as he was concerned. Half of them were on welfare or unemployment, and Rempel considered both of those institutions to be socially parasitic. He worked his ass off and he hated the idea that some of his tax dollars went into the pockets of lazy fucks who couldn't hold a job, or who were too lazy to try.

There were exceptions, of course. There was that stuck-up waitress in 14-E. That broad never even gave him a free refill of coffee when he stopped in the diner. Bitch. And that Irish layabout writer, Kealan Patrick Burke, who just moved here from Columbus. Guy won some awards for some goofy horror stories and thought his shit didn't stink. Thought he was Stephen-fucking-King, and as far as Rempel was concerned even Stephen-fucking-King wasn't Stephen-fucking-King. Not anymore. Not since *The Stand*. Last good book that New England prick ever wrote.

Rempel had not read any of King's books after that, and had not read a word of Burke's, but he was positive the guy was an overrated Mick who was probably a drunk and a wife-beater, too. They all were. Every writer he ever met was a drunk, and every Mick he ever met was a wife-beater. Rempel was positive of this, so he disliked Burke on general principle.

The queen bitch of Sweet Paradise, though, was Dez Fox. Now there was someone who really thought that she crapped little gold bars and peed gin rickeys. And talk about stuck-up? Rempel had asked her over for coffee three times, and each time Dez Fox looked at him like he was a spitty place on the sidewalk.

Granted, she was hot. Bitch had a serious rack of bombs on her, Rempel admired that. Nice ass, too; but she knew that she was stacked and that's why she treated Rempel like crap. Except when something broke in her apartment, then Dez was all sweet, saying "please" and "thank you" like butter wouldn't melt in her mouth.

What made him unhappy was someone making a mess. Which is why he was very unhappy fifteen minutes ago, answering a call at Burke's trailer in the middle of a rainstorm that would have scared the shit out of Noah. The writer called with some kind of hysterical rant about blood or something all over the floor. All over the carpeted floor. Rempel hadn't been able to get a straight story from Burke. The idiot probably cut himself shaving while drunk. Serve him right to bleed to death, the frigging Irish sot. But he grabbed his tool kit, pulled on his yellow rain slicker, and slogged through ankle-deep mud to the writer's trailer.

When he got there he started cursing at once. The door to Burke's trailer was wide open and the rain was pouring in. But as Rempel approached the trailer he slowed, frowning in consternation. The runoff that dripped out of the trailer was tinged a rust red. Christ, what the hell did Burke do? Cut his own head off?

Rempel mounted the three metal steps to the open door and peered inside.

Burke was nowhere to be seen. However, Mrs. O'Grady was lying flat out on the floor just inside the door.

"Shit!" Rempel rushed inside and dropped to his knees beside her, ignoring the blood that pooled around her. The old lady had been terribly brutalized. Some mad bastard had beaten her face in. Literally beaten it in. Mrs. O'Grady's false teeth lay shattered and scattered around her, and from the bridge of her nose to her chin the skin was torn away and the bones smashed to pieces. Rempel stared in mute horror at the exposed splinters of bone that stuck up through the mangled flesh.

He couldn't believe what he was seeing. This was the work of a madman, a maniac. Could Burke have done this? Rempel tried to imagine the soft-spoken Irish writer going apeshit like this. He didn't like Burke, but this didn't fit at all.

It was hard to imagine anyone doing this to a nice old broad like Mrs. O'Grady. Killing her was bad enough, but disfiguring her was . . .

Well, Rempel thought, it was just plain crazy.

Rempel got up and moved cautiously through the trailer. No sign of Burke. No sign of a mad killer, either. He pulled his cell phone out of his pocket and punched 9-1-1. The phone went immediately to a "No Service" message. Not even a ring.

"Shit." He tried 4-1-1 and got the same thing, and he had no better luck with Burke's home phone. It made a weird electronic beeping sound, but there was no dial tone. Rempel had two thoughts about that. The storm and the killer. In the movies it was the killer who disabled the phones, but that wouldn't explain the lack of a cell phone signal.

He heard a sound behind him and turned, expecting it to be Burke.

It was Mrs. O'Grady.

She stood a few feet away from him, her eyes wide and dark and empty, and her face a ruin of jagged bone and ripped flesh.

Rempel stared blankly at her.

"What—" he asked.

She answered with a bite. Not with her old false teeth—they were destroyed—but with a new set of teeth formed by the jagged bones of her exposed jaws. It was a disjointed, improbable weapon, and he should have been able to block her, evade her, sweep her aside. Rempel was easily twice her size. Mrs. O'Grady wasn't even particularly fast.

It was all about shock. All about impossibility.

Rempel stared in shock one second too long.

Which is how so many in Stebbins died that night.

And it was why so many of the dying spoke the same last word. A single syllable, spoken with fear and wonder.

"No."

Dez slowed to a cautious walk as she approached the trailer park. Even from a hundred feet away she could tell that the wave of the infection had already reached here and swept through it.

Two of the trailers were burning.

Doors were open, cars stood idling and empty.

There was no blood, not in this rain, but she saw the glint of shotgun shells on the ground.

Dez wasn't sure how to react to this. On one hand, the violence seemed to have rolled around her rather than over her. On the other, she felt like she was losing what little grasp she had on exactly what was happening.

How long had she been asleep in the back of the cruiser?

It was full dark, and she didn't think it was an early dusk caused by the storm. This was night. The dead of night, she thought, and shivered at her own joke.

She moved into the park. The closest trailers were dark except for Rempel's, but he wasn't home. She wasn't sure if she was happy or disappointed that he wasn't the main course in a monster feast.

A moment later the implications of that thought hit her. It wasn't another bad joke. She really had been disappointed that Rempel wasn't dead, and that was really bad thinking.

I'm losing it.

As she continued deeper into the trailer park she tried to knock down that observation, but it dodged every blow.

God . . . how far gone am I?

How do I even know if I'm crazy or just in shock?

At the corner of Rempel's trailer she paused. Her own double-wide was sixty feet across open ground. No cover except for some flower gardens that had withered in the cold and were now beaten flat by the rain. She was about to sprint for it when she saw a figure come walking out from between her trailer and her neighbor's.

It was a teenager. One of the Murphy twins from the F-section of the park. He was dressed in jeans and a white sweatshirt. No shoes or coat. Even from twenty yards Dez could tell that he was dead. The realization drove a knife into her heart.

The twins were thirteen. Still kids.

She raised her pistol and aimed. The distance was far too great for an accurate shot, but she suddenly found herself running forward, the gun leading the way, her feet making the quick, small steps she was taught in the military. Large steps jolt and jerk the body, spoiling aim; small steps roll the body forward, keeping the gun level. She ran toward the boy and, as he turned toward her and began to reach, Dez fired a single shot from eight feet away. It took the boy in the forehead, blowing an apple-sized chunk out of the back of his head as the impact snapped the child's neck.

Even with the roar of the rain muffling the blast, the gunshot seemed too loud. It would draw them. She knew that for a fact, which meant that she had just blown a hole in her own future.

Hurry, you bitch.

She ran to her trailer, jammed the key in the lock, opened the door, jumped in, and shut and locked the door behind her.

Byron Rempel sat on the floor, dead but newly awake, inert because there was no prey to follow, when Desdemona Fox ran past the open doorway.

The sight of her. The smell of her. The living reality of her triggered a response in the parasitic hive mind that now ruled his body. It was not a thought, merely a reaction. An impulse to follow, to attack, to feed, and to transfer larvae to a new host. To another host. One of many.

Rempel and Mrs. O'Grady struggled to their feet and shuffled slowly out of the trailer, following the scent of fresh meat. Other figures emerged from trailers all along the path the running woman had taken.

CHAPTER SEVENTY-SIX
SWEET PARADISE TRAILER PARK

The trailer was dark. There was no backup generator, no emergency lights.

Dez unclipped her flashlight and used its beam to find the stove. It was gas, so she lit all four burners. The light filled the kitchen and dining room. She fished in the cabinets until she found a box of candles. She didn't have any of the thick girlie-girl scented candles. All she had were thin colored candles left over from JT's birthday, so she lit those and carried a fistful of them into her bedroom. Since she couldn't hold them all and do what she had to do, she grabbed her metal trashcan and dropped the candles on the balled-up tissues, used makeup sponges, torn-up bills, and a card from Billy Trout that she had thrown away unopened. The tissues caught right away and then the rest, throwing bright yellow light into the room.

Dez set the can down on the bedroom carpet, fished in her pocket for her keys, and fumbled the right one into the lock. The Yale clicked open and Dez lifted the lid.

It was all there. Handguns in wooden boxes. Shotguns. Hunting rifles with scopes. Stacked boxes of bullets. Knives. Everything.

For the first time in hours, Dez Fox smiled.

And then the dead began banging their pale fists against the walls and windows of her trailer.

CHAPTER SEVENTY-SEVEN
DOLL FACTORY ROAD

Billy Trout drove across town like a madman. At the corner of Doll Factory and Meetinghouse Road he saw a National Guard Humvee.

"Thank God," he breathed. Guardsmen were mostly local guys, if not from Stebbins then at least from this part of the state. If anyone would understand, they would; and if anyone had the resources to turn this thing around, they would. The feds might be willing to wipe Stebbins off the face of the earth, but he did not believe that of ordinary guys.

The soldiers turned at the sound of his horn. Trout flashed his brights at them. He was looking for a sign, a wave, a smile. Anything.

The soldiers leveled their weapons at him.

Trout slowed the car, still forty yards from them.

He tooted the horn again.

There was a two second pause as the Guardsmen bent their heads together to consult. Trout began to smile.

Then they opened fire.

Mud popped up in lines all the way to his car and then Trout was down, cringing and curling himself onto the seat, screaming as the bullets tore into the grille and hood and punched holes in the glass.

"Jesus Christ! What the fuck are you crazy bastards doing?" he yelled.

There was a lull in the gunfire.

The entire windshield was a lace curtain of cracks and holes.

Trout raised his head, risking a glance over the dashboard.

The soldiers were advancing on him, their barrels smoking in the rain but still aimed his way.

Trout reached out and threw the car into reverse and then shot upright in the seat and kicked down on the gas pedal. The Explorer lurched and jumped backward, rolling fast away from the soldiers who immediately opened fire.

"I'm not infected!" he screamed.

He knew that they could not hear him over the roar of their own guns, but Trout was furious. He kept yelling that as he hit the brakes, shifted into drive, spun the wheel and went diagonally across Doll Factory Road. More bullets stitched a line of ragged holes in the passenger side. Both side windows blew out and Trout was peppered with flying bits of glass; but the car was gaining speed now, clawing across the gravel parking lot of a closed down Denny's, cutting over to a side road and blasting away from the soldiers. Bullets continued to whang and ping off the back of the car for a quarter mile.

Trout was panicking now. Wind and rain battered his face as he drove. He kept thinking, *They didn't care if I was infected or not. They didn't care. God Almighty, they don't care.*

CHAPTER SEVENTY-EIGHT
THE SITUATION ROOM
WASHINGTON, D.C.

The president of the United States sat in his big leather swivel chair, fingers steepled, brow knitted, staring at the satellite map of Stebbins County. Phones rang all around the crisis room as his staff worked to implement the Wildfire protocols. Above the main screen were several smaller screens, one of which was a Doppler radar display of the storm. The National Weather Service was giving a fifty-fifty chance that the storm could veer northeast or continue to stall over Stebbins County. If the latter happened, the computer models estimated that it might be as much as six hours before helicopters could fly. Six hours during which ground visibility was compromised.

Another screen showed men working in a raging storm to load thermobaric devices onto a row of parked Apache gunships.

The president's mouth was dry, and he sipped water. There were a lot of people in the Situation Room, and it took effort to keep his emotions off his face as he studied the weapons being installed.

Thermobaric devices. Fuel-air bombs. Massive cluster bombs that explode in two stages, the first of which creates a cloud of explosive material which is then ignited. As a general had told him once, "Mr.

President, this is the most powerful nonnuclear weapon currently in existence. It is, I can assure you, the very definition of hell on earth."

Those words had been said with pride by an officer fighting the endless war in Afghanistan. Now, however . . .

He picked up a file from the table and opened it. The top page was a printout of the estimated rate of infection if Lucifer 113 could not be contained within Stebbins County. The numbers were impossible. They were bad science fiction. They were a horror story.

The president closed the folder and leaned forward to watch the loading of the fuel-air bombs.

"Dear God," murmured the president.

PART FOUR

THE LAST MEETING PLACE

But I've a rendezvous with Death
At midnight in some flaming town.

—Alan Seeger, "I Have a Rendezvous with Death"

CHAPTER SEVENTY-NINE
SWEET PARADISE TRAILER PARK

Dez looked up from the arms chest and snarled at the sound of hands beating on the thin skin of her trailer. She hurried to the window, peered out, and looked right into the face of her landlord, Rempel. There were others out there, too. Half the goddamn residents of the trailer park were out there.

"You fuckers," she said, but the bravado was thin and fragile, nailed to the walls of her heart by rusty pins. She tried not to think about what she was seeing in rational terms. None of them were friends, but she did not even want to see them as her neighbors. She could not afford to pay that kind of coin, not if she was going to get to the school . . . and right now everything was about the school.

If the school is even there.

A nasty inner voice whispered it to her every few minutes, but Dez could not afford to hear that, either.

She tore open a closet and pulled out a big gray canvas ski bag, threw it onto the floor, and began stuffing as many guns and boxes of ammunition as she thought she could carry. She strapped on an extra gun belt, crossing it with her regulation belt so that both draped across her hips like a gunslinger's rig. Dez pulled on a nylon shoulder rig and snugged a Sig Sauer nine into that. Magazines were stuffed into every pocket. They were so heavy that she had to cinch her trousers belt tighter. The last thing she pulled on was a heavy leather biker jacket Billy Trout had given her for Christmas two years ago. She pinched the thick leather.

"Bite through this, motherfucker."

As she slung the bag over her shoulder, Dez caught sight of herself in the floor-length mirror that hung from clips on the bedroom door. She looked like a character from a video game. One of those improbably busty, impossibly well-armed superchicks who could do acrobatics and hit the kill zone even while firing guns from both hands during a cartwheel.

"You look fucking ridiculous," she told herself.

Her reflection grinned back at her. Dez picked up a Daewoo USAS-12 automatic shotgun, slapped in a ten-round magazine, faced the door, and drew a deep breath.

"Yippie ki-yay and all that shit."

She kicked open the door and jumped out into the rain.

CHAPTER EIGHTY
STEBBINS LITTLE SCHOOL
STEBBINS COUNTY, PENNSYLVANIA

Corporal Wyckoff let the Humvee roll to a stop just inside the big wrought iron gates of the Stebbins Little School.

"Holy God," he said softly.

Beside him, Sergeant Polk stared openmouthed.

The entry road wound upward from the gate to the block school that sat like a medieval castle on a knoll surrounded by neat rows of ancient oaks. The school looked solid enough to withstand a mortar assault, but that wasn't the problem.

The road leading to the school was choked with dozens of crashed and abandoned school buses. Hundreds of passenger cars were clustered around them. A few were burning, several were overturned. Even in the downpour, two of the trees were burning as well, the fire having spread from a wrecked yellow bus that still smoldered. And everywhere—everywhere—were the infected.

"Jesus Christ, Nick . . . there are hundreds of those things."

"Thousands," murmured Polk. "Oh man . . . we are so fucked."

The dead surrounded the school like an invading army laying siege. Wyckoff and Polk heard a few pops of small-arms fire, but whoever was shooting was either in the crowd, in which case he was dead the second he ran out of bullets, or inside the school, and in that case he might as well be on the moon.

Wyckoff stabbed a finger at the scene. "We're supposed to go in and secure that? Not a chance."

"I know."

"Why'd they send us down here?"

" 'Cause no one knows what the hell's going on, that's why. They don't know how bad this shit is. We got no air reconnaissance, Nick; we're the first ones to put eyes on this." Polk pulled his map out of its case and studied the position of the school, pointing out landmarks to Wyckoff. "Okay, here's the school and here's us. We have two squads, so we're sure as shit not going in there. Beyond the school is some forestland, what looks like a stream that feeds into a series of ponds, part of a golf course, and then the Maryland state line. That stream is going to be a river right now, so that's good news. No one's crossing that, and sure as hell not those awkward sonsabitches. That leaves the western side. There's a soccer field and a parking lot, and another fence. The east is a fence and then a couple of farms." He chewed his lip. "We might be luckier than I thought."

"How?"

"We have a combination of natural and man-made barriers that could contain the infected at least for now."

"What if they come this way?" Wyckoff asked.

"We hold them."

"With two squads?"

Polk didn't answer. Instead he grabbed for the radio and called in a situation report to his commanding officer, Captain Rice. Each squad was composed of two four-man fire teams. That gave him sixteen men to hold a gate and the road. It was ugly math, but at least the infected seemed to be focused on the school. None of them had noticed the vehicles sitting at the base of the long entry road.

At least for now.

CHAPTER EIGHTY-ONE
SWEET PARADISE TRAILER PARK

Dez landed too hard, the heavy bag driving her into the mud with so much force that her legs screamed in pain and buckled. She went down to her knees in the rain, but she kept the shotgun barrel out of the mud, and, as the first of the dead turned toward her, Dez fired.

There had to be forty of the monsters clustered around her trailer. Dez fired and fired.

Each 12-gauge shell was packed with nine lead pellets. The blast caught a woman in a bathrobe full in the face and blew half her head away. The dead man behind her caught some of the pellets and one went down with a hole through his eye.

Dez forced herself to her feet and fired, turned and fired, spun and fired. Rainwater hissed on the barrel as it flared hotter with each blast.

The dead were so close to her that she barely had to aim and couldn't miss. Not every shot was a kill, though. Her own awkward gait as she slogged through the mud and the twitchy shamble of the dead threw wild cards into the point of impact. She blew the left arm off of Donny Phelps and caught Lisa Davis on the shoulder. Seven of them went down before the magazine went dry. Dez kicked one of the dead in the thigh, knocking him back as she reached for a second mag and swapped it out. This was worse than her worst day on the Big Sand. This was a different kind of hell.

Rempel's Tundra was parked thirty feet away, in the slip by the office, but there were so many of the infected, and more were coming from the other trailers, drawn by the blasts of the shotgun. She fired and fired, and the dead fell away, their faces splattered, their bodies pirouetting sloppily as they fell.

Tears ran down Dez's cheeks but she didn't know it. She tried not to name the dead as she killed them. She knew that to allow them to be her neighbors, to be the people she knew, was going to kill her. The process had already begun. So she opened her mouth and roared out an incoherent bellow of rage and grief and need and kept firing.

Then Rempel himself was there, and he was the last one between her and the Tundra. His Tundra. As Dez pulled the trigger to fire the last round in the second magazine, she remembered something from that morning. After the hot water had cut off in her shower Dez had thought that she could put a bullet into Rempel's brainpan without a single flicker of regret.

The blast caught Rempel on the bridge of the nose and the top of his head leapt off with a geyser of blood and gray matter, and Rempel was falling.

"God!" Dez screamed as she leapt over him. "I'm sorry! I'm sorry . . . God I'm sorry!"

She reached the Tundra.

Which was locked.

Of course it was locked.

Dez dropped the heavy bag of weapons, whirled and charged back, swapping in the last magazine for the shotgun, firing at the Mc-Gill twins and old Mr. Peluzzi, destroying them, erasing their faces while burning their names into her mind.

She knelt by Rempel, trying not to look at his ruined head, and fished in his pockets as the dead drew closer and closer, their moans louder than the rain. The keys rattled in his left front pants pocket and Dez dug into it, scrabbling at them with one hand while pointing the shotgun at the approaching monsters with the other. Then she had then and was scrambling away. She put the leather key ring between her teeth and took the shotgun in both hands, firing as one of them reached over Rempel's corpse to grab her. The blast caught Max Scheinhert in the throat, pitching his body backward but dropping his head right in the mud between Rempel's outstretched legs.

Dez gagged as she got to her feet and fired again, walking backward, killing the ones closest to her, trying to buy a second's room to breathe.

Then the gun was empty. Dez threw it in the face of the closest infected person, then she leapt for the door of the Tundra, jammed the key in the lock, opened it, threw the bag inside, and climbed in as cold fingers began clawing at her thighs. She kicked at them and jerked the door shut.

She put the key in the ignition and it roared to life without hesitation. Dez pawed tears from her eyes, put the truck in gear, turned the wheel, and smashed her way through a line of things that had been her neighbors.

"I'm sorry," she said with each sickening impact. "I'm sorry . . ."

CHAPTER EIGHTY-TWO
BEAVER ROAD
STEBBINS COUNTY, PENNSYLVANIA

Billy Trout's panic eased down one notch but not any further. His narrow escape from the National Guard had made him far more cautious, but it also filled him with equal parts rage and hopelessness.

They don't even want to know if we're infected.

It was a staggering idea but he knew that this was true. The Guard were not here on a rescue mission. It was a hard, ugly truth but it was irrefutable. If he had any doubts, then what he saw over the next few minutes clarified things for him.

As he turned onto Beaver he saw a silver Lexus askew in the middle of the road, both front doors open. Heather Faville, mayor of Stebbins, lay sprawled in the street a few feet from her husband, Tony. Neither of them bore the signs of infection: no bites, no black goo, nothing. However, they had been gunned down so comprehensively that the car and both bodies were ripped apart. Hundreds upon hundreds of shell casings covered the road. Trout stared. He knew the Favilles, liked them. He wondered if he would live long enough to grieve for them.

The scene was almost a duplicate of what had almost happened to him. The Favilles had seen the Guardsmen and had stopped, probably relieved. They'd gotten out of their car . . . and died in a hail of bullets.

This wasn't an attempt to contain the infection . . . this was murder. The genocide of an entire town.

From then on, Trout went slower, checking each street to make sure there were no soldiers. White-faced things kept coming out of the rain and most of the time he managed to veer around them, but several times he saw them too late and the big SUV slammed into them. After the third impact he felt some eccentricities manifesting in the steering, and there was a disheartening knocking under the hood. However, the tires hadn't blown and the motor still worked, so he kept going.

There were so many of them on the streets, though. Block after block he saw the infected staggering toward the sound of his engine. He did not see a single living person. Not one. That tore at his heart. This thing was spreading so fast. Even with the rain. It was far worse even than Volker had suggested, and he prayed that the National Guard barricades would hold. That thought felt weird in his head. On one hand he hated the soldiers for what they were doing, and on the other hand he was glad they were there.

He had his doubts, though, about whether the soldiers could adequately monitor and defend the perimeter of the entire town. After all, he had been able to sneak into Stebbins without detection. That thought conjured a flicker of horrific memory—Marcia sliding inch by inch beneath the Explorer's wheels.

God.

He was almost to the center of town when he heard more gunfire. Trout slammed on the brakes and the SUV skidded forty feet into a sideways stop. He cranked down the window and stared at the scene unfolding before him in the big parking lot around Wolverton Hospital. A mass of about a hundred of the infected, most of them wearing lab coats, surgical scrubs, and pajamas, was lumbering its way toward a pair of National Guard Humvees. Soldiers stood atop each vehicle, alien in their white hazmat suits, and fired pedestal-mounted machine guns at the crowd. Trout didn't know models or calibers of machine guns, but these brutes were tearing the front rank of the crowd to pieces. Literally to pieces. Arms and hands and heads flew into the rain and were sent flying by the gusting wind. The mass of the dead never paused though. Their bodies soaked up the bullets, and the ones that didn't fall kept moving, kept reaching.

A figure came staggering out of a side street. He was heavily tattooed and dressed in the uniform of a corrections officer. Trout knew him. Michael McGrath, the sergeant in charge of the county lockup. McGrath staggered jerkily toward the soldiers, a pistol in one hand and the other raised. He called out to them in a voice that was completely human, and with horror Trout knew what was about to happen. He'd once done a story on this man. McGrath always walked like that. He had spastic cerebral palsy and yet was able to maintain his job as a tough corrections officer.

The soldiers did not know this. They turned and saw another shambling, twitching figure coming toward them. Trout tried to yell a warning, but his cry was drowned out by bursts of gunfire. McGrath's body shuttered and danced as the bullets tore into him. His pistol felt from his hand and his face drained of expression. He took a single, final step, and then fell.

The wave of the infected pressed forward, and the soldiers abruptly yielded ground to them. Maybe they were low on ammunition, or maybe this kind of butchery was becoming intolerable for those poor young men in the hazmat suits, Trout didn't know which; but the Humvees began rolling backward, and then in the parking lot of a Burger King they turned and raced off along a side road.

Heading where? Trout wondered, though he already knew.

There was only one thing down that road.

The school.

He cursed, threw the car into gear, spun the wheel, and headed down a small side street.

CHAPTER EIGHTY-THREE
SCHOOLHOUSE ROAD
STEBBINS COUNTY, PENNSYLVANIA

As she drove, Dez listened for news on the walkie-talkie. None of it was good. Squads and platoons were encountering pockets of the dead, and several of the teams were overrun. Dez knew that each soldier who died would rise as one of the dead, adding to their numbers.

The chatter between NCOs and officers was increasingly hysterical. Some of the soldiers were refusing to gun down innocent civilians. These weren't terrorists. They didn't look different from the soldiers, which made it even harder. No difference in skin color, no difference in dress. No way to separate us from them, Dez knew. The soldiers were looking down the barrels of their guns and seeing men, women, and—worst of all—children. Pulling the trigger on them, whether or not they were infected, was simply not something every man could do.

The officers were alternating between trying to sound inspirational with a lot of "God and Country" stuff and using flat-out threats. Dez knew that it was all breaking down. The only chance to maintain control was to pull everyone back to the perimeter. The Q-zone. Pull back and wait for the rain to end so they could bring in helicopters. It was so much easier to kill from five hundred feet in the air. Hellfire missiles and Sidewinders didn't have hearts that could break.

Dez was tempted to cut in and say something on the radio, to beg them to protect the school, but some of what she heard made her doubt that civilian protection was any part of the operational plan. She heard the phrase "contain and sterilize" several times, and that sent chills down her spine.

She busted through some backyard fencing and drove completely off the street grid, angling toward the school. Schoolhouse Lane was the only road that went to the school, but not the only way to get there. Dez broke through a white picket fence and was on the ninth hole of the Stebbins Country Club. The grass was still green despite the cold, but the Tundra's wheels tore apart the perfectly maintained lawn. Fuck it. She agreed with Mark Twain that golf was a "good walk spoiled."

Over the next rise she could see the upper floor of the school. There were columns of smoke rising to meet the black storm clouds, visible only by reflected firelight, but they were in front of the school, and as she bounced over the hill she saw trees, buses, and cars on fire. The school was untouched.

She rolled to a stop and considered what to do. Schoolhouse Lane and that part of the fence line was completely blocked by National Guard vehicles. It was hard to see through the rain to tell what they were doing, but it looked like they were erecting a sandbag barrier. Muzzle flashes were continual and in their glow she could see the thousands of dead in the school compound.

Dez's heart sank. So many?

There were fewer than eight thousand people in the whole county, and it looked like at least half of them were down there. Then she realized that it wasn't just the county folk, but kids from neighboring counties who were bussed in to attend the regional schools. And the families of those kids who'd come to the shelter to fetch their children. Lambs to a slaughter.

There was an army of the dead inside the gate, and an army of the living outside.

And her.

The only possible way in was to smash through the side gate.

The upside was that she'd get to the school and maybe help save whoever was still alive inside.

The downside was that she'd open a door for the dead to escape. Not that there weren't plenty of the bastards out here, but . . .

Even while she was debating it, she began rolling down the hill toward the gate. At first she let the car coast, picking up speed through gravity, and as she did this she picked up the walkie-talkie and keyed the Send button. She'd listened long enough to pick up the key names.

"Break, break, break, this is Officer Desdemona Fox, Stebbins PD calling for Lieutenant Colonel Macklin Dietrich. I know you're on the line, sir. Please verify that you can hear me, over."

There was a confusion of voices and Dez repeated her call. And again. Finally Dietrich's gruff voice responded.

"Who is this?"

"Already told you that, sir. Officer Fox, Stebbins, PD."

"This is a military line and—"

"Excuse me, sir, but cut the shit. Far as I know I'm the last surviving police officer in Stebbins, and I am going to enter the Stebbins Little School to look for and protect survivors."

"The hell you are, officer—"

"Pardon, sir, but the hell I'm not," she barked. "There are a couple of hundred kids in there."

"Everyone in that compound is compromised, Officer Fox. You need to report to a checkpoint and—"

"And get shot? No thanks, sir. Besides, I see muzzle flashes coming from the second floor of the school. Those dead sonsabitches can't shoot a gun, so someone's alive in there."

"Officer Fox, I am ordering you to stand down."

"Sir, I'm calling to inform you, not to ask permission. And to tell you to secure the hole in the west gate."

"What hole?"

Dez answered with a rebel yell as she gunned the engine and sent the Tundra smashing through the wrought iron at seventy miles an hour. The windshield cracked, metal crumpled, and glass flew into the air and was whipped away by the wind. The engine coughed but did not die and Dez fed it gas all the way across the lawn and up the far hill.

There was a new crackle of gunfire and she looked in the rearview mirror to see a Humvee with a top-mounted .50 caliber come racing along the fence line. The gunner was firing in her direction, though the range was too great and more than half the bullets hit the fence.

Trying to get my attention, she thought. *Okay, dickheads, you have it. Now let's play.*

She gunned the engine and raced across the parking lot, swerving only enough to avoid smashing into living dead who staggered toward the sound of her roaring engine. Dez recognized faces and could put names to a few of them.

Behind her, the army Humvee was inside the fence now and continuing to fire. Dez cut in and out between parked cars, letting them soak up the rounds from the heavy .50 caliber. A few of the dead went down, too, their bones shattered by the foot-pounds of impact as the bullets pounded them.

Dez circled the building to see what was what. She didn't like what she saw. There were thousands of the living dead in the parking lot. Littered among them were at least fifty corpses who lay unmoving in the rain. Somebody knew how to kill these things. As she shot past the crowd of monsters, they surged after her, and that effectively blocked the pursuing Humvee. She could hear the constant machine-gun fire as she rounded the corner again.

The real problem, the thing that drove nails of ice into her flesh, was what she saw at the back of the school. There were far fewer dead back there—fifty or so—but the back door of the school was open.

As Dez watched, two zombies shuffled inside.

"You bastards!" she yelled and angled toward the door, then suddenly thought better of it and cut left in a tight circle, coming up behind a parked school bus and stopping. The engine idled roughly, the sound like the throaty growl of a wrestler waiting for the next round. She looked from the knot of dead milling near the back door to the corner of the building. "Come on, come on . . ."

The Humvee roared around the side of the school and then slowed as the driver tried to spot the Tundra. From where she sat, Dez was sure she could see them but they would have a hard time spotting her. The dead near the back of the building turned toward the Humvee, which was fifty yards closer to the building than Dez's Tundra was, and they began moving toward the soldiers. A few moved at a loping run, the rest tottered on clumsy legs. The soldiers immediately began firing at the living dead.

"Perfect," Dez said, grinning. She grabbed the stick shift, stepped on the gas, and shot out from behind the bus, driving at full speed in a straight line toward the Humvee. The driver and the gunners never saw her coming.

Dez gave the truck all the gas it could take and the huge pickup slammed into the Humvee with the force of a thunderbolt. With that much momentum and the rain-slick ground, the Humvee was slammed sideways. Dez kept her foot pressed to the floor, driving the other vehicle across thirty yards of asphalt. Then the Humvee's far-side tires collapsed and it canted down to the blacktop. It slammed everything to a teeth-jarring halt, and the Tundra's airbag deployed hard enough to punch Dez to the brink of unconsciousness.

But her mind was racing now, revving with fear and need. She struggled to remain conscious as she fished in her jacket pocket for a knife, flicked the blade open, stabbed the airbag, and slashed it down to ribbons. She kicked the door open and staggered out. The world took a few sickening sideways steps and she followed with it, then she grabbed the crumpled hood to steady herself. The closest dead were thirty yards away and closing.

The Tundra was a wreck, but she didn't care. It was Rempel's anyway. The Humvee was also a pile of junk. The driver was slumped over, dead or unconscious. Dez could not afford to pare off a slice of compassion. She knew they were following orders, but that cut no slack with her. The gunner had been flung out of the vehicle and was on the ground, groaning and clutching a broken arm. A third man, a rawboned guy wearing sergeant's stripes stenciled on his hazmat suit, was struggling to get out of the Humvee through the shattered window. Dez ran around to his side, grabbed him by the neck, and hauled him out. He thumped down on the ground and looked up at her face from behind the plastic mask of the biohazard suit. He reached for his sidearm and Dez kicked it out of his hand as the weapon cleared the belt holster. Dez reached out and tore off his hood, mask and all, and screwed the barrel of her Sig Sauer in the man's eye socket.

"Freeze, motherfucker," she said.

"God! No, please . . . don't!"

"What's your name?"

"Polk. Teddy Polk. Sergeant, Pennsylvania Army National—".

"Skip that bullshit." She pulled the pistol out of his eye and hit him on the top of the head with it. Not hard, but hard enough. Not a love tap. "Okay, Polk, why were you trying to shoot me?"

"We have to. You're infected . . ."

"Do I fucking *look* infected?"

"How can I tell? It's easy to hide a bite."

"I wasn't bitten."

"We were told that some of them spit infectious materials and—"

Dez stiffened. The Russian woman had spat the black goo at her. So had Andy Diviny. Had she gotten any of it on her skin? She was almost certain she hadn't.

Almost.

"I'm not infected," she said again, her voice hard and cold. "Point is, you fuckers didn't even bother to check."

Polk's eyes shifted away toward the approaching dead and came reluctantly back. "I . . . they said . . ."

"They said what?"

He flinched. "We were told that *everyone* in town was infected."

"Christ. Well, news flash, Einstein, they're wrong. Your commanding officers are lying to you. I'm not infected . . . The people in the school aren't infected, the—"

"Were you in there?" he cut in.

"No, but—"

"Then you don't know. Everyone outside is infected."

"Someone inside is shooting. Have you seen any of them fire a gun?"

"Some of them drive cars and—"

She hit him again. Harder.

"Ow! Goddamn it . . ."

"You dumb shit. If they're driving a car or shooting a gun—or *speaking*, for Christ's sake—then they're not infected. Are you asswipes just killing everyone in town?"

Polk did not answer.

The rain was thinning, the roar of the wind was less intense, and they could hear the moans of the approaching dead.

"Please," he said desperately.

Dez felt her anger flare to the boiling point. "'Please'? Seriously? How many of the infected said that to you? Please?"

She wanted to shoot this son of a bitch so bad it made her teeth hurt.

"We only know what we were told. What were we supposed to do?"

Dez said nothing. Polk was right and she was picking a fight with someone too many pay grades below policy level.

She backed away, keeping the gun on him.

"Listen to me, Polk," she said sternly, "I'm going into the school. I know that there are people in there. Uninfected people. Kids. This is the shelter for the whole county. This is where people go because it's supposed to be safe. You hear me?"

He nodded.

"You get back and tell your commanding officer that Officer Desdemona Fox, Stebbins PD, is in the school with the survivors. I'll make sure everyone who isn't infected is kept safe and in one place. I'll get the uninfected to safety inside the school."

"What if there are infected people in there?" he countered. "They said this thing spreads so fast that it can't be contained. Once a person's bitten or whatever, they're done. It's just a matter of time, and not much time, either."

"The people in there are fighting back. They're not sick." She said it with venom, but in truth the gunfire from the upper window had stopped and she had no idea at all about what waited for her inside that old building.

Polk was staring at her, reading the doubt on her face. "They're probably dead inside there . . ."

Dez raised her hand to backhand him across the face and he flinched, but she did not hit him. Instead she lowered her hand. "What did they tell you about this thing? How did it start? What is it?"

Polk rubbed his bruised head and looked past Dez.

She smiled without turning. "Yeah, I know, company's coming."

"We got to get out of here—"

"Talk to me, Polk, or I'll kneecap you and leave you here for those dead fucks."

He squirmed as if weighing his need to run against the chances she'd really gun him down. "They didn't tell us much. Mostly about how to avoid the infection."

"They must have told you something . . ."

"Terrorists," said Polk. "They said that this was a terrorist bio-weapon." He licked his lips as he looked past her again. "Come on . . . please . . ."

Dez smiled. She could feel the ice in her own lips. "Yeah, Polk . . . the big bad monsters are coming to get you. Sucks, doesn't it? Sucks to be afraid. Now— imagine how those kids in that school feel? They were counting on you. People believe in you guys. You're the heroes, you come and save people."

He said nothing.

"Except when you don't," she sneered.

There was a sound behind her. Dez turned in place and fired four shots. Double taps. One to the chest, one to the head. Twice. Two of the infected fell. The others were still far out of reach.

Dez turned back and pointed the gun at Polk. "You remember what I said. You tell them that people are alive in there."

"It won't matter what I say," he said. "They won't care."

Dez stepped forward and touched the hot barrel to his upper lip. Polk hissed in pain.

"Make them care," she said.

Polk stared up at her. His eyes were filled with doubt and fear and anger. But in the end he nodded.

Dez lowered the pistol and stepped aside. "Get your friends and get the fuck out of here. I'll cover your ass."

As he rose he continued to stare at her. "Why?"

"Because," Dez said with a faint smile, "that's what we're supposed to do. Now go on. Git!"

Polk went past her, giving Dez a wide berth. He pulled the groggy machine gunner out of the crumpled turret. The man was badly banged up, but he was able to walk after a fashion. Together, he and Polk pulled the driver out of the wrecked Humvee. The man, a corporal, groaned but did not wake up. Polk and the gunner lifted him and they hobbled off at a limping pace. Dez watched them go and then turned to the wall of living dead that was coming toward her.

When the three soldiers were at the fence, Polk paused and looked back at Dez for several seconds. She was tempted to shoot him the finger, but she didn't; and before he turned way Polk gave her a single, short nod.

Dez frowned, trying to ascribe meaning to it.

A moan drew her attention and as she turned, her bravado melted away like fog on a hot morning. There were dozens of the things. Mangled faces torn to raw meat, eyes missing, legs twisted . . . and with all that they kept coming. Dead things pretending to be alive, their mouths working with hunger.

The open door of the school was on the other side of them. Seventy yards. Might as well be on the moon.

"Shit."

Dez holstered her pistol and quickly searched through the wrecked Humvee and found two M4s. She did not have time to look for extra magazines. They had to do the job or the job wasn't getting done.

She pulled the bag of weapons out of the Tundra, slung it over her shoulder, groaning a little at its ponderous weight. She slung one of the M4s on the opposite shoulder, worked the bolt on the other, and stepped out from behind the wreck of the two trucks. Dez took a breath, set her jaw, then set the selector switch on the M4 to semiauto and started running, cutting to the left of the leading edge.

The dead turned to follow her, but she didn't fire. Not yet.

She moved in a wide arc, hoping to draw more of them away from the entrance so she could make a run at the doorway. They came for her, hungrier for her flesh than they were for whatever waited inside the building.

Finally, she had no choice, and she fired a burst at the closest infected. The unfamiliar weight of her burden threw off her aim and the bullets stitched holes in the chests of the dead closest to her. She corrected, steadying the gun, and fired again. One of the monsters staggered back with two new black holes above its empty eyes. As it fell, Dez fired again and again. Some of them went down, but by the time she'd burned through the magazine, only five of them were down. With the gun bag on her shoulder she had no aim at all. Without stopping, she dropped the first M4 and unslung the other, tried to aim better, fired, fired, fired. And it clicked empty.

"Shit!"

She dropped the second rifle and pulled her Glock. The rear security door of the school was closer now and she could see a couple of the creatures standing just inside. She fired at them, dropping one but wasting three rounds on the brick doorframe trying to hit the other. The angle was all wrong.

She ran into the rain, toward the school, sloshing through the muddy grass, firing at everything that moved. She was only halfway there when her foot came down on a Frisbee lying in a puddle and she was sent sprawling onto the grass. The big bag of guns came off and went sliding away into the darkness. She kept her grip on the Sig, but the barrel punched three inches into the mud, totally clogging it.

Something moaned and she rolled onto her back as Harvey Pegg, the school's gym teacher, lunged at her. His hands closed around the open *V* of her jacket and his head ducked down to bite her arm with terrible force. Dez screamed and brought her knee up into Pegg's crotch, knocking him forward and over her. As he tumbled over, she tore her arm out of his mouth and gave it a quick, desperate look. Pegg's teeth had scored the leather but hadn't bitten through.

"Thank you, Billy Trout," she said between gritted teeth.

Dez started to get to her feet even as Pegg got to his. He was a second sooner and began to rush at her, and there were three other dead behind him. Dez fired two shots and then the slide locked back.

Shit.

There was nowhere to run and no time to grab another weapon. She was done and she knew it.

Then suddenly the world was filled with bright light and noise. There was a huge *crunch!* as a black SUV slammed into the infected, splattering them and flinging their bodies away like rag dolls. The car slid three-quarters of the way around and its engine died with a broken rattle.

Dez stared up in total shock as the driver jumped out.

Voiceless with the impossibility of this, she mouthed his name. "Billy?"

CHAPTER EIGHTY-FOUR
STARBUCKS
BORDENTOWN, PENNSYLVANIA

Goat trudged through ankle-deep mud for miles. He was not built for this kind of physical activity, and by the time he was halfway to the highway his muscles were screaming at him. He tried to buck himself up with images conjured from a thousand news stories he'd watched. Soldiers humping fifty pounds of gear through twenty-five miles of desert under relentless Arabian suns. Medical teams for Doctors Without Borders walking for days through malaria-filled jungles in order to bring medical supplies to remote villages. Stuff like that. It helped, but not much.

What really kept him going was Dr. Volker's voice. He had his earplugs in and as he walked he listened to the recording Billy Trout had made at the doctor's house. It had scared him then and it scared him worse now.

When he finally reached the highway he thumbed a ride with a guy driving a semi from Akron to Baltimore. Goat spun a story about his car breaking down. The driver didn't care and seemed disappointed that he wouldn't have company for longer than the five miles it took to get to Bordentown. The trucker had the radio tuned to Magic Marti, who said that the storm showed signs of weakening. From where Goat sat it was hard to tell. Well . . . maybe the rain was a shade less intense.

The trucker dropped Goat at the Starbucks, accepted a coffee for the road, and left.

Goat brought his coffee with him as he searched out the most isolated corner of the coffeehouse. He opened his laptop and went to work.

The first thing he did was to download the files from Volker's flash drives and e-mail them to himself at several accounts. He copied the e-mail to Trout and their editor, Murray Klein. Then he updated his Twitter account with a "Breaking News Coming Soon" post. With that done, he downloaded the interview as MP3 files.

Then he waited for Trout to call.

CHAPTER EIGHTY-FIVE
STEBBINS LITTLE SCHOOL

Billy Trout had rehearsed this moment fifty times since bypassing the National Guard out on the highway and sneaking back into town. Not this exact moment—in none of his fantasies did he imagine that he'd swoop in and rescue Dez Fox—but the moment where they'd meet again. In most of his scenarios, Dez's mouth would soften from the angry stiffness it wore since the last time they'd broken up; her eyes would glisten with unshed tears, and the two of them would fly into each other's arms, realizing the rightness of them here at their darkest hour. He knew it was a chick flick ending, but he secretly believed that such tender moments could happen. In each scenario they would kiss. The kind of kiss Bruce Springsteen could get a number one record out of.

So he was already smiling and reaching for her when Dez stared up as he looped the equipment bag over his shoulder and got out of the Explorer.

"Billy—"

"Hey, Dez," he said warmly. "I knew you'd be here . . . I knew you'd still be alive."

She said, "What in the deep blue fuck are you doing here, you asshole?"

Trout's smile faltered. "What? Um . . . I'm . . . rescuing you?"

"Oh, great. So what am I supposed to do now? Swoon into the arms of the big, strong 'Fishing for News with Billy Superman Trout' hero of the day? Give me a fucking break." She dropped-out the empty magazine and slapped a new one angrily into place.

"Huh? No, Dez, I—"

"You should have gotten your ass out of town, Billy."

"I *was* out of town," he snapped, his own anger flaring, "but I came back for you."

"Oh, please. With all this going on? You expect me to buy that shit? You came back for a Pulitzer and a ticket out of this shithole. The only thing you care about is your next byline."

"You know that's not true, Dez." He shook his head in disgust. "Where's JT?"

"He left me. Just like the others."

"Left you? You mean he was infected?"

Her eyes shifted away from his. "I don't know what happened to him. He just left."

"Just like that? No mitigating circumstances?"

"No, not just like that, okay? They arrested us and put us in separate cruisers. His crashed. My driver got attacked. JT never came back to look for me."

"Did you look for him?"

"I tried."

"You try his house?"

"No . . . there wasn't time."

Trout took a step toward her. "Dez . . . JT didn't abandon you. You do know that, right?"

"He left me alone. It always happens. The trooper, too . . ."

Trout came closer still. There was a strange light in Dez's eyes that he'd caught glimpses of before. Now it burned like a torch. "The trooper didn't leave you. He died. He was taken. It was something that was part of his life drama, and its effect on you, scary as it must have been, was a side effect. It had nothing really to do with you. Same goes for JT. You said his car crashed. Either he escaped from the backseat, injuring himself in the process, or he was taken. I don't think that in either case he was thinking, 'Yeah, this will really fuck over Dez. This will show her.'"

"Show me what?"

"That you should be abandoned. That it's what people do to you."

"That's bullshit. I'm not making this shit up. I mean . . . *you* left me."

"Really? This is the conversation you want to have right now? Fine, 'cause God knows we have nothing else pressing. So, here's the truth, Dez: you left me the first four times, and the only reason I bailed that last time was because you were screwing that biker. Maybe I read that wrong, but it seemed to have 'fuck off' written pretty clearly on it."

She said nothing.

"God knows this isn't the time for you to try and catch up on fifteen years of very heavily needed therapy, Dez, but you have some serious issues. You always think people are abandoning you. Your mother did it . . ."

"She had cancer . . ."

"And your father did it."

"He was killed in the war."

"I know, Dez. I'm the guy who does know this stuff. Maybe you told JT, too, but I doubt there's anyone else you opened up to about it."

"You think I'm crazy?"

"Of course you are. You're crazier than a barn owl on meth, and you damn well know it. Look at your lifestyle. There's nothing about your daily habits that doesn't speak of self-loathing. You drink too much. You'll screw anything with even a high school level pickup line and a tight ass. You're a bitch of legendary proportions. And you've done just about everything you can—which is saying a lot—to make sure that nobody likes you. And definitely that nobody loves you. What makes it all so cheap and dime-store is that it's pretty much textbook stuff. Child abandonment issues played out with sex, drugs, and rock 'n' roll here in backwoods Stebbins County. Tell me if I'm wrong."

Dez did not tell him he was wrong. She glared at him for a two count, and then she drew her Glock and pointed it at his face.

"You better run, Billy."

"Jesus Christ, Dez . . . let's not go totally over the edge here . . ."

"Run!" she screamed, and fired. The bullet burned through the air an inch from his ear. Trout heard a wet thwack behind him and turned to see a zombie pitch backward with a neat black hole in the center of its pale face. Behind it were a dozen more, and at least a hundred of the things were coming around the sides of the building.

"Oh . . . shit!"

Dez shoved him hard to one side and fired again and again. "Get the duffle bag!"

Trout looked around and saw the canvas bag on the ground. He ran at it and bent to scoop it up, but it was far heavier than he expected and the weight jerked him back. He felt sudden pain flare in his lower back.

"Stop fucking around and get the bag!" Dez yelled.

"I'm getting the bag, Officer Hitler," he muttered under his breath as he bent and used his knees to lift the bag. He slung the strap over the same shoulder that was supporting Goat's equipment, hugged the bulky bag to his chest, and looked around.

"Go wide," shouted Dez, pointing.

Trout nodded and went left, cutting a wide line around the closest mass of zombies. The way Dez was indicating would take him behind the line of parked faculty cars. There were no dead visible over there. He understood her plan. Run wide around a big obstacle, get the dead to follow, and then cut between the cars and head to the open door. Good plan, except that with every step pain shot down the back of his left leg. He realized that he must have pulled his sciatic nerve when he grabbed the bag.

"Well, that's just peachy," he growled, but he kept going, gritting his teeth against the pain.

Dez was right behind him, walking backward while she fired at the oncoming wall of the dead. Trout kept looking over his shoulder, watching with horror as Dez brought them down, one at a time. The girl who worked at Mario's Pizzarama; Archie from the Allstate office; the school's vice principal; Melissa Crawford, mother of new twins; and others. Trout knew almost every face, could put a name to almost every one of them. He knew that Dez did too, and he knew that this must be killing her. Just as it was killing him.

The rain was thinning more and more, and Trout could see all the way to the wrought iron fence. The National Guard were there in force, and they had to be able to see what was happening . . . but they did nothing.

Bastards! Trout thought, but his real rage was not directed at them but at the insect-brained generals and policy makers who were so willing to accept a scorched earth policy rather than find a solution that would save American lives. Trout was moderate enough, even as a liberal, to accept that military power was necessary and that even some wars needed to be fought. He wasn't a fool. On the other hand, he didn't like the obvious disconnect between the human element and most military theorists and the generals who paid them. Year after year he lost ground to the cynical view that humanity was far less important than either tactical advantage or financial gain. When he heard politicians use the phrase "in the best interests of the American people" he knew that it was always a profit-based decision. And it wasn't just in war. The cold detachment was evident in the mishandling of Hurricane Katrina, the hesitation to provide financial support for the health needs of the Ground Zero workers, and the apparent abandonment of returning U.S. vets, especially those wounded and requiring expensive medical treatment.

Here was another example, one that was biting him in the ass right now. Solving the problem of the Lucifer 113 outbreak would clearly be easier and less of a political nightmare if there were no survivors. Wipe the slate clean, maybe kick out a few bucks for a memorial, and do some spin control to blame it on terrorists, the former administration, the policy makers on the other side of the aisle, or on anyone who was the target du jour. Even if he lived through this, Trout doubted he would ever see the name Volker in the papers, and certainly no mention of Lucifer 113 or the CIA. That would all be erased because the truth would cost too much to tell.

To hell with that, he thought as he bit down on the jolts of pain. But what was the answer? How did he and Dez and Goat fix this? Could it, in fact, *be* fixed?

As he ran—as he listened to Desdemona Fox, the woman he loved, shoot their neighbors down—he began to get an idea. A really wonderful, ballsy, nasty idea.

Dez fired her last shot and swapped out the magazines.

"How we doing?" she yelled.

Trout looked ahead. "Clear . . . but only if we haul ass."

"Then let's haul ass," she barked. She fired two more shots, spun, and sprinted to catch up with him. When she saw that he was limping, she grabbed him by the shoulder and hauled him roughly along with her.

With the storm abating slightly the moans of the dead filled the air. It was such a horrible sound that it made Trout's knees buckle, but then as he thought about what those moans meant—the insatiable hunger of the parasitic zombies—he bared his teeth and willed more power to his legs.

They ran down the far side of the faculty cars. A zombie lunged at them from behind a parked Highlander.

"Dez!"

"Got it!" She pivoted and shot the dead man through the mouth just as the thing spat black goo at them. The bullet snapped its head back, and the black liquid geysered straight up and splashed back on the zombie's face as it fell. A few drops landed on Dez's sleeve, but there was still plenty of rain to wash it away. Or so Trout hoped.

At the end of the row they cut toward the school. Most of the infected—frightening but without intelligence or imagination—had followed them on their wide course and only three of the dead were lingering by the open door.

Dez pulled out in front, bringing her gun up in a two-handed grip and changed her pattern of running so that she took smaller steps to steady her body as she aimed.

The zombies heard them coming and turned toward them. Trout saw that one of them was the attorney for his second wife. When Dez shot him, Trout expected to feel a nasty little thrill in his chest. He didn't. This wasn't a video game and that man was someone he knew. It didn't matter that Trout didn't like him. This wasn't about who liked who; this was a human being who did not deserve what happened to him. As he fell, Trout made himself say the man's name, quietly to himself.

"Mark David Singer."

All at once that began a ritual that Trout knew would be with him throughout this crisis. No one should have to die without a name, without some recognition of their humanity.

As Dez shot the second zombie—needing two shots to bring her down—Trout fished for her name. She was the music teacher here at the school. He had interviewed her last year about the Christmas pageant. She was sixty, with gray hair and a corpulent figure. A nice lady. She loved the kids she taught.

He watched her fall with the right side of her face blown to red ruin by Dez's bullets.

"Sophie Vargas," Trout said as he ran past her falling corpse.

The last of the infected outside the school was a stranger. Dressed like a businessman. Probably the father of one of the kids, Trout guessed. Come here to pick up his child. The businessman grabbed Dez's left arm and tried to bite her wrist, but Dez used her right to bring the barrel of the Glock to the man's temple. The blast knocked his head sideways and he crumpled at Trout's feet.

Dez was at the door now, pointing the gun inside.

But Trout stopped. He looked over his shoulder. The other zombies were closing fast, but Trout was trapped by the needs of his new ritual. He bent down, hissing at the pain, and patted the man's pockets until he found a wallet. He pulled it out, shoved it in his jacket, spun, and hobbled to the door with two yards grace. He staggered inside, dropped the heavy duffle, twisted around, grabbed the door handle and gave it ferocious pull. It slammed, but not shut, and with horror Trout saw that a hand was caught between the door and jamb. He had to pull on the door to keep it from being whipped out of his hands.

Behind him, Dez was still firing her pistol.

"Dez!"

"Not now, Billy!" she fired back.

So, he took the big risk. He stopped pulling and shoved on the door, slamming it outward into the faces of the crowd of infected. So many faces. Torn and bloody. They spit black blood at him, and Trout cried out as it splattered on his jacket. With a snarl of rage and fear, he raised his leg to kick out at the zombie whose hand was caught in the door. With a jolt he realized that the man fighting to get in was Doc Hartnup.

"Doc?"

Hartnup's dead eyes looked right through him, but his mouth was a hungry snarl. Hartnup spat black blood at him, which splattered on Trout's chest.

That sent Trout into a panic. Doc or not, he lashed out with his foot and caught the dead man in the stomach. Again and again before it lost its hold and Trout fell backward, hauling on the crash bar of the door so that the heavy metal panel swung all the way shut with a huge clang.

Closed. Locked.

Fists pounded on the door from the other side. Trout tore off his jacket and flung it into a corner then pawed at his shirt, looking for traces of the black mucus.

Nothing.

"God almighty," he wheezed. Another gunshot made him turn and he saw Turk, the little guy who owned the Getty station, go tumbling to the ground.

"Turk," Trout murmured. "Danny Turkleton."

Dez stood with her back to him, her shoulders heaving with exertion. Four other zombies lay on the steps. Trout knew two of them and he spoke their names aloud. The others were strangers. A corrections officer and an Irish guy Trout recognized from Dez's trailer park but couldn't name. Trout pulled the wallet out of his pocket and flipped it open to the driver's license.

"Kealan Patrick Burke."

"What?" Dez asked sharply, then saw what he was looking at. Her expression changed slowly, and Trout could see that she somehow understood what he was doing. She looked down at the bodies around her and nodded.

"Did you know them?" Trout asked.

She nodded. "All of them." She said their names, and he repeated them.

They looked at each other for a fractured moment, the stink of cordite, blood, and human waste in the air, the steady pounding on the door, the bodies sprawled in what, for them, was a "second death."

"It's all impossible," she said. "You know that, right?"

"It's worse than impossible," he said.

Dez narrowed her eyes. "What do you mean?"

"I know how this started," he said. "And it's a lot worse than you think."

A voice spoke from the shadows behind Dez. "Then you'd better tell us everything, Billy."

They turned and stared as a big man came walking out of the shadows. His clothes were torn and he had makeshift bandages wound around his head and left arm. His face was battered and bruised, and his eyes were haunted by the things they had seen. But for all that, he looked powerful and dangerous, and he had a hunting rifle held in his strong brown hands.

"JT!" cried Dez.

As Trout watched, she ran to him and wrapped her arms around him and buried her face against his chest, and sobbed.

Son of a bitch, Trout thought with an inward rueful smile. *That's my goddamn scenario.*

JT Hammond gave Dez a fierce hug and he kissed her hair.

Then Dez pushed herself away, glared up and him, and slapped him across the face.

"You asshole!" she yelled. "You fucking left me!"

And that's my girl, Trout thought, and this time his smile reached his lips.

CHAPTER EIGHTY-SIX
OUTSIDE OF STEBBINS LITTLE SCHOOL

He stood as silent as a tombstone. A few of the Hollow Men pounded on the door, some of them milled around, drawn by trace scents of fresh meat that were tricks of the storm winds. But Doc Hartnup and most of the others stopped moving and stood staring at the closed door.

Hartnup had recognized the two people his body had been chasing. Desdemona Fox, whom he'd known for years, and the reporter, Billy Trout. Even as his hands tried to grab them and tear them apart, his mind tried to communicate with them. He screamed their names. His screamed his own name. He begged them to shoot him. Dez Fox had shot so many of the others, and now they lay still and unmoving. Hartnup wondered—hoping, praying—whether they were really and completely dead now. He had seen others gunned down by the police and later by the National Guard. Taken down with bullets to the brain. He believed that this was the trick. Any bullet was a magic bullet as long as it struck the brain. He had to believe that or there was no God, no hope, and all was red madness forever.

Dez Fox had not shot him. Each time she fired in his direction there was another one of the Hollow Men to take the bullet. Some died, some were with him now, pounding or milling or standing.

Please, he cried within his darkness. *Please . . .*

CHAPTER EIGHTY-SEVEN
STEBBINS LITTLE SCHOOL

JT rubbed his face and grinned.

"I didn't leave you, kid," he said. "It took about six state troopers to keep me from you after you fell." He touched his battered face. "They weren't very nice about it, either. Officious pricks."

"Wait, wait, hold on," said Trout, "why were you fighting the state troopers?"

"They thought we were on a killing spree," said JT, and he quickly explained the chain of events that started at Doc Hartnup's.

"Doc's outside," said Trout. "He's one of them."

"I know. I saw him from the upstairs window but I couldn't get an angle on him," said JT, though he looked sad. "Anyway, the staties put Dez in one cruiser and me in another and that was the last I saw of her."

He glanced at Dez, who nodded. "I know." She explained what happened to her, and about the death of Trooper Saunders. Then told them about the Guardsmen, the fight at the trailer park, and meeting Trout.

JT said, "We were run off the road by the Guard. As they were driving me to the station the trooper got a call that all state police were being ordered out of Stebbins. Right now, no questions. But that isn't what happened."

"I can guess," said Trout.

JT sighed. "It was an ambush. Guess they didn't want any armed infected in town, and they've pretty much decided that we're all infected. I was in the back of the cruiser when a Humvee opened up on us. We crashed and they drove off. The trooper with me was hit pretty bad. He managed to unlock the back and take off my cuffs, but by then the dead were closing in around us. It was all I could do to get out of there. Wish I could have helped the trooper, but he was dying already. Two rounds, one in his chest. I fought my way out and went to the station, but that was a total loss." Sadness darkened his eyes. "I had to . . . um . . . take care of Flower."

"Oh shit, Hoss," Dez said, touching his arm.

"I'm sorry," said Trout.

JT nodded. "That was almost the worst thing today."

"Almost?" asked Trout.

"Yeah . . . worst thing was the thought that my girl here was gone."

"Thanks, Dad," Dez said with a twisted smile. "But I got home from the prom unmolested."

Their grins were forced, and they didn't last.

"After the station," continued JT, "I decided to head over here. It was already a mess. Couple of these things attacked the middle school kids while they were getting onto the buses to come here. By the time the buses arrived, the infection was rampant. Things went south from there."

Trout looked past him to a set of closed fire doors. "What's the situation in here?"

"One of the parents came out through this door to try and reach his car. His kid wasn't here." JT shook his head. "He left the door open and about twenty of those things got in. Me and a bunch of teachers have been searching the building. I think we got most of them, but we still need to check the top floor—and I'm down to six rounds—"

Dez nudged the duffle bag with her toe. "Merry Christmas, Hoss."

JT glanced at her, then knelt and unzipped the bag. Trout peered over his shoulder and saw all the guns and boxed ammunition.

"Sweet Jesus on the cross," murmured JT, lifting out a Mossberg shotgun. "I'm so happy I could cry."

His tone was light, but Trout could see the tension in the big man's face, feel it vibrating in the air around him. Shadows moved behind JT's eyes. Trout knew that, strong as he was, this was going to ruin him, too.

Dez looked up the stairs. "What about the kids?"

"Everyone's in the auditorium," said JT. "We have a couple of guys in there with guns. They're watching the doors, but they only have a couple of rounds each. We got kids from both schools, a lot of parents. Some townsfolk."

"How many?"

"In all?" His eyes shifted away for a moment. "Eight hundred, give or take."

Dez brightened. "Eight hundred kids? That's great!"

"No," JT said softly, "eight hundred all told. Kids, parents, and everyone else. We lost more than half the kids when those monsters attacked the buses. Some ran away, but . . ."

Dez closed her eyes. "Ah . . . God . . ."

"I wanted to call in some backup," said JT. "I wanted to tell the damn National Guard that we needed help, that we're mostly safe in here. But they aren't listening. They shot at us. They killed a couple of the teachers who were trying to help the kids. Maybe they thought the teachers were attacking . . . I don't know. With the rain and all, I just don't know. We can't seem to get them to understand . . ."

"They're not here to help us," said Trout. He and Dez told JT about their encounters with the Guard.

"That's nuts," said JT. "We're *not* infected."

"They don't care," said Dez. "They've been told to keep this from spreading at all costs. End of story."

JT shook his head. "Do they even know what this thing is? Is this something that's happening everywhere or is it some kind of toxic spill? We don't know anything about this infection."

"It's not an infection," said Trout. "Not exactly. It's an infestation, and it started with Homer Gibbon."

"What?" demanded Dez. "Gibbon . . . ?"

"His body was shipped here after the execution," Trout explained. "His Aunt Selma was going to have him buried on her family farm-land. It's a long story, but the short version is that his body is infested with a genetically engineered wasp larva. Parasites. Most likely Doc got it from Gibbon and it spread from there."

"How do you know that?" asked JT.

Dez pushed past JT and grabbed a fistful of Trout's shirt. "What do you know?"

"I know everything," Trout said quietly. "And . . . you're not going to like what you hear."

"Well, gee, Billy, I guess I've spent so much of today laughing my tits off that I suppose I could use some depressing shit to balance it all out."

Trout gently pulled her hand free and smoothed down the front of his shirt. He took a breath and told his story, starting with the call from the prison guard, the visit to Aunt Selma, and the horrifying discussion with Dr. Volker. He told them everything, and by the time he was finished, Dez had gone dead pale and JT looked like he wanted to throw up.

"This is totally fucked," Dez said at last. "I thought this was going to be some kind of terrorist thing."

"Terror begins at home," said Trout, and she shot him a withering look. "Oh, come on, Dez . . . you're too smart to think that we're only ever the white hats. Wake up."

"No," she said, letting out a breath. "It's just . . ."

She shook her head. There were no adequate words to express how she felt, and Trout understood that.

"Knowing how it started doesn't help us much," said JT, " 'cause we sure as hell know how it's going to end. I think the only reason they haven't nuked us back to the Stone Age is the storm."

"No," said Dez, "they wouldn't nuke us. They'd firebomb us. It's safer for them and the fire—"

"—purifies," finished Trout. "I thought of that."

"Great," JT said. "That's just great. The storm's already lessened. Pretty soon they're going to be able to put birds in the air and fry our asses."

"I have a walkie-talkie," said Dez. "We can talk to them."

"Let's give it a try," said JT. "We have eight hundred people in here."

Dez turned on the walkie-talkie and adjusted the squelch. There was steady, overlapping chatter and it took her several tries to get through. Trout produced a small video recorder and began taping.

"Break, break, break, this is Officer Desdemona Fox, Stebbins PD, calling for Lieutenant Colonel Macklin Dietrich. Please respond."

The chatter slowly died down and then Dietrich's gruff voice responded. "This is a secure military channel, Officer Fox. You are not authorized to broadcast on this—"

"I think we've been through this already, Colonel. Let's cut the crap and get right to it," Dez said forcefully.

"What is the reason for this call, officer?"

"Trying to make it to the end of the day without dying, sir."

A pause.

"What is your location?"

"I'm at the Stebbins Little School. There are eight hundred people in here. None of us are infected. We have steel security doors and this building is the town evacuation shelter."

"The infection has spread throughout the entire town, officer," said Dietrich. "I'm sorry to have to inform you of this, but—"

"The town, yes. Maybe. But the school is a secure facility. This is where the survivors are. We need you to come and get us out."

"I don't believe you understand the nature of this event, officer."

"Colonel Dietrich, you are incorrect, sir, when you say that we are unaware of the nature of this event. We are very goddamn aware. And we are asking how you intend to help."

There was silence on the line. When Dietrich spoke his voice was tight. It was hard to tell if it was anger or fear. "There's nothing we can do. If you're in the thick of this then you should be able to comprehend that."

"I comprehend some of it, Colonel. What I don't comprehend is why you're not even trying to rescue or protect the uninfected. This isn't an airborne disease. It's spread through spit or a bite or some other fluid contact."

As she spoke, Trout panned the camera to show the dead zombies on the floor and the black goo around their mouths. He zoomed in to focus on the wriggling threadlike worms in the muck. Then he panned back up to Dez. In this light, with her disheveled hair, her hard beauty, her Valkyrie bone structure, she looked like a hero out of legend, a warrior woman who could have belonged to any of the great battles of history. Trout never doubted that he loved Desdemona Fox, but at the moment he felt like he wanted to shout the fact.

Dietrich said, "You are a police officer, I believe, in a small town? Not a biologist or medical doctor?"

"Yes, sir, I'm a small-town cop. I also spent a couple of years in Afghanistan taking orders from cocksuckers like you, so I know when someone's blowing smoke out of their ass."

"Watch your mouth, Officer Fox."

"Or what? You want to come here and arrest me? Go ahead. Otherwise stop acting like you're in command of this situation. I'm asking you—*telling* you—to get in touch with your boss and tell him to get in touch with his, as far up the line as you have to go. Tell them that we know who let this monster off the chain and who's responsible for killing an entire town . . . and who now wants to try and cover it all up by pretending that the surviving witnesses are infected just so you can slaughter us all. You tell them that."

No reply.

"Colonel . . . ?" No reply. In fact there was no further chatter on the walkie-talkie. Not one word.

Dez shook her head and stared at Trout, who was still taping. "They're going to let us die here. God . . . they're going to murder all these kids." Tears broke from her eyes and rolled down over her cheeks. She weighed the walkie-talkie in her hand and then with a snarl turned to hurl it against the wall but JT scooped it out of her hand.

"No," he said, "we might need that."

"I blew it," she snapped back. "I pushed too hard and blew it. God, why am I always such a bitch?"

"Actually," said Trout, turning off the camera and lowering it, "I thought you were magnificent."

"Oh, shut up, Billy."

"No," said JT, "boy's right. You were great. You smacked that officious prick's ass."

"That'll look good on my tombstone. Let's face it, I played the wrong card. He knows that we're a liability and now he's going to burn this town down just to keep us from telling the world." She glared at Trout. "Why the fuck are you smiling?"

"I taped that conversation you just had. Dietrich's voice is crystal clear."

"So? We can't do anything with it. The Internet and cell service is as dead as we're going to be."

Billy Trout unslung the equipment bag he carried and bent down—hissing a little at the pain in his back—to unzip it.

"You're not the only one who brought goodies to this party, Dez." He produced a device and showed it to them, his smile never wavering. "This is a satellite news uplink. If we're going to go down, babe, then let's at least go down swinging."

CHAPTER EIGHTY-EIGHT
PENNSYLVANIA ARMY NATIONAL GUARD
COMPANY D, 1-103RD ARMOR

Lieutenant Colonel Dietrich set his walkie-talkie down and stared at it for five long seconds. Across the table from him, Captain Rice stood in silence, not daring to intrude into this moment. He could see the fires that rage were lighting under the colonel's skin. His commanding officer's mouth was a tight knife slash; his nostrils flared wide like a charging bull.

Rice tried to make himself invisible. He expected Dietrich to suddenly dash everything off the table, or hurl the walkie-talkie the length of the room. But the colonel said and did nothing as the seconds splintered off the clock and fell like debris on the floor.

Dietrich walked over to the window and looked out at the storm.

"The wind's dropping," he said. His tone was quiet, calm, and that surprised Rice, who had heard the full exchange between Dietrich and that crazy female cop in Stebbins.

"Yes, sir," said Rice. "Weather service says that we've seen the worst of it. The storm front is turning north by east. Winds are down to—"

"How soon before we can get some birds in the air?" asked Dietrich.

Instead of directly answering, Rice made a call, spoke to another captain, listened, and hung up.

"As soon as the wind drops another fifteen miles per hour, sir. We're still at the outer range of unsafe."

Dietrich nodded. He clasped his hands behind his back and continued to stare out the window.

"That cop is well intentioned," he said quietly, "but she does not understand what's at stake."

Rice cleared his throat. Very quietly. "No sir. She was totally out of line. Probably stress . . . or the onset of the disease."

"Probably," agreed Dietrich coldly.

"Your orders, sir?"

Dietrich said nothing for almost twenty seconds. Rice waited him out. Then the colonel turned.

"Sound draws these things, correct?"

"The infected, sir? Yes, that's what we've heard from our people on the ground."

Dietrich nodded. "Then here is what I want to do."

Rice listened in silence. Dietrich's plan was as solid as it was brutal.

As Rice hurried out of the office to set things in motion he said a silent prayer for the people in Stebbins.

CHAPTER EIGHTY-NINE
STEBBINS LITTLE SCHOOL

"Are you sure this will work?" asked JT as Trout set up the satellite equipment.

"Goat said it would, and he knows this stuff pretty well," said Trout. "I'm no damn good at all in a fight. I do this or I go hide in a closet." He handed the unit to JT and showed him how to work it, then he stepped away and ran his fingers through his wet hair and straightened his soaked shirt. "How do I look?"

"Like a drowned golden retriever," said Dez.

"Thanks."

"But a good-looking drowned golden retriever," she said, giving him a small, crooked grin.

Trout flashed her a brilliant smile. "That's probably the nicest thing you've said to me in two years."

He expected her to smile at that, instead he saw a flicker of pain dart through her eyes; and he felt like an ass for making a bad joke at a time like this. He busied himself with clipping the lavaliere mike to his shirt collar.

"Ready," he said.

JT held up crossed fingers. Dez merely nodded, her expression on the doubtful side of neutral. Trout cleared his throat and gave JT the nod to start recording.

"My name is Billy Trout," Trout began. "I'm a reporter for Regional Satellite News in Stebbins County. Please watch this video. This is not a hoax, this is not special effects or a gag. This is real. People are dying and more will die. There's a good chance I'm going to die. Maybe today."

Trout paused and took a breath. He was sweating and used his fingers to wipe the sweat out of his eye sockets. From behind JT, Dez gave Trout a thumbs-up, and he plunged ahead.

"If you've been watching the news you know that the big storm is centered over southwestern Pennsylvania right now. You may also have heard of some problems here in Stebbins. Rioting and looting. However, I am here to state for the record that there is no rioting in Stebbins. There is no looting. However a lot of people are dying here. I am going to tell you the truth about what is happening here in Stebbins. If I live through this, I'll probably go to jail. That's okay, as long as the story gets out. Please watch this video. Please post it on YouTube. Put the links on Twitter and Facebook and everywhere else you can think of.

"I am in the Stebbins Little School, the elementary school here in town. There are eight hundred people in here with me. More than half of them are children. A lot of people have died here today, but unless we all work together, a lot *more* are going to die. I repeat . . . this is not a joke. This is not a hoax. This is real and it's happening right now."

He took a breath. His hands were shaking.

"This is Billy Trout, reporting live from the apocalypse . . ."

CHAPTER NINETY
BORDENTOWN STARBUCKS

It seemed to take forever, but the call finally came through on Goat's Skype account. Routing it through the main RSN satellite was a firing offense and almost certainly illegal. Fuck it. So was turning people into zombies.

Trout sent him three videos. One was for immediate release, the other two were to sit in their chambers until Billy told him to pull the trigger.

Goat used his earphones so no one else could hear the call, and he set Skype to record everything as a backup to the straight satellite feed, which was automatically recorded on the RSN server, which was in Pittsburgh not Stebbins. Goat copied the whole thing on his hard drive, too. Then, as soon as it was done, he e-mailed it to himself at three different accounts. That would give him copies in his sent folder as well as the three in-boxes. All of this took a few seconds and now there were copies in places the government could not easily block, access, or confiscate.

After the broadcast was done, Goat got a private Skype call from Trout.

"Did you get them?"

"Yes I did, Billy, and I'm sweating high-caliber bullets right now. Tell me this is all true. The National Guard's actually shooting people?"

"They're shooting everyone."

"Aren't they testing them first?"

"No."

"Then how do they know who's infected or—"

"Goat—they're shooting *everyone*. No questions asked."

"Oh, man . . ." Goat felt the room beginning to spin. "How safe are you going to be in that school?"

Trout was a long time answering.

"Billy?"

"You got to get this out. Listen, kid, this is a million times worse than anything Volker said it would be. Goat . . . everyone's dead. Marcia, Gino . . . everyone."

"Marcia . . . ?" Goat asked hollowly.

Trout told him what he'd seen and done . . . and been forced to do. When he described the encounter with Marcia, Trout broke into tears.

"Oh, shit, man . . ." said Goat in a voice choked with his own tears. He looked around the Starbucks, but the place was so deserted that there was no one near, no one to see or hear. "Those *fuckers*. Marcia? Goddamn it, Billy, we can't let them get away with this."

"I have no intention of letting them skate, kid. We're going to ram this up their asses."

Goat wiped his eyes and nose on his sleeve. "What do you want me to do?"

CHAPTER NINETY-ONE
STEBBINS LITTLE SCHOOL

"Watch out!" yelled Trout, and Dez whirled around as a zombie came at her from the shadows of the top landing. Dez fired three shots, one to the chest and two to the head, and the dead woman spun into the wall, then slid bonelessly to the floor.

"I don't know her," murmured Trout. Dez glanced down.

"Peggy Sullivan," she said. "Secretary here at the school."

"Peggy Sullivan," echoed Trout. He nodded and they moved on.

They were a few steps from the second floor landing. Dez was on point, but she had turned to look down at the small body of a little boy who lay twisted on the midpoint landing. The child had been shot, but it was clear that he had been infected before he'd been put down. Dez was only distracted for a second, but it was enough for the other zombie to blindside her. This impact knocked her sideways, but she twisted around and put two rounds into the creature's face.

"You okay?" JT asked from the bottom of the stairs. He was watching their back trail and carrying the heavy duffle of weapons. Trout was in the middle, unarmed and hypervigilant.

"Yeah," Dez breathed. She took her pistol in both hands and went up the last few steps, checking the corners. "Clear."

They followed her up and waited for her to check the hallway.

"I thought you cleared these things out of here."

"We locked some of those things in the first two rooms," said JT. "More upstairs."

Dez moved cautiously forward. The classroom doors had frosted windows, but she could see awkward shapes shift and move behind the heavy glass. When she bent to listen should she could hear the low, hungry moans.

"How many are in there?"

JT came up beside her. "Six in that room, two in the other." He nodded down the long, dark hallway.

"Can't leave them here," said Dez. "They'll get out one way or another."

He drew in a ragged breath. "Damn," he said, but he nodded.

"Wait," said Trout, "what are you going to—"

Before he could finish, Dez kicked open the door and she and JT rushed inside. All Trout could see from the hallway were shadows and bright flashes, and all he heard was the thunder as Dez and JT emptied their guns into the living dead.

When they emerged, their faces were wooden.

"Dez, I—" Trout began, but Dez pushed past him to the door on the other side. She and JT paused to reload, then they nodded to each other, kicked open the door, and went in shooting.

Trout stared in horror. Not because they were doing so much killing, but because so much was necessary. When JT pushed open the door and stepped into the hallway he looked ten years older. So did Dez. They stood there, faces dirty with gun smoke, reloading their weapons, their eyes fixed onto the middle distance and empty of all life. Like the eyes of the dead things they had just slaughtered.

Dez dropped a bullet and Trout saw that her fingers were trembling. He knelt to pick it up, and when he handed it to her she closed her fingers around his for a moment. She squeezed her eyelids shut and fought to keep her mouth from twisting with barely suppressed sobs. Then she released him, took the bullet, and finished reloading.

"The auditorium's down and around the corner," said JT gently, but Dez pushed past him.

She knew every inch of this old school. These drafty corridors and echoing fire towers were part of her childhood. She'd been a lonely girl who loved playing in her imagination, and the school was a castle under siege or a grand palace filled with knights and ladies, an old haunted house or the lair of a crafty wizard. She could walk the halls blindfolded. She hurried along, her gum-rubber soles making almost no sound. JT was as quiet on his feet, but after two flights of stone stairs he was huffing like a dragon; behind him, Billy Trout limped along. With each step, the sciatic pain was worse and his pace slower. It made him feel old and intensely vulnerable.

JT had grown up in Fayette County and his family had not moved to Stebbins until he was in high school, but Trout knew this old place every bit as well as Dez. He remembered the lonely, lovely little blond-haired girl, and he had loved her from afar even then.

He thought about that as they hurried through the pale glow of the emergency lights. *All this time and I'm still no closer to having her*, he thought. *Or, maybe I'm further away.*

It saddened him as much as the tragedy in town, and he could totally understand—now more than ever—Dez's feelings of being abandoned by those she loved and trusted.

"Ah, Dez," he whispered in a voice he knew could not carry to her ears. "You're crazy but I do love you so. How sane does that make me?"

Up ahead, Dez paused by the double doors that led to the auditorium, looking back over her shoulder almost as if she had heard him after all. Their eyes met and she gave him a brief, sad smile.

What does that mean, he wondered. Was it an acknowledgment of feelings as viewed from two sides of an uncrossable field of wreckage? Possibly. Or, was it a good-bye? Did Dez believe that they were all going to die here? Neither she nor JT had shown much faith or enthusiasm for the videos he'd sent. Though they did not say so, it was clear that they did not think Trout could make his plan work.

He wasn't entirely sure himself. Nor was Goat. It was a gamble of a kind he had never imagined making before, not even in his wildest Hollywood dreams.

Trout held eye contact with Dez, wanting to preserve the moment, to make this communication, however tenuous, last. But timing was against them and that connection was too fragile to support it. Dez turned away and reached for the door handles.

CHAPTER NINETY-TWO
BORDENTOWN STARBUCKS

Goat was quickly going crazy.

He kept nervously toggling back and forth between Twitter, YouTube, and Facebook, watching the hits, the retweets, and reposts of Billy's video. In the first hour it was on YouTube it had fewer than a hundred hits, and most of the comments posted by viewers were cynical and mocking. They did not believe the video was real. Then something happened a few minutes into the second hour. There was a significant jump in hits. Goat backtracked and saw that the new rush was being driven by Twitter. A couple of key players had retweeted the URL. Some of these were conspiracy theory nuts who thought this was an early Christmas present, some were anarchists of the kind who thought Julian Assange's WikiLeaks posts in 2010 were holy writ, but a lot of them were serious players in the media. Goat had posted the link everywhere and had sent it in mass e-mails to everyone in his media listservs. Thousands upon thousands of people in print, broadcast, and digital media. Some of them apparently knew Billy Trout, and that's where the traction started. They reposted the link to their contacts and included personal endorsements of Trout. The secondary wave of posts went out in a massive ripple. Someone who knew Billy also knew a producer on CNN and that person included the link in a news update. That sort of thing happened again and again. By the time ninety minutes had passed, the spread was viral.

Viral marketing. Goat considered that, and for a moment he thought that it was an unfortunate choice of words; then he looked at it from a different perspective. It had a flavor of poetic justice to it.

By the end of the second hour the number of hits on YouTube had climbed to the high five figures and every time Goat refreshed the page the number jumped by hundreds. And then by thousands. The spread was geometric.

But Billy Trout did not call back.

Even though Goat's system could accept a satellite call via his Skype, the connection did not work in reverse. Goat could not reach Trout.

Goat licked his lips and drummed his fingers and drank too much coffee. And felt his nerves burning down to the gunpowder.

Finally he couldn't take it anymore and he posted the second video. This was the one where Billy was videotaping Dez Fox while she argued with the National Guard Colonel on the walkie-talkie. If the first video was a slap in the face, then this was going to be a full swing-of-the-leg kick in the nuts.

He kept glancing at the door as if expecting federal agents to come busting in any second. *Well*, he thought, *too bad if they do . . . but it's already out there. So, fuck you.*

CHAPTER NINETY-THREE
THE WHITE HOUSE SITUATION ROOM
WASHINGTON, D.C.

The president of the United States watched the monitors on the wall. The rain and wind had diminished significantly. Two minutes ago he gave permission for the six Apache helicopters to take off, with four Blackhawks flying close support. The Apaches each carried fuel-air bombs as well as their usual complement of Hellfire missiles, machine guns, and rocket pods. There was enough firepower aboard those helos to destroy an average-size American city. Far more than was necessary to wipe Stebbins off the face of the earth.

The order he had given was to fly to Stebbins. Nothing more. Not yet. He couldn't imagine how he could shape his mouth to give the kill order for this.

Scott Blair, the National Security Advisor, came hurrying into the Situation Room. He waved away the staff members sitting closest to the president and then bent to speak in a confidential tone. "Mr.

President? We've just learned that someone in Stebbins is sending out messages."

"What kind of messages, Blair? And to whom?"

"The wrong kind, Mr. President," said Blair. "What's worse is that they're being posted on the Internet. YouTube, mostly; fed by links on Twitter, and other social media sites. We're working to control those sites . . . but the Internet is volatile. The National Guard units in Stebbins are attempting to locate the sender and shut him down."

"What's he saying?"

"I can play it for you, sir. Do you want me to clear the room?"

"If it's already on the Internet, there's no point. Play it."

Blair nodded and punched some buttons on a computer built into the table. The screen switched from the weather report to a page of the YouTube Web site. Blair pressed Play and a good looking white man with blond hair and a pinstripe shirt appeared. The man was soaked and his face was lined with stress. His eyes, which were robin's egg blue, stared into the camera with laserlike intensity.

"My name is Billy Trout . . ."

Everyone in the room stopped to watch and within seconds there wasn't a sound. Not a murmur or side comment. The president felt his throat constrict as he watched the video. The video included footage of infected bodies, mangled and partially consumed, torn by bullets, splashed with black mucus. There were two other people in the video, both police officers, both showing signs of injury and stress. A white woman and a black man. Trout named them and gave their badge numbers. The last few lines of the video hit the hardest.

". . . this is not a natural disaster and this is not a terrorist attack. This is a man-made disaster, and I know who is responsible and how this occurred. Please post the link to this video. The only thing that can save the lives of all these people, all of these *children*, is the truth. Call your local papers, call the news services. Contact your local congressperson. This is not a local problem. This is not Pennsylvania's problem. This is a threat to the entire country, if not the entire world. Please . . . we are alive in Stebbins and the devil is at the door. Do not let them commit mass murder. Save the children of Stebbins County."

The video ended but the room remained absolutely silent. All eyes were on the president.

"You're sure this isn't a hoax?" he asked.

Blair shook his head. "Billy Trout is a reporter for Regional Satellite News. Small time but well respected. Officers Desdemona Fox and JT Hammond are with the Stebbins police. She's former army. DMV searches match them to their photo IDs. This is real."

"Several hundred people? That's great news! I want the Guard to get to those children. Protect them and get them out of—"

"Mr. President . . . I don't think you appreciate the complexity of this. Our Wildfire containment protocols have six different response models for suburban outbreaks. All of them offer options for many aspects of the problem, but on one point they all agree. If hard containment is possible, then that is the only safe and reliable course of action."

The president stared at him. "No way, Blair. I can't accept that. You're saying that a Red Wall response is our *only* response?"

"Regrettably, sir, that is correct."

"No. That is unacceptable."

"Sir . . . you've seen the reports, you know that we can't let a single infected host out of the Q-zone. Not one. This isn't cholera or typhus. We can't inoculate against this. No one has a natural immunity to these parasites. Each host is one hundred percent infectious. One drop of blood contains enough larvae to—"

"I know, damn it."

Blair adjusted his glasses. "Then, sir, you have to understand the severity of this. We don't have diagnostic protocols for this. We don't have prophylactic measures beyond sterilization."

"So, what would you have me do? Drop fire bombs on that town while someone is broadcasting it to the world? There are seven thousand people in Stebbins County. I don't think I want to go down in history as the president who slaughtered more people than were killed in the entire war in Afghanistan! Twice as many as died on 9-11."

Blair sighed and shook his head. "Given the field reports we've received, Mr. President, I doubt as many as ten percent of those people are still alive."

"Those are estimates, Blair, not hard numbers, and you damn well know it. There could be four or five thousand people still alive. I won't authorize a strike unless we have exhausted all other possible options."

"Well, sir . . . whether we drop bombs or not, sir, we have to stop the sender. So far nothing he's said is damaging to your administration, Mr. President, but we can't take any chances."

"How would you suggest we stop him?"

Blair did not have to spell it out; his look was eloquent enough.

"Christ," growled the President. "Is that the best we can do? React like thugs?"

"This is a commanding response to a very real threat to this country, Mr. President. This isn't a hurricane or broken levies. If we drop the ball on this, or if we're too cautious in our response, then we could be looking at a pandemic that would make the Black Death look like—"

"Skip the dramatics," snapped the president.

"Your pardon, but I'm not being dramatic. If anything I'm *understating* the nature of this threat."

The president shook his head. "I'm not going to authorize a sanction against someone who is trying to save American lives. I've compromised a lot since taking office, Blair, but I haven't slipped that far."

Blair took a breath. "I understand your concerns, Mr. President, but our scientific advisors are in a panic over this. They are urging us to implement Red Wall. *Urging*, sir."

"I understand," said the president wearily, "I've ordered the choppers in. Once they're over Stebbins airspace, we'll see where we are."

"Thank you, Mr. President."

CHAPTER NINETY-FOUR
STEBBINS LITTLE SCHOOL

Dez Fox looked out at a sea of faces. Hundreds of them, young and old. More young than old. All turned toward the open doors, their faces pale with fear and their eyes bright with hope.

They must have heard the gunshots, Dez thought. *God . . . look at all the little ones. In here. Thinking they're safe.*

She wanted to find the two teachers JT had left to guard the door.

Find them and kick the living shit out of them for abandoning their posts, and for abandoning these kids.

She felt JT and Trout move up to flank her, filling the doorway.

The kids looked at them and at the guns they carried, and at the uniforms they wore. Suddenly, and all together, they jumped to their feet, screaming and applauding. Dez felt her lips part into a silent "oh" of surprise. She turned to JT in confusion.

Trout leaned close and whispered in her ear. "They're applauding because the cavalry has just arrived."

"But," she said, "but . . . we're not . . ."

"Smile and wave, Dez. That's what they're looking for. Smile and wave. Be the hero. Let them know you're here for them. After all, it's the truth, right? So let them know it. Let them know that you're here for them, to protect them, and that you won't abandon them. That you won't let the monsters get them."

Dez looked into Trout's eyes for a long time even as the applause rolled like thunder around the big hall. She looked for the mockery, the joke in his eyes. And she did not find it.

She slowly raised her pistol over her head and forced a smile onto her face.

The applause rose in intensity. Teachers and parents made their way through the sea of kids, and they shook Dez's hand, and Billy's, and even JT's.

"Are we getting out now?" asked a woman who held a two-month-old baby in her arms.

"Soon," Dez lied. "The . . . um, National Guard is still clearing things up outside. We have to sit tight for a bit. Might be a few hours, might be all night, but help is on the way. They need us to cooperate as best we can."

Her use of key words like "National Guard" and "they" worked their magic. They promised order and answers.

A woman—the stick-thin school principal, Mrs. Madison—came hurrying through the crowd and gave Dez a fierce hug. That got applause, too. The crowd gradually settled down as teachers and some adults quieted the sections near them. It looked orderly, and Dez guessed that Mrs. Madison had appointed these adults as section leaders. Good call.

"Thank you," said Mrs. Madison. "God, thank you. Do we know what's happening?

Dez held up her hands to stop the flow of questions. Then she gently pulled Mrs. Madison into the hall and away from the other adults. "Listen, we don't have a lot of time, so please pay attention. We're not leading a cavalry charge right here. And the National Guard are not our friends at the moment. They think we're all infected in here, and until we clear the real infected out of here we can't prove that it's safe for the Guard to come in and rescue us. That means we have to make sure that anyone who's been bitten is secured."

Mrs. Madison frowned. "Secured?"

Dez gave her a brief explanation of Lucifer 113 and how it worked. "Anyone who has been contaminated—no matter how, and no matter if they don't look sick yet—will become like those *things* out there. Everyone who has this thing is going to have to be put down."

Mrs. Madison blanched. "Officer Fox . . . we have *kids* with bites. Surely you can't expect us to shoot children? That's insane. It's inhuman. We have them in classrooms. We're giving them medical attention . . ."

"Then give me an alternative. If we allow the infection to stay inside the school we'll all die. This is easy math."

"God . . ."

"JT and I will take care of it," snapped Dez. "Mrs. Madison, I need you to stay inside the auditorium. Once we leave, keep the doors locked until either JT or I tell you it's safe to open the doors. Otherwise you *do not* open up to anyone, understood?"

The principal nodded. "Mr. Chestnut is somewhere in the building. He heard some sounds and he took two of the janitors with him to investigate."

"Lucas Chestnut?" Dez asked. Chestnut had been a very young teacher when she had attended the school. He must be well into middle age by now. "How long ago?"

"Why, he left just after Sergeant Hammond did. I'm surprised you didn't see him."

"Shit," said Dez. Mrs. Madison began to say something but didn't; instead she sagged back with a hand to her throat.

"Stay here and don't let anyone else leave," ordered JT. "You understand me? No one. Now—go back inside and put a smile on your face and tell everyone to sit and wait until we get back. Don't tell anyone else how things really are. Not yet. Got it?"

The principal nodded, and JT led Dez out into the hallway. They listened at the open stairwell but heard nothing. "Let's try the top floor," said JT. "It needs to be checked anyway."

Dez looked up at him. "You be careful, Hoss. No heroics."

He snorted. "I'm fresh out of heroics, girl."

They smiled at one another and were about to enter the stairwell when Trout came running out of the auditorium.

"Hey! Dez!"

She wheeled on him. "Where the hell do you think you're going?"

"With you. But I need a gun."

"Not a chance, Billy. Stay here with the kids. I don't trust you."

"What? How the hell can you say—"

"With a gun, dumb-ass. You don't know how to shoot, remember? Go find a baseball bat or something and stay the hell in there."

"Dez, I—"

She got up in his face, and though her mouth was hard, her eyes were pleading. "Billy . . . stay with the kids. *Please.*"

"Ah . . . fuck," he said, but he nodded. "Okay, Dez."

There was a brief look of relief in her eyes as she turned away and hurried down the hall with JT. For just a moment, and despite all of his conscious reasoning to the contrary, it felt to Trout that Dez was not running off to a fight, but that she was running away from him. It made no sense, but it opened a little door of insight in his head.

He turned away and Dez watched as the auditorium doors closed behind him.

Dez watched him go and she had to smile. At his willingness to help. At the courage he'd shown in coming back to town. At his ass. He had a great ass, she decided. She sighed and turned away, aware that the members of her "team" were watching her.

JT murmured, "I thought you were done with that boy."

"I am."

"Doesn't look like it to me."

"Yeah, well I thought you didn't walk with a limp," Dez said.

"I don't."

She got up in his face. "Want that to change?"

"Um . . . no, I don't."

Dez nodded. "All right then, end of discussion."

If JT planned to say more it was cut short by a piercing scream of terrible pain that floated on the sluggish air from the darkened stairwell.

CHAPTER NINETY-FIVE
OLD FAIRBANKS ROAD
NEAR BORDENTOWN

Homer Gibbon heard the sound before he saw them. It was a big, deep, bass sound that filtered through the rain and the radio and the sound of his wipers. The *throp-throp-throp* of helicopter rotors. He pulled to the side of the road, rolled down his window, and leaned out to look.

They came over the treeline like a flight of giant insects from some old monster movie. Homer had never been in the military, but he knew everything related to war. From movies, from books and magazines, from endless jailhouse conversations. These were Apache Longbows, and he was pretty sure they were outfitted with 30mm chain guns, Hellfire, Hydra, Stinger, and Sidewinder missiles. At least that's what he remembered.

Homer smiled.

Nice.

He turned up the radio. Jason Aldean was singing "My Kinda Party."

"Yes, sirree," he said to the radio. Homer put the car back into drive and kept going.

CHAPTER NINETY-SIX
THE WHITE HOUSE SITUATION ROOM

"We have another video from Billy Trout," said Scott Blair.

The president swiveled his chair to face the monitors. "Let me see it."

Blair hesitated. "Sir, this is pretty delicate stuff. This is going to be a political nightmare."

"Run it," said the president firmly.

The YouTube video played. It showed the same female officer standing in a hallway filled with corpses of the infected.

"She obtained a walkie-talkie from a National Guardsman that she attacked."

"Did she kill him?"

"No-o-o," Blair said, dragging it out. "Three soldiers required medical treatment and she wrecked their Humvee."

The president shushed him as the audio played. They sat and watched the one-sided conversation Dez Fox had with Lieutenant Colonel Macklin Dietrich.

Colonel Dietrich, you are incorrect, sir, when you say that we are unaware of the nature of this event. We are very goddamn aware. And we are asking how you intend to help.

There's nothing we can do. If you're in the thick of this then you should be able to comprehend that.

I comprehend some of it, Colonel. What I don't comprehend is why you're not even trying to rescue or protect the uninfected. This isn't an airborne disease. It's spread through spit or a bite or some other fluid contact.

Blair leaned closed. "This is the crucial bit."

I'm asking you—telling you—to get in touch with your boss and tell him to get in touch with his, as far up the line as you have to go. Tell them that we know who let this monster off the chain and who's re-sponsible for killing an entire town . . . and who now wants to try and cover it all up by pretending that the surviving witnesses are infected just so you can slaughter us all. You tell them that.

There was a few seconds more silence as Fox waited for a reply that was not going to come. Then she looked straight into the camera and said:

They're going to let us die here. God . . . they're going to murder all these kids.

Tears broke and rolled down her cheeks, and the tape ended.

Blair flapped his arms. "This was just posted and it's already burn-ing up the Internet. It's everywhere. It's on CNN and FOX and ev-erywhere."

"God . . ."

"And I take it you heard that one line?"

"About her knowing who let the monster off the chain? Yes. Do you think they know about Lucifer 113?"

"I . . . don't know, sir. I can't see how they *could* know."

An aide came hurrying into the room. "Excuse me, Mr. President . . . the helos have crossed into Stebbins airspace."

CHAPTER NINETY-SEVEN
STEBBINS LITTLE SCHOOL

They went up the stairs. Dez first, with her Glock held in both hands; JT was right behind her with a Mossberg 500 Bullpup with dual pistol grips, including one on the pump. Eight steps from the top they paused to listen.

"Oh, god! Help . . . oh, Christ . . ."

"That's Lucas," said JT. They took the last steps two at a time, swiveling their weapons around at each corner, expecting white faces to come lunging out of the shadows. They saw the blood first.

A footprint perfectly outlined in red. A heavy shoe, a Timberland or a good knockoff. Dez pointed with her Glock.

"I see it," JT said quietly as they moved up the steps.

". . . please . . . God . . ." Lucas Chestnut's voice was faint, depleted. Dez already knew that they weren't hurrying up the steps to save him. He sounded hurt, and the day they'd lived through had taught them that "hurt" was a death sentence. No matter how small a bite, it was as good as a bullet to the heart.

They rounded the last turn in the stairwell and found another footprint.

And a foot.

The shoe, ankle, and part of the shin stood on the top step. The rest of their owner was twenty feet down the hall, crawling along, inch by inch, toward a man who sat with his back to the door of the English room. A bloody fire ax lay across the man's thigh, and his body was covered with bites. Dozens of them.

Two other figures crouched on either side of him. One held Lucas Chestnut's arm in both of her hands, and as Dez watched she bent and sank her teeth into the flabby flesh on the inside of the teacher's elbow. The other person, a teenage boy, knelt and worked at Chestnut's abdomen, biting and tearing to get through the tough abdominal wall. The zombie with the missing leg crawled inexorably forward, moaning piteously at the meal it longed to share.

Chestnut was too weak to scream. He sobbed and shook his head over back and forth in a permanent denial of what was happening. Then, as Dez and JT stepped out of the stairwell, Chestnut turned his streaming eyes toward them.

"Please . . ." he begged weakly. "For the love of God . . . please stop this . . ."

Not stop *them*. Stop *this*.

Dez heard JT inhale with a hiss.

"Steady on, Hoss," she said softly and stepped past him. The maimed zombie heard her first and he turned and snarled. Black saliva dripped from his lips. Dez recognized him as one of the janitors. Roger somethingorother.

She raised the Glock and fired. The bullet caught Roger in the temple and the force blew one of his eyes out of the socket. He collapsed forward, the bones of his face crunching onto the hard floor. Behind her, Dez heard JT gag.

Dez did not look. She shifted the barrel of the Glock to the teenage boy.

Bang.

Then the woman, a stranger.

Bang.

Lucas Chestnut raised his eyes to her. Blood bubbled from between his lips.

"Please . . ." he begged.

Bang.

Dez lowered the gun and closed her eyes.

Behind her a door creaked and she whirled just as JT bellowed in surprise, his cry mingling with moans as the dead poured out into the hall. Five of them. No, *more.* Eight or nine!

"JT, look out!"

JT went down under a pile of them and the impact made him jerk his finger on the trigger. The blast hit one of the dead above the elbow and blew away her arm. She did not even pause as she flung herself at JT.

Dez fired three fast shots at the infected who were still standing, killing two and sending one staggering backward toward the top of the stairs. The creature fell and went tumbling and crashing down out of sight.

Under the pile, JT pivoted his big shoulders and smashed the shotgun across a zombie's face, knocking the creature off of him. The dead man fell with a swatch of JT's shirt between its teeth. Another of the dead immediately lunged into the opening and then Dez was there, kicking at them, slamming the steel toe of her shoe into the temple of one, stamping her heel down on another's spine, using her free hand to grab one by the belt and pull him back. When that zombie hissed and turned toward her, she pistol-whipped his mouth away from her and then shot him through the ear. JT rammed the barrel of his shotgun under the chin of the closest infected and pulled the trigger, blowing the thing's scalp and brains all the way to the ceiling.

Dez kicked one of the dead in the cheek and shot another through the eye. Then she grabbed JT and hauled. He kicked his way out and they flopped backward, both of them flat on their backs.

The dead came at them, and Dez took the Glock in both hands and fired, fired. JT blew the knee off of one, and, as it collapsed down, he put the next round through its forehead. He kicked that body back and fired at the one behind it, catching it in the chest and the shoulder and then the face.

The last zombie was an old woman, and Dez kicked her on the point of the jaw with all her strength. The woman's head whipped up and back and her neck snapped.

Then it was over.

The two of them lay there, covered in blood and black muck and bits of flesh.

Dez recovered first. She saw the black mucus glistening on her thigh, and she screamed and scrambled over onto hands and knees and then shot to her feet. JT was up at once. He snatched the big steel fire extinguisher from the wall and turned it on her, using the compressed blast to whip the infectious goo off of her clothes. Then Dez tore it from his hands and did the same. Both of them were making small, almost feral whimpering sounds as they emptied the entire unit. Dez cursed and flung it away.

"We're good," JT said nervously, "we're good, we're good."

But they were not good.

At the far end of the hall was a big set of windows that looked out over the parking lot. Until now that window was as black as the stormy night outside, but all at once it glowed with brilliant white intensity.

"Flares?" ventured Dez.

Then the whole building suddenly began to shake. Heavy vibrations rattled with the drone of huge machines. They bolted for the far end of the hallway and stared out the window as a line of Apache Longbow helicopters came tearing through the night sky over the line of pine trees, ghostly in the glow of the white phosphorous flares that drifted down on tiny parachutes. With them, flying close support, were four UH-60 Black Hawks.

The strain on JT's face melted into a smile. "Sweet Jesus," he said, "I think the cavalry just arrived!" He began waving to the choppers.

A moment later the side door on the lead Black Hawk rolled back to reveal the ugly multibarreled snout of a minigun.

"No!" screamed Dez as she grabbed JT and tore him away from the window a split second before hundreds of rounds chewed the whole wall into a storm cloud of flying glass, torn brick, and splintered wood.

CHAPTER NINETY-EIGHT
THE AUDITORIUM

Trout reached out to Goat. "I'm sending you a lot of stuff," he said. "Get it on the Net."

"Okay, but we're doing this the slow way, Billy."

"What do you mean?"

"The way you've been doing your bits—you know, 'Live from the apocalypse.' That's the key. We should be doing a live stream. We don't need to edit anything. We're not waiting for a broadcast time slot, man. This is raw and immediate, so let's go reality show with it."

"Will anyone watch it?"

"Billy, every-fucking-body is watching this. The whole world is watching, but I don't know how long we have before the feds find me and shut us down. I'm running this through a real maze of off-site bounce-around servers, but they will find me . . ."

"Then let's go live."

Trout began doing interviews in the auditorium. Everyone was in shock, a few were absolutely catatonic with fear or grief. Trout could only imagine what some of them had seen. Family members torn apart by the zombies. Friends and schoolmates dragged out of the buses. Teachers slaughtered while trying to protect the kids. Or, as some people quietly suggested, a few teachers and parents simply running away, so wrapped up in their own immediate needs that they were willing to leave the innocent to their fate. Some of the people, adults and kids, were ebullient with a kind of excitement that was too big, too hopeful, and spoke of a fractured perception. Those were the ones, Trout knew, that would shatter if one more thing went bad.

One little girl stared blankly into the camera and asked, "Mommy?" She said that one word, uttered that single plea, over and over again. At the same time that Trout was aware that this was broadcast gold he was also aware that his heart was breaking. He knew that the little girl's face would haunt his dreams the rest of his life . . . if there would be more life to live.

He kept going, interviewing everyone.

No one was grandstanding, no one was spinning a tale simply because they were on TV. These people were far too badly shaken, their hurt was far too present in their minds for any artifice, and Trout knew that this would be evident to anyone who watched the video. Anyone who was unmoved would have to be more dead inside than the creatures who were laying siege to the school.

A few of the adults he interviewed—a disheartening few—seemed to have found some measure of dignity and courage. On the other hand, many of the kids were displaying genuine courage that bordered on heroism. One eleven-year-old girl in particular, Bailey, had gathered the littlest kids into a corner and was entertaining them with stories. However, Trout saw a broken field hockey stick standing against her chair; it was jagged and covered with blood. He bet there was a story there, and he hoped he would have a chance to see it told.

Another kid, a hulking sixth-grade boy, whom puberty had hit like a runaway train, wore most of a set of football pads over his street clothes and carried an aluminum baseball bat. Trout interviewed the boy, Bryan, who told him about how he'd been chased into the gym by a couple of the dead and found five girls already there, hiding in the big wire cage where they stored the sports gear. Bryan had run into the cage, put on as many pads as he could, including a football helmet, then grabbed a baseball bat and left the cage to attack the zombies. It was a wild story, and Trout might have doubted Bryan's word if not for the five girls who sat nearby giving the boy adoring stares.

Trout did as many short interviews as he could. Some were stories of combat and victory, some were narrow escapes, but most were about terror and loss. And in the case of many of the children, the stories were about abandonment—either by cowardice or, more often, because the parents and teachers had died during the fight. To a terrified child, though, it amounted to the same thing. And that made him think about Dez. She was the same age as most of these kids when her parents died, and even though she knew—with all of her considerable adult intelligence—that those deaths had been beyond the control of her parents, Dez was still caught up in abandonment issues to this day.

As he set up to interview a librarian who had been rescued by a cheerleader, the whole auditorium suddenly froze into a listening silence.

Trout spoke quietly into the mike. "We're hearing gunshots. It sounds like . . . yes, they're coming from upstairs. That's the Stebbins police officers, Desdemona Fox and JT Hammond. They're hunting the last of the infected in order to ensure that this building is safe and secure."

He paused and aimed the mike at the ceiling. The shots continued and Trout wished that he felt as confident about what was happening up there as he sounded. But he needed to convey the message that the school was under control.

"The shooting has stopped," he said and panned the camera to show that every one of the eight hundred faces in the auditorium was tilted upward, eyes wide, expressions showing mingled hope and dread.

The silence in the big room held and held, and then the whole building began to vibrate.

"Helicopters!" said one of the men in the back. "The army's here!"

Wild cheers erupted throughout the hall. Trout goggled at this, but then considered that these people were here in the school long before he got here, so they may not have seen the ruthlessness of the National Guard.

"Listen to this," he said in the mike. "People are cheering because they hear helicopters. They're hoping that the military is coming to rescue them. I had that same hope when I crossed the quarantine zone. And, call me crazy, folks, I still hope that the guys in the white hats *do* come along and save our butts, because I'd love a happy ending here."

He tilted the mike up again, and waited with the others, muttering,

"Come on . . . come on . . . come *on*," under his breath as the heavy *throp-throp-throp* of the rotors beat closer and closer.

And then the miniguns opened up.

The cheers instantly turned into a shrill chorus of screams as the windows exploded inward in storm clouds of glittering glass. The shards swept across the packed crowd, slashing and tearing. Children dove under the seats, adults tried to shield them with their own bodies. Bullets buzzed above the massed people like a swarm of furious hornets.

Billy Trout dove behind an upright piano used for school shows and the bullets coaxed a mad, disjointed tune as they ripped the instrument into kindling. Despite the madness raining down around him, Trout punched the Record and Send buttons and aimed the camera at the windows.

CHAPTER NINETY-NINE
STEBBINS LITTLE SCHOOL

The Black Hawk hovered in the air like a nightmare, the minigun growing like a dragon, spitting hundreds of rounds at the top floor of the school. A second helicopter coasted with monstrous slowness past the far side of the school, firing at the row of lighted windows. Below them, the living dead moaned and reached with aching fingers toward the sky, trying to tear the machines down to tear them open for the meat inside. But the choppers were too high and the dead could not reach them, and the intensity of need within those moans rose to a horrible shriek.

"This is Billy Trout reporting live from the apocalypse!" he yelled. "I don't know if you can hear me, but we are under attack. Please . . . if anyone can hear me, we need help!" He turned up the gain on the lavaliere mike clipped to his lapel so that his words could be heard over the din of screams and automatic gunfire. "We've been begging for help from the government . . . and this is how they respond!"

Dez was curled in a fetal crouch, her arms wrapped around her head, her body bleeding from dozens of cuts. Her eyes were squeezed shut, but her mouth was open as a continual, red-raw scream tore itself from the deepest part of her. A dozen feet away, JT Hammond was curled into a similar knot, trying to shrink into himself. He, too, screamed.

This is not an attack by a terrorist organization. These are not the infected that I've been telling you about.

Billy panned the camera to show the helicopter hovering outside, its cannons filling the air with fire and death.

That is a UH-60 Black Hawk helicopter. It is part of the Army National Guard detachment sent to contain the plague outbreak in Stebbins. It is not firing on the infected. There are no infected where I am. I'm in the auditorium of the Stebbins Little School . . . a regional elementary school. Most of the people in this room are children. There are also teachers and some citizens of Stebbins who were told by authorities to come to this place because it is the county emergency shelter. I repeat . . . the people here are not infected. There are mostly children and people directed here as an official shelter.

Mrs. Madison crawled off the stage and into the sound room. The bullets couldn't reach her in there, and she began waving to people—adults and children—to follow her. It was a risk though. It meant running across the no-man's-land of the stage. A few tried. Not everyone succeeded.

From the booth, Mrs. Madison could see Billy Trout huddled under the piano. She knew what he was doing and could hear snatches of it. Then she saw the big microphone on its silver stand, the one that was provided for the pianist when she sang along with the children. The wires snaked across the stage, and the leads were still socketed into place on the sound board. The auditorium, she knew, was part of the emergency services setup in the school. The backup generator that powered the lights also provided power to essential emergency equipment. Including the public address system.

Mrs. Madison flipped a row of switches and channeled the feed from the fallen microphone into the main public address system, then turned the volume all the way to the right. Suddenly Billy Trout's voice boomed like thunder from every speaker mounted inside—and outside—the school. When Trout heard this, he grinned, reached out and pulled the mike closer.

This cult of secrecy and the military's obsession with owning the worst weapons of destruction has brought us all to this moment. More than six thousand people have died today. They were murdered. Nearly the entire population of Stebbins County. These people are no less victims of terrorism than were the nearly three thousand people who died when the Twin Towers fell, or the two hundred and sixty-six people in the four hijacked planes used on 9-11. Or the one hundred and twenty-five people killed at the Pentagon that day. Or the thousands killed in Iraq and Afghanistan. But what makes it more tragic, more unforgiveable . . . is that the people of Stebbins were not killed by al-Qaeda or the Taliban. There are no terrorist cells operating in Stebbins county. These people were murdered by the U.S. government because some people believe that it is better to kill the innocent than to admit a mistake.

On the other side of the building, the children and teachers and parents and refugees from the storm crawled under the auditorium seats, screaming and crying out in fear and confusion. For many of them the light of hope was blasted out of their eyes, not through injury, but as they tried and failed to grasp the meaning of what was happening. First the infected attacking and slaughtering so many, and now the rescuers—the *army*—turning their haven into a killing ground of flying glass and blood.

We cannot allow ourselves to become a nation of fools and slaves. We cannot allow our own government to serve its own agendas at the expense of the people. I appeal to every true American, every patriot—whether you're left or right—to stand up and say: "Stop!"

Outside the fence line, hundreds of National Guardsmen stood ready, waiting for the helicopters to do their work so that the next phase of the cleanup could start. Sergeant Polk sat among them, listening to the words that boomed from the speakers mounted outside the school. He smoked a cigarette, chain-lighting it from the last. Discarded butts lay in a puddle by his feet.

One of the men in his squad chortled. "Do you hear this bull-crap?"

Polk turned to him.

"What's wrong, Sarge?"

Polk nodded toward the school. "I didn't sign up for this shit."

"Geez, man, what'd that bitch cop do to you? You going all girlie on us?"

Polk drew in the smoke, held it in his lungs, and exhaled slowly. Then he abruptly got out of the vehicle and began walking toward the gate.

"Hey!" yelled the other soldier. "Polkie . . . what the shit are you doing?"

"Taking a goddamn stand."

"What for?"

Polk whirled. "There are people alive in there. Haven't you fucking been listening?"

He turned and kept walking.

A lieutenant started to run after him. "Sergeant Polk, get your ass back to the line right goddamn now."

Polk turned again. "This is *wrong*! We're supposed to be here to help."

"We can't help these people," growled the lieutenant.

"We didn't even fucking *try*!"

He reached the row of parked Humvees and climbed into one.

"Sergeant, I am ordering you to stand down."

Polk started the engine and put the Humvee in gear.

The lieutenant drew his sidearm and pointed it at Polk. "Sergeant, stand down and step out of the vehicle or I will shoot."

Polk took his foot off the brake and let the Humvee roll forward. The lieutenant ran to stand between him and the gate, and a lot of the Guardsmen swarmed with him. All around them was the roar of the choppers, the thunder of the machine-gun fire, and the amplified sound of Billy Trout's voice. Polk pressed lightly on the gas and the Humvee began moving toward the gate.

Other soldiers raised their weapons and pointed them at the vehicle, but the soldiers were cutting looks back and forth between Polk and the lieutenant.

By now the complete file of how this plague started, including a complete confession by Dr. Herman Volker, will have been sent to every major news service in the country. There are no more secrets to defend. You kill us now, it will be act of revenge . . . and everyone will know it . . .

Polk revved the engine, then leaned out of the window. "Either unlock the gate and stand back or watch your ass because I'll roll right over it."

"Sergeant, you are buying yourself a world of hurt with this nonsense. Stand down before I put you down."

Polk revved again.

And a single soldier stepped away from the massed soldiers and began walking toward the Humvee. The lieutenant yelled at him, too, but the soldier held up one fist, forefinger extended. Then he turned and walked backward, his rifle in hand but the barrel pointed to the ground.

"He's right, loot," the man yelled. "This is bullshit. This is wrong."

The lieutenant shifted the barrel of his pistol to cover the second soldier. "Drop your weapon and stand down."

"Sir, I respectfully decline to accept that order."

"On what fucking grounds?" screeched the lieutenant, his face boiled red.

"On the grounds that I enlisted to protect my country and my fellow Americans. Haven't you been listening to what that reporter's been saying? They have proof that this was something of ours. Maybe it was a mistake, or maybe somebody went batshit and released it, but we started this. How the hell can killing Americans be a right and proper military response to that?"

"That's not for you to decide."

The man brought his weapon to port arms. "It is now."

"Fucking right it is," said another man, and the lieutenant turned in horror to see a third man step out of the line and walk toward Polk. Then a fourth. Then five more. Ten.

. . . so, please . . . stop the slaughter. Stop the killing. Save the children of Stebbins County. We're here. We're alive. We need your help . . . Please . . .

As the lieutenant stood there, his pistol still pointed at arm's length, at least half of the men deserted his side of the parking lot and went to stand in a ragged line around Polk's Humvee. Other Guardsmen were hurrying along the fence line to see what was happening.

Another officer, Captain Rice, came to stand beside the lieutenant.

"Eddy," he said softly, "you're about to make the biggest mistake of your life, and I can guarantee that no matter how this all plays out today, it'll be the last one of your career."

"They're deserting during a time of crisis."

"That's one way to see it," said Rice. "But, tell me, son . . . you ever heard of General George Custer?"

Then Captain Rice pushed the lieutenant's gun arm down, turned, and walked across the concrete to stand with the others.

And then the guns stopped. Smoke whipped up out of the barrels to be threshed by the whipping rotor blades and scattered as mist into the rain. The choppers—those two and the others that hovered above the parking lot—still filled the air with thunder, but the madness of the gunfire had abruptly stopped.

Glass tinkled as pieces fell from the shattered window frames.

In the parking lot the dead moaned.

In the auditorium the wounded cried out.

Billy Trout crept cautiously out from under the sagging ruin of the piano, brushing glass from his hair and lacerating his hand without realizing it. He stared around at the damage. Everyone seemed hurt, but no one looked dead. He frowned, trying to understand it. He could see the Black Hawk holding station outside, the gun still pointed into the school.

Why have they stopped? he wondered.

CHAPTER ONE HUNDRED
STEBBINS LITTLE SCHOOL

"Is it over . . . ?"

Dez's voice was tiny, a whisper from a raw throat.

The air thrummed with the sound of the rotors. Inside her head there was a more terrible thunder as her pulse hammered her brain. As she rolled onto her hands and knees, glass fell from her hair and clothes. She stayed there, unable to move, feeling the entire day burning in every bruised bone, every aching muscle, every fried nerve.

JT Hammond crawled slowly to the wall, shedding debris and leaving a trail of bloody hand and knee prints. He grabbed the shattered sill and pulled himself up.

The two Black Hawks pulled back from the building. Beneath them the dead were massing into a huge crowd. The sound of the gunfire and the voice from the speakers drew them from every part of the parking lot. Thousands of bone white hands reached for the birds, thousands of mouths moaned and bit the air.

As the first two Black Hawks moved away, their machine-gun barrels trailing smoke, the other two flew out over the crowds of the living dead.

The cries of the dead rose into the cold drizzle of midnight.

"Is it over?" Dez asked again.

"No," he said.

The guns swiveled up toward the window.

Then there was a mechanical squawk behind them. Dez and JT turned and looked down. The walkie-talkie lay there.

". . . icer Desdemona Fox, please respond. Officer Desdemona

Fox, please respond . . ." The call repeated and repeated. Dez did not recognize the voice.

"Well," said Dez, "ain't that interesting as shit?"

JT laughed. He turned around and slid down to sit with his back to the wall.

Dez climbed painfully to her feet and tottered over to where the communicator lay amid the rubble. She bent over with a groan and picked it up, keyed the Send button and spoke.

"This is Fox."

"Desdemona Fox?"

"No, it's Michael J., asshole."

"Please verify your badge number and the last four digits of your social security number."

After a moment's hesitation, Dez complied.

The voice said, "Confirmed. Thank you, Officer Fox. Please hold the line."

"Is this some kind of trick?" asked JT, but Dez didn't reply.

Another voice spoke, one she hadn't heard before. "Officer Fox?"

"This is Fox. Who's this?"

"This is Major General Simeon Zetter, commander of the Pennsylvania Army National Guard."

A day ago she would have been impressed to the point of speechlessness. A lot had changed since then. "What can I do for you, General?"

"Is Mr. Trout with you?"

"He's in the building. Why?"

"His videos have gotten quite a bit of attention."

"Kind of the point, general. We've got more ready to roll."

"No doubt; however, before you broadcast them I want you both to listen to me," said Zetter. "I'm speaking frankly to you and I want to appeal to your integrity and your patriotism."

"Save the recruiting speech," barked Dez. "We've been playing fair. You fuckers haven't."

"Dez," JT said softly.

Zetter said, "I understand your feelings, Officer Fox. I doubt apologies would carry much weight right now."

"Not much, no."

"I have just taken tactical command of this situation."

"What happened to Dietrich?"

"He's been relieved of his duties, Officer Fox. I am speaking to you now on the direct orders and behalf of the President of the United States."

"I didn't vote for him," she said, just to be pissy.

"That doesn't make him any less your president or any less my boss," said Zetter. "I give you my personal word, for whatever you think that's worth, that we are willing to listen to what you have to say."

"That's not enough, general," she fired back. "I'm looking out the window at a bunch of gunships. If we hadn't posted those videos we'd be dead right about now."

"Yes," agreed the general, "you would. And I make no apology for that. We are facing a terrible crisis and the nature of it has forced us to make some very hard choices."

"Like slaughtering an entire town?"

The general paused only a moment, Dez had to give him that. "Yes," he said. "As horrible, tragic, and regrettable as that is. The disease pathogen at large in Stebbins has no equal on earth. Though it will sound harsh to say it, I believe that it is because of God's mercy that we had this hurricane, because without it the plague would doubtless have spread much farther than it has. That is not a fatuous comment, Officer Fox, and it is not as heartless as it sounds."

"I'm sure we're all touched by your concern."

"The president wants me to assure you that everything that should and must be done *will* be done to bring those responsible for this disaster to justice."

"That doesn't do much for the people of Stebbins, General. And it doesn't do much for the kids here in the school. I want to know what you're going to do to resolve this situation."

"The simple truth is that the best and safest way to protect the entire country would be to carpet bomb Stebbins with thermobaric weapons. That plan was approved prior to the posting of your second video."

"That's what you have in the Apaches?"

"Yes."

"And now . . . ?"

"Now this has become a different matter. Even as we speak the entire country is raising its voice in protest. Stebbins is on everyone's tongue. The White House switchboard has been totally jammed for two hours. No one is talking about anything else."

"So . . . does that mean you're going to get us the hell out of here?"

"We are discussing options on how to do that," said Zetter. "I need to know that you understand how serious this is."

"We're trapped in a school surrounded by zombies, General. Yeah, we get how fucking serious it is."

"Then tell me . . . if you were in my shoes, knowing what you know about this disease, what would you do?"

"Nice try," said Dez, "but I'm not a general, a scientist, or the president. We want you to solve this."

"We can't. The best we can do is either eradicate it or wait it out. The thermobaric option has a ninety-three percent estimated chance of success."

"What are the odds on quarantine?"

"To be frank, fifty-fifty at best. I advised the president that it is a gamble not worth taking. I stand by my comment. If one infected person breaks quarantine then we are likely to be facing an apocalyptic plague. Those words are chosen with precision, Officer Fox. This would be a biological apocalypse."

"Okay," Dez said tersely, "So why are we talking? I'm still looking out the window at rockets and miniguns."

"My scouts said that the back door of the school was open for a significant length of time, and they reported gunfire from inside the school. That suggests that some of the infected are inside the school."

"All of the living dead have been taken care of," said Dez.

"What about people with bites or exposure to the black blood? Do you know what that is?"

"Yes."

"Anyone who has had contact with that is likely to be infected, even if they are not yet showing signs."

"We have a few bite victims, but they've been quarantined in locked rooms. Everyone in the auditorium is uninfected."

"That's not good enough, Officer Fox. If you want us to help you, then you need to help us. There can't be a single infected person in that building. There can't be a single suspected case. Not one. Are we clear on that?"

Dez looked at JT, who was sitting with his head in his hands.

"Christ," he said, "he's talking about kids and friends of ours and—"

"JT," she whispered, "what choice do we have?"

He shook his head. "You're killing me here, Dez."

Into the walkie-talkie she said, "We'll do what has to be done."

"Send the infected out of the building," said the general.

"Are you going to quarantine them? Are you going to take them to a secure medical facility?"

Zetter paused. "I'm sorry, Officer Fox, but that is not possible. Not with this plague."

Dez closed her eyes.

"And what about us?" she asked hoarsely.

"You will be under quarantine for an indefinite period. We are trying to determine the absolute outside range of the parasite's life cycle. That means that you survivors are a community in there. We'll air-drop food, weapons, medical supplies, hazmat suits, and other materials. None of my people will enter the building. Anyone who leaves the building before the quarantine is lifted will be terminated. No exceptions. That order comes down from the president of the United States, Officer Fox."

"What about the rest of Stebbins? There may still be people out there . . . pockets of resistance?"

The general sighed. "Officer Fox . . . there *is* no 'rest of Stebbins.' Not anymore."

Dez almost threw the walkie-talkie out of the window. Instead she walked over and sat down next to JT.

"Okay," she said into the mike. "And goddamn you all to hell."

CHAPTER ONE HUNDRED ONE
STEBBINS LITTLE SCHOOL

Billy Trout was covered in blood. Some of it was his; a lot of it belonged to the children in the hall. After the shooting stopped, he and the other adults swarmed through the hall, coaxing children out from under chairs, herding them and carrying others onto the stage and into the dressing rooms and greenroom backstage. It disturbed Trout that so few of the children were crying. Right now even hysterical screams would be more normal than the drawn faces and empty eyes of these kids. He had seen this kind of thing before, mostly in newsreel footage and photos of children in Iraq and Afghanistan, in Somalia and Chechnya, in war-ravaged places around the globe. The hollow stares of hollow children who have been emotionally and psychologically gutted by fear, horror, and the betrayal or abandonment of those who were supposed to be there to protect them.

The only relief, and it was a small one, is that there were no casualties. Despite injuries, some serious, to everyone in the room, no one had been killed. In Trout's view, as far as miracles went this one was kind of left-handed.

He could hear the helicopters outside and wondered why they had stopped.

His camera was on a stool at the edge of the stage. The Record and Send buttons were still locked down. The images of bloody children crawling out from their marginal niches of safety did not need a narrator, and Trout was too busy anyway.

He thought about the diatribe he'd given during the attack. The phrasing was probably too colorful, a bit over the top. On the other hand, this whole thing had a "worst-case scenario" flavor to it.

There was a knock on the door and everyone froze. The teachers with guns rushed over, grimacing with impotent anger. Trout ran with them. If this was another attack, then Team Stebbins was going to rack up some points.

The knock came again. Three hits, then two, then three.

"It's Dez!" Trout said as he shouldered his way past the armed teachers. He unlocked the doors and pulled them open.

Dez Fox and JT Hammond stood there, bloody and shaken, looking as battered and abused as the people inside. Even though he had no invitation, no right, no permission to do so, Trout took Dez in his arms and pulled her into a fierce embrace. For a moment she tensed to push him back, but then wrapped her arms around him, and they held each other, feeling unuttered sobs tremble beneath each other's skin.

"God, Dez," Trout whispered, kissing her hair.

The teachers lowered their guns. And Trout slowly, reluctantly released Dez. She did not move away from him, and he was glad of that.

JT still stood in the hallway, apart and alone, his shotgun held in his bloody hands. The expression on his face was indescribable. It was a bottomless sadness mixed with a realization of the worst horrors.

"We heard from the National Guard," he said. "They called Dez on her walkie-talkie. They offered us a deal."

The crowd pressed close to listen.

"What kind of *deal*?" asked Trout cautiously.

"A bad one," said Dez softly. "But it's all we're going to get." Trout watched her eyes as she looked out at the sea of faces. Most of the little children were backstage now, but there were teenagers here, and babies in the arms of people who had probably rescued them from the things that had been their parents.

"Tell us," said Mrs. Madison.

She told them.

That's when the weeping began. Shock from the helicopter attack crumbled in the face of this new grief.

"How many bite victims do we have here?" asked Dez.

Mrs. Madison shook her head, refusing to say.

One of the other teachers put her hand on the principal's shoulder but looked at Dez. "Fifteen adults. Three . . . children."

Dez sagged back against Trout and he caught her.

"You can't send the children out there," insisted Mrs. Madison. "It's inhuman."

"It's a plague," snapped JT so harshly that it silenced everyone. "If the infected stay in here they will get sick and die, and then they will reanimate. Even if you keep them locked up, you can't save them. All you can decide is whether they die a slow agonizing death or go . . . more quickly . . ."

His voice broke at the end, but his words hung in the air.

Mrs. Madison turned to the other teacher and buried her face in her shoulder and wept. Everyone stood there and watched her thin back hitch and buck with each terrible sob.

JT, Dez, and Trout went to do what had to be done. They asked for volunteers and got none. Not one.

The three of them closed the auditorium doors and walked down the hallway to the classrooms where the infected were being kept in isolation. Trout thought that it felt like walking that last mile from a jail cell to the execution chamber. It had the same sense of finality at the end of it, the same enormous dread of the unknown.

But what he said aloud was, "With everything that's happened, we've kind of lost sight of how this started."

"Volker?" asked JT.

"No . . . Homer Gibbon. Volker said that he'd be different than the other infected. That he might still have some conscious control over his body. I wonder . . . could he be out there now? Is he the reason this spread so fast? Is he going around like some monstrous Johnny Appleseed, spreading the plague?"

JT said nothing.

Dez shook her head. "If he is, then the Guard will have to hunt him down."

"Right now," JT said softly, "it's hard to say who's worse. Gibbon, Volker, or the people in the government who allowed *anyone* to work on the *Lucifer* thing. They're all monsters."

Dez nodded, and Trout agreed wholeheartedly.

The bite victims were in one room; those sick from the black mucus were in another.

"Billy," said Dez, "you unlock the door and then get behind us. We're going to have to go in guns out just in case they're turned."

Trout looked at her. "Would it be easier if they have?"

JT and Dez said it at the same time. "Yes."

But none of them had. They were all there, still alive, but terribly sick. They sat slumped in chairs with their heads on the little desks; or they lay on the floor covered with coats and anything else that would keep them warm.

Trout looked around the room and then at JT and Dez. "We're all going to hell for this."

"Already there," said JT. He knelt by a man who was a friend of his, Greg Schauer, who owned a little bookstore in town. He touched his shoulder and rocked him gently. "Hey, man . . . hey, Greg . . ."

Schauer opened his eyes like a sleeper after a long night, but his gaze remained vague and disconnected. "JT . . . ? What's going on, man?"

"C'mon, Greg," said JT as he tucked his hands under Schauer's armpits and pulled him to his feet. "Time to go, brother."

Schauer peered at him with dreamy eyes. "Go? Go where?"

"Outside . . . they're waiting for us."

"Who?"

"The National Guard."

Schauer managed a weak smile. " 'Bout time the cavalry arrived."

JT sniffed back tears. "Yeah. The good guys are here to take care of us."

He shot a look of black hatred at Dez. It wasn't meant for her, and she knew it; he was sharing what could not be expressed, and she met him with equal intensity.

The good guys.

The words were like a curse, or the punch line of a bad joke told in front of good people.

One by one they helped the sick people to their feet. Dez produced her last pairs of polyethylene gloves from the compartment on her utility belt. She gave one pair to Trout and dragged the others over her own lacerated hands.

There was no trouble, no resistance. The people were too sick and frightened, and those who had the energy to be involved in what was happening were guided along by the thought that they were walking toward rescue and medical treatment and safety. Even though none of them had been told that beyond JT's cynical comment.

The good guys are here to take care of us.

When the infected were all out in the hall, Dez reached for the doorknob to the second quarantine room. That was where the three children were kept. Trout stepped up and pushed her hand away.

"No," he said. "I'll do this . . ."

It meant so much to Dez that Trout understood this about her, and she smiled through her tears. "No," she said, and she opened the door.

The children were small. There were two boys of about kindergarten age and a girl who looked to be in second grade. All past-tense designations now. These little ones would never go back to school. They would never learn, never play, never grow up. They would always be remembered as children, if there was anyone among the survivors who knew them.

Despite the risk of infection, Trout bent and picked up one of the little boys. The child was on the edge of a fevered coma, but his eyes were still open. He looked despairingly at Dez, who nodded.

He understands, she thought.

JT picked up the other boy and cradled him in his big arms. The child had a bite on his arm that was already festering.

"We have to do this quick," he said.

Dez went to the little girl. The child was as hot as a furnace, but her eyelids fluttered open as Dez gently picked her up.

"Are . . . we going home now?" the little girl asked.

A sob broke in Dez's chest and for a moment she stood there, clutching the girl to her chest, her face crumpled into a knot of grief.

"Yes," she whispered to the little girl. "Yeah, baby . . . we're going home now."

She led the way out of the room and down the hall. JT and Trout waited for the staggering adults to follow, and then they came last. A procession of the dying and the broken.

They walked to the stairwell and then down the cold tower that was no longer part of a knight's castle or a princess's glittering palace or a wizard's lair. Now it was cold stone, as lifeless as the stones on the walls of a crypt.

They stopped at the back door and, still holding the girl, Dez unclipped the walkie-talkie and keyed the Send button.

"We're bringing out the bite victims. Three of us are *not* sick. Two cops and a civilian in a blue shirt and khakis. Do not fire on us."

"Roger that," said a voice. Not Zetter.

"We don't want to get overrun either. Can you draw the infected away from the door long enough to let us bring them out?"

"Yes, ma'am. You'll hear it."

Trout grinned at Dez. " 'Ma'am'? You'd have threatened to knee-cap me if I ever called you that."

"That still applies, so don't get any ideas."

Suddenly outside a siren began howling. Another joined it, and another. Dez leaned close to the door to listen. The sound began to move, to fade.

"They're using sirens to draw them away."

JT nodded approval. "First smart thing they've done."

After a couple of minutes the walkie-talkie squawked.

"You're clear, Officer Fox," said the voice. "It's a tight window, so hurry."

JT pushed on the crash bar and the door opened. There were bodies outside, crumpled and broken. JT looked around for movement and saw none.

"It's clear."

He stepped outside and held the door as the line of infected people shambled out. Trout and Dez came last, still holding the children. The soldiers had popped more flares, but they were on the far side of the parking lot, and trucks with sirens were parked on the other side of the fence.

"Are they going to help us?" asked one of the bite victims.

"They're coming," said Dez, hating herself for the lie inside the truth. She told the wounded to sit down by the wall. Some of them immediately fell asleep; others stared with empty eyes at the glowing flares high in the sky.

For a moment it left Dez, JT, and Trout as the only ones standing, each of them holding a dying child. The tableau was horrific and surreal. They stared at each other, frozen into this moment because the next was too horrible to contemplate. Then they saw movement.

JT peered into the shadows. "They're coming."

"The Guard?" asked Dez, a last flicker of hope in her eyes.

"No," he said.

They heard the moans. For whatever reason, pulled by some other aspect of their hunger, a few of the dead had not followed the flares and the sirens, and now they staggered toward the living who stood by the open door.

"We have to go," said Trout.

"And right now," agreed JT. He kissed the little boy on the cheek and set him down on the ground between two sleeping infected. Trout sighed brokenly and did the same. "Dez, come on . . . ," murmured JT.

But Dez turned half away as if protecting the little girl she held from him.

"Please, Hoss . . . ?"

"Dez."

"I can't!"

"Give her to me, honey. I'll take care of her. Don't worry."

It took everything Dez had left to allow JT to take the sleeping girl from her arms. She shook her head, hating him, hating the world, hating everything.

"Better get inside," JT warned. Some of the zombies were very close now. Twenty paces.

Trout ran to the door. "Dez, JT, come on. We *have* to go. We can't leave the door open."

Dez retreated toward the door, backing away from the child she had to abandon. Trout reached down and took her hand, and when she returned his squeeze it was crushingly painful. He pulled her toward the door as the first of the dead stepped into the pale light thrown by the emergency light.

"JT, come on, let's go!" Trout yelled.

The big cop did not move. He held the little girl so gently, stroking her hair and murmuring to her.

"JT!" cried Dez. "We have to close the door!"

He smiled at her. "Yeah," he said, "you do."

They waited for him to come, but he stayed where he was.

"JT?" Dez asked in a small, frightened voice. "What's wrong?"

JT kissed the little girl's forehead and set her down with the others. Then he straightened and showed her his wrist. It was crisscrossed with glass cuts from the helicopter attack.

"What?" she asked.

Then she saw it.

A semicircular line of bruised punctures.

Dez whimpered something. A question. "How?"

"Upstairs, when those bastards tackled me. One of them got me . . . I didn't see which one. Doesn't matter. What's done is done."

Then the full realization hit Dez. "NO!"

It was all Trout could do to hold her back. She struggled wildly and even punched him. The blow rocked him, but he did not let go. He would never let go. Never.

"No!" Dez screamed. *"You can't!"*

The dead were closing in on JT. He unslung the shotgun. Across the parking lot the last flares were fading.

"Go on, honey," JT said.

"No goddamn way, Hoss," she growled, fighting with Trout, hitting him, hurting him. "We stand together and we fucking well go down *together."*

"Not this time," JT said, and he was smiling. Trout could see it even if Dez could not, that JT was at peace with this. "I'm going to keep these bastards away from those kids as long as I can. I need you to go inside. I need you to tell the National Guard to do what they have to do, but make sure they do it right. They got to wipe 'em all out. All of them."

What he meant was as clear as it was horrible.

"JT—don't leave me!"

He shook his head. "I won't ever leave you, kid. Not in any way that matters. Now . . . go on. There are kids inside that building who need you. *You* can't leave *them."*

And there it was.

Dez sagged against Trout, and he pulled her inside and held her tight as the door swung shut with a clang.

They heard the first blasts of the shotgun. Trout didn't hear the next one because Dez was screaming.

CHAPTER ONE HUNDRED TWO

JT Hammond stood with his back to the line of bite victims, holding the shotgun by its double pistol grips, firing, pumping, firing. There was almost no need to aim. There were so many and they were so close. He emptied the gun and used it as a club to kill as many as he could before his arms began to ache. Then he dropped the gun and pulled his Glock. He had one full magazine left.

He debated using the bullets on the wounded, but then he heard the whine of the helicopters' rotors change, intensify, draw closer; and he knew what would happen next. He just had to keep the monsters away from the children until then. Soon . . . soon it would all be over, and it would happen fast.

He took the gun in both hands and fired.

And fired.

And fired.

Then one of the dead came at him from his left and JT turned to see that it was Doc Hartnup. He almost smiled.

"Sorry, Doc," he said, and fired.

Doc Hartnup saw JT Hammond fighting for his life. He would have given everything to help this man, to save a single life. It would not repay all of the lives he'd taken . . . but it would give him at least a moment's grace. However he had no control over the body. It staggered toward the officer, legs moving quickly as the hunger built to insane levels.

His white hands reached for JT, ready to grab, to rend and tear and expose all of that fresh meat.

Then JT turned toward him and raised the pistol.

Hartnup looked into the barrel of the black automatic. It was bottomless and as dark as forever.

"Sorry, Doc," said JT Hammond.

There was a moment of intense white, brighter than the sun. Then everything went black. Hartnup felt his body falling.

Then he felt something else. Inside the hollow body he felt *himself* fall. Moving. Being pulled down into a well of darkness. He panicked and tried to fight it but it was like being pulled into the gravity well of a black hole. Hartnup fell and fell, and as he fell he could feel the connections to his stolen body snap and fall away, as if the scaffolding that kept him in position within the empty shell was collapsing.

He could not feel the body of the Hollow Man.

He could not feel anything. Not the hunger, not the pain. Nothing.

And soon, he could not think anything.

As his body fell to the bloody ground, Doc Hartnup fell into the black well of death and was truly and completely gone.

JT Hammond stood above the children, his smoking gun in his hand, the slide locked back, the gun empty. Searchlights swept across the sea of zombies and focused a burning ring around him. JT raised his arms out the side, letting the pistol fall. The living dead swarmed him.

The Black Hawks opened fire.

The heavy bullets tore into the zombies, punching through meat and shattering bone, knocking the dead backward and off their feet. Exploding skulls and tearing limbs from their sockets.

In the White House Situation Room, the president of the United States sat with his aides and Scott Blair, National Security Advisor, and watched the slaughter of the infected.

"What have we done?" whispered the president.

Blair took off his glasses and rubbed his face. "We did the right thing, Mr. President."

The president shook his head. "No," he said, "no we did not."

Inside the school, huddled together on the floor, Dez and Trout held each other as the bullets hammered like cold rain on the walls. It seemed to go on forever. Pain and noise and death seemed to be the only things that mattered anymore. The barrage began chewing through the walls, showering them with debris.

And then . . . silence.

Plaster dust drifted down on them as the rotors of the helicopters dwindled to faintness and then were gone.

"It's over," Trout whispered. He stroked Dez's hair and kissed her head and wept with her. "I won't ever leave you, Dez. Never."

Dez slowly raised her head. Her face was dirty and streaked with tears, and her eyes were filled with grief and hurt. She raised trembling fingers to his face. She touched his cheeks, his ear, his mouth.

"I know," she said.

Dez wrapped her arms around Trout with crushing force. He allowed it, gathering her even closer. They clung to one another and sobbed hard enough to shatter the whole ugly world.

CHAPTER ONE HUNDRED THREE
BORDENTOWN STARBUCKS

Goat looked out at the storm. The night sky was still black, but the rain had slowed to a gentle drizzle. From where he sat he could see the lines of red taillights and white headlights on the highway. He wondered how many of those travelers knew what was happening?

Probably all of them by now.

The story was everywhere. It was the only story on the news right now, and Goat suspected that half of those oncoming headlights were reporters trying to get to Stebbins while the story was still breaking. He had already seen ABC, CBS, and CNN vans come through.

He trolled the online news. FOX was the first to pull the word "zombie" out of the info dump of the Volker interview. "Zombie Plague in Pennsylvania." Goat snorted. It sounded like an SNL skit. Wasn't funny at all.

He looked down at the clock on his laptop. Ten minutes to one. It wasn't even twenty-four hours since this thing started. It felt like a year.

The news feeds broke into the story to announce that the president was going to address the nation at 3:00 a.m. Goat wondered if he would pass the buck onto the previous administration, or to spooks within the intelligence community who still clung to the glory days of the Cold War. Or, would the president take the hit, be the captain of the ship? Either way, a lot of things were going to change.

Goat sipped his coffee and wondered when Billy would call. The last message from him said that they were going to take the infected outside. Since then . . . nothing.

Headlights flashed as a car pulled into the lot. Goat flicked a glance. A metallic green Cube. Ugly. Same make and color as the one in Aunt Selma's front yard. It made him think of that, and how it all started.

Then his mind ground to a halt as the driver's door opened up and a man got out.

A tall man. Bare-chested despite the cold.

A grinning man, with a tattoo of a black eye on each flat pectoral.

Goat wanted to scream but he had no voice at all. He wanted to run, but he was frozen in place.

The man walked the few steps between car and door in an awkward fashion, as if his knees and hip joints were unusually stiff.

Goat's fingers were on the keyboard. Almost without thinking, his fingers moved, tapping keys as the bare-chested man pulled open the door and stepped into the Starbucks. The few remaining customers turned to look at him. The barista glanced up from the caramel macchiato she was making. She saw the bare chest and the tattoos. She saw the caked blood and the wicked smile.

The man stood blocking the door. Grinning with bloody teeth.

Goat's fingers typed eight words.

The barista screamed.

Goat loaded the address of the press and media listserv into the address bar.

The customers screamed.

Goat hit Send.

Then he, too, screamed.

In Bordentown. Homer Gibbons. Quarantine failed.
It's here . . .

CHAPTER ONE HUNDRED FOUR

This is how the world ends.
    This is how the world ends.
    This is how the world ends.
    Not with a bang . . . but a bite.

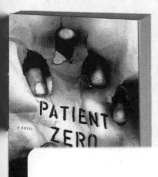
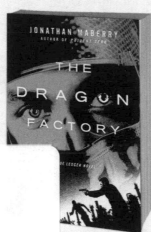

Benny Imura couldn't hold a job, so he took to killing.